Family Connections

Anna
JACOBS

Family Connections

CANELO

First published in the United Kingdom in 2007 by Severn House Publishers
Ltd

This edition published in the United Kingdom in 2019 by

Canelo Digital Publishing Limited
57 Shepherds Lane
Beaconsfield, Bucks HP9 2DU
United Kingdom

A CIP catalogue record for this book is available from the British Library.

Print ISBN 978 1 78863 612 4
Ebook ISBN 978 1 78863 431 1

Look for more great books at www.canelo.co

Printed and bound in Great Britain by Clays Ltd, Elcograf S.p.A.

Chapter 1

Perth, Western Australia. March

It was the first month of autumn but the weather was still hot. Gina Porter wiped the sweat from her brow as she braced herself mentally to clear another room of her father's possessions. His hoarding had been a joke in the family for years but now that he was dead, it wasn't funny any longer, because there was only her to deal with the house.

'You should have cleared out some of this stuff yourself, Dad,' she said aloud as she looked round the cluttered room.

She almost tossed the crumpled plastic bag on the pile of rubbish then inspected its contents 'just in case'. Inside was a brown paper carrier bag, its creases worn, its string handle greyish and limp. How old must this be? She hadn't seen one like it since she was a child, though paper bags were now back in fashion again.

'Oh, thank goodness!' Here were the various certificates for births, marriages and deaths, things she'd been hoping to find, because she was desperate to find out about her father's family. There were also quite a few photos, though the faces and even the names on the backs meant nothing to her. Relieved, she began to gather them together to take home for future investigation. Then something on her parents' marriage certificate caught her eye and she smoothed it out again.

Her father's name, Daniel James Everett, was there, but the woman's name beneath it wasn't her mother's. And the date was wrong too. It said 1942 not 1955.

She jumped in shock as a voice called from the hall, 'Mum?'

'I'm up here, love.' She hastily bundled the papers together and slipped them into the carrier bag again. She didn't want to share this puzzle with anyone yet.

Her daughters had said she should simply call a charity and give everything to them, but she couldn't do that, just – couldn't. And she had been proved right. In the spare rooms her father had rarely used, under mounds of papers, books, old photos, bric-a-brac, tools, she'd found some pieces of furniture which he'd picked up in junk shops years ago when they were short of money. They were quite valuable antiques now and she was sending them to auction.

But the latest find was much more precious because it had upset her not to know anything about her family background. She turned to smile as her daughter Lexie came up to join her, carrying her three-year-old grandson.

'Hi, Mum. I got off work early today so I've brought you some more boxes and bags. How long have you been here?'

'What? Oh, since about nine this morning.'

'That's quite long enough. Ben and I are taking you out for tea. I do wish you lived nearer to me then we could do it more often.'

'Lovely.' Only when she got to her feet did Gina realize how stiff she was. She bent to pick up the precious bag.

Lexie looked at her accusingly. 'You're not taking any more rubbish home, surely?'

Gina hugged the package to her chest. 'These are old family papers. They're important.'

'You're as bad as Pops was. I give you warning, when you die I shall just hurl everything into a bin and have it carted to the tip.'

'I'm not so old that you need to worry about that!'

They both stopped short as knife-edged memories sliced into them. Gina's husband hadn't been that old, either, but he'd been wiped out at the age of forty-six by a drunken driver.

'Sorry, Mum.' Lexie gave her a hasty one-armed hug and Ben offered a sticky kiss. 'I didn't mean to remind you of Dad. You know me, open mouth, put foot straight in.'

Ben began struggling to get away from his mother, reaching out towards the piles, his chubby fingers waggling in anticipation.

'Don't put him down! I've sorted those out.'

Lexie muttered something under her breath and hitched her son into a more secure position.

'These things you consider rubbish are important to me,' Gina said quietly, remembering the marriage certificate and wishing she was alone to study the rest of the documents.

For a moment she was tempted to share the news with Lexie, but dismissed the thought quickly. Neither of her daughters really understood her deep and abiding sadness at her lack of family connections.

She turned to lead the way out, wiping her eyes quickly on her arm and hoping Lexie wouldn't notice. 'You're right, though. I have done enough for today. And it would be great to have tea with you and Ben.'

She let Lexie take her to a nearby Chinese restaurant which her father had loved and to which they'd often gone as a family during the past few years. As usual, the cook made Ben a small omelette, which the little boy ate with messy enthusiasm while the two women shared szechuan beef and chicken chow mein.

Half an hour later Gina smiled and sagged back in her chair. 'I think everything's catching up with me now. That drive home always seems longer at night, so would you mind if I left now?'

'Course not. I can't stay out late with Ben anyway or he'll be unbearable tomorrow.'

They walked out to their cars each holding a hand of the little boy, who was drooping and quiet. The air was balmy after the hot March day and Gina stopped for a moment to gaze up at the sky. 'Your father always loved summer evenings like this.'

'I still miss Dad.'

'So do I. But it's three years now and I've moved on.'

There was silence as they reached the car park, then Lexie picked Ben up and said in a rush, 'I don't think you have, Mum. Moved on, I mean. I think you've sat still.'

Gina stared at her in shock. 'I've done all sorts of new things since your father died.'

'Cosy little things – joined a reading group, gone out for meals with your friend, who's also a widow. That's not exactly living it up, is it? Some women get new jobs or even start dating again. But you haven't. You live in the

4

same house as before and you're still working part-time in that craft shop. You're only fifty-one and young-looking for your age. I hope I last as well as you have. Why, your hair isn't even grey yet, apart from a few threads. I think you should get a new job and go out to places where you can meet some unattached men. Dad wouldn't want you to spend the rest of your life alone.'

Gina swallowed hard. 'I don't need this just now.'

Lexie leaned against the side of her mother's car. 'There's never going to be a perfect time to tell you.'

'I suppose you and Mel have been discussing me.'

'Of course we have, but she doesn't agree with me. Well, she wouldn't. She always wants things to stay the same. Other people put down roots; Mel puts down a mine shaft. But I'm worried about you and the future. I was going to talk to you about it in the restaurant, only I chickened out. But when you said you'd moved on, I just couldn't hold back any longer. It's like that thing you've got on the wall at home. I've always hated it. It says 'Go placidly'. Who wants a placid life? I think you should run joyously forward and have some adventures before it's too late. I love you to pieces, Mum, but I had to tell you.'

Gina swallowed hard. 'Well, consider me told.'

Lexie leaned forward and gave her a final kiss on the cheek. 'You're the best mum in the world, but promise me you'll add a little excitement to your life. Get out and meet new people. Promise me!'

'I'll think about it.' Gina unlocked her car and waited till Lexie had unlocked hers and fastened Ben into his car seat. They were two parking spaces away but she felt as if they were miles apart.

Lexie started up the engine then stuck her head out of the car window and bellowed, 'I nearly forgot. Can you come over and babysit for me tomorrow night, please?'

Gina started to say no then realized Lexie had rolled up the car window and switched on her CD player. She'd simply assumed her mother would agree.

And Gina would. Why not? She had nothing else to do because she hadn't moved on, had she? That accusation rankled. As for Lexie's advice, Gina had never been the sort to run forward joyously and have adventures, even though she'd have liked to travel overseas. Her husband had been even quieter, a home-loving man. And the two of them had been perfectly happy together in their own way.

Move on, indeed! Where to? Everyone she loved was here in Western Australia.

As she turned on to the Freeway to drive south to Mandurah, she wondered yet again why her father had never told her he'd been married before.

She drove slowly, not sure she wanted to get home because she now had two things to worry about in the dark reaches of the night: what her younger daughter had just said and unravelling the mystery of her father's first marriage.

–

Lexie's way home led near her sister's house, so she made a small detour. Since there was a light on downstairs she stopped on impulse, looking up admiringly at the brand new two-storey residence that was Mel's pride and joy. She rang the front door bell and tapped her foot impatiently as she waited.

Mel opened the door, staying behind the security grill till she saw who it was. 'Lex! What on earth are you doing here at this time of night?'

'I wanted to talk to you about Mum. Are you busy?'

'Just sitting watching TV. Simon's gone out. Come in.'

'I'll get Ben. He's asleep in the car.' She carried her son inside and laid him gently down in the corner, his head on a cushion. 'Where's my gorgeous niece?'

'Asleep, thank goodness. Emma's been a terror this evening, came home from school in a temper because she'd fallen out with her best friend.'

'I'll be glad when Ben goes to school. It'll make things so much easier.'

'In some ways. But schools don't keep them until the working day ends, so you'll still need babysitters. And kids catch everything that's going around once they start, so you'll have trouble when he's ill.'

Lexie shrugged. 'There's always Mum. She pulled you out of a hole when Emma got flu so badly.'

'Yes. Mum's been great. But you can't have it both ways. If she does what you want and gets a more exciting life, she might be too busy to babysit for us.'

'She'll still do it now and then.'

'What if she decides to travel overseas?'

'Mum's not the travelling sort.' Lexie flung herself down on the couch with a sigh.

'Glass of wine?'

'No thanks, not when I'm driving. But I wouldn't mind an orange juice, if you've got one.' She bounced to her feet and followed her sister into the kitchen. 'You all right? You look very pale. You're not coming down with something, are you? Thanks.' She raised her glass. 'Here's to us.'

'Let's go and sit down. I'm exhausted.'

'You try to fit too much into your life, you know. Um – I've just been talking to Mum about moving on.'

'Wow. I didn't think you'd actually do it. What did she say?'

'She got a bit huffy – you know that look she gets.'

Mel rolled her eyes. 'Don't I ever? I bet she doesn't change things, though. How's she going with clearing Pop's house?'

Lexie sighed. 'She's still taking things home. She had a big bundle of old papers today.'

They were both silent for a moment or two then Mel cleared her throat. 'I've got a bit of news of my own.'

'Yeah?'

'I'm pregnant.'

Lexie gaped at her. 'But you said you weren't having any more children after being so sick the first time. You swore once was enough to go through nine months of chucking up.'

'It is – was. Only, good old Mother Nature has decided otherwise. Take it from me, the only safe method of birth control is complete abstinence. I told Simon after Emma was born that he should have a vasectomy, but he wouldn't, damn him!' She snatched a tissue and mopped her eyes. 'Sorry. Hormones have gone haywire.'

Lexie went to sit next to her, rubbing her back gently. 'You poor love.'

'Simon's pleased, but it's not him who'll be getting fat and feeling sick for months on end, is it? All he can say is, he always wanted another kid. Men are so selfish.'

'You've quarrelled?'

'Have we ever! He stormed out of the house in a huff tonight and I don't know where he is.' She reached for another tissue.

'You'll sort it all out.'

'I suppose so.' Mel stared down at the dregs of her orange juice. 'But I'm already throwing up several times a day and I feel even worse than last time.'

'You were bad with Emma.'

'And you were fit as a flea when you were expecting Ben. I hate you.'

Lexie grinned at her. 'No, you don't.'

'I do at the moment. Why can't I be like that? I can't afford to stop work. We need my salary to pay the mortgage on this place. I suggested to Simon that I have a termination. That's what tonight's quarrel was mainly about.'

Lexie gaped at her. 'But you're married! There's no reason for you to have an abortion.'

'Except that I don't want another horror pregnancy. I'm only just over two months and it's like looking down a long, dark tunnel. I can't face it, Lex.' Her voice wobbled, a tear escaped and she mopped her eyes again.

'I thought you were looking pale.'

'Yeah, and this is the best time of day for me. You should see me in the mornings. Not a pretty sight. Thank heavens for make-up.'

'Well, you can always sell this house and buy some-where smaller. You'll make a huge profit. Then you'll be able to live off Simon's salary and things won't seem as overwhelming.'

Mel sat bolt upright. 'We sell this place over my dead body! I put down roots here when we moved in and I'm not pulling them up again, whatever anyone else wants.' She took a deep breath. 'I'm hoping Pops' money will help us through until I can go back to work properly. Wasn't it kind of him to leave us something? Only, I can't seem to start planning. My brain's turned to mush and I get so tired.' She stared down at her hands for a moment, brushing away another tear with a scowl that defied her sister to comment. 'So… how's the new guy?'

'OK. Fun, but not a keeper. Look, I'd better get Ben home to bed and leave you to sleep.'

But as she drove away, Lexie wondered how bad the row had been between Mel and Simon. And surely her sister wasn't serious about a termination?

Lexie looked down at Ben as she carried him into the house. He was all soft and floppy, like a rag doll, and she loved him to pieces. For all her troubles with her ex, she wouldn't be without her son for anything in the world. She was glad his father had gone to work in Sydney because she didn't want to share Ben with the Rat.

She laid the little boy carefully in his bed then walked slowly along to her own bedroom. Mel must be feeling really bad to talk about terminations!

–

Brad Rosenberry picked up the mail when he got home from work on that hot autumn day, shuffling through the pile and stopping at the sight of an airmail letter from the UK. The others were only bills, so he put them down and turned the letter over to see who it was from. But there was no address on the back.

He didn't open it, because he'd done the shopping on the way home and had some frozen stuff to put away. Helen had always done that and since her death he'd followed similar patterns. He still missed having her around. They'd been through troubled times in their marriage but had grown a lot closer since the kids left home, and even more so during the years she'd been fighting breast cancer and had needed his support so desperately.

He realized he was still standing there clutching a packet of frozen raspberries and quickly put the last few things away. There. All neat and tidy, and he'd eaten at a café near the supermarket, so didn't need to mess the kitchen up again till supper time.

Pouring himself a glass of red wine he took it and the strange letter out on to the back patio, his favourite place to sit on warm evenings. He studied the envelope again, unable to decipher the postmark. Who would be writing to him from England? He seemed to hear Helen saying, 'For goodness' sake, open it and find out, Brad!' but he enjoyed guessing what letters contained.

Since this one offered no clues, he tore it open and spread out the thin sheet of paper.

Dear Mr Rosenberry

My name is Rosie Quentin and I think you knew my mother, Jane, seventeen years ago when she was visiting Australia. She was Jane Carroll then.

My mother didn't know she was pregnant with me when she left Australia. If you're the right Bradley Gerald Rosenberry, you're my father. I only found out Dad couldn't be my biological father when we were doing blood groups and genetics at school.

I found your address in the Australian white pages online. There wasn't another BG Rosenberry listed. Then I found out you'd written a couple of training manuals and the bio put you at the correct age, too. You can find nearly anyone on the Internet these days.

I hope you don't think I'm cheeky, but it's terrible not knowing what sort of background I come from, so could you please write and tell me something about yourself? I would really like to meet you one day. I'm going to do a gap year starting in fifteen months, before I go to university – well, I hope I'll be going to university. I'm planning to go backpacking with a friend and we both want to visit Australia. Would you mind if I came to see you? I feel a bit lost at the moment about who I am.

I've enclosed an international reply coupon, so please, even if you're not the right man, could you let me know because I'll have to start searching again? Only, I have a hunch you are the right man and my hunches aren't usually wrong.

Rosie Quentin

PS I'm sorry if I've not written this tactfully, only I've tried six times and this was the best I could manage.

Brad stared at the letter, then re-read it slowly.

'Jane Carroll,' he murmured as memories came flooding back. She'd worked in a café near his office, so bright and full of energy and enthusiasm. He hadn't meant anything to happen, but he and Helen had been going through a bad patch just then and Jane had been lonely because her travelling companion had met a guy and moved on without her.

He wasn't normally the unfaithful sort and the thought of his children had made him finish the affair a few weeks later and try harder to make his marriage work, but he'd never forgotten the cheerful English girl. He'd wondered from time to time how she was doing, but had no way of finding out because she'd not given him her address in England.

She'd had a daughter! His daughter!

Why the hell hadn't Jane told him? He'd have helped her financially and... Then he remembered how short of money he and Helen had been in those days and knew it'd have not only have been a struggle to support Jane and her child; it'd have been the final straw that destroyed his fragile marriage.

A daughter! Was she called Rosie because of his surname? He smoothed out the letter, touching the signature, not knowing whether he was glad about this or not. But the words touched his heart. 'I feel a bit lost at the moment about who I am.' Poor kid.

A sentence near the end of the letter caught his eye again. 'I have a hunch you are the right man and my hunches aren't usually wrong.' He was prone to hunches, too, uncanny feelings about the people he loved. And his weren't usually wrong, either.

Psychic, his mother had called it, and said it ran in her family. He didn't know about that. He wasn't into ghosts and all that woo-woo stuff. But he had to admit that he did have hunches from time to time.

He couldn't think of anything else but Rosie all evening, lost track of his favourite TV show in the middle of the episode, drank a second and then a third glass of wine, and eventually went to bed to toss and turn.

At three o'clock the solution to all his problems came to him and he lay smiling as he thought out the details carefully. It would work, he knew it would!

–

When she got back home from her meal with Lexie, Gina could wait no longer. She spread out the long, thin piece of green and white paper that was headed Certified Copy of an Entry of Marriage and studied it intently. Daniel Everett, bachelor and soldier, had married one Christine Pirie, nurse, at the Register Office, Blackpool, in June 1942.

So it had been a war-time marriage.

She knew her father came from Lancashire, because he'd never lost the accent, but she'd thought he came from near Preston from something she'd overheard once. Perhaps Blackpool was his first wife's home or he'd been stationed there.

Here in faded black ink, for the first time, she found her paternal grandfather's name and the information that he was a shopkeeper. She mouthed the name and touched it with one fingertip. Why had her father always refused point-blank to speak about his family? The old resentment surged up. She'd begged him to tell her about them so many times and he'd insisted she was better off without 'that lot'. And her mother had just shrugged and said she had no close relatives left, and begged her not to upset her father.

Clearly Dad had quarrelled with his family, but Gina had never been able to understand how that could have happened, because Dad had been a calm man, the best of fathers, a loving husband, a generous friend.

What had happened to his first wife? She must have died very young, poor thing, because Gina knew her parents had married in 1954, the year before she was born.

She re-read the marriage certificate, this time noting that the bride's family were also shopkeepers. Then she let the piece of paper drop and sat staring at nothing, losing herself in her thoughts.

Blackpool. Her father's family had come from there, not Preston. She'd seen the famous seaside resort on television a few times. There had been a drama series set there quite recently. It looked an amazing place. She'd wanted to visit the UK, but her Tom had hated flying. They'd once flown across Australia to Sydney and he'd been white-knuckled all the way, so they'd never gone overseas.

With a sigh she turned to the other papers in the bundle and what she found made her cry out in shock and seriously consider burning the whole lot in the garden incinerator.

She didn't, of course. She stuffed them back into the carrier bag and shoved it into a cupboard. She'd have to find a better hiding place than that. She didn't want her daughters finding out.

It was a long time before she got to sleep that night.

Chapter 2

Perth, Western Australia

The following day Brad put his plan into action as soon as he got to work. He went to see his manager, and watched Rodney shuffling papers around, as usual trying to give the impression that he could hardly spare the time to talk to anyone.

Brad fought hard to restrain the smile that was twitching at the corners of his lips. He was going to enjoy every second of this meeting. Rodney was a fool, a pompous, self-opinionated fool. But the manager's job had come up when Helen was terminally ill and Brad hadn't even bothered to apply. He'd felt from the start that things wouldn't go well for Helen, though he hadn't said that to her, of course. Another of his hunches, one he could have done without.

For all his lack of sleep, Brad's brain felt crystal clear this morning. 'I turn fifty-four tomorrow,' he announced when Rodney looked up.

'What? Oh. Happy birthday. Don't forget to bring us some of that fantastic chocolate cake.'

There was a pause as Rodney realized his faux pas.

Brad took a deep breath. Helen had been famous for her cooking, sending in luscious cakes each year to celebrate his birthday. 'Look, I need—'

'I'd like to talk to you about—'

They both spoke together then broke off. Determined not to be sidetracked, Brad quickly dived in before Rodney could start again. 'Fifty-four,' he repeated loudly. 'One year away from retirement.' Ah! Now he had his manager's full attention. 'And I want to retire early.'

'Isn't it a bit premature to discuss this? I mean, you have another year left before you're eligible to stop work. And anyway, you've still got a lot to give to the organization. When I consider—'

Brad interrupted ruthlessly. 'I have six months' long service leave accrued. If I take that on half pay, it'll double the time and bring me to retirement age. I not only want to retire; I need to. So I'm telling you first, since you're my manager.' He pushed a couple of pieces of paper across the table and added with great relish, 'Here. These are the forms you'll need to sign to OK that.'

Rodney pushed the pieces of paper hastily back, shaking his head. 'I'm sure you don't mean this, Brad. It's—' he paused and his voice took on a solicitous tone that was as false as his smile, 'the anniversary of Helen's death soon, isn't it?'

Brad nodded, feeling his face muscles tighten. He had never discussed his feelings with Rodney and never would.

'You're bound to be feeling a bit down. Look, why don't you take a week off? We can manage without you for a few days, though it won't be easy.'

'No.'

Rodney puffed out an angry breath. 'I'm trying to give you time to think things through properly. You should—'

'I shan't change my mind. If it weren't for my super-annuation entitlements, I'd have gone two years ago.'

Rodney glared at him. 'Well, I won't approve a year's leave. I do have the power of veto on such things, you know. Your services are going to be needed on the big new training project.' He took the papers, ripped them in half and tossed them in the bin.

Brad shook his head, trying not to smile. 'I'll have to see the doctor then and ask about sick leave. I've been feeling rather depressed lately. In fact, that might actually be the best way to do things from a financial point of view. I've got lots of accrued sick leave. Yes, that's a great idea, Rodney. Thanks. You're doing me a favour by refusing, really.'

He stood up and walked towards the door, turning only at the last minute to frown and say, 'On the other hand, I'd rather do it my way by using up my holiday leave. Fewer hassles, you know. I'm really not up to hassles at the moment.'

With a loud, patently false sigh, he left, but couldn't help smiling broadly once he'd closed the door. He strolled back across the big open area to his office at the far side, a rare cubicle of privacy on the perimeter of a group of desks, ringing telephones and staring faces. For once, he didn't stop to speak to any of his colleagues.

But he couldn't settle to work. His thoughts kept returning to Rosie and to the idea he'd been toying with for a while, of going to England and travelling round Europe. It all fitted together so neatly, as if it was meant to be.

–

Gina woke up with a start, covered in sweat, and gaped in shock at the glowing green numerals on the clock/radio. Nine o'clock! She couldn't remember the last time she'd slept so late. She usually enjoyed getting up early, especially during the hotter months, waking at six or even earlier.

Then she remembered what she'd discovered among her father's papers, something which had kept her awake until the small hours, and she groaned softly. It couldn't be true, it just couldn't. But as she showered and snatched a hasty breakfast, she knew it was, didn't even need to look at those papers to check.

She pulled them out of the bag and checked anyway. Yes, she'd remembered the date on the second marriage certificate quite correctly.

Her parents hadn't got married until she was ten years old!

She didn't mind about them living in unwedded bliss, but she did mind them pretending they'd got married the year before she was born, counting off the supposed number of years each wedding anniversary and including her in their little celebrations.

They'd lied to her!

She minded that very much indeed.

There were some envelopes with faded Australian stamps in the carrier bag, addressed to members of his family in England. Jake Everett was the name on some of them, Peggy Everett on the rest. That wasn't his wife's name, so who were these people? Children? Did she have a half-brother and sister? The mere idea of that made her clutch the envelope to her bosom and close her eyes. So often as a child she'd longed for a brother or sister.

Or were these people her father's siblings? In which case she had an aunt and uncle.

Why had the letters been returned unopened, though?

She studied them. They all had the same address, scored through with a heavy hand and 'Not wanted at this address, return to sender' written in big capital letters.

She wondered whether to open them, but didn't feel she ought to. It would seem like prying into something very private.

Then she gasped as another thought occurred to her. Perhaps she could go and find these people, give them the letters in person? Surely after all this time they'd have lost their anger and be prepared to hear what her father had to say.

She went to make herself a cup of English Breakfast Tea, her favourite in the mornings, and sat staring into space for so long it went cold.

'Snap out of it!' she told herself. She still had to finish clearing out her father's house.

Putting the letters away, she ate a bowl of cereal and set off. It took a full hour to drive up the freeway from Mandurah to her father's house, what with major road works and the busy Saturday traffic. When she pulled up on the drive, she stood by her car for a minute or two, staring at the old weatherboard house with its sagging veranda, suddenly reluctant to go inside. She hoped desperately that there wouldn't be any further shocks lying in wait for her.

The house looked the same as ever. Only the garden betrayed a lack of care and attention. It had been beautiful before, her father's hobby, with roses, petunias and flowering bushes to attract the birds. Now, it was merely tidy and she'd put the bird feeder away. She hadn't time to do anything except weed the front, make sure the reticulation system was working and pay a man twenty dollars to mow the lawn every couple of weeks. Grass grew so quickly in the hot weather and the place had to look neat so that it could be sold.

When she went inside, her strange mood evaporated and the house felt, as it had always done, peaceful and welcoming. She'd had a very happy childhood here. It suddenly came to her that what had happened didn't change that and feeling better, she settled down to work on clearing the final bedroom.

Her parents weren't stupid or spiteful. They must have had a very good reason for what they'd done.

At two o'clock there was a banging on the front door and Lexie yelled through the letter box, 'Open up, Mum. We're here to kidnap you again. It is Saturday, you know. You don't have to work 24/7.'

Gina hurried to unlock the door, wishing her car hadn't given away the fact that she was here. Today she'd far rather have been left alone.

Lexie stared at her. 'Why did you lock the door? Are you all right? You look tired.'

'I didn't sleep very well.'

'Why not?'

Gina shrugged, wondered whether to explain why, then decided not to, not yet anyway. 'It's upsetting me, clearing out Dad's stuff.'

'I told you it wasn't worth the effort. You should have given everything to a charity and let them clear the place.'

'We'd all be several thousand dollars poorer if I'd done that.'

Lexie stared at her. 'You mean those horrible, lumpy old pieces of furniture are worth that much?'

'So the valuer told me. At least they've taken them away now, so I shan't be worrying about the house getting broken into. There's probably nothing else of value left.'

'I've got this afternoon free, so I can help you if you like, speed things up a little.'

Ben began tugging at his grandmother's jeans, holding his hands up to be cuddled so she picked him up. 'Thanks for offering, Lexie love, but I need to do this myself. And anyway, you'd just throw everything away.'

Lexie grinned. 'Yeah, well, someone has to or you'll never get it finished.'

'Look, I've got everything sorted out into piles and you know what Ben's like. Let me finish it my way. You could make me a cup of tea before you go, though. I've brought some of my own tea bags. Dad used to drink cheap rubbish.'

'You and your fancy teas! Have you had any lunch?'

'I'm not hungry.'

'You always used to nag us to eat sensibly, so I'm going to return the favour now. I'll go and buy you a sandwich at the corner deli and I'm staying to make sure you eat it. We don't want you fainting when you're babysitting Ben tonight.'

Damn! Gina had forgotten about the babysitting. She would normally have brought her overnight things with her to save an extra journey, since Lexie's house was the other side of her father's from hers.

When her daughter came back from the deli, Gina obediently ate the sandwich.

'Mum… Did you know Mel's pregnant again?'

Gina gaped at her. 'No, I certainly didn't, though she didn't look well last time I babysat. But she said she'd been doing extra hours at work. Why on earth didn't she tell me?'

'She's upset about it because she's sick as a dog again.'

'Poor darling. My mother said she was the same when she was carrying me.' Gina screwed up the piece of paper the sandwich had been wrapped in and threw it into a bag of oddments destined for the tip. 'Time for you to leave now, Lexie. I'll never get anything done with this young man messing up my piles.'

'All right. See you tonight!'

'What? Oh, yes.' Damn! She'd have to leave early to go home and fetch her things. She was getting a bit tired of all the babysitting, something she'd never expected to feel in the first flush of joy at having grandchildren. No, she'd buy a cheap nightie and go as she was to Lexie's. It was a warm day. She didn't need anything else, could leave early tomorrow morning to go home.

Since Tom's death, both Lexie and Mel simply assumed Gina would be free any time they wanted her help, which had been three times last week, and she'd had to miss her book club meeting. If this went on she'd have no life of her own. She needed to put her foot down about it.

She began to go through the final bits and pieces in grim readiness for any other nasty surprises. But she couldn't settle to it with her usual efficiency, because one thought kept coming back to her.

She might have half-brothers or sisters in England!

The thought of that made something deep inside her ache, the same desperate longing for family that had haunted her childhood, something she thought she'd outgrown after she married. Tom had an older brother and a few relatives in Sydney, but apart from that one visit, he hadn't kept in touch with them beyond a card at Christmas. None of them had bothered to come across to Western Australia for his funeral, which had seemed dreadful to her.

She'd have kept in touch if she'd had a brother or sister. It must be so wonderful to have big family parties and…

Oh, she was a fool! Always wishing for the moon lately.

–

Brad couldn't stop thinking about the girl who said she was his daughter. The letter writer must be telling the truth… mustn't she? Surely no one would lie about a matter as important as that? And she knew about him and Jane.

The mere thought of this Rosie, another child of his begetting, made him catch his breath in wonder and stop whatever he was doing to contemplate the idea. What did she look like? Did she take after his side of the family or Jane's? He dearly loved the two children he had raised. He didn't always agree with them or approve of what they were doing with their lives – which seemed a natural parental reaction to the next generation – but that didn't stop him loving them. They were flesh of his flesh and that made all the difference.

He would be happy to love another child, however belatedly.

Why hadn't Jane told him?

He replied to Rosie the day after receiving her letter, noting that she'd given him a PO Box, not a street address, and wondering if that was significant. It was a difficult letter to write, even for a man supposed to be skilled with words, but he assured her that he was indeed the correct Brad Rosenberry and that he wanted very much to meet her, would have done so sooner if he'd known of her existence.

He wanted to say so much more, to ask about her current life and interests, her childhood, what had happened to her mother, what Jane thought about this… but decided after several abortive attempts that it would be better to keep his first communication short and wait until they were face to face to do some real talking. He did ask if next time Rosie could send him a photo, though. He didn't even know what colour her hair and eyes were.

Why hadn't she emailed him about this? It'd have been so much quicker. Everyone of her age was on email these days and most people his age, too. He included his email address in his reply, just in case.

He hadn't told Michael and Joanna what he was doing. Better to present his two children with a fait accompli about both the retirement and the trip to England. They'd grown absurdly protective of him since Helen's death and wouldn't like him going off on his own.

He, on the other hand, was excited about it.

And if he was too old to climb any tall mountains at fifty-four, he wasn't too old to climb a few hills, surely?

Chapter 3

England

In a neat detached executive residence in Poulton, near Blackpool, Peggy Wilkes got her husband's breakfast ready while he took his shower. Nervously she adjusted the spoon and dish as she listened for his footsteps on the stairs.

When Hartley came down, he looked at the table then at her. 'My coffee?'

She hurried across the designer kitchen to fill the plunger, suddenly aware that she'd been staring out at the weak April sunshine instead of paying attention to what she was doing. She usually had his coffee waiting for him when he came down.

'I don't know what's got into you lately, Peggy. You can't even prepare breakfast efficiently!' His voice had that icy tone that always made her want to curl up and die.

'I've been feeling a bit tired lately.'

He sighed. 'Then go and see the doctor. That's what he's there for.'

'I have done and he wanted to give me some anti-depressants. I've tried those before. They make me feel worse.' She pushed her spectacles higher up her nose then added in a rush, 'I was – um – thinking of going to that new Women's Wellness Centre instead.'

'No.'

'Why not? It looks—'

'You know what I think of those places. They're run by man-haters and lesbians. I won't have *my* wife going to one.'

She realized the coffee was ready and got him a cup, but her hand was shaking and she spilled some into the saucer.

With a muffled exclamation Hartley took it from her and went across to the sink, wiping the saucer and the bottom of the cup carefully before carrying them back to the small table at which they ate breakfast, all other meals being taken properly in the dining room. 'My eggs?'

She went to put them on as he shook out the newspaper, boiling the eggs for exactly four minutes and serving them with great care.

But she'd forgotten the butter and it was still hard from the fridge.

The annoyance on his face deepened, but he didn't say a word.

When he'd gone to work, she collapsed into a chair and made herself a pot of tea. She sat sipping it slowly as she ate her toast, relaxing now that Hartley had left for the day. After clearing up the kitchen, she set off for the shops.

While she was in the supermarket Peggy caught an unexpected glimpse of herself in a surveillance mirror and stopped in dismay. She looked tired and haggard, far older than her sixty-six years. And yet her hair was only grey at the temples and she was slim enough. She ought not to look like that.

When she got home, she put the shopping away, then went to stare at herself again in the hall mirror. She wished… she hardly dared even think it, but sometimes she wished quite desperately that she could leave Hartley and live on her own in peace and quiet. Even the tiniest bed-sitter would be paradise compared to her life in this chill residence decorated in white, grey and stainless steel, Hartley's choice of a colour scheme. The house was far too big for the two of them, but Hartley had insisted on staying here. He didn't have to clean it, though, and she was tired of cleaning rooms that were never used.

He'd always been a bit fussy and picky, but after the daughter he adored moved away from Poulton to live near Manchester, he'd become much more critical and exacting, wanted every detail of his life arranged just so. The trouble was, Peggy had never been the sort of person who could organize details to that degree and lately she seemed to upset him more often than please him.

On the rare occasions when Cheryl came home to visit them, he gave their daughter the royal treatment and insisted on being with her all the time so the poor girl couldn't relax. Girl! Cheryl was thirty-six now and still unmarried. It had been over a year since she'd stayed for more than a couple of hours. Hartley had mentioned that last night with one of those heavy scowls that always made Peggy shiver with apprehension.

'It's your fault,' he'd said. 'Why should she come home to chaos and mess?'

Peggy felt upset that he'd say such a thing. It wasn't true. The house was immaculate by anyone else's standards. But Cheryl had confided last time that she hated her father's fussy way of living. That had surprised Peggy, because her daughter didn't usually confide in her. Cheryl had moved in with a man, it seemed, but hadn't told her father that either. Peggy didn't blame her. He'd have thrown a fit.

She sighed and got herself another pot of tea. She couldn't see any way to leave Hartley. At sixty-six she had no way of supporting herself and was quite sure she'd take away very little from this marriage if they did split up. The house was in his name, as were all the bank accounts.

By the time he came home from work that evening, she had tea ready. And for once she'd made a stand – if you could call it a stand.

He stared at the dining table with its single place setting then at her. 'Where's yours?'

'I'm not hungry. And I'm not eating with a man who does nothing but complain. I had a snack earlier. I'm going to watch TV.'

'You stupid bitch!'

He muttered the words, but there was nothing wrong with her hearing. She served his meal then went into the conservatory and switched on the little TV set there. He didn't come to join her after he'd eaten. She made no attempt to join him.

But she could feel his presence. And his anger. He'd been permanently angry since head office had suggested a date for his retirement, a suggestion everyone knew was really a way of getting rid of him.

She tried to concentrate on the programme, one she liked to watch when he wasn't in, one he said was designed for morons. But she couldn't get interested in it tonight, so in the end she picked up a book.

Only her thoughts kept intruding and she couldn't make sense of what she was reading.

Things were going from bad to worse between them lately and she didn't know what to do about that.

And when he retired, he'd be there all the time! She didn't think she could bear that.

Chapter 4

Australia

A few days later Brad went along to beard Rodney in his office, putting the next stage of his plan into operation. 'Are you actually refusing to accept my leave forms and resignation? Because if so, I'm going to call in the union.'

Rodney gobbled with indignation and lost himself behind a tangle of unfinished sentences. As everyone knew, he'd do anything to avoid union trouble because that wouldn't look good on his record as a manager.

Brad plonked another set of completed forms on the desk and left.

The following morning he found a note in his in-tray from Rodney, insisting that he talk to the Staff Counsellor before doing anything rash.

He grinned and strolled obediently along to Judy's office. 'Are you busy?'

She looked up. 'Oh, hi, Brad. No, of course I'm not. Come in and close the door.'

He sat down, still feeling relaxed, and cocked one eyebrow at her. 'I presume dear Rodney's been speaking to you about me?'

'Yes. Are you here to discuss whether you should retire early?'

'No. I'm going to retire early, but he insists he won't sign the forms till I've seen you. I don't mind what you call our discussion. Hell, I don't mind if you broadcast this conversation to the whole office because whatever you say, I shan't change my mind. I'm already out of here mentally.'

She was fiddling with a pen. 'I do have one concern, Brad – and it's quite independent of Rodney. Have you really thought out what you'll do with yourself afterwards? You know, once the first flush of freedom is over? You're too young and energetic to potter around the garden all day, surely?'

'Apart from the fact that I'm not into gardening, which was Helen's thing, I don't intend to settle down at all. I'm going to England to visit family I've not seen for years. Then I'm going to see something of Europe. I want to visit lots of places I've only read about.'

'What do your children think about your plans?'

'I haven't told them yet. They'll miss me but I suspect what they'll miss most of all is my babysitting. They're at that frantically busy yuppie stage of life: raising kids, climbing corporate ladders, going to the gym and giving dinner parties. Their lives are like a treadmill with every half-hour mapped out. Makes me feel exhausted even to listen to them talking about their schedules. Helen and I were never so ferociously active.'

'I know what you mean. My niece is the same.'

He looked at his watch. 'Well, are you going to support me or not, O wise and noble Counsellor?'

She leaned back, smiling at him. 'What if I don't?'

'I'll go to my GP and get signed off on sick leave. I'm sure he'll support me if I get all upset and tell him I can't cope any more with this job.'

She got up and came across to hug him and plant an unexpected kiss on his cheek. 'Of course I'll support you, you fool. But I'm going to miss you. You're one of the sanest people in this madhouse.'

He clasped her nearest hand for a moment between his. 'Thanks, Judy.'

'I hope we can keep in touch afterwards.'

The message in her eyes startled him. It looked – why, it looked as if she was offering him encouragement to treat her as a woman, something he'd never seen signs of before. He felt flustered by that unspoken message. He hadn't looked at another woman since Helen died. They'd had to stop sharing a bed even before that, which his body had protested about regularly. Still did.

Well, it could just protest. No way was he risking chance encounters with strangers. Nor did he intend to get tied down again by marriage. He was going to do things for himself now, travel, meet people briefly and then move on. He'd had enough of running a beautiful house and putting in the long hours needed to get a showy garden.

One day, he supposed, he'd come back to Western Australia and settle down, but not for a year or two. It was remotely possible that he might meet another woman he could love, but he didn't think so. He was good at making friends with women, not so good at making lovers of them.

–

The day after Brad had spoken to Judy about his plans, Rodney came into his office and scowled down at him.

'If you're so determined to act foolishly, I'll allow you to retire early.'

'That's great.'

'But I have to say, as your superior officer, that I'm sure you'll regret it. And what's more, I don't think much of someone who'd leave us in the lurch like you're doing. So don't ever come to me for a reference.'

Brad tilted his chair back and grinned. 'I won't regret it at all. And I shan't be going back to work so why would I need a reference? I intend to enjoy the rest of my life.'

The only response to that was a sour look and – was it possible? – a flicker of envy in Rodney's pebbly grey eyes.

For the first time in ages Brad felt energy and excitement coursing through him. He watched through the glass panels as the other man strode across the main work area and into his office. As soon as Rodney's door was closed, Brad stood up, raised both his fists in the air and let out a whoop of delight.

That brought his colleagues crowding into his office.

'It's all arranged,' he told them. 'I'm leaving… retiring… escaping.'

He sent out for a big cake for morning tea. Rodney was conspicuous by his absence from the little gathering but Judy was there, smiling across at him and raising her mug of coffee in a silent toast.

She waited till everyone else had gone to ask, 'How soon are you leaving?'

'As soon as I can.'

'Don't be a stranger afterwards.'

'No. No, I won't.' There was a silence and she looked at him with a question in her eyes, at least he thought she did. But he still couldn't pluck up the courage to ask her out for a date. He was terrified of making a fool of himself. What if he was mistaken? What if she was just being friendly? Worst of all, what if she thought he was sexually harassing her? One had to be very careful these days, especially in the workplace.

–

Early one evening in the middle of the week Gina's door-bell rang and she found Lexie grinning at her through the security screen. 'Surprise!'

'What brings you down to Mandurah?'

'I've got this chance to go out to a really super party tonight – and would you believe it, it's in Mandurah. I tried to ring only you must have been out and you hardly ever switch on your mobile, so I took a chance you'd be able to look after Ben for me.'

Gina stared at her in shock.

Lexie twirled round to show off her outfit. 'It's this new guy, Jon. He's fun but he's into parties not small children. Definitely a case of FOC.'

'FOC?'

'Fear of Commitment.'

'Well, you've got a small child.'

'I know. But I'm lucky. I've got you as well. Jon knows I'm not looking for another husband, just a bit of fun and sex.' She glanced at her watch, squeaked in dismay and rushed back to her car to fetch her son and his things. 'See you in the morning, Mum! I'll pick Ben up really early – could you have him ready by seven? – so that we can get back to Perth in time to leave him at the child-minding centre – they do hate you to be late.'

As soon as his mother left, Ben started to cry and wanted to be cuddled. It was one o'clock before Gina got to bed and even then she lay awake for ages, annoyed at herself for letting her daughters think they could take advantage of her like this. She'd had to cancel going for a drink at a friend's house to look after Ben.

That settled it. She had to work out a way to gain more independence from her family. Last week it had been Mel, who had looked awful and shouldn't have been going out at all, but had an important office function. Gina was getting very worried about her elder daughter. Not only was Mel unwell, but there was a palpable tension between her and Simon.

Next morning the alarm woke Gina from a deep sleep at six and even so, it was hard to get Ben ready on time. He wasn't a morning person, had always woken grumpy and scowling, even as a baby.

Lexie breezed in just after seven, snatched the piece of toast from her mother's hand and demolished it in two bites. 'Why am I always so hungry after a good night's sex?'

'Do I wish to know that?'

Lexie grinned. 'I deserve some fun after my years with the Rat, don't you think?' She went across to pick up her son and plant a smacking kiss on his cheek. 'Don't turn away, young man. A kiss is a valuable thing.'

Not Lexie's kisses, Gina thought. Her younger daughter scattered them on everyone she knew. She was openly affectionate. An uncomplicated sort of person, everyone said. Gina wasn't so sure. Lexie had hidden depths and the divorce had hit her harder than she let on, even to her family.

'I've got Ben's things ready.'

'You're a doll, Ma. I don't suppose you could come up and babysit next Saturday, could you?'

'I don't think I—'

'Thanks. You're the best.'

And Lexie was gone without waiting to hear what she'd been about to say, leaving behind the quiet after the storm – and the mess, too.

Gina put some more toast on for herself and began to clear up, muttering, 'If you don't do something drastic, my girl, you'll end your days as the family drudge.' She went to stare at herself in the mirror, wondering if she looked like a soft touch.

She didn't look anything much. Nondescript was the word that sprang to mind. She'd been pretty as a girl, had kept herself nice for Tom as she grew older. Lately, it hadn't seemed to matter what she wore as long as she was neat and tidy. Maybe she'd go out and buy some new clothes, get a different hair style? Yes, why not?

And maybe after that she'd do something that would surprise everyone.

She kept thinking of the relatives she had in England – well, she might have – and wondering if she dared go and visit them. Would they turn her away as they had her father's letters?

She'd never been overseas, but it wasn't hard to get to England by plane. People did it all the time. She rather fancied the idea of shocking her daughters rigid by climbing out of her rut.

Lexie had been right. Gina had to move on. And as a first step, she was going to get a more modern haircut and buy a few new clothes.

Brad was surprised by the farewell party. It wasn't just drinks after work, but a proper 'do' at Judy's place with enough food to feed a starving army. Rodney wasn't there, but a lot of people whom Brad had known and liked during his long years in the public service were. Some of them had already retired. Some were younger and envious of his new freedom.

He spent a thoroughly enjoyable evening, and when Judy pulled him towards her in a dark corner of the patio and gave him a passionate goodbye kiss, he found himself responding, returning it, holding her close… tempted.

She pulled away a little, still keeping hold of him. 'Want to go to the theatre next week? A friend can't make it and I have a spare ticket.'

He stared at her, looked up at a star twinkling down on them, then blurted out, 'It's the wrong time to start anything up between us, Judy. I'm leaving for England in a few weeks' time.'

She was silent for so long he wondered if he'd upset her.

'That wouldn't have mattered if—' She reached up to caress his cheek. 'It's all right, Brad. The spark isn't there for you, is it?'

'You're a very attractive women.'

She shrugged and took a step backwards. 'No need to sugar the pill.'

'I'm telling it as I see it. You are attractive, but at the moment I'm rather preoccupied about a private crisis you don't know about.'

She patted his arm, summoned up an unconvincing smile and walked away.

He stood by himself for a moment or two, then went to join the others.

By the end of the evening he was tiddly and for once, he didn't care. It was good to say your farewells properly, he thought, leaning back in the taxi and letting the street lights flow past like a string of gold-haloed beads. He couldn't remember the last time he'd let himself go like this. He wasn't really a drinker. An occasional beer or wine and that was it. But you only retired once and even if he didn't retire officially until next year, as far as he was concerned, now was the moment of severance.

'Freedom,' he murmured, raising an imaginary glass in a heartfelt toast. 'You can't beat it.'

When he entered his own house, however, his euphoria vanished abruptly. The big hallway seemed to echo round him. The rooms Helen had once loved and been so proud of seemed soulless now with their neatly aligned furniture. When Helen was alive, this place had been a home, and a beautiful one at that, because she had a knack when it came to home-making and decorating. Now, it was just a piece of real estate, quite valuable because it was in an inner suburb that had zoomed up in value. He wouldn't be at all sorry to let the house go, would probably buy himself a luxury flat instead.

He slept badly. Increasingly his body was proclaiming its dissatisfaction with the celibate life, and the feel of Judy's soft body against his had stirred it up again. You'd think desire would be fading at his age, but it seemed to be making a come-back lately.

Judy was right, though. The spark wasn't there with her.

Perhaps he would never find another woman he felt comfortable with. He certainly wasn't going out hunting for one. The mere thought of that made him shudder.

–

Gina decided her father's house was now ready to bring in the charity people she'd contacted to take the clutter of things away. She supposed she could have had a garage sale and made a little extra money but couldn't be bothered. She had other things on her mind since finding those papers.

There were a couple more car loads to take home for herself, things she couldn't bear to part with – though where she was going to put them, heaven alone knew. And then she would bring in a few estate agents to give her some preliminary valuations.

She glanced inside the letter box, though since she'd put on a sticker saying 'No junk mail' it had mostly been empty. Today, however, there was an airmail letter postmarked England, quite a thick one, too. The return address said simply Jones & Black, with a PO box in Blackpool. She hurried inside, clutching it tightly. Blackpool! That was where her father's English family came from.

In the kitchen she sat down, staring at the letter, suddenly reluctant to open it and let out more secrets. 'Don't be silly!' she muttered and tore open the envelope to find several sheets of paper. The printed header on the covering letter said 'Jones & Black, Private Investigators'. She blinked at it in shock. What was her father doing with a private investigator?

Dear Mr Everett,

I'm writing to advise you that I now have all the information you requested. I've attached details of the family members in whom you're interested and have added a couple of other names to the rough family tree you sent me.

I shall be happy to help you further in any way, should you require it.

I've enclosed my final invoice, payable within 30 days as usual.

Kind regards,

Allyn Jones

Gina heard the kettle bubble violently, then click and switch itself off, but didn't bother to make a mug of tea. She re-read the letter then spread out the next piece of paper, swallowing hard at the sight of a family tree... her family tree.

As she studied it, she pressed one hand against her lips to hold back a sob. It wasn't fair! She ran her finger over the names of the generation below her father's on the family tree. Peggy and Jake were indeed her half-brother and sister! They were older than her but please, whatever fate was guiding her life, let them still be alive! 'Margaret Wilkes and Jacob Everett.' She murmured their full names like a mantra. If she met no one else from the English side of her family, she had to meet these two.

Then she remembered that the letter had contained other papers and spread them out. Each gave the address of one person and a few precious details. Margaret née Everett, known as Peggy, mother of one daughter

(Cheryl), housewife, married to Hartley Wilkes, manager of an insurance office. He must be close to retirement. Peggy would be sixty-six now, fifteen years older than Gina. What was her sister like? *Her sister!*

And Jake, her brother, was divorced, had taken early retirement a few years ago, was the father of a daughter and had a granddaughter of twenty. He was sixty-five. Did he look like her father? she wondered. Their father.

She had two nieces and a great-niece in England, as well as the brother and sister, and she didn't even know what they looked like. It was too much. The years of suppressed longing burst out of her in a bout of sobbing and crying that exhausted her.

When she'd calmed down, she stayed where she was, head resting on her hands on the table.

Lexie had said she should get out of her rut. Well, she would. She was definitely going to go to England and meet her relatives. She'd write to them first and... A dreadful thought suddenly occurred to her. What if her father done something so terrible that they refused even to see her? They'd returned his letters unopened, with 'not wanted at this address' on them, instead of the usual, 'not known'.

She couldn't ask him about it now, but at a guess he'd probably left his first wife and run away with Gina's mother. What else could have caused this sort of reaction?

Well, she wasn't going to let her brother and sister turn her away, whatever it took. She'd not write because they might send back her letter unopened. She'd just turn up and tell them who she was. At least that way she'd see them.

She wondered if there were any other members of the family. The letter said 'family members in whom you're interested'. There might be others, more distant relatives.

The world suddenly seemed brighter. It was a while since she'd had a purpose in life, but she had one now! She'd get some brochures today and start making travel plans before she told Mel and Lexie about any of this. They wouldn't like her going on her own, they were so protective of her.

But this was something she had to do.

–

Brad decided the time had come to tell his two grown-up children what he was doing. He felt guilty that he'd not even told them about retiring early, but he'd not wanted them to interfere. He invited them round for tea – without their spouses and children, for once. 'I've something important to tell you,' he'd said and refused to explain further on the phone.

They came after work, Michael still wearing his business suit and Joanna wearing the female equivalent, looking immaculate, as she always did.

Brad settled them down with a glass of wine each. 'I've taken early retirement.'

Joanna stared at him. 'How can you retire at fifty-four? I hope you haven't done anything foolish, Dad.'

Brad wondered when they'd started considering him too stupid to make his own decisions. 'I'm also selling this house. It's far too big for one person. Can you sell it for me, Michael?' There had to be some advantages to having a son in real estate.

'Yes, of course. It'll go quickly in the present boom. Where are you going to buy?'

'A luxury flat in an inner suburb, though I won't be here to live in it for very long.'

Dead silence as they exchanged worried glances.

'You're not – ill?' Joanna faltered at last.

'No, of course not. Oh, darling!' He pulled her to her feet and hugged her. 'No, I've not felt as well for a long time. Truly. It's just that I'm going travelling. You know I've always wanted to, but your mother didn't enjoy it.' He waited until his daughter had sat down again, by which time Michael had more questions.

'Where are you going?'

'To the UK first, then who knows?'

'You're just taking off round the world – with no plans? Are you sure that's wise, Dad?'

'I'm sure it's what I want to do. I fancy having a few adventures before I'm too old. And there's something else I need to tell you.'

They looked at him warily then stared in shock as he told them about Rosie.

'You mean – you were unfaithful to Mum?' Joanna exclaimed. 'Dad, how could you?'

'Helen and I weren't getting on very well at the time and Jane was very attractive. It just sort of happened. I'd had to turn down a good job in the eastern states because your mother refused point-blank to move and I was very upset about that.'

'I didn't know,' Joanna said. 'Why wouldn't she move?'

'She didn't want to leave her friends or her house.'

44

'It doesn't excuse what you did.' She turned to her brother. 'Why haven't you said anything? Surely you don't condone what Dad did?'

Michael shrugged. 'It happens.'

'You men always stick together.' She turned back to her father. 'Did Mum know about this woman?'

'I don't think so. She was too bound up in motherhood and domesticity to notice what I was doing – or what I needed, either. I'm not making excuses, but our marriage wasn't perfect, then or at any time. I stayed with Helen mostly for you two. You were – and are – very important to me. But don't mistake me, she and I rubbed along pretty well. It wasn't a bad marriage, just… not a wonderful one.'

'So you're going to England to meet this Rosie,' Michael said.

'I was going anyway. I'm just changing the order of what I do there. Meeting her now has a higher priority than catching up with my cousins.'

The minute the sound of their cars had faded, Brad poured himself another glass of wine and wandered out into the garden. Heat met him like a wall, even though it was six thirty in the evening. He took a sip and rolled the Chardonnay round his mouth, enjoying its woody taste, then sighed and got out the hose pipe. He'd need to keep the garden looking good if he was to sell the house quickly – and he'd need to remove a lot of the furniture from inside the house, to show off how spacious it was. Helen had been a hoarder. He felt the need now to divest himself of all that baggage, to tread more lightly through life.

He was going to go travelling this time, he really was. And it felt right, too. That inner sense of his wasn't sounding any alarm bells.

Chapter 5

England

Ignoring Hartley's prohibition, Peggy nerved herself to visit the Women's Wellness Centre. She parked her car and got out, but couldn't bring herself to walk inside so stood by the car, looking at the angular modern building with its huge expanses of glass.

'They don't bite, you know,' a cheerful voice said behind her.

She swung round, her heart pounding because she'd been so lost in her thoughts she hadn't seen anyone approach.

The other woman smiled at her. 'Sorry. Didn't mean to make you jump. It's just that I felt like that the first time I came here. Took me three visits before I walked through that door. How about I take you inside and give you the grand tour? You can just walk out again afterwards with a handful of brochures, if you like. People do it all the time.'

'Well – er – yes, why not?'

The receptionist called a greeting to Peggy's companion then went back to her computer.

The tour didn't take long. 'There are various consulting rooms to the right. The doctors here really understand what it's like to have a woman's body, not a man's. Can't tell you the difference it's made to me. And there are counsellors too, if you need them.'

She didn't wait for a reply but turned to the left and pointed to doors which led to a series of small meeting rooms. Then she allowed Peggy a quick glimpse through a glass panel in the door of a much larger room at the rear, where a meditation class was taking place.

The women's faces looked so serene Peggy felt a surge of bitter jealousy. 'How much does it cost? That sort of thing, I mean. Meditation.'

'Whatever you can afford to pay. Most of us give a couple of pounds. There are some who can't afford even that. No one bothers.'

'I've always wanted to learn to meditate.'

'There you are. Why don't you sign up for the next beginners' class?'

'My husband is – well, he doesn't believe in that sort of thing. I don't want to upset him just now.'

The other woman glanced quickly sideways. 'Oh? Well, if he's giving you grief physically, there's help for that sort of thing, too.'

Peggy shook her head. 'He's never touched me, he's just... sarcastic. So I don't—' She couldn't continue, stared down at her feet. Her companion's silence felt warm and friendly, not like Hartley's disapproving silences. 'I shouldn't let it get to me,' she confessed. 'I'm probably over-reacting.'

'Maybe. But if it's upsetting you, why should you put up with it? Mine used to bash me, but I've left him now. Haven't been so happy in years.'

Peggy was afraid of revealing more about her life, didn't want to go down that path, so glanced at her watch. 'Oh, dear! Look how late it is. I'd better be going. Thank you so much for the tour.'

They walked back to the entrance.

'Want some brochures?'

'No, better not.' She knew if Hartley saw them he'd go mad.

'Here. Let me give you my phone number. If you want to meet for a coffee some time…'

Peggy backed away quickly. 'It's very kind of you, but I'm rather busy, shouldn't really have come here.' She was relieved when the other didn't follow her or make any protest. As she drove out of the car park, she avoided even looking towards the entrance.

But she thought about the centre quite a lot. It had felt so friendly and welcoming. Perhaps if she… No, she irritated Hartley enough as it was. He'd be furious if he knew she'd come here and he'd mock the very idea of meditation classes.

It simply just wasn't worth it.

But what was worth doing these days?

–

In England Jake Everett whistled as he dug over part of his vegetable garden, ready for a new planting. When he heard a car draw up, he ambled round the house, through the side gate he was always forgetting to close. His daughter Mary and granddaughter Lou got out of the car.

'Now this is a pleasant surprise!' He blinked at the colours of Lou's hair – a right mess it looked with those jagged ends, not to mention the paler streaks standing out against the dark brown! But remembering his own long-haired days in the sixties and his parents using exactly those words about his chosen hair style, he bit his tongue.

Then he noticed the expressions on their faces, the way they were avoiding looking at one another and his heart sank. Another quarrel. There had been huge quarrels last year when Lou refused to go to university and took a catering and waitressing course instead, then found herself a job in a café. 'Something wrong?'

'I've brought Louise round to see if you can talk a bit of sense into her, Dad.'

Lou glared at her mother. 'You're just being stupid about it.'

'Stupid! My only daughter wants to go backpacking round the world with some fellow we know nothing about, instead of doing the advanced catering course that a hundred other girls – sensible girls! – would give their eye teeth to get a place on. I mean, if you must do catering, then you should do it properly, get well qualified and—'

'Mum—'

Mary glared at her daughter. 'I think I'm the only one talking sense in our house, because she's wound her father round her little finger as usual.'

Jake gestured them through. 'The front door's locked so come around the back way.'

Lou gave him a peck on the cheek. 'Sorry to interrupt your gardening, Gramps. It's all a storm in a teacup, really.'

Mary marched ahead and once in the kitchen began without a word to pile up the dirty dishes on the draining board, turning on the hot-water tap.'

'Leave that!' Jake reached across her to turn it off. She was a right old bossy breeches, his Mary.

'I can easily wash up while we talk,' she protested.

'I wash up once a day now, as you well know. There's no need to do it more often with only me in the house. The less detergent people tip down the drains, the better for the environment. Now, do you want a cup of tea?'

'No, thanks. I've just had one.'

'Take your coats off? No? Come and tell me what this is all about, then.' He shepherded them into the front room, which he only used in the evenings, and sat down in his favourite armchair, watching them undo their coats and Mary fuss over her handbag. 'Well?'

'She's planning to go gallivanting round the world,' Mary repeated, glaring at her daughter.

'Lots of young people do that,' he said mildly.

'Wait till you hear what she's intending to do in Australia…' She paused dramatically then threw the words at him. 'Find your father, if he's still alive, and see if we have any long-lost relatives out there.'

He stilled and stared at Lou. 'Nay, then.'

She gazed back at him defiantly. 'Why shouldn't I, Gramps?'

'You know why not. You were told when you found those papers in my sideboard.'

'Just because you and Auntie Peggy hate your father doesn't mean the rest of us have to hate him and his family.'

'I don't hate him, exactly, just… don't want anything to do with him.'

'Anyway, we don't know that he ever had any family in Australia,' Mary snapped. 'And even if he did, they might not want to know us.'

'Then why are you getting your knickers in a twist at the mere thought of me going there, Mum?'

'Because… because you always meddle. You'd no right to go nosy parkering in your grandad's cupboard in the first place, and you've no right to interfere in this, either. Sometimes it's best to leave things as they are.'

'I was only looking at the photo albums that time, not nosy parkering, as I've told you a million times. And if I hadn't found the papers, you'd never have told me about my great-grandfather in Australia, would you?'

'You don't need to know about him,' Jake said mildly. 'My father's nothing to us now, made himself nothing when he abandoned us. Why, he never even tried to write to us. What sort of man does that, cuts off his own children because his wife won't divorce him?'

Lou looked at her grandfather reproachfully. 'He's still kin. And if he had any more children out there, they'd be close relatives of ours. Why, you might have half-brothers or sisters. Don't family connections count for anything with you?'

'Of course they do, but they didn't count for much with my father, did they?' He frowned at her. 'I agree with your mother about this, Lou. Best to let sleeping dogs lie. I want your word that you'll not try to contact them.'

She looked at him for a moment then shook her head. 'I'm sorry if this upsets you, Gramps, but I want to know about them. They're my relatives too, you know.'

He searched his mind for a sanction to apply that would stop her doing this… and could come up with nothing.

'Well!' Mary said in scandalized tones. 'I never thought to hear you defy your granddad.'

'I'm grown up now, Mum. Sometimes a person has to do what seems right.'

'Who are you to decide what's right about this?'

'Someone who's earning her own living, someone who has her own opinions and thoughts.' Lou spoke quietly but firmly.

'You'll break your granddad's heart.'

'No, I won't. If it didn't break when grandma left him, it won't break over me looking for our long-lost relatives.'

There was dead silence in the room as she brought up this other forbidden topic.

Jake stared at the rug as the image of his former wife rose before him. She'd been as bad as his father, chasing off and leaving her family, and he'd never forgiven her for that, didn't even speak her name now.

'You'll do as you please, you always have done.' He stood up. 'So I'll not waste my time arguing.'

'I'm not doing it to hurt you,' Lou said softly, coming over to give him her usual hug.

He turned aside, didn't want hugging, was too angry with her.

Mary came across to pat his shoulder. 'I'm sorry, Dad. I can't do anything with her these days. I don't know what the world's coming to.' She turned to leave, then swung back again. 'I nearly forgot. The settlement date's been fixed and we're moving next month.'

'I'll miss having you nearby.'

'You'll still have Lou – or you would if she wasn't going off round the world. She's refused point blank to come with us. Contrary, that's what she is.'

Lou sighed. 'I keep telling you: my friends are all here and I like living near the sea.'

'You always have to have the last word, don't you?'

Jake managed a smile, at least he hoped he did, as he waved them goodbye then went back to his digging. But he spent more time leaning on his spade than turning over the earth.

He felt guilty now about refusing Lou's hug, but he still thought she was betraying the family. It was the one thing they'd always been very solidly together about until now, his damned father. It still hurt that the man hadn't written to him and Peggy when they were children. He should have kept in touch and shown that he still cared about them, even though he and their mother didn't get on.

It was no use getting in touch now. The time for that had passed.

Jake hoped desperately that there were no Australian relatives for Lou to find. He didn't think he could bear anyone raising those old ghosts again. They'd had a bad year or two after their father left, he and Peggy. Oh, not financially, he'd left them all right for money, but emotionally. His mother had gone to pieces and young as they were, it'd been up to him and Peggy to run the house and look after her.

Pride had made them keep this to themselves, and they'd done the housework and shopping when they got home from school, sharing the chores, trying to jolly their mother out of her miseries.

It had been a very bad time.

Some things you could never forgive.

Chapter 6

Australia

Of course Brad didn't get away with things as easily as that. He'd known he wouldn't. Michael invited himself round for a drink a few evenings later and tried very earnestly to persuade him not to sell the house until he returned from his trip.

'Prices are rising fast, Dad. If you wait a few months you could get a lot more money, I'm sure.'

Brad listened for a while then laid a hand on his son's shoulder, not in the least moved by this careful persuasion. 'I need to sell this house before I can move on. Nothing you say or do will make me change my mind.'

'We'll miss you, the kids especially.'

'I'll miss you all, too. But I have to meet Rosie and make sure she's all right.'

'I always thought you'd do some more writing when you retired.'

'I had a couple of human resource training books published. I haven't written anything for several years. And now that I'm retiring, I'm not exactly going to be staying up to date. So what would I write?'

'You could try short stories or poetry. There's a writers' group that meets in our local library.'

Brad closed his eyes and prayed for patience as he repeated slowly and emphatically, 'I want to travel. After I've seen Rosie, I'm trotting off round Europe and maybe America. Now, you get this house on the market and find me a flat somewhere nice, or I'll find someone else to do it.'

Michael produced the papers for him to sign, but was still radiating disapproval when he left.

Brad knew that would fade. Michael never stayed angry with anyone for long.

As for him, he had another daughter to see in England. If nothing else came of her making this tentative contact with him, he had to make sure she was all right, for his own peace of mind. Oh, hell, who was he kidding? He wanted to see her, love her, be her father properly. Michael and Joanna were off his hands now. This Rosie was younger than them, she would be at a more vulnerable time of life.

What did her mother think about it all? Jane had been a strong, confident woman, which was what had attracted him at a stage where Helen seemed to be settling all too early into middle age and stodginess. He was surprised that she'd pretended her husband was Rosie's father, though. Why would they need to do that? There wasn't the stigma about children born or conceived outside marriage nowadays.

And what was the man like who'd raised his daughter? What would he feel if the biological father turned up? That might be difficult for him

Brad didn't want to upset their family, but he had to meet Rosie, just had to.

Mel woke feeling so nauseous she could hardly make it to the bathroom in time to throw up. When she stared at herself in the mirror, she was shocked at how ill she looked. She saw Simon's reflection behind hers and looked at him accusingly. 'I can't go through this again.' She couldn't stop her voice wobbling.

He came to put his arms round her and she leaned against him – sagged, really.

'Let's get you back to bed, darling. I'll bring up a cup of tea and a piece of dry toast. That used to help a bit last time.'

She threw his arm off and stumbled across to the bed. 'Nothing helped, as you well know. I was sick for the whole nine months – morning, noon and night. I can't face it again, I just can't!'

'I'm not murdering our child. I'll have a vasectomy after this one's born and—'

'No need! I'll be having my tubes tied. I'm not relying on you any more.' She burst into tears and turned away from him, burying her face in the pillow. When she heard him go out, she let herself cry for a while, then lay there feeling exhausted. Maybe she'd take today off work, give herself a good rest.

When she heard footsteps coming back up the stairs, she scrubbed her eyes on a corner of the sheet and scowled at him as he set the tray down beside the bed.

'Hot water with ginger and lemon in it. I read some-where that it can help and—'

But the nausea was rising again and she shoved him out of the way as she bolted for the bathroom.

'Was it really this bad last time?' He frowned at her as she stood up from where she'd been kneeling. 'I don't remember you looking so ill.'

She leaned over the wash basin, rinsing her mouth out and splashing her face with cold water. 'Yes. For the first three months. You may not remember, but I do. I had to carry a bucket with me everywhere because there were days when I couldn't even make it to the bathroom in time to be sick. And I had to stop work. But I'm not doing that this time!'

'I'm sorry. If I could do it for you—'

'If men had babies, if they had to go through this, there would be fewer children born.'

It was an old quarrel between them.

'Sexist claptrap,' he said absently as he put his arm round her and guided her back to the bed. He put a glass into her hand. 'Try it anyway. Just have a sip or two.'

She sighed and did as he asked. It wouldn't help. Nausea was still roiling round inside her. But the warmth of the glass was comforting and she put both hands round it. 'I'm not going to work today.'

'Good.'

'Just today. Giving myself a bit of a boost, so that I can cope.'

'We shouldn't have gone out last week.'

'It was an important function. I was trying mind over matter… only it didn't work. I don't think anyone noticed when we slipped away, though.'

'You should stop work completely, Mel. Or at least take sick leave. You are definitely sick. If we downsized, you could stop work completely and we could manage perfectly well on my salary.'

She didn't answer, just stared down at the glass of steaming liquid because the nausea was still heaving around in her stomach, pressing for release. When Simon stayed beside the bed staring down at her, she snapped, 'Go away. I prefer to do my throwing up in private. If you want to help me, get Emma off to school and yourself to work.'

But when he'd left the house she was sorry she'd snapped at him, wanted him back, wanted his arm round her shoulders. Most of all she wanted to be rid of this sickness. There were seven more months of this to endure.

She buried her face in the pillow and began to weep – loud, ragged sobs and scalding tears.

–

Gina opened the door, took the business card the real estate agent offered and showed him round her father's house. It was looking as well as it could without her redecorating or spending money. She'd got rid of the clutter and placed a couple of pot plants strategically to hide stains in the carpet.

'I'm glad to see you haven't done much to tart it up,' he began, saw her frown and added hastily, 'not that it isn't clean and tidy. In fact, it's well presented, for a house of this era.'

She cut in ruthlessly because selling her childhood home was proving to be more painful than she'd expected and she wanted to get these interviews over with quickly. 'Let's get straight to the reason you're here. How much is the house worth?'

He named a figure that shocked her, it was so much more than she'd expected. 'You can't be serious!'

'It's a very good neighbourhood, close to the city. Gentrification has started – look at the improvements in the next street. This place will be snapped up by developers, who'll probably knock it down and put three units on the block.'

She'd guessed that. 'I see. Is that a realistic price or are you exaggerating?'

He cocked one eyebrow, studied her through narrowed eyes and reduced his price by ten thousand dollars. 'I think that's what you'll actually get, but we'll ask what I originally said to give us some leeway for bargaining. I sold one near here six months ago for considerably less. Real estate is booming in Western Australia, you know.'

The next two agents told the same tale, give or take a few thousand dollars, though the female agent seemed more knowledgeable.

That evening Gina was sitting wondering who would be the best person to sell the house when the phone rang.

'Marla here. I came to value your father's house today. Look, Mrs Porter, I've got an offer for it, quite a good one, too. Are you interested?'

Gina gasped. 'How much?'

The figure named was ten thousand dollars over the highest estimate given her.

'Why on earth is he offering more?'

'Because he wants your answer within twenty-four hours,' Marla said. 'There's no negotiation on that or the price. Quick decision or he looks elsewhere.'

'I'll – um – consult the other beneficiaries and get back to you in the morning.'

'I'm here till ten o'clock tonight if you come to any decision.'

Gina rang her daughters. 'If someone wants to pay that much so quickly, we could probably get more for it,' she cautioned them. 'Though you can never tell.'

Both her daughters recommended selling immediately.

'It's worth it to avoid any hassles,' Lexie said.

'I've not got the energy to do anything about it,' Mel said. 'But the money will be a big help, the way things are.'

'Still feeling sick?' Gina asked.

'Yeah. Even worse than last time.'

'I'm so sorry, love. Maybe you could stop work and—'

'I'm *not* giving up work. We'd have to sell this house if I did that.'

Gina bit back a sharp response. Mel was totally unreasonable about that home of hers. It sometimes seemed that she cared more for it than she did for her husband and child. But neither of her daughters was prone to listen to advice, so Gina had stopped offering it.

She rang the agent and agreed to meet at eight o'clock the following morning to sign the contract, which would make the sale binding.

It felt strange. It would leave a big gap in her life. For the past few months she'd done a lot of to-ing and fro-ing, first to help her father and then to clear up after him. Now, all of a sudden, it was over.

I have the time and money to do something for myself now, she thought. And she hadn't changed her mind about what she intended to do.

That afternoon she went and had her hair re-styled and was delighted with her new look, though she refused to have it coloured. Why should she? She liked her own colour and a few grey hairs didn't worry her.

The day after she bought some new clothes, casual but smart, suitable for travelling.

She was going to do it, she definitely was!

–

Gina phoned her daughters to arrange a meeting and tell them what she was planning. During their conversation, Mel had to rush away to be sick and Simon took over the phone.

'She sounds really bad,' Gina said, worried.

'She is. But she's still dragging herself into work and won't listen to sense. You'll be shocked when you see her. She's lost so much weight. Try to talk a bit of sense into her, will you?'

'When could anyone make Mel change her mind once she'd decided on something?'

He sighed. 'She's certainly got her full quota of stubborn genes.' There was a moment's silence, then he said in a strangled voice, 'I can't take much more of this, Ma watching her run herself into the ground and… Ah, there you are, Mel.'

'You all right, love?' Gina asked when her daughter came back on the phone.

'Obviously not. But I'll survive. A pregnancy doesn't go on for ever. Now, you wanted to see me and Lexie. What was it about?'

'I'll tell you when we meet. It's quite important. In the circumstances, I think it'd be best if we came to your place. How about tomorrow evening? Are you going into work? All right then, I'll bring a casserole for tea, with enough for us all, Simon and the children too. You'll only have to come home in the evening and take it easy. Tell the after-school sitter that Emma can come straight home tomorrow. I'll be there.'

Mel's voice softened. 'Thanks, Mum. That'll be a big help.'

Gina phoned Lexie about the meeting then tried to watch TV, but she couldn't concentrate for worrying about poor Mel.

—

After his talk with his children, life speeded up so much that Brad started to wonder if he was going crazy.

He looked at several flats and chose one which had views of the city. The lights at night should be pretty. It had three bedrooms and a spacious living room and kitchen combined, two bathrooms, plus a balcony big enough to entertain a few friends.

To his dismay, he had grossly underestimated the time it would take him to clear out the house, and in the end, he had to call in Joanna and Michael to help so that he could be out by settlement date. He hadn't realized how many of Helen's things were still packed away in various cupboards, not to mention stacked in the roof, and deciding what to throw away gave him a few wakeful nights.

When removal day came at last, he stood around feeling useless, watching the men carry his life out of the front door, piece by piece. The boxes looked so anonymous and the furniture scratched. It was cruelly revealing, that sunlight. He'd buy some new furniture when he came back from his travels.

After the removal men had gone, he took a last stroll round the empty, echoing house, dashing the tears from his eyes and muttering, 'Bloody fool!'

Then he went outside, locked up carefully and got into his car. No regrets, he told himself fiercely as emotion still threatened to overcome him.

–

A couple of weeks later, when Michael popped in to see him, Brad invited him and the whole family out for a farewell meal.

'Come and have dinner at our place on Friday, instead,' Michael said. 'You can stay over and I'll drive you to the airport early on Saturday morning.'

'Thanks. And Michael… I just wondered if things are all right at home? You and Sheila seemed to be very distant with one another last time I was round.'

Michael looked at him and grimaced. 'You don't miss a thing, do you?' He took a deep breath. 'Sheila and I aren't getting on all that well at the moment. She's met someone else.'

'Oh, no!'

'It's a bit… um, difficult.'

'Are you sure you want me to stay the night?'

'Yes. Sheila's very good a putting a normal face on things for the kids' sake. She should have been a damned actress! The kids will want to say a proper goodbye to you and we'll invite Jo's lot over too.' He gave his father a wry smile. 'I take after you. I love having kids. If Sheila tries to take them away from me when she leaves, she's in for a big battle.'

'Family is what matters most,' Brad agreed quietly. 'And thanks for all your help with the house and flat, son. I really appreciate it.'

'It was my pleasure. Got to go now.' Michael drained his glass, then as they both stood up, gave his father a big hug. 'I'm going to miss you like hell.'

'I'll miss you, too.' He hesitated. 'Do you want me to postpone things?'

'No. There's nothing you can do to help my marriage. You go and sort out our baby sister.'

Chapter 7

England

Lou had had it with the rows and threats at home, and the fuss her mother was making about moving house. It was driving everyone crazy, not just her.

'For two pins I'd pack my bag and leave tomorrow,' she told her boyfriend Rick that evening as they walked down the street.

'Why don't we?'

'I thought we were going to wait for the end of the college year, so that you could get your credits.'

He shrugged. 'I'm going to fail. No credit in that.'

'You should do some of the work, enough to scrape a pass at least.'

He shrugged and grinned at her, his teeth very white against his dark skin. 'I can't face it. They want me to draw and paint in their style. This group of lecturers doesn't seem to go for pictorial work and that's what I like to do. Crazy, isn't it? I chose the wrong college, I think, but I didn't know any better then. No one in my family's ever studied art.'

'Oh, Rick. You're not going to drop out?'

He shrugged. 'I've dropped out already. Haven't attended any classes for the past week. Haven't told my dad about it, though. You know how ferociously respectable and follow-the-rules he is. He'll go through the roof at me.'

'Will you have enough money to pay for your share of the trip?'

'Sure.' He grinned. 'They might not like pictorial work at college, but it brings in a steady flow of punters who want their likeness sketched at the shopping centre every weekend. And I can earn more money while we're away doing the same thing.'

She frowned at him, thoughts chasing one another round in her mind, then straightened her shoulders. 'All right. Let's go and find out about tickets tomorrow. Mum's driving me mad with her nagging and I'll have nowhere to live once she moves because I'm not going to live with them in Birmingham. And Rick?'

'Yes?'

'I want to go straight to Australia to find my family. We can do a few side tours on the way back.'

'OK. Still at odds with your Ma?'

'Very. And with Gramps, too. They're so unreasonable about my great-grandfather. He wasn't a serial murderer, just a man who left his wife for another woman. It happens all the time.'

'What are you going to do about your things?'

'Beg Gramps to let me put them in his garage. He won't refuse.'

'And how will you find these relatives when we get there?'

She smiled. 'There was an envelope in among the photo albums. It wasn't opened, but on the back it had my great-grandfather's name and address in Australia: well, it's either him or he had a son called Daniel Everett. I didn't mention that I'd found it, just memorized the address. Gramps was so angry with me that I didn't dare ask him why he hadn't opened the letter.'

'His father's probably dead by now.'

'Well, he wasn't dead a few months ago and that's when it was posted. Even if he is dead, his address gives me somewhere to start, doesn't it? He may have family out there. That'd be cool, wouldn't it?'

'So we're on for our trip, Missy Lou?' he asked in a mock American voice.

'We certainly are, Mr Rick,' she replied in the same accent.

Solemnly they shook hands, then he kissed her and she melted in his arms as she always did, loving his tall, strong body but most of all loving the fact that he was such a darling.

Her mother hated her going out with a black guy. She hadn't said it straight out, but she was always very stiff with Rick. Well, that was something her old-fashioned, narrow-minded mother would have to get used to. Her father was more concerned about his new job, even more than he'd been about his old one. She tried to remember the last time he and she had talked, really talked, and shook her head. They never had and probably never would.

She smiled wryly against Rick's shoulder. He was as much a misfit in his family as she was in hers. They refused to call him Rick, which was what he liked, insisting on 'Richard', with which they'd christened him. Richard didn't suit him at all. He was so laid back nothing seemed to faze him and his family were all uptight about life.

They'd made it clear to Lou that they considered their son too young for a steady relationship. During it his father had called her 'white' in such an officious tone that she'd told him straight out that she was pink, not white, thank you very much. He hadn't liked that. Too bad. He could lump it.

And actually, Rick wasn't black. He was coffee coloured, café latte, lovely skin he had.

Coffee and roses, they joked sometimes as they held hands. Now he signed his notes to her with a little sketch of a cup of coffee and a rose. Was that romantic or what? She smiled at the thought.

'What are you grinning at?' he teased.

'You. Coffee and roses. Us.'

He put his arm round her and they walked on, not saying much, simply happy to be together. They were good with one another and if it was up to her, their relationship was going to be permanent, whatever anyone said about them being too young. Age had nothing to do with recognizing your soul mate.

Rick hadn't actually said anything about a long-term relationship yet, but he would soon, she was quite sure of that. And just as sure of her answer.

–

After school Rosie and her friend went to pick up Mandy's family mail from their post office box. Mandy grinned and held out a letter. 'He's replied.'

'Oh, no! I can't believe it!'

Rosie took the letter her friend was holding out and stuffed it in her pocket.

'Aren't you going to open it?'

'Only when I'm alone. It's scary stuff, Mandy. I can't open it in the street. What if I cry or something?'

'You'll tell me what he says, though.'

'Mmmm.'

When she left her friend, Rosie went to sit in a sheltered corner of a park near her home, tearing open the letter with hands that trembled a little.

Dear Rosie

Your letter came as a great surprise to me, but a very welcome one, I promise you. I am indeed the correct Bradley Gerald Rosenberry and I remember your mother very fondly, so it seems I must indeed be your father.

It feels strange, doesn't it, to have such a close relationship with a complete stranger?

I'd love to meet you and I'd already planned to visit the UK next month, so you don't need to save up to come to Australia. My wife died a few years ago and I've just taken early retirement, so I'm going to do some travelling.

Are you all right with me coming to meet you? If so, it'd be nice if you gave me a proper address and a phone number.

Do you still live with your mother? How does she feel about this? If you haven't told her you've been in touch with me, you really should.

There are so many things I want to ask you... but I think they'd better wait till we meet.

You have a half-brother and sister here, both older than you. Joanna is 32 and works in executive placement. She has three children. Michael is 30 and is in real estate. He has two children. So that makes you a five-fold aunt.

I'm looking forward very much to getting to know you.

Love,

Brad

PS I had trouble thinking how to sign this letter, since you have another father and I don't want to usurp his place after all these years.

She swallowed hard and read the letter again, then held it to her breast and tried to think coherently. But she couldn't! She felt dazed at how easily she'd found him.

And he was already planning to come to England. She'd only have a short time to prepare for their meeting, the main things being to convince her mother that it was a good idea and to make sure her Dad wasn't too hurt by it all.

When she got home, she stopped short in the doorway of her bedroom at the sight of her mother standing staring at a piece of paper. 'What are you doing?' she demanded. 'Those are my things.'

'I was getting my emails from the computer, then I decided to clear up this pigsty of yours so that I could vacuum. I knocked that box off the shelf. I didn't mean to pry, but everything fell out.'

Rosie went a little closer and gulped as she realized which letter her mother was holding. She could have kicked herself. She'd written it so many times and kept a copy of her final effort. 'So now you know that I've written to him.'

'How the hell did you get Brad's address?'

'From the Australian white pages online. You told me his middle name, which made it easier.'

'I did?'

'Yes. Bradley Gerald Rosenberry. You were being sarcastic, but I remembered it.'

'I wish you hadn't done this, Rosie.'

'I know. After I realized Dad couldn't possibly be my biological father from our science lessons, you made it plain that you didn't want me finding out about my real one. I think it's weird that you never told me.'

'Schools have a lot to answer for, the way they teach science!' Jane snapped. 'And Stu's been a good father to you, he doesn't deserve this.'

'It doesn't stop me loving Dad, but we both know he's always cared more about Casey than me. No, don't deny it! You know it's true.' She watched her mother close her mouth on a protest and avoid looking directly at her. She couldn't help her voice wobbling as she added, 'I never understood why. I thought there must be something wrong with me. Once I understood, well, I felt a lot better about myself. So it was a good thing for me to find out.'

'I'm sorry. I didn't know.'

Rosie shrugged. She hadn't realized how much it mattered, either.

'Can't you let it drop at that? You hurt Stu badly when you confronted us about your parentage. This'll hurt him even more.'

'And you? Doesn't it hurt you at all? I mean, you must have loved this Bradley person once.'

'Brad. He never used his full name.' Jane ran one hand through her unruly hair and sighed. 'I was telling you the truth when I said he was just a holiday romance. It meant no more to me than that because I knew by that stage of my travels that I'd never want to settle anywhere except England. I didn't even know Brad was married at first and when I did, well that made a difference too. I didn't want to be responsible for breaking up a marriage.'

'So he was unfaithful to his wife.' Rosie didn't like the thought of that.

'These things happen. People don't mean to be unfaithful, but I was lonely and he was unhappy. He'd just had to turn down a job in Sydney, a job he wanted very much, because she refused point-blank to move from Perth. And he was not only married, he had two children. He loved them to pieces. I soon realized he'd never leave them.'

'Would it have made a difference if he'd known about me?'

'I doubt it.' Jane sighed and stared into space for a moment or two. 'I didn't know I was pregnant myself till I got back to the UK. I decided not to tell him and almost immediately I met Stu. He's the man I love properly, as one should love a husband.' She hesitated, then begged, 'Please, darling. Don't do this. Don't push it any further.'

Rosie stared at the floor, testing out the thought of agreeing in her mind, then shaking her head slowly because she knew she couldn't stop here. What was driving her was too important to abandon. Some primal urge to know your kin, she supposed. They didn't teach you about that in biology, just the mechanics of how human beings bred more human beings, and how blood groups interacted. 'I'm sorry, Mum, but I just have to meet him. I don't know why, but I have to.'

Jane screwed up the copy of the letter and threw it on the floor. 'I'll make sure you don't. I'm not having you do something which will tear Stu apart, especially not now.'

'What's so special about now?'

Silence, then, 'Nothing.'

Rosie stared at her mother. 'You always say 'Nothing' in that tone when there is something.'

'Nothing that I intend to tell you about at the moment.' She turned and walked out of the room, slamming the door behind her.

Rosie went and sat on the bed, staring into space till her brother Casey came in and flopped down beside her.

'I couldn't help overhearing.' He kicked a shoe to one side. 'How long have you known Dad isn't your father?'

She grabbed his arm. 'Shh! Mum will go ballistic if she finds out you know.'

He lowered his voice. 'How long?'

'Since last year.'

'That means we're only half-brother and sister.'

'Doesn't make any difference to me. You're a pain in the arse, but better the pain you know...'

He grinned. 'Yeah. You're a pain, too.'

She could tell he was relieved by her response, though he'd never admit it.

'Scary stuff, eh?'

73

'Tell me about it. Casey… do you know what Mum means about Dad when she says she doesn't want him worrying "especially now"?' Rosie waited, then nudged him. 'You do, don't you?'

'I did happen to hear them talking the other evening.'

'You mean you eavesdropped again. You are a little shit.' He was always doing it, which drove her mad when she had friends round.

Casey shrugged. 'A guy has to keep an eye on things.' He began drawing patterns on the carpet with his toe.

'Well? What did you overhear?'

'Dad's been given a hint that he might not get the job as head of the Learning Resource Centre when they merge the two schools. There's a guy in the other school who's put in for it too, and you know Dad doesn't get on with the headmaster. So he may have to look for another job.'

'He'll hate that. He loves that job of his, and it's only just down the road.'

'We might have to move to another town, you know,' Casey added.

'He won't do it. He's a real stick-in-the-mud, grew up round here, bought a house here, doesn't really like going on holidays even. And I wouldn't want to move, either. Not when I've only another year at school.'

They sat in silence. After a while Casey stood up, patted her arm awkwardly and ambled out without saying anything.

Rosie sat for a bit longer staring into space. Would her mother be able to stop her from communicating with Brad? No, definitely not. She was using her friend's family's PO Box and as Mandy emptied it for her parents on the way back from school every day, they wouldn't know about it, either. She'd give Brad her mobile phone number when she wrote back so that he'd be able to phone her when he came to England, then they'd see about meeting one another.

If only her mother didn't use the same computer for emails, she'd have emailed him now that she had his email address, but she hadn't dared risk that.

She didn't want to hurt her parents, sometimes wished she'd not found out. As Casey had said, it was scary stuff. But she had to follow it through. Dad always said she was like a terrier, never letting go. Mum said she was pig-headed. Whatever. It was how she was.

She wouldn't stop what she was doing, but she really wished her mother was on her side. She hated deceiving her parents.

Chapter 8

Australia

Gina arrived early at Mel's house, let herself in and stared round in shock. She'd never seen the place in such a mess. She didn't hesitate to do a quick tour of the rest, collecting dirty clothes from the bedrooms. Going into the laundry, she set on a load of washing. After that she began to clear up the kitchen.

When her granddaughter arrived home from school with a friend from the same street, she gave them a piece of fruit each and sent them out to play in the backyard, where she could keep an eye on them. Complaints about wanting to watch TV left her unmoved. In her opinion, today's children watched too much TV and spent too much time sitting in front of computers and other gadgets. Not that she had anything against computers.

By the time she heard Mel's car and the whine of the automatic door on the garage, she had a second load of washing going. She went to greet her daughter and stopped dead.

'What's the matter?' Mel demanded.

'You look dreadful.'

'I feel it.'

'Go and sit down. I'll bring you a drink.'

'Just fruit juice.'

Gina stared at her, taking in the haggard, gaunt cheeks and dark-circled eyes. 'What have you eaten today?'

Mel shrugged. 'Nothing much. I can't keep things down in the mornings, and lunch time isn't much better. I should be able to have something for tea, though.'

'Not good enough. You've a baby to feed as well as yourself.'

'Don't nag, Mum. You're as bad as Simon. I'm not stupid, I'm doing my best to eat. Right? But I just throw it up again.'

'You're trying to do the impossible by continuing to work, if you ask me.'

'I didn't ask you.' Mel closed her eyes for a minute, then stumbled across to a chair. 'Could you get me that orange juice, please? I can sometimes keep a sweet drink down at this time of day.'

Gina poured one, hearing the washing machine chime out to announce that it had finished its load. 'I've been doing your washing. I'll just put that lot on to dry so that I can iron it for you before I go.'

As she passed her daughter, Mel caught her hand. 'Sorry I was so sharp, Mum. I'm not at my best. But I'm grateful for your help. Very.' Her voice wobbled on the last word.

Gina gave her a quick hug and went to deal with the washing.

When she returned, Mel had gone upstairs and the glass of juice was only half empty.

Resolutely refusing to tell her news until Ben and Emma were in bed, Gina served dinner and relaxed with a glass of wine. 'I'm assuming I can stay the night?'

'You know you can.' Mel pushed her plate aside.

'Can't you eat just a little more?' Gina pressed.

'No. I can sometimes keep down a small meal, but never a large one. I'll save the dessert for bedtime. So, what's the big news?'

Gina took a deep breath. 'As soon as we've sorted out Dad's estate, I'm going to England.'

Three faces registered amazement and shock.

It was Lexie who broke the silence. 'But why?'

'Because of what I found in Dad's papers.' She explained about the family in England.

'And he never said a word!' Lexie exclaimed indignantly.

'He must have had his reasons,' Simon said. 'Don't you think you should contact them first, Ma? Find out if they want to see you?'

'No. I've decided to present them with a fait accompli. I'm not giving them a chance to say no. They didn't even open the letters Dad sent, just sent them back unopened. But he obviously wrote for several years, several times the first year, then at Christmas and one other time for each of them, which I suppose must have been their birthdays.'

'They may still refuse to have anything to do with you,' he said.

'Then they'll have to refuse to my face and I'll at least see them.'

'What about this?' Mel indicated her belly. 'I was counting on you to help.'

Gina took another deep breath. 'I know. You and your sister have both been counting on me rather too much. Babysitting for you so often has been disrupting my life. I don't mind doing it occasionally, but not several times a week. And as Lexie pointed out, I'm young enough to move out of my current rut and do something with the years I've got left. So that's what I'm planning to do.'

She saw Lexie wince and Mel bite her lip.

'What about your job, Mum?'

'It's not much of a job and we all know it. I can find another just like it when I come back or go temping, even. I've been using the computer a lot since Tom died and I've done a touch-typing course on it. Makes things so much easier.'

Dead silence.

'I know you were counting on my help, Mel darling. But if you continue to make decisions that involve me giving up my life to support yours, then I'm afraid you're going to have to find other ways through your problems. To be frank, you're ill and need to rest. You only have to look in the mirror to know that. But you won't listen to Simon or me. It seems as if you care more about this house than you do about your baby – or about *my* life.'

Mel stood up so abruptly that she knocked her chair over. 'I never wanted this baby, so it's not fair to ask me to give up things I love for it.' She turned as if to run out of the room, gave a gasp and collapsed.

Simon ran round the table to kneel beside his wife. 'She's unconscious!'

As two or three minutes passed and Mel showed no signs of regaining consciousness, Gina picked up the phone. 'I'm calling an ambulance. Mel needs help.'

Simon nodded, still clasping his wife's hand in his. 'Maybe I should have let her seek a termination.'

Gina shook her head. 'No. Terminations aren't for babies who're merely inconvenient.'

'But she's ill – and making herself worse. I don't want to lose her.'

'I don't either.' But his words had struck terror into her. Mel wasn't that bad, surely?

'I've been beating my head against a brick wall for weeks, Ma, watching her get weaker and weaker. How she's found the strength to continue at all on so little food, I don't know. She wouldn't even go and see the doctor, said he was no help last time and she wasn't wasting what energy she did have left sitting around in a medical centre waiting on his convenience.'

Lexie spoke from across the room, where she was watching through the window for the ambulance. 'I've tried to talk sense into her as well, Mum. But you know Mel. Once she's set her mind on something she won't listen to what anyone says.'

Gina felt guilty now for what she'd just said to Mel, but could do nothing except stay crouching next to Simon. Her worry deepened as her daughter remained unconscious.

'She's fainted twice before, but she came around quickly each time. It wasn't like this.' Simon's face was ravaged with anxiety. He was still holding his wife's hand.

By the time the ambulance arrived, Mel had regained consciousness. But she didn't protest about what they'd done, merely lay back and closed her eyed with a murmur of 'Too tired.'

To see her stubborn daughter so quiescent was the most frightening thing of all to Gina.

–

Brad needed to hear from Rosie before he could finalize his plane flight. He grew impatient, taking long walks to fill the hours and reading a lot.

He was tempted to get in touch with some of his old friends from work, but decided against it. Better a clean break for the moment. Maybe he'd call Judy when he got back. But the thought of her didn't stir up any feelings in him other than friendship and she was clearly attracted to him, so on second thoughts, it was best to leave things alone.

At last the letter he'd been waiting for arrived and he tore it open impatiently, standing by the mailbox with the sun blazing down on him.

It was disappointingly short. Rosie had given him only a mobile phone number. Did that mean she didn't trust him? He hated the thought of that, absolutely hated it. And she said she couldn't email because her mother used the same computer.

He dashed off a quick reply to her, promising to ring as soon as he arrived in Lancashire. Then he booked the next available flight to the UK and found a large hotel in Blackpool that was offering a very tempting special price if you booked for a whole week.

–

Lexie stayed with the children while Gina followed the ambulance to the hospital. There they wheeled Mel away, then Gina and her son-in-law sat for what seemed a long time in the casualty area. Eventually they were summoned into a tiny bare cubicle of a room to speak to a doctor.

'We need to admit your wife, Mr Tesker. She's in a very bad way, severely malnourished. We can only hope the baby hasn't suffered. You really should have sought help before this.' He frowned at Simon as if it was his fault.

'I've been trying to get her to see a doctor, but she wouldn't.'

'My daughter can be rather stubborn,' Gina said. 'And I have to say, the doctors didn't help her much last time with the nausea.'

'I think it's worse this time,' Simon said, 'but she's been trying to hide how bad, even from me.'

When they took Mel up to a ward, Gina offered to go home and pick up some things for her daughter. 'You stay here, Simon.'

'Thanks.'

Her thoughts were very sombre as she drove back to Mel's house. She didn't see how she could leave for England now. It was one thing to leave a healthy daughter to her own devices, but not one who was so ill.

No, she'd definitely have to put off her trip.

She was surprised at how deeply disappointed she was.

Chapter 9

From England to Australia

Lou told her parents she was leaving early for her trip and flying straight to Australia.

Her mother regarded her sourly. 'We would prefer you to help us move and settle in. Surely you can wait a few months?'

'You're trying to take me away from Rick.'

'He's not a good influence.'

'I love him, Mum. Can't you understand that?'

'I can understand that you're going to ruin your life. You're too young to be settling down with the first fellow you meet, especially one who's failed his college course.'

'He hasn't failed, he quit!'

Her mother raised one eyebrow in that infuriating way she had.

'I'm not coming with you.' Lou hesitated. 'Can you take some of my things, though?'

'No. You're not using us as a furniture store if you're not going to live with us.'

Lou looked at her, disgusted at this refusal to help her. 'Do things your way or get out, is that it?' she asked in a choked voice. 'All right, I'll find somewhere else for them.'

It was like living with an angry wasp. And her father was rarely around because he was working longer hours than usual to finalize projects at his current place of work. He wouldn't have stood up to his wife anyway. It had always been clear who was the boss in their house.

'How can you do this to us, Louise?' Mary raged yet again that evening. 'Don't you care anything for me, for your grandfather?'

Lou tried to stay calm. 'Of course I do. But I care about the rest of my family too – having one, that is.'

Her mother's blank look spurred her on to try to explain what was driving her. 'Look, I'm your only child. Cheryl is *your* cousin. She's not only much older than me, but looks down her nose at our side of the family. I have no relatives in my generation here. If I've got any down under, I want to meet them. If I like them, I'm going to stay in touch with them. And nothing – nothing at all – will make me change my mind about that.'

Her mother got one of her puckered-mouth looks. 'Do as you please, but don't come begging me to help you if things go wrong.'

It wasn't the best note on which to leave for Australia, but her mother was as hard as a rock underneath that quiet exterior. You either did things her way or suffered the penalties. But Lou knew that if she really did need help, if she got into trouble overseas, help would be forthcoming – together with a great deal of grumbling and scolding afterwards.

She and Rick went to take her things round to her granddad's in the car of a friend of his. She didn't even consider asking her dad to help with this. The friend drove off and Rick helped her stack the boxes in the garage.

'Cheer up, love. Your parents will come around.'

She looked at him. 'In their own time. They're not—' she hesitated then said it, 'the most loving of parents, are they? Thank goodness for my granddad.'

Rick gave her a long hug then they went into the house and had a cup of tea.

'Are you still mad at me, Gramps?' she asked afterwards as they were being taken on the usual tour of his vegetable garden.

He looked at her, his eyes sad. 'Not angry, just disappointed that you're so intent on stirring up things best left alone.'

'I'm sorry to upset you.'

'But you're not changing your mind.'

'No.'

He changed the subject.

When they were walking away down the street she looked at Rick. 'Do you think I'm being unfair to my family?'

'I can understand your need to do it. And I'd be a fine one to tell another person what to do about her family. I've upset my own so badly by dropping out of art college that they've thrown me out. I'll be sleeping on the floor at my mate Cole's flat till we leave.'

'Oh, Rick, why didn't you say?'

'I thought you had enough to worry about.'

She stopped walking to pull him to her for a quick kiss. 'You're a darling.'

He grinned and smacked a loud kiss on each of her cheeks in return. 'I know.'

'And so modest with it.' She sighed as they started walking again. 'I'll be glad when we leave.'

But she didn't feel glad as the plane took off; she felt sad and disoriented. Her mother hadn't relented and had hardly said a word to her during the final week. Lou reached for Rick's hand and held it tightly. 'Here we go, then.'

He gave her one of his gentle smiles. 'We'll be all right, Lou.'

'Will we?'

'Yes. Whether you find your Australian family or not, you and I are going to have a ball and fill ourselves with mind-blowing experiences. And I'm going to come home with a sketch book full of stuff for future paintings which will make our fortune. You'll see.'

She wondered what new understanding of the world she would take home. They said travel broadened your mind. She'd had quite a narrow life up to now. Her parents were extremist stick-in-the-muds. Absolute dinosaurs.

She'd miss Gramps most of all. He was quite with it in his own tranquil way, what with organic gardening and save the planet stuff. She admired that in him. And even though he disagreed with what she was doing, he hadn't gone on at her or sulked as her mother had.

–

Peggy opened the door and blinked in shock to see Cheryl standing there. 'Darling, why didn't you phone? I've not got your room ready or anything.'

Cheryl shrugged. 'I was in the district so I thought I'd pop in.'

'Are you able to stay overnight?'

'Yes. If that's all right.'

'It's always all right, you know that. I'll just ring your father and let him know.'

'He knows already. I phoned him at work. I'll put this in my bedroom, shall I?' She carried her overnight case and computer upstairs and called down, 'Mum, where shall I put the ironing?'

Peggy went rushing along to the bedroom. 'Sorry. I've not had time to do it today.' She gathered it up and stood for a moment, unable to think where to put it. There was nowhere, really. Hartley had taken the second largest bedroom for his home office and had his computer set up there. And he had the fourth bedroom for his models. He had several display cabinets full of them, had been making them for years. He'd not thank her for dumping un-ironed washing in there. 'Um – do you think I could leave it on this chair? I mean, if you're just staying overnight, it won't matter to you, will it?'

Cheryl pulled a face. 'I hate seeing piles of washing lying round. Why do you iron so much anyway?'

'Your father is rather – fussy.' Peggy hugged the washing to her breast then put it on the chair. 'Don't tell him it's here.' She glanced uncertainly towards Cheryl, who was hanging up a skirt and top.

Her daughter looked back. 'You shouldn't let Dad bully you.'

'How do I stop him?' When her daughter just shrugged, she asked, 'How's the guy you've moved in with?'

Cheryl's face softened. 'He's great.'

'Maybe you could bring him home to meet us?'

'Not yet. It's too soon. You haven't said anything to Dad about him?'

'No, of course not.'

'That's all right then.' She smiled. 'And I won't say anything about the ironing.'

Peggy tried to get the dinner perfect, she really did, but the steaks were tough, even though the butcher had promised they'd be nice and tender. She'd rather have shopped at the supermarket, where prices where cheaper and you could get everything under one roof, but Hartley was friends with the butcher so he had an account there. It was a good thing she had steaks in the freezer and could pull an extra one out. She'd take the toughest one for herself.

Cheryl came into the kitchen as she was preparing the vegetables. 'Any chance of a cup of coffee?'

Still smarting from her daughter's unkind remarks, Peggy nodded towards the cupboard. 'You know where everything is.'

'I've just redone my nail varnish. I don't want to scratch it till it's fully set. They call it quick drying, but it isn't.'

Suppressing a sigh, Peggy got up and pulled out the instant coffee jar.

But Hartley walked in from the garage just then, saw the jar of coffee and frowned. 'I think we can do better than that for our daughter, Peggy. And you can make me one, too.' He got out the percolator, then swept Cheryl off to the sitting room. Laughter came from there as Peggy continued her preparations.

The meal wasn't one of her best, but it was all right.

Hartley took a bite of steak. He didn't comment, but the way he grimaced at his plate and turned to Cheryl, pointedly not addressing any more remarks to Peggy, showed her his opinion of the meal. He could do that sometimes with no more than a lift of the eyebrows. She couldn't finish her food, felt tears well up in her eyes and made an excuse to go into the kitchen and wipe them away.

The evening seemed interminable. Cheryl was having problems at work and was asking her father's advice. It sounded to Peggy as if her daughter was acting like a prima donna, but Hartley was on her side as usual.

It was a relief that Cheryl had to leave early the next morning to visit a client in a town an hour's drive away.

Hartley looked at Peggy after he'd waved his daughter goodbye. 'Not your best effort at being a hostess.'

She watched numbly as he went to fetch his briefcase and left the house. Only when the sound of his car engine had faded into the distance did she allow the tears to fall.

–

Lou and Rick arrived in Australia early one morning to discover a world where the air seemed clearer and the colours brighter. Even the sky seemed to be higher above their heads, arching over them like a colossal blue dome.

He stood outside the Perth airport building staring round in delight. 'Will you look at that light! Lou, I've got to paint this.'

She tugged at his arm. 'First we have to find the backpackers' hostel and get our bearings. Do you mind moving on?'

He grinned at her. 'OK, slave driver. But you realize you're stopping me from thinking deep artistic thoughts here.'

She grinned back as she hitched her backpack higher. 'Yeah. Right. Now let's find our way to Bakpak Heaven.'

The double bedroom at $25 a night, sharing a bathroom with others, seemed fine except for having two single beds. But at that price you couldn't expect perfection like a lovely double bed.

Even though it was the middle of the morning here, Lou yawned and looked longingly at the beds.

Rick hauled her out for a walk. 'Experts say that you need to get the sun on your face when you change time zones.'

They lasted till four o'clock then gave up fighting the drowsiness and crashed for a long night's sleep.

Tomorrow we'll to go shopping, Lou decided as she snuggled down in bed. If we get ourselves some bits and pieces of food it'll be cheaper to use the cooking facilities here than buy meals out. And the day after tomorrow, I'm going to look up my great-grandfather.

She smiled as she put one arm round Rick. They'd pushed the beds together and tied the legs to keep them together. It felt so right to be sleeping openly with him, not just sneaking off furtively to make love and then pretend they hadn't.

Families!

–

Gina settled in at Mel's house while her daughter was in hospital. She'd put her own plans on hold because someone had to look after Emma – and after Mel too when she came out of hospital.

They had Mel on an IV drip and were giving her anti-emetics. The doctor told Simon this was one of the worst cases of pregnancy sickness she'd ever seen.

'I'm to blame,' he said to his mother-in-law the next evening when he came back from the hospital. 'I should have had a vasectomy like Mel wanted me to.'

Gina looked at him over the rim of her wine glass. 'She could have had her tubes tied. It takes two to make a baby, you know.'

'Yeah. I suppose so.'

'What we need to do is make plans for after she comes out.'

He looked round with a groan. 'They don't think she'll be able to go back to work, not if she wants to keep the baby. She'll be upset to lose this house, but I won't. You know, Ma, it feels like a burden to me and always has done. I don't know why we took on so much debt, why Mel had to have everything so perfect.'

'I think she wanted to put down roots. You'll have her grandfather's money, don't forget. That may tide you over till she can start work again.'

'I suppose.' He reached out to pour himself another glass of wine. 'But it'd be stupid to spend that nest egg.'

'You can't decide anything till she comes out of hospital.'

'Mmm.' He stared into the glass for a few moments, then looked up. 'I was asking the guys at work. One has a partner who's a midwife and she sent me an email. Vitamin B6 is supposed to help and she knew one woman who was helped by green cordial, of all things.'

'The doctor at the hospital may have some suggestions too.'

'Yeah. But nothing worked last time. You can't get away from that, can you? And it's Mel who's suffering, not me. She's barely a third of the way through, poor thing.'

Gina watched him take another slurp of wine but didn't comment. If he wanted to drink too much tonight she'd not say a word, though if he made a habit of it, she'd have to speak up. She wasn't going to spend her evenings with a drunk. Nor did she intend to become the authority figure for them both.

They had to work out their own problems – and let her deal with hers.

Only… Mel's fragile state of health looked as if it was going to get in the way of Gina's plans. It was so frustrating. Not that she'd refuse to help her daughter, of course she wouldn't. But she'd been looking forward so much to her first trip overseas.

Chapter 10

England

Rosie woke up feeling dreadful. Her skull was full of cotton wool, her throat itched and her head was thumping. She staggered along to the bathroom, stared at the white face in the mirror and groaned.

As she was coming out she met her mother.

'You look dreadful, darling.'

'I think I've got 'flu. It's going around at school.'

'You'd better stay home. Go back to bed and I'll bring you up a cup of tea.'

'Thanks.'

When her mother brought the tea, she said, 'I'll ring school and let them know.'

Rosie meant to ring Mandy but dozed off and by the time she woke up, she knew her friend would be in class.

She slept through the lunch break, so missed contacting Mandy then as well. She was annoyed with herself but seemed unable to do much else but doze.

Well, if there was a letter from her real father, it would still be waiting for her when she got better.

—

Peggy couldn't seem to pull herself together after Cheryl's visit. And Hartley was being very cool and distant with her, treating her as if she'd let him down. He didn't need to say a word, just looked at her, and she knew what he was thinking.

Then there was an incident at the supermarket. So humiliating. She did the shopping, then offered her card at the checkout.

It was refused and she had to leave all her shopping there till Hartley came home from work and could come with her and use his own credit card.

'My foolish wife,' he'd told them, 'forgot to check the shopping account. I'll top it up tomorrow and this won't happen again.'

'Why did you say that?' she asked as they went back to the car.

'What?'

'About it being my fault. It wasn't. It was yours.' And she was quite sure he'd done it on purpose to punish her. 'I don't see why you can't allow me a little leeway with the shopping money.'

'I'm the one who earns the money and I'll be the one who'll decide how it's spent.'

The look he gave her made her bite back any further protests, but she felt angry all evening. He seemed to control every little details of her life and gave her no breathing space… as well as no respect.

Suddenly she remembered the Women's Wellness Centre. The woman who'd shown her round had said there were counsellors there. Did you have to pay for them? If so, Hartley would be bound to find out because he kept a firm hand on her outgoings and would only let her have a debit card attached to a special housekeeping account.

Would it do her any good to see someone? Would they help her to accept her daily life with him?

No. She didn't need help. She was managing all right.

She was so lost in thought the following evening that she forgot to start cooking the dinner and it wasn't ready on time.

Hartley looked pointedly at the clock as she served the meal half an hour late.

She lost the last vestiges of her appetite and turned to leave the room.

He was up and barring the way before she realized what he was doing. 'Where are you going?'

'To watch TV. I've told you before I don't enjoy my food when you're so… critical.'

'I didn't say a word.'

'You don't have to. It's the way you look. Nothing ever satisfies you.'

'Sit down. You can at least keep me company.'

She hesitated, trying to pluck up the courage to say she didn't feel like being shouted at, but couldn't find the courage to be so honest. 'I may be sickening for something. I think I'll go to bed.'

'I hope you haven't got the 'flu that's going around. Make up the sofa bed in my models room before you go to bed and I'll sleep there. I don't want to catch anything. I've got some important meetings coming up in the next few days. Where's my magazine? I might as well read if I'm going to be on my own.'

'In its usual place.' She escaped, her heart fluttering, her whole body tense. He went into the living room for the magazine she'd laid next to his armchair, taking it back to read while he ate. From the top of the stairs she heard the rustle of a page being turned, the sounds of his knife and fork, and tears filled her eyes.

It hadn't occurred to him to worry about her not feeling well, let alone cosset her a little. He didn't really care for her, just found it convenient to have a wife to serve his needs. But what could she do about that? She wouldn't even have enough money to run away on.

Run away! Oh, she often wished she could just vanish, dreamed of finding a little flat for herself and living quietly and frugally. As if.

Her thoughts churning round and round, she took his pyjamas and dressing gown into the models room, struggled with the sofa bed, put his toiletries in the guest bathroom and went back into the bedroom they usually shared. It was heaven to shower slowly in the en suite and slip between the sheets on her own. On an afterthought she screwed up some tissues and dropped them on the bedside table to make it look as if she'd been blowing her nose.

When she heard him come up, she closed her eyes and pretended to be asleep. She heard him open the bedroom door and stand there, so she lay very still.

With a mutter of annoyance he went away, closing the door with a thump. She heard him using the other bathroom, banging about in the room next door and finally getting into bed.

Only then did she relax and try to settle down for the night.

But it was no good. Sleep eluded her and she lay awake, seeing the illuminated numbers on the clock radio in the darkness, watching them flick through the minutes as she followed her own dark thoughts.

She didn't wake till just after nine and lay there for a few moments, feeling totally disoriented. The house was so still that Hartley must have gone to work. Well, he never let anything make him late for the office, did he?

She stumbled downstairs, feeling heavy-headed as if hung over, to find chaos instead of the usual order. When she peered into the dining room, she saw that Hartley had opened a bottle of red wine with his meal the previous night. He must have drunk most of it because he'd knocked the bottle over, making a small puddle on the white tablecloth. It hadn't occurred to him to put the cloth to soak.

In the kitchen was the debris of his breakfast. You'd think a grown man could put the milk back into the fridge and his dirty crockery into the dishwasher. But he was useless in the house.

Automatically she cleared the dining room first, taking the tablecloth into the utility room and running the stain under the tap. She then used vinegar and bicarbonate of soda to remove the mark. As the cloth grew white under her ministrations, anger welled up and boiled over – anger at him but most of all at herself for being such a doormat.

She stood there motionless and then, before she could change her mind, she grabbed her handbag and keys, got into the car and drove to the Women's Wellness Centre. Not allowing herself even a second's hesitation, she parked the car any old how and marched inside, walking up to the counter. 'I need to see a counsellor.'

Only then did she burst into great strangling sobs.

Brad got off the plane in England feeling exhausted. He was too tall to fit comfortably into those tiny seats, so hadn't been able to sleep, only doze for an hour or so during the twenty-hour journey from Australia. He wished he'd been able to afford to travel business class but this trip was going to cost enough without splashing out on luxuries like that.

He stared enviously at those sitting further forward who could afford it. They looked so much more comfortable, not to mention having a lounge to sit in during the two-hour wait in the airport at Dubai.

In Manchester Airport he yawned several times as he went to collect his luggage and go through customs. Afterwards he stood surrounded by family reunions, watching the joy on strangers' faces as they met loved ones. He was surprised at how much he wished he had someone to meet him.

Finding his way to the car hire firm, he took possession of the keys to his temporary vehicle and tried to take in the directions for finding it in the vast airport car parks.

What he really wanted was to lie down and sleep – under a table, in some secluded corner, anywhere. He'd know another time to book into a hotel near the airport but he hadn't made a long journey like this before and had assumed he'd sleep on the way. For now, he had no choice but to pick up the car and drive it away.

He found a café in the airport and ordered a black coffee, shuddering at the greasy food on display. Hopefully the caffeine would keep him awake while he drove to Blackpool.

'M61,' he muttered as he settled into the car and studied the map again. 'Then M55.'

It was easy to find his way to the motorways because there were big signs painted on the roads at crucial points as well as signs on poles. Roundabouts kept the flow of traffic going. The West Australian road engineers could learn a few things about road design, he decided as he moved easily into a new line of traffic. Back in Perth it was all stop-start at traffic lights.

Even with a hold-up for road works, he was in Blackpool in just under two hours.

He got lost in the town centre, however, and a few cars hooted their displeasure at his slow, hesitant driving. People seemed to drive more quickly here than in Australia, nipping with ease through the narrow gaps between the parked cars that littered the streets like discarded toys.

There were so many hotels on the seafront, it took him a while to find the one he'd chosen from the Internet.

'I may sleep right through till morning,' he told the receptionist. 'It's a big time difference coming from Australia. Could you give me a wake-up call about eight o'clock tomorrow morning?'

'Of course. Just put the Don't Disturb sign on your door handle until then, sir, so that they don't come in to turn down your bedcovers this evening.'

Sighing in relief he wheeled his suitcase up to his room, took a shower and fell into bed.

He knew nothing more until the following morning when he woke to the patter of rain against the window and looked out at grey skies and a heaving, brownish-coloured sea. Further along from his hotel was a pier. There were no pedestrians around.

He grinned. Well, what did you expect? This was Lancashire, famous for its rainy climate.

He had a quick shower and went down to eat a hearty breakfast. It sometimes embarrassed him how much he ate, but he never put on an ounce.

He would, he decided, ring his English daughter tonight after she got home from school. In the meantime, he'd go out for a nice long walk along the seafront, rain or no rain.

–

Mandy found another letter for Rosie in her family's post office box and wondered what to do about it. She decided to call in and see her friend, who hadn't been at school today. She could pretend to be giving Rosie information about homework.

Mrs Quentin opened the door and made no effort to invite her in. 'Rosie has bad flu, Mandy, and your mother won't want you catching it.'

'I'll just stand in the doorway of her bedroom and have a quick chat.'

'I'm afraid that'd be unwise. Anyway, she's sleeping at the moment. Thanks for calling.' She closed the door firmly.

Mandy frowned and walked slowly along the garden path. At the gate she met her friend's brother and grabbed his arm. 'Casey, can you give Rosie a message for me?'

He shrugged. 'I suppose.'

She fumbled in her pocket for the letter and dropped it. The wind caught it and they had to chase it across the garden. Laughing, she pounced on it and handed it to him. 'Give her this.'

He stared at it. 'What is it?'

'Just a letter.'

'It's from Australia.'

'So maybe she's got a pen friend. Don't let your mother see it.'

He looked at her then stuffed the letter in his pocket without a word, unsure whether she knew who Rosie was writing to in Australia.

As she went away Mandy began to wonder if she'd done the right thing. No, Casey wouldn't betray Rosie to her parents. He was all right, for a boy.

–

Jane didn't normally spy on her children but Mandy's obvious desperation to see Rosie had made her feel suspicious so she went to watch her through the front room window.

'Ah,' she said softly as Mandy stopped Casey, pulled out a blue envelope then had to chase it across the garden. 'So that's how Rosie got the letters.'

When her son came in, Jane was waiting. 'I'll have that letter.'

He took a hasty step backwards. 'It's for Rosie.'

'Do you know who it's from?'

He hesitated, caught her eye and nodded.

'So do I. Give it to me.'

He fumbled in his pocket and held back. 'You're not going to open it, Mum?'

She snatched it from him before he had realized what she was doing. 'Just forget you ever saw it.'

'But she wants to meet him.'

'And I don't want her doing something that could tear our family apart.'

'Only if you make a fuss about it. People do it all the time, meet their biological parents. It wouldn't worry me, so it's only you and Dad you're thinking of.'

'I'll decide that, thank you. And I want your promise that you'll not say a word about this to Rosie.' She waited.

He looked at her pleadingly.

'Promise me you won't say a word to her or you'll be grounded for the next month.'

'I promise I won't say a word.'

The way he was looking at her made her feel guilty, but she had to protect Stu. 'Just remember your promise. Now, come and get a snack then you can get on with your homework. And you're not to go near your sister. She's got flu and I don't want you coming down with it as well.'

—

Casey tried twice to slip into Rosie's room but both times his mother seemed to materialize from nowhere.

'I shan't tell you again to stay away from your sister,' she said the second time.

In the end he had to wait till after he'd gone up to bed and his parents were watching one of their favourite programmes on TV. But when he slipped into the next bedroom he found Rosie fast asleep, her cheeks flushed, her breathing heavy. He'd already scribbled a note to her, so that he wouldn't have to break his promise not to say a word. He shoved it into Rosie's iPod case and went to bed.

She'd be using the iPod tomorrow, he was sure. She always had some music or other playing and their mother didn't like loud noise, so they had to use headphones.

His mother didn't usually open their letters. They weren't little children, so what she'd done sucked big time.

Chapter 11

Australia

Lou and Rick asked directions and set off to brave the public transport system of a strange city, but the buses didn't seem to run very often.

'I was talking to a guy at the hostel,' Rick said. 'He reckons you need a car if you're going anywhere in Australia except city centres. Even hitching lifts is uncertain, there are such big distances between towns.'

'Well, we've got plane tickets that'll take us on to Melbourne, so we only have to get around Western Australia.'

He smiled. 'Bet you didn't get high marks for geography.'

'So?'

'You could fit ten Britains into Western Australia, it's that big, so even if we only wind up only seeing the southern part, that's a lot of driving. Up north is wild country, where tourists get killed if they're not careful. I'm no nature boy, so I don't intend to risk myself up there.'

'You must have studied Australia at school.'

He grinned. 'Not really. But I studied it in the college library before we came here. Better than painting silly blobs and pretending they mean something. If you have to talk up a picture, it's not communicating as it should, visually.'

When they got off the bus, they had to ask directions again and walk for about twenty minutes before they got to the right street. But when they arrived at the house they found it deserted, and a For Sale sign plastered with a Sold sticker standing in the front garden.

'Oh, no! He can't have died!' Lou wailed softly. 'Not when we've got so close.'

'He may just have gone into an old folk's home. We need to ask the neighbours,' Rick said. 'Come on.'

They knocked on three house doors but got no answer, then at the fourth one, the door opened and an old lady peered through a mesh security screen at them.

'We're looking for Mr Daniel Everett,' Lou said. 'I think he's my great-grandfather.'

'Oh, dear! Oh, I'm so sorry. You're too late.'

'He's not— dead?'

'I'm afraid so. He died a month or two ago.'

'Did he have any relatives?'

'Yes. A daughter.'

Lou squeezed Rick's hand in excitement. 'Do you have her address?'

'No, I don't. Sorry.'

'Is her surname Everett too?'

'Dear me, no. She's married. Or she used to be. Her husband was killed by a drunken driver a few years ago. Terrible shame it was. Now, what is her surname? I know her first name is Gina.' She wrinkled her brow. 'No, I'm afraid I can't bring her second name to mind. I'm getting so forgetful lately.'

Lou stood still, hoping against hope that she'd remember, but the old lady shook her head again.

'I'm sorry I'm not much use to you. And Gina cleared the house out before she sold it, so she won't be coming back again.'

They went to stand in front of the house.

'Surely the estate agent will know who she is?' Lou said.

'But will he tell us?'

'We can only try. And I'm going to leave a note in the letter box, too.' She went to sit on the veranda steps and pulled out her travel diary, frowning in thought as she wrote a message, tore the page out and pushed it into the letter box near the gate.

'Come on,' she said. 'Let's go and find this estate agent.'

–

Gina was feeling restless. Mel was still in hospital, improving slowly, but alarmingly lethargic, so unlike her bustling, energetic self that they were all worried sick about her.

Signing, Gina looked out of the window, feeling like getting out of the house for an hour or two. Just a drive round would cheer her up. She decided to go and have one last look at her father's house before they knocked it down. She'd take a photo of her old home, too, as she hadn't been able to find one among his things.

When she got there she stood in front of it, feeling sad. She'd lived here as a child, visited regularly since getting married. It'd be better not to come back once they'd knocked it down, but to remember it as it was today.

She almost expected to see her dad come out and start deadheading the roses.

Before she left, she decided to check the mailbox and see if it had brought any more surprises. A wind was getting up and blew her hair into her face as she fished inside the old-fashioned metal box on a pole, pulling out a pile of advertising brochures and flyers. One piece of torn paper blew out of her hands and floated off down the street. No use running after it. Anyway, if it'd been a proper letter it'd have come in an envelope.

She stuffed the junk mail into the wheelie bin and went back towards her car. Just as she was about to get in, old Mrs Besham came out of a nearby house and waved to attract her attention.

'Gina! Have you a minute?'

'Yes. How are you?'

'I'm as well as can be expected. Not getting any younger. I just wanted to tell you that some young people were knocking on doors asking about your father. The lass said he was their great-grandfather. They sounded English to me.'

Gina looked at her in shock.

'I saw them write a note and push it into the letter box.'

The piece of paper that had blown away! Gina stared at her in horror.

A car drew up further down the road and Mrs Besham turned round. 'Ah, there's the lady who takes me shopping. Sorry, dear, can't keep her waiting.' She hobbled away.

Gina hurried down the street in the direction the paper had been blown, but though she looked into every single garden, there was no sign of it.

Feeling immensely sad she made her way back to the car.

So near and yet so far!

There was no way she could think of to trace two young people whose names she didn't know and who might be anywhere in Perth.

Nothing was going right for her lately, nothing!

–

Lou rang up the estate agent who'd sold the house and explained her dilemma.

'The person who sold it is on leave, I'm afraid and I couldn't possibly give you a client's phone number,' a man's voice said. There was a blur as if he was covering up the phone and answering someone else. 'Sorry, got to go.'

She glared at the buzzing phone then looked at Rick. 'Did you hear that? He put the phone down on me.'

'Yes.'

'I'm not giving up. I'm going to go and see that man and I won't stop pestering him till he rings up the daughter of my great-grandfather and asks her if she'll see me.'

'In that case, I think it'd be better if we hired one of those cheap rental cars that guy we met last night was telling us about. The bus system here is pitiful.'

'That's an added expense.'

'So I'll draw a few more pictures and make the money up. This is important to you.'

She had to give him a hug. He was the most easy-going guy she'd ever met, and the most lovable too. It wasn't that he was weak. He just didn't approve of violence and he liked to help other people. 'I love you.' The words were out before she could stop them.

He put his hands on her shoulders and held her at arm's length. 'You've never said it in that tone before.'

She felt suddenly shy. 'What tone?'

'Serious. Did you mean it seriously?'

She nodded.

He folded her in his arms. 'Good, because I've been waiting for you to realize that this thing between us is important. I love you too, Lou. There aren't enough words to say how much.'

They stood there for a few moments, pressed closely against one another, then she looked up at him and he kissed her. But after a moment he drew back breathing deeply. 'Not now. We'll need the rest of the day to get hold of a set of wheels and then find this office.'

They walked out into sunshine that seemed twice as bright as before and into a world full of smiling people.

'Actually, I'm going to have to do quite a lot more portraits,' he said as they walked along the street.

'Why?'

'To buy you a ring.'

She stopped dead. 'A ring?'

He nodded. 'I'm old-fashioned that way. If my girl loves me as much as I love her, I'm thinking marriage.'

'But people don't usually get married straight off. They just – you know – shack up with one another.'

'Have I ever been like other guys?'

'No, definitely not. Thank goodness.'

'And I'm not starting now. So… will you wear my ring? And in a few years will you do the whole thing and get married in style?'

She nodded. Until she met Rick she'd had a scorn of marriage, because her parents were so lukewarm towards one another. But she felt utterly comfortable with Rick, so right… She smiled at him, spun round in a circle and did a few dance steps for good measure, she felt so warm and happy. 'Yes, of course I will.'

He laughed and bowed to her, sweeping her into a quick waltz to the next corner. When an old man stopped to stare disapprovingly at them, Rick stopped to say, 'She's just agreed to marry me.'

The old man's wrinkles multiplied into a broad, crevassed smile. 'Good luck to you both of you, mate.'

Rick took hold of her hand. 'Brill. Now that's settled, let's get hold of some wheels.'

Chapter 12

England

Jane hesitated over her daughter's letter, her desire to protect her family warring with her sense of what was right and wrong. In the end family — and her husband's needs in particular — won and she opened it.

The handwriting was familiar. Hard to forget, because Brad had such a slashing, powerful style and a way with words, too. Written words. He hadn't been as good at putting his emotions into spoken words. She'd thrown the few letters he'd sent her away before she left Australia, but she hadn't been able to throw away her memories of him. Stu, bless him, wrote a truncated style of English and couldn't produce a flowery phrase, written or spoken, to save his life.

She read the letter carefully, then read it again to make sure she'd missed nothing. Brad was coming to England and would ring Rosie on her mobile phone as soon as he'd had a night's sleep. And then maybe they could arrange to meet if she would give him her address. He was looking forward very much to getting to know her.

However, before they did that, he felt Rosie should tell her mother that she'd been in touch with him.

The letter was so fair and reasonable Jane felt her face flame as she folded it up. But at the same time she was calculating that if he only had Rosie's mobile number, he wouldn't be able to trace them. She could stop all this now, stop it once and for all, because he'd believe Rosie had changed her mind.

Guilt clutched at her stomach as she crept up to her daughter's bedroom, but it didn't stop her. Stu was in such a fragile state at the moment. She had to protect him, keep the family on an even keel – whatever it cost. Rosie had managed perfectly well for seventeen years without knowing Brad and could continue to manage without him.

In the bedroom the mobile phone lay in its usual place on the charger and Rosie was tossing restlessly in bed.

Jane stood near the door, hesitating, then Rosie woke up and stared at her. She walked across to the bed, forcing a smile to her face. 'How do you feel, love?'

'Awful.' Rosie swung the covers aside. 'I'm burning up.'

Jane stood back to let her go along to the bathroom. 'I'll get you some hot lemon and honey to drink. You need to keep up your fluid intake.'

As the bathroom door closed, she turned back and pulled out the connecting wire. She slipped the mobile into her jeans pocket then ran downstairs and put the little object into her handbag. Rosie would never think of looking for it there.

She'd never think her mother had taken her phone and letter, either.

When Jane went back upstairs, Rosie was lying in bed again and had to be bullied to drink the whole glass of juice.

'Can I get you anything else?'

'No.' Rosie frowned at her. 'Shouldn't you be at work?'

'I was a bit worried about you, so I took the afternoon off.'

'You didn't need to. I'll sleep myself better. You know I always do.'

'Well, it's my normal day off tomorrow, and you should have turned the corner by Friday, so I'll go back to work then.'

Rosie smiled sleepily at her. 'Good old Mum. Always looking after us.' She snuggled down and closed her eyes.

The feeling of guilt was even stronger as Jane went downstairs, but not strong enough to make her put the phone back.

Only, what was she to do with it?

Experimentally she switched it on. At that minute it rang and she jumped in shock, staring at it, terrified to answer.

–

Brad went up to his hotel room after consuming a hearty breakfast and took out his new international mobile phone. He tapped in Rosie's number and waited for it to ring. It did, several times, and just as he was going to stop calling, someone answered.

'Hello?'

'Rosie? Is that you?'

Silence at the other end, so he said, 'It's me. Brad.'

'This isn't Rosie. It's Jane. And she's changed her mind, Brad, doesn't want to meet you now. So please, leave us alone.'

The phone cut off abruptly.

He stared at the tiny gadget in his hand, then sank down on the bed, feeling so crushed with disappointment that he couldn't move or think for a few minutes. Meeting Rosie had become the main object of this trip. He'd almost forgotten his cousins, wasn't nearly as interested in seeing Europe, but Rosie... he was longing to meet her. He stared at the phone, then looked out of the window at the brown, heaving sea.

Why had she changed her mind about seeing him?

And even if she had, why hadn't she told him so herself? Why ask her mother to do it for her? It didn't seem right.

He stiffened. It wasn't right. Suddenly he was quite sure of that. Jane had answered the phone, not Rosie. And Jane hadn't even explained, just shut down on him.

He picked up his own phone again and pressed redial.

'The number you have dialled is not available,' a mechanical voice answered.

He looked at it grimly. Someone must have switched the phone off. Rosie? Had his daughter even been present? Or was this all down to Jane?

He didn't intend to make himself obnoxious, didn't want to upset the family, but until he heard from Rosie herself that she wanted nothing more to do with him, he wasn't going to give up hope. She had initiated the contact. Surely she wouldn't chicken out without even meeting him once?

In the meantime, what the hell was he going to do with himself on such a day? Rain was still sweeping across the promenade, scouring the pavements. A tram went past and he watched it idly, then turned to his clothes. Because it was nearly summer in England, he'd brought nothing suitable for a cold, rainy day like this. He might as well go and do some shopping. Then he'd try that phone again.

–

Jake looked out of the window and saw nothing but grey skies. No gardening today, though the plants would appreciate a good soaking.

But the trouble with rainy days was they allowed you too much time for thinking. He was sorry now that he'd been so hard on Lou, kept wondering how she was getting on.

He still wished she wouldn't try to contact his father. At least he thought he did. He already knew that the old man had lived to a ripe old age. What he'd not been able to understand was why their father had suddenly written to them a few months ago. Peggy said she'd destroyed her letter, but he'd kept his – unopened. Somehow he couldn't bear to read it.

Guilt flooded through him. He was a fine one to talk about keeping in touch. When was the last time he'd seen Peggy? It must be months now and she only lived a few miles away. Trouble was, he couldn't stand that bugger she was married to or the way Hartley treated her as if she was a servant, and a stupid one at that.

On that thought he picked up the telephone and dialled her number. There was no answer and he didn't want to leave a message, but he made a mental note to ring again later. She was probably out.

–

Rosie felt well enough by mid-afternoon to want to listen to some music. Her mother had gone shopping, so she slid out of bed and picked up her iPod. As she took it out of its case, she found a scrap of paper stuffed in with it. How had that got there?

She was just about to throw it away when she realized it was a note from Casey.

> Mandy brought an airmail letter for you from you know who. Mum took it off me and opened it. Thought you should know. C.

Rosie stared at the note in dismay. Then she heard a car turn into their drive and contemplated going down to confront her mother. No, best to ring Mandy up first and check what had happened.

But her mobile wasn't there. She knew she'd left it charging up, she did that automatically as soon as she got home.

She checked the floor and under the bed, in case it had been knocked off the surface, but there was no sign of it.

Had her mother taken that, too? Why?

She made her way carefully down the stairs, feeling exhausted by the time she got to the kitchen.

Her mother turned from the sink and stared at her in surprise. 'What on earth are you doing out of bed?'

'Where's my mobile phone?'

'How should I know?'

'You're the world's worst liar, Mum. Where is it?'

'I took it away. You'll never get better if you're nattering on that thing.'

'You're still lying. And there was a letter for me, too.'

'How did you—'

Rosie felt the room swirl round her and staggered across to one of the chairs in the eating area.

'You definitely shouldn't be up.'

'Give me my phone and my letter and I'll go straight back to bed.'

There was silence then her mother shook her head.

'The letter was from him, wasn't it? Brad.'

Her mother's mouth went into a tight, disapproving line. 'You shouldn't have started all this without consulting us.'

'I need to meet him, Mum. It doesn't stop me loving Dad and considering him my father, but I need to know this other guy too. Surely you can understand that?'

'No, I can't. And I'm not having it.'

'Why not?'

She hesitated. 'Because, Stu's job is at risk and he's extremely upset about it. He's got all the trouble he can take at the moment.'

'I thought he'd be a shoo-in for the new job.' She hadn't believed Casey when he told her Dad might not get the job.

'He's been at loggerheads with Binnings, who's going to be the head of the new school and he's hinted pretty broadly that Stu should look for a job elsewhere.'

'Well, if Dad doesn't get that job, he can find another, surely? They're always talking about a shortage of experienced teachers.'

'Stu wants to live here, near the nursing home where his father is.'

'Grandpa doesn't know whether we're here or not now. He doesn't recognize anyone. I'm not going to see him again. I'd rather remember him as he used to be.'

'Well, your father does want to be near him and he also wants to stay in the area where he grew up. You know what a homebody he is. And you also know how much he loves that job of his, what a success he's made of the Learning Resource Centre.'

'Yeah.' Rosie shifted uneasily in the chair. 'Poor Dad. But this isn't just about him. I have my own needs.'

'At the moment Stu comes first. Unless you'll promise me not to contact Brad again, I'm not giving you your phone back. And I'm definitely not giving you the letter.'

'I can't believe I'm hearing this! You've no right to do that.'

'I'm your mother. You're under age. I have every right. And I repeat, you're not the only one who matters here.'

And from that decision Rosie couldn't move her. She felt so woozy that after a while she went back up to bed. But she wasn't going to give up.

When Casey came home from school there was another row downstairs and he came stamping up to his room.

Rosie raised her aching head to call, 'Casey!'

He came into her bedroom and sat on the end of her bed. 'You look awful.'

'Yeah, you're beautiful too. Look, I heard Mum shouting at you. Was it about me?'

He shrugged.

'Thanks for giving me the heads up about the letter. She won't hand it back, though, and she's taken my mobile off me.'

'You can borrow mine.'

'How can he contact me on that?' Her eyes filled with tears and she rubbed them away on the sheet. 'I haven't given him our address. He'll not be able to find me. He'll think I don't want to see him.'

Casey grunted something, patted the bump under the bedclothes where her feet were and left.

Rosie scrubbed at her eyes. But however hard she thought about it, she could see no way of getting in touch with Brad. And she wanted to so desperately.

She hadn't said anything to her dad, because he'd been looking pretty grim lately. But she would if her mother didn't relent. Dad was usually very fair about things.

–

When Brad had finished shopping, he got into the car and drove aimlessly out of the centre of Blackpool. Seeing a sign to Poulton, he turned in that direction because it was the town where Rosie's post office box had been.

He stopped the car near the centre of town, waited for a heavy shower to pass, then got out and asked the way to the post office. He stood by the rows of post office boxes, with their neat little keyholes and found the number he had sent letters to.

On a sudden impulse he went inside and bought a prepaid envelope and a notepad. Taking it back to the car, he found a long-stay car park and settled down to write to Rosie. It took several attempts because he wanted to get it just right.

By that time he was hungry so he went and bought a snack, taking the scribbled note out of his pocket to study as he ate. He made a couple of small changes and nodded. Yes, he'd explained how he felt, said he was puzzled that she hadn't spoken to him herself. He hadn't tried to blame anyone but had wondered if she knew what was going on.

If she really didn't want to see him then he would, very regretfully, leave her in peace.

Going back to the car, he wrote it out carefully, giving the address and phone number of his hotel and writing that on the back of the envelope as well.

When he went to post it, he hesitated for a minute, then raised the letter to his lips and wished it luck as he dropped it into the letter box.

Chapter 13

Australia

Gina spent the whole day worrying about the note that had blown away. There had to be something she could do to trace the person. It must be one of her relatives from England. Surely it was?

When she went to the hospital, Mel was sitting up in bed, pale and limp still, but looking better than she had for a while. Gina kissed her cheek and offered a novel by one of her daughter's favourite authors.

Mel looked at it and gave a faint smile. 'Thanks. But all I seem to do is sleep.'

'Your body must need it. How's the sickness?'

'A little better, but that stuff they're giving me clouds my brain so that I can't think straight.' Tears came into her eyes. 'They said I shouldn't go back to work, should just take things easy until the baby's born. Nearly six more months! We're going to lose the house.'

'Most women would be more concerned about whether they were going to lose the baby.'

'The doctor says the baby's all right, developing normally. It's me who's malnourished.'

Gina hadn't intended to start this discussion, but if Mel wanted her sympathy, she wasn't going to get it. 'Just be thankful for what you have got. If you have to move somewhere smaller, it's not the end of the world.'

Tears rolled down Mel's cheeks. 'You don't understand.'

'No, I don't. I've not got a husband any more. I certainly understand that. And I've had to put my whole life on hold to help you. I understand that, too.'

Mel gasped.

'Sorry.' Gina stopped and fought to control her irritation. 'I didn't mean to speak so sharply when you're in this condition, only I'm not having you oozing self-pity all over me – or anyone else.'

'You said something similar the night I collapsed, didn't you? About me interrupting your life.'

'Yes.'

Mel started fiddling with the edge of the sheet. 'I'm sorry, Mum.'

'You're not being ill on purpose. These things happen. You know I'll always help you when you're in trouble, but you have to help yourself, too. No one can turn the clock back, so we have to make the most of what we've got.'

Mel lay back with a sigh and a nod. 'Thanks for the book. And thanks for all you've done for me.'

'You're my daughter. I love you very much.' Gina kissed her, received a big hug in response, then left her daughter to sleep. When she looked back from the doorway, Mel's eyes were already closed.

It was as Gina was walking back to her car that she remembered Mrs Besham saying 'young people' about the two who'd tried to find her. If they were young, they might be staying in a backpackers' hostel. That was the cheap way to travel. It was worth a try, surely?

Only how did you leave messages for people when you didn't know their names?

–

When she got back to Mel's house, Gina started ringing round the backpacker hostels, but as she'd expected, they said they couldn't really to help her. They got lots of English people passing through.

Only when she pressed them did they agree to put up a notice to say she was looking for some young people believed to be relatives of Daniel Everett, but they doubted it'd do any good.

Frustrated, she waited until Emma came home from school, gave her a quick drink of fruit juice and bundled her into the car. Then she drove round to Mrs Besham's to ask for a better description of the young woman who'd been looking for Gina's father.

The old lady opened the door and stared at her in surprise. When Gina explained her reason for coming, Mrs Besham insisted they have a cup of tea while she tried to remember.

Her description of the young woman could have fitted a hundred other young women. 'They all look alike these days, with that stripy hair and clothes that look too small for them,' Mrs Besham muttered.

'Oh, dear! How am I going to find them, then? Did you say she had a companion? What was the other person like?'

Mrs Besham's face brightened. 'He was dark. Nice-looking young man, not got crinkly hair or anything.'

Gina sat forward. 'You mean he was black?'

'I just said he was dark, didn't I?'

Gina set down her cup, plonked a quick kiss on the old lady's cheek and took her leave. She felt a great urgency because the young couple might be setting off any moment for their next destination.

When Emma began grumbling, she said sharply, 'Be quiet, dear! This is very important.'

'But I'm hungry, Gran.'

'We'll stop and get you a burger and fries.'

Emma brightened. 'Mummy doesn't let me have those.'

'She won't mind this once.'

Back at the house, she sat Emma down and went back to the phone, calling all the hostels again. If it was humanly possible, she intended to find this young woman.

—

Not without difficulty, Lou and Rick found their way to the office of the estate agents. The receptionist seemed completely impervious to their problem and kept saying sorry, she couldn't give out clients' phone numbers.

Frustrated, Lou leaned forward and said very loudly, 'We've come all the way from England to trace my relatives and I'm not stirring from here until you ring up this woman and ask her if she'll speak to us.'

A man came to join them. 'Is there a problem?'

Once again, Lou explained.

'Oh, I think we can ring up Marla's client, don't you?' He smiled at the receptionist. 'Have a go now.'

Muttering, she got out the file and casting a suspicious glance at them, opened it on top of a filing cabinet behind the counter so that they couldn't see its contents. She rang a number and waited, foot tapping impatiently, but no one answered. When the answering service started she put the phone down.

'Why didn't you leave a message?' Lou demanded.

'It's not my place to harass clients.'

'Your client would *want* to see us! And she won't think much of this firm if you refuse to help.'

The same man, who'd been listening from across the room, called, 'Tell us where you're staying and we'll ring your relative again later. After that, you really must leave us to get on with our work.'

Lou wrote down the name and address of the hostel then went outside.

'I bet they throw away the piece of paper.'

–

It was a very busy day at the real estate office, one of many during a frenzy of house buying that had sent prices skyrocketing. The receptionist tried the number once more then set it aside until later.

As one of the sales staff walked past, the piece of paper wafted off the desk and floated underneath the filing cabinet.

The receptionist got on with her normal work, keeping one eye on the clock. She had a hot date that evening and was counting the minutes till she could leave. She didn't even think about making the phone call.

Chapter 14

England

After Peggy had at last stopped weeping, the counsellor brought her a cup of tea which she sipped gratefully.

'Ready to talk now?'

Peggy looked at the other woman, saw no scorn, only sympathy in her expression and nodded. 'I think so. But what good will it do?'

'It never hurts to share your problems with an impartial listener.'

Impartial, Peggy thought. Yes, she needed that. There was no one in the family she could talk to. Well, they didn't even keep in touch with one another, did they? Hartley said he didn't want her family coming round and her brother was a loser, no wonder his wife had left him. Jake said Hartley was an arrogant bastard who expected the whole world to revolve round him and Peggy should stick up for herself.

In fact, when the two men got together they were like bristling dogs, always on the verge of quarrelling.

She looked up at Gillah. 'I've never heard that name of yours before.'

'It's Jewish, means Joy of the Lord. I chose it myself when I made a new start in life.'

'It's pretty.'

Gillah nodded and waited.

'I can't think where to start talking,' Peggy blurted out. 'I don't know how it all came to this.'

'Start anywhere you like. This isn't a test.'

So the worries tumbled out, how Hartley had always been – well, the only way to describe it was *superior* in attitude towards her. How he'd grown so much worse since their daughter left home. Finally, her voice breaking with the humiliation of it all, she described Cheryl's visit and the way they'd left her out of everything. Only then did she look up, sure she'd catch a scornful look on Gillah's face as well.

But there was only an understanding expression, which gave her the courage to say, 'I feel such a fool at my age. I'm sixty-six, for heaven's sake. You'd think I'd have sorted out my life by now. And what will I do when Hartley retires next year? He'll be at home all the time then. I can't face that. I can't!'

She hadn't let herself dwell on how worried she was about his retirement until the words came tumbling out. She clapped one hand to her traitorous mouth and looked at Gillah again, feeling helpless and stupid.

'You're not a fool, Peggy, and I'm so glad you came to the centre. People can become unhappy or need help at any age. Though I think you must have been unhappy for a long time. Am I right?'

Peggy nodded. She had been, she saw that quite clearly now. It was as if she'd been hiding from the truth before.

'When people retire it can be very stressful building a new life. A surprising number of marriages break up over that, people your age. So let's talk about your worries and—'

'But talking to you won't change a thing, will it?' Peggy blew her nose again. Her eyes felt swollen and tender. She jerked to her feet and went to stare at her face in a small mirror near the door. 'Just look at me! What am I going to do? If I go home looking like this Hartley will know something's wrong and he'll—'

'He'll what?'

'Probe. Force me to tell him why I was crying. Mock me. Forbid me to come here again.'

'Is there anywhere else you could go tonight? A family member, perhaps?'

'I've never gone away overnight before. Never. Hartley might – come after me, make a scene.'

'If you're that afraid of him, we could find you a temporary place in a women's refuge.'

Peggy stared at her in horror.

'Why don't you take some time to think about this? I don't want to influence you because you need to make your own decisions.' Gillah looked at her watch. 'I have another client to see in a couple of minutes, but we've got a room here where you can sit in peace and privacy. No one will disturb you in there if you close the door. And then in an hour's time, I'll come and see you so that we can discuss some practical options.'

'I'd like that.' The thought of an hour's peace and silence was blissful.

Peggy let Gillah show her to the room in question, which had some comfortable chairs, a hand basin with a little mirror over it and a box of tissues nearby. There was a low table full of magazines and a small circular table in one corner with a Buddha figure about two hand spans high. He looked so serene. Beside him was a shallow, oval bowl of water with petals floating on it. Frondy green plants around it cradled him in greenery. The whole effect was both pretty and calming.

When the door had closed behind Gillah, Peggy didn't move for a moment or two, letting the peace of this small room wash over her. She heard herself sigh aloud, but no one else could hear her so she sighed again, because that seemed to lighten the pressure on her chest.

Gillah had pointed out the tea and coffee machine in the corridor just outside and suggested she help herself, so before she sat down Peggy peered outside to check that no one was around to see her swollen face and got herself a cup of tea. It tasted stale, as machine-made tea always did, but it was warm and she felt as if she needed the comfort of that warmth.

After she'd drunk it, she sat staring at the Buddha figure while her thoughts went around her head in tight circles.

It was a while before she looked at her watch. If she was going home, she really ought to be making a move now or she'd never get tea cooked on time. Only she couldn't bear the thought of going back there. And when she looked in the small mirror over the washbasin, her face looked so bad she knew she couldn't face Hartley.

A few things crystallized suddenly. She didn't want to go home at all. She dipped a fingertip in the little pool, making gentle ripples, watching the patterns as the petals bobbed about. When the water had grown still again, she went to stare out of the window at a small garden full of bright flowers.

As she moved back to her seat she caught sight of herself in the mirror: puffy eyes, wrinkles, glasses slipping down her nose and grey hair in a tangle. She looked every day of her age – and more.

Her main feeling now was of shame. At her age, to come to this! Oh, the humiliation of it!

Only – she couldn't take any more of Hartley's sneering, she just couldn't.

She didn't want to go to a women's refuge, though. The mere thought of that made her cringe.

But where else was there?

–

When the phone rang, Jake had just come in from the garden and was feeling ravenous. He nearly didn't answer it, then picked it up and barked, 'Yes?' impatiently. If it was telemarketers, he'd give them an earful. He hated them with a passion. In fact, he made a note of any company they were representing and went elsewhere for his supplies.

'Mr Everett?'

'I don't want to buy anything, thank you.'

'It's about your sister. Peggy's here with me and she's very upset. Could you come and see her, do you think?'

'Where's that husband of hers?'

'He's the reason she's upset.'

'Oh.'

'Will you come?'

'Yes, of course. Tell me where…'

He broke the speed limit driving to the Women's Wellness Centre, wondering what on earth had happened to his sister.

When he went inside, a group of women had just arrived for a meditation class and he hovered uncomfortably near the door till the chattering group had filtered off towards the left. Then he moved forward. 'I had a phone call from someone called Gillah. My sister's here, apparently. My name's Everett.'

'Just a minute.' She picked up the phone. 'Gillah, I have a Mr Everett here.' She smiled at Jake. 'Please take a seat. Gillah won't be a minute. She's one of our counsellors.'

He nodded and waited till a woman came out of a side corridor and moved towards him. She walked with an easy flowing movement and her gentle smile made him think of a group of narcissi at the back of his garden that nodded to him every spring in just that way. He'd always preferred them to the showier daffodils nearer the house.

'I'm Gillah. I'm so glad you were willing to help. Would you mind coming into my room for a minute and I'll explain the problem before we go to see Peggy?'

Her voice was low and calm, the soft sounds slipping easily into the ears. Baffled by all this but instinctively feeling that this woman wasn't a fool, he followed her. He listened incredulously as she explained what had happened.

'Our Peggy?'

'Yes. She was distraught when she came here. We've managed to calm her down a little, but she bursts into tears at the mere thought of going home. Could your sister possibly stay with you tonight, Mr Everett?'

'Of course she can.'

'You won't – call in the husband?'

'Of course not! I can't stand the fellow.'

'Oh, good. Come this way.'

When he saw Peggy, Jake bit back an exclamation of shock. Her face was so swollen with crying he hardly recognized her. He didn't try to talk to her, simply folded her close, making soothing noises and rocking her slightly, as he had done to his granddaughter Lou when she was little.

It was a while before Peggy was ready to leave but as they walked out, he kept his arm round her shoulders and she put her arm round his waist.

'Sorry for being such a nuisance,' she kept saying, 'but I've nowhere else to go.'

'You're family. Of course you can come to me.' But he had to keep reassuring her of that because she didn't seem able to take it in.

When they were seated in the car, he frowned in thought. 'Do you want to stop on the way home and buy a nightdress or something?'

She looked at him blankly for a minute then shook her head. 'I can't afford it. Hartley hasn't given me the housekeeping money yet this week.'

'Don't you have a credit card?'

'He doesn't believe in them, except the one for grocery shopping.'

'Does he have a credit card?'

'Yes. But he says he knows how to use it wisely.'

Jake knew what he thought of men who treated their wives like that. 'Well, we'll go into the supermarket and I'll buy you a few things.'

She shrank down into her seat. 'I'm not fit to be seen in public.'

'Then we'll go straight home. I can always nip out later. That superstore stays open twenty-four hours a day. I never thought I'd be glad of that.'

At the house he fussed over her, got her a cup of tea and set about preparing some food.

'Not for me, thanks. I'm not hungry,' she said.

'You have to eat something and I don't like eating alone. Just a small helping, eh?'

He watched her force down a few mouthfuls then put the knife and fork down.

'Don't be angry, Jake. I just can't eat any more.'

'Now why would that make me angry? I'm worried about you, not angry, love.'

She studied his face and seemed to relax a little at what she saw.

As he was clearing the table, he asked, 'Do you want me to ring Hartley up and let him know you're safe.'

She looked at him in horror. 'I don't want him to find out where I am. Gillah said you wouldn't contact him.'

'But he might go to the police and report you missing.'

'Gillah said she'd ring him for me.'

'That's all right then. Now, come and have a walk round my back garden. It's looking a picture if I say so myself.'

Peggy enjoyed the tour and sat with him on a bench for a while. He could see from the way she turned up her face that she was enjoying the late afternoon sunshine. She wouldn't let him go out and buy her anything, though, and seemed utterly terrified of being left on her own, so he found an old t-shirt for her to sleep in and lent her his best dressing gown. But he heard her moving around for a long time after they went to bed.

And he had difficulty getting to sleep himself.

What on earth had that bugger been doing to his sister? Peggy had always been timid, even as a child, but now she seemed afraid of her own shadow and was downright terrified of encountering her husband. And yet, what would she do if she left Hartley? She wasn't suited for building a life of her own.

Well, if necessary, she'd have to stay here. At least for the time being.

The trouble was, Jake enjoyed his quiet life. He had friends when he wanted them and solitude when he preferred it.

He was very disappointed in Cheryl. She ought to have seen that her mother was upset. He hadn't had a lot to do with his niece, but it was obvious that she always sided with her father against her mother. Hartley had idolized her as a child in a way that was sickening to see. He supposed that was because it had taken Peggy a long time to fall pregnant. Cheryl was in between Jake's daughter and granddaughter in age but no one had treated Lou like a little princess and she'd grown up into a sensible, practical young woman.

He'd been wrong to get so angry with her about going to find their relatives.

But he still hoped she hadn't found any.

He had enough complications in his life just now.

—

Casey found Mandy waiting for him after school. His friends sniggered and made remarks about older women, so he gave them the finger and turned his back on them.

'Will you give Rosie a message from me?' Mandy asked as soon as she had his full attention.

'Yeah.'

'You won't let your mother find out?'

'Nah.'

'She – your mother – rang up my parents and told them about the letters. They've taken away my key to the post office box and they're going to give your mother any letters that come for Rosie. Tell her I'm sorry. There's nothing I can do.'

He looked at her in dismay.

His bus came then and he had to run to catch it.

'You won't forget?' she called.

'Course not.'

When he got off the bus, he walked slowly home, kicking at pieces of waste paper, trying to work out what to do. He'd heard Rosie and Mum arguing last night, but Dad had just sat in the kitchen and stared into space as if he'd gone suddenly deaf.

When he got in, he took the milk out of the fridge and poured it carefully into a glass instead of chugging some straight down out of the carton, which always sent his mother mad. Best not to upset her at the moment.

She came into the kitchen. 'Did you have a good day at school?'

'Mmm.'

'You're not to go and see Rosie. In fact, you can do your homework down here tonight and sit with us.'

'But I need my computer.'

'I'll come up and sit with you while you use it.' She gave him one of her Ice Queen looks as she added, 'I don't trust you after you broke your promise to me to say nothing to Rosie.'

'I only promised not to *say* a word, and I didn't say it.'

The look she gave him would have withered a whole rosebush. 'Go up and change quickly.' She followed him up and stood on the landing, arms folded. 'I'm not going down until you do.'

He muttered under his breath as he changed out of his school uniform and sorted out his homework. It was going to be a very long evening.

It was even worse than he'd expected because around seven Mandy's mother popped round with a letter. He pretended not to be watching, but he could tell it was from Rosie's Australian father by the way his mother looked at it.

'It's not fair,' he said loudly when the visitor had left. His mother ignored him and went into the kitchen.

'What's not fair?' his father asked.

'Mum opening Rosie's mail like that.'

His father stared at him. 'Come again?'

'She's opening Rosie's mail from her biological father. The two of them were going to meet.'

'Oh, that. I'm sure your mother knows best.'

'Don't you even care?'

'I have other things on my mind at the moment.'

When Casey had finished his homework, his mother made him help clear up the kitchen and take out the rubbish. It was as he was putting the transparent plastic shopping bag of rubbish into the dustbin that he saw it: an envelope that was torn into four lying on top of the scraps from dinner. Only one letter had come into the house since tea time. With a furtive glance back at the kitchen he took the pieces of the envelope out of the bag, grimacing at a smear of gravy on one, and stuffed them into his pocket.

When he came back inside, he heard sharp voices from upstairs. Rosie and Mum were arguing again.

With a sigh he went and sat in the living room, forced to watch old-fashioned rubbish on the TV with his parents as if he was six years old again.

It wasn't fair.

And if his mother thought she'd change Rosie's mind with this sort of treatment, she had rocks in her head. His sister would win a gold medal in the Stubborn Olympics any day. She took after their mother in that.

When he went up to bed, his mother followed him and fiddled around in her bedroom until he'd finished in the bathroom and gone into his room. She came to stand by the door. He scowled at her.

'I know you think I'm being cruel, but I'm doing it for all of us, so that we can stay a family.'

'You're doing it for yourself. Rosie wants to meet that guy and you don't want to see him again.'

She flushed bright red and whisked out again, slamming the door behind her.

Only when he'd heard her go downstairs did he take the pieces of paper from underneath his pillow and piece them together. The guy must be staying in Blackpool, because it was the address of a hotel. He wondered what his mother had done with the letter.

He put the pieces into a side pocket of his schoolbag and tried to go to sleep.

But he couldn't settle because from Rosie's room he could hear muffled sobs. He'd normally have gone in to see her, but tonight he didn't dare.

He couldn't remember ever being this angry with his mother.

Then the idea came to him, and with such force it took his breath away for a moment. He considered it for a while and the more he thought about it, the more right it seemed. Smiling broadly, he made a triumphant fist in the darkness. Mum had taken Rosie's mobile away from her, but she hadn't taken his. He was going to ring that hotel in the morning and tell the guy where they lived. And he didn't care if his mother grounded him for weeks when she found out.

It upset him to hear Rosie crying like that. She never cried.

Chapter 15

Australia

Lou was feeling a bit down so Rick took her out for a drink, but that didn't help, so they went back to the hostel.

'I don't want to go to bed yet,' she said as they went inside. 'Let's go to that room at the back and see if there's anyone interesting to talk to.'

When they walked into the big room, all the talking stopped and everyone stared at them. Even the trio playing pool stopped hitting balls and turned in their direction.

Lou exchanged puzzled glances with Rick and then turned to the nearest group. 'What's the matter?'

'You're wanted.' One of the guys pointed to the notice board.

Thinking someone was playing a joke on them, she went across to see a new notice with a big red arrow pointing to it.

URGENT!

Lady is looking for two people (a girl and a black guy) who were trying to contact the Everett family. Please ring this number.

Lou clutched Rick's hand tightly, then turned to him, her eyes alight with excitement. 'Perhaps that receptionist did ring them up, after all?'

He smiled and took down the notice. 'She must have. Let's go and find out what it's all about.'

But when he took out his mobile phone and offered it to her, she was suddenly afraid. 'What if they don't want to see me? What if they tell me to mind my own business?'

'Then it's best to find out straight away.' He dialled the number, then shoved the phone into her hand. 'Do it!'

–

Gina was just getting ready for bed when the phone rang. Someone picked it up and she continued to brush her hair, almost absent-mindedly.

There was a knock on the door. 'Ma, it's for you. Are you decent?'

'Yes.'

She opened the door and took the handset from her son-in-law.

'Hello?'

'Are you Daniel Everett's daughter?'

She gasped and saw Simon turn back and mouth, 'You all right?'

She nodded vigorously.

'Hello? Is anyone there?'

'Sorry. I was just a bit surprised. And yes, I am his daughter.'

'Oh, what a relief! I've been trying to contact you. I went to his house, but I was too late. It'd been sold. A neighbour said he'd died. I'm sorry about that because he was my great-grandfather.'

'Oh, my!' Gina plumped down on the bed.

'Are you all right? I'm not… upsetting you?'

'I'm fine, just a bit surprised. Actually, I've been trying to find out about my father's English family, so this is… Look, where are you staying? I rang several hostels and left messages. You see, the note you left in the letter box at Dad's blew away so I didn't know where to contact you – not even your name.'

'We went to see the estate agent who sold the house and asked them for your address but they wouldn't give it to us. Did they ring you?'

'No. I spoke to the neighbour and left messages everywhere I could think of.'

Gina heard a mutter of voices, then the girl said, 'Sorry! I've not introduced myself, have I? I'm Lou, short for Louise Lorrie. Sounds awful, like a stage name, doesn't it? That's why I prefer Lou. My granddad is Daniel's son by his first wife.'

'I'm delighted to meet you, Lou. I'm Gina Porter. Can we get together?'

'Yes, please! We've hired an old car, so we could come and see you tomorrow, if that's all right?'

'Of course. Who's "we"?'

'Me and Rick, my boyfriend. We're backpacking together. Just a minute, Rick's getting something to write on.'

Lou repeated the address back to her to check she'd got it right.

Gina gave her directions and agreed to meet at ten o'clock. She stared at the phone as she put it down, bemused. Such a cheerful young voice and with a similar northern accent to her father's. It took her a minute to pull herself together then she went to find Simon and tell him what it was all about.

'They must come and stay,' he said at once. 'They'll be watching their money if they're backpacking and we have another spare bedroom. Obviously we need you here while Mel's in hospital, but you'll want to spend as much time as you can with them.'

'Thanks, Simon. There are two of them so they can have my room and I'll go into the smallest bedroom. Isn't it exciting?'

She went to bed again but couldn't sleep. She had longed all her life for relatives, now she was about to meet one. And there were others in England. Even if she couldn't go to find them as she'd planned, one of them had come to find her. It was wonderful, just wonderful.

Tomorrow couldn't come soon enough.

Chapter 16

England

Brad found a message pushed under the door of his hotel room when he returned there after breakfast. He picked up the slip of paper and read it.

> Casey rang. Rosie does want to see you, but
> her mother's taken her mobile away.

An address and phone number were scrawled below this message.

Who was Casey? And how had he known to contact Brad here at the hotel? The only person in England who knew where he was staying was Rosie.

If Jane had taken away her daughter's phone, perhaps... there was no perhaps about it: she must have got hold of his last letter.

Was this Casey person telling the truth? If he was, Jane had been lying when she said Rosie had changed her mind about meeting Brad.

Oh, hell, what should he do? He went to stand by the window. It was fine today, if still somewhat brisk for an Australian used to warmer summers. He put the piece of paper carefully into his wallet – not that he needed it now, because he'd memorized the address – and went for a walk. He always thought better while walking.

He strolled along the promenade, lost in thought. When he grew tired of walking he stood by the wall, overlooking the beach. Who was Casey? A brother? A boyfriend? He hadn't meant to cause trouble in Rosie's family, but clearly he had done. Only… he ached to see his daughter and she clearly wanted to see him. That was only natural, surely?

In the end he came to the conclusion that it was Rosie whose wishes should be considered first, not her family's. He'd read enough to know that adopted children could have a burning need to meet their biological parents.

And he had a burning desire to meet his child.

–

When Peggy awoke, she couldn't for a moment think where she was. Then it all came rushing back to her and she buried her face in the pillow, wishing it wasn't true, wishing she was still in her own home.

Footsteps went past her room.

'Jake? Is that you?'

Her brother opened the door and peeped in. 'You're awake, then?'

'Yes. What time is it?' She reached for her spectacles because she needed them even to see her watch properly these days. 'Ten o'clock! You should have woken me.'

'Why? Your appointment with Gillah isn't till this afternoon. I reckoned you must need a good sleep. Do you want me to bring you up a mug of tea?' When she didn't answer, he said, 'Peggy?' in a questioning tone.

She blinked and looked at him. 'What? Oh. Tea. No, I'll get a quick shower and come down.'

'All right.'

She'd washed out her knickers and bra overnight and though they were still a bit damp, at least they were clean. She had a quick shower and got dressed.

Jake was waiting for her downstairs. He didn't say much, but made her some breakfast. To please him she forced down a slice of toast and marmalade, but it might as well have been cardboard for all she tasted, and there was no way she could eat a second piece.

'Do you want to go shopping?'

She hesitated then shook her head. 'I'd rather speak to Gillah first, work out what to do.'

'You should leave him.'

Jake's voice was harsh, so unlike his usual gentle tone that she looked at him in shock.

'For years I've watched Hartley turning my sister into a timid mouse and I've kept my mouth shut. It got so that I didn't even see you any more, and I wanted to. He kept putting me off coming. I should have insisted, come around when he was at work. I blame myself for that. But when I saw the state you were in yesterday… well, I can't keep quiet any more. Leave him, Peggy love. Make a new life for yourself.'

'How can I? I'd not have anywhere to live. Or any money to live on.'

'You could get social security to help you, I'm sure. And there's your old age pension plus you'd be entitled to a share in the house.'

'It's in his name.'

'It's the marital home, you've contributed to the family by running it. I'm pretty sure you have some rights there.'

'I – can't seem to think straight. And I don't want to leave my home, Jake.'

'Even with Hartley in it?'

She bowed her head, not knowing the answer to that because her thoughts were so tangled. She waited for Jake to say something cutting but he only patted her arm.

'Sorry, Pegs. I shouldn't be pressing you. It's a hard decision to make, I'm sure.'

She smiled at him gratefully. But his very kindness was a lesson after the scornful way Hartley treated her.

'If you've finished, come out into the garden. A bit of sunshine will cheer you up.'

It was a lovely oasis, and she sat again on the bench strategically placed to overlook the flowers and behind them she could see vegetables standing in sturdy rows. For the moment, it was enough just to sit here and wait for her appointment.

Jake left her in peace, going to pull up a few weeds, remove a caterpillar, smile down at his neat row of young cabbages. 'I'll just take some stuff out to the front,' he said and went to unlock the side gate, before turning back to get his wheelbarrow.

Suddenly the side gate banged against the wall and Peggy opened her eyes in shock as the peace was fractured by a voice roaring, 'There you are, you stupid bitch! I might have known I'd find you here.'

She opened her eyes to see Hartley advancing across the garden towards her and screamed in sheer terror at the fury on his face.

Without making a conscious decision about his destination, Brad drove to Poulton again, still worrying about whether he was doing the right thing or not. With the aid of the satnav he found his way to the address Casey had given him. At least the house existed, he thought as he drew to a halt in front of a neat, semi-detached residence in a street of very similar dwellings.

He sat for a minute or two gathering his courage, then got out of the car and went to ring the doorbell.

There was no answer and he was about to ring again when he heard footsteps. The door swung open and he found himself facing Jane. Older, but he'd have known her anywhere, even though she wore her hair short now and had grey threads at her temples. He smiled. 'Long time no see.'

She stared at him in shock, her mouth forming his name, then tried to shut the door in his face.

'Ah, Jane, don't do that!' he pleaded. 'Surely we can talk this over?'

'Go away, Brad! We don't want you here.'

'But Jane—!'

'Go away!'

'When I hear Rosie say that, I'll leave and not until.'

'If you don't go now, I'll call the police.'

'That'll create an even bigger fuss.' He kept his hand on the door, holding it open. 'Is Rosie in?'

'No, she isn't. She's at school at this time of day.'

That hadn't even occurred to him. His grip on the door must have slackened because Jane slammed it in his face.

He felt foolish now. He'd been so excited, hadn't thought about it being a weekday. It was such a disappointment. Sighing, he turned away. He wasn't giving up, though. He'd come back later.

–

Inside the house Rosie heard the doorbell as she was going back to her bedroom from the bathroom. She was feeling better today, but still a bit wobbly.

She heard her mother walk along the hall below and open the door, stiffening in shock as she heard her say harshly, 'Go away, Brad! We don't want you here.'

It couldn't be him, could it? No, surely not? How would he know where she lived?

Then she heard him saying her mother's first name, pleading to talk about this, to see Rosie, and she knew it really was him. Without thinking, she flung on her dressing gown and rushed down the stairs in time to see her mother closing the door and sagging against it, an expression of distress on her face.

Jane looked up and scowled at Rosie. 'Go back to bed this minute.'

Her mother was bigger than her and far stronger, so Rosie turned and fled up the stairs. But she didn't go to her own room, she ran into her parents' bedroom and flung open the window. 'Brad! Don't go!'

He turned round and she stared down at him, unable to say another word, marvelling that this was the man who'd fathered her. He was staring up at her with equal intensity.

She heard her mother running up the stairs and shouted desperately, 'I do want to see you. Don't let her send you away.'

Her mother tried to pull her away from the window and she fought back, begging, 'Don't do this to me, Mum! It's not fair. I need to see him.'

And suddenly her mother let go of her and leaned against the wall, fighting against tears. 'Please, Rosie.'

'I don't want to hurt you. I don't. But I have to meet him. Can't you try to understand? He's my *father*!'

Her mother swallowed hard then spread her hands in a helpless gesture. Pushing herself away from the wall as if it was a huge effort, she moved to the open window, calling down, 'Come back in half an hour, Brad. We'll talk about it then.'

He stood frowning up at her, then nodded and walked away.

Jane looked sideways at Rosie. 'I hope you don't regret this.'

'I'm sure I won't. He – looks nice.'

'Oh, yes. He's a good-looking man, even now. He must be what… fifty-four or five?' She stared at her daughter as if she'd never seen her before then said sharply, 'You'd better go and get a shower before you dress. You won't want to meet him looking like that.'

As Rosie turned she saw her reflection in the long mirror on the wall and gasped in horror. 'Look at my hair! It's like rat tails. What will he think of me?'

She rushed into the bathroom and slammed the door. A minute later the water started running.

Jane stayed where she was, feeling disoriented. Brad hadn't changed much, still had that rangy, long-limbed look that had attracted her to him in the first place. And he still had that crooked smile, too. 'I wish you hadn't come, Brad Rosenberry,' she whispered, turning to examine her own face in the mirror and wondering what he'd thought of her.

But it was her daughter's face she saw in her mind's eye, so like Brad's. Why had she never realized that before?

Because she hadn't wanted to, that's why.

And what was Stu going to say about all this? He was so lost just now. He needed stability more than other people, her Stu did, and this world didn't give you much of that, it seemed. Even if they did offer him another job, she couldn't imagine Stu agreeing to move home and family to a different town. He'd lived here all his life, except for his time at university, and he'd been horribly homesick then.

Maybe it'd do them all good to move somewhere else, though. Maybe they'd been here too long, lying cosily in the same velvet rut. Only… they'd been happy here, hadn't they? And there was Stu's father to think of. He couldn't have long to live now.

Stu had been a good father, especially when the kids were young, though he'd got a bit engrossed in his work in the past few years. But fairness obliged her to admit Rosie was right. He did favour Casey just a little, looked at his son with an degree of extra fondness.

She hadn't realized Rosie had noticed or that her daughter felt diminished by this. She ought to have. They ought to have been open about her birth from the start. Only Jane had met Stu almost as soon as she got back to England from Australia and when he found she was pregnant, he'd begged her to marry him anyway and put him down on the birth certificate as the father.

And now – now she would have to try to persuade him to let Rosie and Brad get acquainted with one another. That was going to be very difficult indeed.

Was it even possible?

–

Jake stepped between Peggy and her irate husband.

Hartley drew himself up and said in that sharp, icy tone that always made Peggy shrivel, 'Get – out – of my way!'

Jake held his ground. 'I'd like you to leave my garden.'

'I'll leave with my wife. Go and get your things at once, Peggy!'

As she shrank back behind her brother, Hartley lunged forward and tried to elbow him aside, then suddenly rammed into him hard, trying to knock him out of the way.

Jake had grown up in a rough street and automatically side-stepped, letting Hartley's momentum carry him past. Recovering quickly, he stood ready for anything.

But Hartley had lost his balance and with a yell, he fell into a muddy patch that had recently been watered. He stared up at Jake for a minute, a ludicrous expression of shock on his face, then pulled himself to his feet, trying to brush the mud off his clothing. 'Look what you've done! You attacked me. I'll damned well sue you for that.'

'Nonsense. You attacked me and I acted only in self-defence.' Jake turned to Peggy for support, but she was curled up on the seat, face buried in her hands, sobbing. And the sight of her, looking so abject, upset him so much that he turned back to yell at his brother-in-law, 'You're not only trespassing but you've damaged my prize flowers. If you don't leave, I'll call the police.'

Even as he was speaking, Bob from next door popped his head over the fence, proving that as usual he was eavesdropping. Only this time Jake was glad to have a witness.

'Need some help, lad?' Bob glared at Hartley as he added, 'I can testify that you acted in self-defence because I saw it all through the gap in the fence.'

'I might need some help if he doesn't leave now.' Jake turned to look at his brother-in-law and repeated, just to make things plain in case of future trouble, 'Please leave my property.'

'Not till my wife comes with me.'

Weeping, Peggy stood up. 'I'd better go.'

Hartley let out a snort of triumph. 'Go and get your things this minute. And don't try this sort of thing again, you stupid bitch!'

Jake took a hasty step forward before he could stop himself, fists clenched.

Peggy stepped back a pace, staring at her husband. 'What did you call me?'

'Stupid!'

'You said bitch as well and your tone…' Her voice broke for a moment and she wrapped her arms round herself. 'Is that what you really think of me?'

'Well, running away like a silly child wasn't the brightest thing to do, was it? It's not as if I've been beating you or anything.'

Jake watched, praying that she'd not let that bugger browbeat her into going back to him.

'Go – and get – your things!' Hartley repeated, speaking in a staccato manner.

She took a deep breath and said in a voice which wobbled, 'I've an appointment this afternoon with a counsellor. I'll decide whether to come home or not then.'

Jake watched, almost holding his breath, willing her to stand firm against this bully.

Peggy studied her husband as if she'd never seen him before then shook her head. 'I can't carry on as we have been doing, Hartley, I just can't. And when you retire, it'll be a lot worse, because you'll be there all the time. I've been worrying about that for months, the thought of you watching me, criticizing me all the time. Every single minute.'

As Hartley's hands bunched into fists again and his face turned dark red, Jake stepped forward hastily. 'Go into the house, Peggy love. I'll see him off the premises.'

She nodded. 'Thank you.' She still had her arms wrapped round herself and her shoulders hunched as she turned away and walked quickly towards the house.

'I'm going straight to my lawyer about this,' Hartley yelled after her. 'You'll be sorry, Peggy Wilkes!'

She didn't turn around or respond in any way as she disappeared from view.

Letting his breath out slowly in relief, Jake gestured towards the side gate and repeated, 'Please leave my property now.'

'You'll be sorry as well.'

'Not as sorry as I was the day she married you. I've been sorry about that every time I've seen her since. You're a bully, Hartley Wilkes, and you don't deserve a nice, gentle lass like my sister. Why the hell she's stayed with you, I've never understood. Go and consult your damned lawyer.

We'll get one for Peggy and I think you'll find she has rights, too.'

He stood and watched the intruder leave, then went to slide the bolt at the bottom of the side gate, so that it couldn't be opened from outside.

From his post by the fence Bob said chattily, 'He's a nasty piece of work, that one.'

'Aye. Thanks for joining in.'

'My pleasure. You'll want to watch your back from now on, though.'

'What can he do to me? But if he does go to the police…?'

'I've only to tell the truth about him attacking you. But he won't do it. They're cowards underneath, that sort are. Bullies, I mean.'

'I'd better go and see our Peggy now.'

Inside the house Jake found her standing by the sink with a kettle under the tap. She didn't seem to have noticed that it was full and the water was overflowing.

'I'll see to that.' He took it out of her hand and turned off the tap, then hesitated before putting an arm round her. They weren't a demonstrative lot, the Everetts, but if ever there was a time for showing affection, he reckoned this was it.

She stood rigidly.

'Am I being stupid?' she asked in a voice barely above a whisper.

'No. I think you've come to your senses.'

He guided her to a chair then put the kettle on and rinsed out the mugs they'd used at breakfast.

'I am stupid, though,' she announced as he handed her the tea.

'Don't say that, love.'

'But I am. I've let him bully me all these years. Anything for peace, that's me. A real coward.'

He sat down opposite her and said earnestly, 'You're just a gentle soul, always have been. But you have let him ride roughshod over you all your married life.'

'He wasn't so bad at first.'

'That's a matter of opinion.'

She looked at him in surprise.

'He always had to be top dog and he put you down right from the start. That upset me.'

She took a sip, brow furrowed in thought. 'I never knew you felt like that. Why didn't you say something?'

'I didn't like to come between man and wife. And who was I to advise about marriage when my own wife had left me?'

She stared into her mug, cradling it in her hands. 'Hartley's got much worse since Cheryl left home. He idolizes her, you know. So he left me alone while she was around – well, more or less. But now... I can't do anything right and he's getting worse. When he retires I can't face it, Jake, I just can't.'

'Well, I reckon you're doing the right thing, going to see Gillah.'

His sister nodded, but her expression was bleak.

'She'll know your legal position – about the house and other things.'

'I was hoping she might help me persuade him to get some counselling, try to change. I don't really want to break up my marriage – well, I don't think I do. I don't want to leave my home. I just want things to be different, easier.'

Jake didn't comment on that. He felt there was about as much chance of Hartley Wilkes changing as there was of a rocket full of purple aliens landing on the beach at Blackpool. 'You can stay here with me till you've got things sorted out, if you like.'

'Thanks, Jake. I'll try not to be a nuisance.'

That made him feel angry. 'Just be yourself, Peggy. No creeping around on tiptoe here.'

Then he thought of something positive. 'I'll enjoy your cooking. You're a splendid cook. Can you still make that apricot cake?'

A faint smile crossed her face. 'Yes. Can you still eat as much of it?'

He grinned. 'I certainly can.'

She leaned across to kiss his cheek. 'Thank you.'

'It's what family are for, helping one another.'

Chapter 17

Australia

Gina heard the car pull into the drive and went to open the front door, staring avidly at the girl who got out of it – bounced out would have been a more accurate description. Her heart was beating and she was both excited and nervous at the same time. She held out one hand and the girl clasped it with a beaming smile.

'Gosh, you look so like my auntie Peggy when she was younger! Mind you, she always looked a bit nervous, but you don't.' She laughed. 'What a way to introduce myself. It is lovely to meet you. Can I call you Auntie Gina?'

'Yes, of course.' Gina smiled at her and turned to shake hands with the tall young man who followed her to the door. 'You must be Rick. Won't you come in?'

Lou beamed and followed her inside. 'Wow, this is a gorgeous house!'

'It's my daughter Mel's, and it's her pride and joy. She's in hospital at the moment so I'm helping Simon look after the kids.' She led the way into the family room and gestured to the seats. 'Won't you sit down?'

But Lou had gone straight to the window to stare out at the back garden with its swimming pool and matching outdoor furniture. She whistled in amazement. 'It's like a Hollywood set.'

Gina smiled. 'Mel's put a lot of effort into getting the house just right. I'll show you round afterwards, if you like.'

'Is she very ill?'

'She's pregnant and so sick she can't keep anything down. She was bad when she was carrying Emma, but she's much worse this time. She collapsed a couple of days ago.'

'Poor thing. One of my cousins on Dad's side was like that. I felt so sorry for her. Has Mel tried ginger beer first thing in the morning?'

'I don't know.'

'It helped my other cousin.'

'I'll tell Mel, then. Or you can do that yourself if you're staying long enough to meet her. Coffee?'

Gina got them mugs of coffee and cut slices of the cake she'd baked early this morning when she couldn't stay in bed for excitement.

Rick took a huge bite and beamed at her. 'I'd love the recipe for this. It's delish.'

'You cook?' she asked in surprise.

'When I can get Mum out of the kitchen, yeah. I enjoy it. But I wouldn't like to make my living from it, as Lou does.'

Gina could hold back her curiosity no longer. 'Tell me about them, Lou, my half-brother and sister. Just before he died, Dad had a detective looking for his relatives over there, but I only found out that I had any when I cleared out his house. He never told me anything about his first family, not a single word. In fact, I didn't even know he'd been married before.'

Her voice went shaky as she said that and she felt a hand on hers, looking down to see Lou's slender fingers. She clasped them for a minute then said, 'A great-niece. Goodness, that makes me feel old.'

'Well, you don't look old enough to be a great-aunt. You must be nearer Mum's age than Gramps'.'

'Tell Gina about your family, Lou,' Rick prompted, smiling his acceptance of another piece of orange almond cake as he spoke.

So she talked about her great-aunt Margaret, known as Peggy, whom they hadn't seen for years because no one liked her bully of a husband, her cousin Cheryl —should that be second cousin or first cousin once removed? Neither of them knew for certain. Cheryl was a spoilt brat, it seemed, even though she was years older than Lou. Then there was her beloved grandfather Jake and her mother, who had moved to live in Birmingham recently.

'Is that all your close relatives?'

'No, there's Auntie Bridget. She's eighty-two and she's great fun, not at all old in the head. She has a computer and goes on the internet and has all sorts of friends on line.'

The phone rang just then and Gina excused herself to pick it up.

'Mum?'

'Mel darling, how are you?'

'A little better. They say I can come home tomorrow if there's someone to look after me. I'm sorry to be such a drag, but you will be able to stay on a bit longer, won't you?'

'Yes, of course. Are you keeping food down now?'

'Sort of. They're going to get a nurse to come every day at first then every few days, to keep an eye on me. And I'm not to go back to work – well, I couldn't anyway. It exhausts me just to have a shower.'

Gina could hear by her tone how unhappy that made Mel. 'I'm sorry, love. You really like that job, don't you?'

'Yeah. But I'm using up my sick leave before I resign, just in case.'

That comment reassured Gina more than anything else that her daughter was a bit better. She told her about her relatives, but could hear that Mel was sounding weary so didn't go into any detail. Putting the phone down, she went back to join her guests.

'I hope nothing's wrong?' Lou said.

'Not exactly. Mel's able to come home tomorrow, but she'll need looking after. So I'll definitely have to put off my trip to the UK. It's selfish of me, I know, but I was so looking forward to meeting my family.' She pulled a wry face and changed the subject. 'What about you two? Simon says you can come and stay here for a while, if you like. There's a spare bedroom and it'll save you money.'

'Are you sure?' Lou asked. 'I mean, if you have Mel to look after, you won't want us as well.'

'You're family. And anyway, who said you're getting the five-star hotel treatment?'

'We can help with the cooking, if you like,' Rick offered.

They both beamed at Gina and their enthusiastic acceptance cheered her up a little.

But when they'd gone to get their things from the hostel, she sat for ages staring out into the garden before she got on with the housework.

Life didn't always let you have what you wanted. She should be used to that by now. She'd better ring and cancel her provisional flight booking. Trouble was, the information was at home. Well, a day or two wouldn't make any difference.

Chapter 18

England

Brad returned to Jane's house after the specified half-hour had passed, a very long half-hour during which he looked at his watch every minute or two, amazed to see how slowly the hands were moving.

Jane opened the door for him, grim-faced, and he went inside, feeling bad about upsetting her. She led the way into the living room without a word.

Rosie was standing facing the door. She didn't say anything, but she looked at him as if trying to memorize his face. He smiled as he did his own staring. Her hair was dark and curly, her face piquant and full of life.

'Do you want me to stay?' Jane asked her daughter, pointedly ignoring Brad.

'No, Mum. I told you.'

'Well, I'll be in the kitchen. Just call out if you need me.'

When the door had closed behind her, Rosie looked at him apologetically. 'She's only trying to protect me.'

'I know.' Brad walked across and took her hands, holding her at arm's length. 'Let me look at you properly. You're a bit like my daughter Joanna, a bit like your mother, but the final mixture is very much yourself.'

'And you don't look old. Mum said you were fifty-five.'

'Only fifty-four!'

She grinned at him. 'You're wearing well.'

'And you haven't even started wearing yet. Shall we sit down?'

She plumped down on the couch and after a moment's hesitation he took a chair opposite, from which he could watch her.

'I have a half-sister and brother, haven't I?'

'Yes. Joanna and Michael. Do you want to see some photos?'

She nodded, so he got out his wallet and passed the photos to her. 'And here are their children.'

She stared at them in delight. 'That makes me an aunt, doesn't it?'

'Yes.'

'Cool.' She studied the photos intently before passing them back to him. 'Did you tell Joanna and Michael about me?'

'Yes. They were surprised – and rather upset that I'd been unfaithful to their mother.'

'Was it a grand passion? You and my mum, I mean.'

'It was a grand attraction. She was very pretty and lively with it. I shouldn't have… but I can't regret it because she lifted my spirits during some very dark times. And of course, our relationship created you.'

'How does it feel to have an extra daughter?'

'Awesome – in a literal sense. I love being a father, you see. I'm sorry, though, that I've had no part in your life until now. I'll always regret missing your childhood. But I hope you'll let me see you sometimes from now on.'

'I'd really like that. But Dad will always be – well, my dad. So I think I'd rather call you Brad, if that's OK with you.'

'Of course it is.'

They chatted for a few more minutes then Jane came in and the atmosphere chilled perceptibly. 'Would you like a cup of tea or coffee, Brad?'

He looked at his brand-new daughter and shook his head. 'I think I'd better leave now. Rosie's looking tired.'

'She's just recovering from flu.'

'I want to see you again, Brad,' Rosie said immediately. 'Perhaps we could go out together somewhere on Saturday?'

'I'd like that.' He turned to Jane. 'Would you be all right with that?'

'I'm not all right with any of this, as you both know. I'll have to ask her father. He's the one who's going to be most upset.'

He gave them the piece of paper he'd prepared. 'I'm at this address for the next week, then I'm considering finding a self-catering place.'

Jane looked at him in dismay. 'I thought you were just passing through!'

'No. I want to explore the north of England, because that's where my family comes from. But most of all, I'd like to spend some time with Rosie. There are other relatives in England that I want to visit later as well.'

'I'll see you to the door.'

Rosie winked as she shook hands with him. 'See you on Saturday, Brad.'

'I'll look forward to it. Ten o'clock suit you?'

She nodded.

When he'd driven off, Jane slammed the front door and came back into the living room. 'How did he find out our address?'

'I don't know. It wasn't from me. Mum... don't be like this. Please. He seems very nice. I can see why you fancied him. Tell me—'

'Well, I don't fancy him now and I wish he hadn't come back into my life. What happened between us is long gone. And what your father – your real father – will say about Brad coming to see you, I dread to think.'

Rosie bent her head and let the tirade wash over her. Her mother had already said all this – several times. But it was never any use arguing when her mother was in this mood. She and Casey had found that out years ago.

She was dying for her brother to come home so she could tell him about Brad. He at least would understand and wouldn't treat her like a criminal.

It was a relief when her mother went to work in the afternoon. But she didn't give Rosie her mobile back and she made her promise solemnly not to phone anyone, not even her friend Mandy.

Why was Mum acting like this? Rosie wondered rebelliously. And how would Dad be?

–

Stuart was late getting home from work and when he came into the kitchen, Jane could see at a glance that something had upset him.

'What is it?'

'They've given the Special Educational Needs Co-ordinator job in the new school to someone else. It's not even the guy from the other school, it's an outsider.'

She rushed to put her arms round him and they stood close together for a minute or two. 'I'm so sorry, darling. Have they – offered you anything else?'

'Not exactly. There's to be one other teacher in the Learning Resources Centre. I may or may not be offered that position. It'd be a step down in status, though it wouldn't affect my salary. As if money is all that matters!'

He stepped away from Jane, reached into the fridge and pulled out a bottle of wine. 'If I don't get that other job, I can work in the new combined school as an English teacher or I can find myself a job elsewhere and they'll give me glowing references, because they really appreciate what I've achieved.' His voice dripped with sarcasm, but broke on the last word and he dashed one hand across his eyes.

'Well, surely there's a shortage of Special Education Needs teachers?'

'Not round here, there isn't. Everyone wants to live close to the coast, it seems. And anyway, most of the vacant jobs have been filled for the coming school year by now.' He poured himself a glass of wine and took a big gulp before pouring one for her.

'What are you going to do, then?'

'I don't know, can't seem to think clearly.' He swallowed more wine with an audible gulp.

Casey came in, opened his mouth to speak then closed it again and looked from one parent to the other. 'Something wrong?'

'Your father didn't get the SENCO job.'

'Oh, no. Sorry about that, Dad. They must have rocks in their heads after what you've done for that school.' His father nodded but didn't say anything, so Casey turned to his mother. 'Can I have something to eat, then I'll go up to my room and – um – leave you two in peace?'

Jane thrust the biscuit tin at him and grabbed two cans of lemonade out of the fridge. 'Take one to your sister. And don't either of you come down till I call you for tea.'

Casey nodded and ran upstairs.

Jane turned back to her husband and went to stand behind his chair with her arms round him. 'I don't know what to say. I was so sure you'd get that job.'

'I've crossed swords with Binnings too often. I suppose he wanted a meeker person running the new centre.' He lifted the glass to his lips again. 'You're not drinking. Aren't you going to help me drown my sorrows?'

She hesitated then went to pick up her glass and raise it in a silent toast as she sat down across the table from him. 'Here's to all this leading to something better.'

He looked at her as if she had suddenly turned into an enemy. 'I don't want something better. I want what I created. One of the best damned learning resource centres in the north. I did it against all sorts of stupid odds and regulations. I helped raise money for extras, put in all those hours at home, making aids and designing computer programs. If there was any justice in the world, that job ought to be mine!'

He slammed the glass down and buried his head in his hands, trying to muffle his weeping.

Jane hesitated, wondering if he wanted her to cuddle him. She'd never seen him so upset about anything.

He stood up abruptly, looking through her, not at her. 'I'm not fit company for anyone tonight. I'll go into the den. I don't want any tea.'

She didn't protest, just watched as he picked up the glass and bottle of wine, and walked blindly across the hall to the tiny den, two and a half metres by three in size, which had been labelled the 'office' on the house plans. He had spent many an evening working there on projects for his beloved centre, had given it so much.

How could they hand the job to someone else? She could weep – only that would do no good. Her role now was to support him and keep any other troubles away from him. And that included Rosie's latest obsession with her biological father.

Damn Brad Rosenberry! Damn all biology teachers too! If they hadn't taught Rosie about genetics, she'd not have realised that Stu couldn't be her father.

–

Peggy sat in Gillah's cosy office, wondering why the other woman wasn't saying anything. 'Aren't you supposed to tell me what to do?' she asked at last.

'No. I'm supposed to help you decide what to do, not do it for you. You're the only one who knows how you feel, after all.' She smiled. 'For the moment, I don't think you're ready to make any major decisions. I think we should talk about your legal situation and you should try to understand it before you do anything.'

'But I can't impose on Jake for too long. I need to get things settled.'

'Has your brother said that, or is it something you've dreamed up yourself?'

Peggy wriggled uncomfortably. 'He said I could stay for as long as I like. Only how can I? I've no money, no clothes.'

'You can go home and get them.'

Peggy shivered. 'I'd not dare.'

'We could get a policeman to accompany you.'

She was horrified. 'What would the neighbours think of that?'

'Who cares what the neighbours think? It's you we have to help.'

'Would you really come with me?'

'Yes. As long as your brother comes too.' Gillah looked at her watch. 'He's retired, isn't he? Give him a call. I've got a free hour and we could go there right now. You still have a key?'

'Yes.'

When they got there, Peggy sat in the car and stared at her home. Only it didn't feel like hers any more. She couldn't understand why that was because she'd only been away from it for a day.

'You all right, love?' Jake asked.

She nodded, took a deep breath to brace herself and got out of the car. They followed her and waited as she fumbled for her front door key and tried to insert it. But it wouldn't fit. She looked at Jake in bewilderment.

'Here, let me do that for you.' He too failed to fit the key in the lock and frowned at it. 'Are you sure you've got the right key, Peggy?'

'Of course I am.'

'This one doesn't fit the lock.'

'It must do!' She stared at the key and then at the lock, suddenly realizing why it had seemed different. 'The centre part's all shiny and new looking.'

'The bugger's changed the lock on you!' Jake exclaimed.

Peggy looked from one of her companions to the other. 'What am I going to do?'

'You have a perfect right to break one of your own windows if you want,' Gillah said with a smile. 'Not that I'm urging you to do that, of course.'

Peggy gaped at her. 'I can't break a window!'

'Why not?'

'It… I…'

'Break one round the back,' Jake said cheerfully. 'In fact, I'll break it for you.'

'No,' Gillah said. 'If anyone does it, it should be her because it's her home.'

Peggy felt shivery inside as she led them round the back, then relief flooded through her as she remembered something. 'How silly of me! We don't need to break anything. I know where the spare key to the back door is hidden.'

She went across to the flower bed and scraped the earth aside. But there was no key in the usual place. 'He's taken that too.'

Anger was rising in her now, driving her on. She seized a garden ornament and went towards the window of the utility room. 'Stand back.' Not even waiting to check that they'd done so, she smashed the window and used the concrete frog to clear the shards of glass from the frame.

The neighbour peered over the fence as she was doing this. 'Oh, it's you, Peggy! I thought you had burglars.'

'No, just forgot my key, that's all.'

'Seems rather drastic to break the window.'

'I need to get inside urgently.'

'Well, you know best. My Fred would go mad if I did that.' She went back into her house.

'Interfering busybody,' Peggy muttered, reaching carefully inside the window to open the door.

It was anger that carried her along as she piled her clothes into bin liners, hesitating as to what to take then deciding to take nearly everything. She didn't want to have to break in again.

She was glad Jake and Gillah didn't try to make her chat, though.

'That's it,' she said when she'd finished.

'Do you want to leave him a note?' Gillah asked.

Peggy considered this but she couldn't imagine what she'd say. 'No. He'll see that my clothes are missing and Mrs Nosey-Parker next door will tell him I broke the window.'

As they went downstairs she hesitated, then drew herself up. 'We're going out through the front door, not creeping round the side like thieves.'

'Well done, Peggy,' Gillah said as they went towards their cars.

She nodded. To her surprise she was feeling quite proud of herself. And it had felt good to smash that window. For two pins she'd pick up a stone and smash a few more. She realized the counsellor had said something and was waiting for an answer. 'Sorry? What was that again?'

'I said there's a meditation class starting at the Centre tomorrow night. I wondered if you'd like to go. It's very calming.'

'I don't think—'

Jake interrupted before she could finish refusing. 'I'll take her there and pick her up afterwards. Sounds a good idea. She can't sit in the house all the time.'

Peggy didn't particularly want to go, but realized it'd give him some time on his own. 'All right. I suppose I could give it a try.'

Gillah gave her another of those approving nods.

'You're the best brother ever,' Peggy said to Jake as he drove her home. 'Are you sure you won't mind me staying with you?'

'Of course not, love. But I do want you to go to this meditation class.'

She was already having second thoughts. 'I'm not sure.'

'You need to make new friends, start building a new life. And it would be very calming without you needing to use tranquilisers. You do need to calm down, you know. You're so anxious about everything.'

Peggy stared at him in amazement. 'I never thought to hear you telling someone to try meditation.'

'You don't know much about what I've been doing lately. I've started looking into Buddhism, for one thing, and conservation for another. If you live on your own you have to get out and do things or you rot.'

'I think I'd enjoy some quiet rotting time,' she said bitterly.

'No, Peggy. You've cowered inside that house of yours, waiting on that bugger hand and foot for years. Do this one thing for me: go out to that class and meet a few other folk. They'll all be women. Nothing for you to fear there.'

She hesitated. 'You'll take me and pick me up?'

'I promise.'

'All right.' But she knew she was going to hate it.

Chapter 19

Gina went to fetch Mel home from hospital, together with a sheaf of instructions about diet, permitted medications and danger signs.

Her daughter walked out to the car quietly and sank into the seat with a sigh, saying in a thread of a voice, 'I feel so tired, Mum. All the time. As well as sick.'

'Perhaps we shouldn't have invited Lou and Rick to stay.' Gina studied her anxiously. 'It'll be too much for you.'

'I doubt it'll make much difference to me. It's you who'll have all the trouble of looking after them. I keep falling asleep. It's this travel sickness stuff they've given me. It helps stop me throwing up but it makes me sleepy.'

'I doubt Lou and Rick will be any trouble. They both love cooking and they're so cheerful, it's a pleasure to have them around. Emma fell asleep on Lou's knee last night watching TV.'

'She did? That's not like her.' Mel fell silent, leaning back with her eyes closed as they headed south.

When they got home, she smiled faintly at the sight of her house. 'I'm sure I'll feel better now I'm home. Thank goodness for Granddad's money.'

'You're still going to try to keep the house, then?'

'Of course I am.'

Gina didn't comment on the foolishness of that. Now wasn't the time to try to talk sense into her daughter. She got the suitcase out of the car boot and went inside. They were greeted by the smell of cooking and she looked anxiously at Mel to see whether this would make her nauseous. But Mel didn't seem to notice, just walked into the kitchen and collapsed into a chair in the casual eating area.

'Let me introduce you to Rick and Lou. Lou's a first cousin once removed of yours.' They'd worked out the exact relationship last night.

Lou came across to give Mel a quick hug. 'What a time to have visitors!'

Rick beamed from across the room and waved a spoon in greeting. 'I though some soup might go down more easily than solid food. It's a pleasure to cook in this kitchen. I hope you don't mind us making ourselves at home.'

But Mel sat up suddenly, clapped one hand to her mouth and rushed along to the bathroom. She came out a few minutes later, looking boneless and exhausted.

Gina studied her anxiously. 'You ought to be in bed.'

Mel dropped into the nearest chair. 'I've had enough of bed in the past few days. I'll go mad all alone up there.'

Lou looked at her thoughtfully. 'That big couch of yours in the living room is as good as a bed. How about we get some sheets and blankets and make it up for the daytime? Auntie Gina said you had to rest, but you can do that just as easily down here as upstairs. And you'll have company.'

Mel smiled gratefully. 'I can see we're going to get on well, Lou. The couch it is.'

She allowed them to help her settle, accepted a tiny bowl of Rick's soup and took some more tablets. When Gina looked in on her she was asleep, but even in sleep she was frowning. She was so unlike her usual assertive self, it was terrifying.

Gina sighed, her last faint hopes fading. There was no way she could leave Simon to look after Mel on his own.

–

For the next two days, Lou and Rick went out during the day but came back mid-afternoon, leaving Gina to look after her daughter and keep up with the family's washing. Mel continued to spend a lot of time sleeping so wasn't much company and the daytime hours seemed to move very slowly.

Their young relatives were the easiest guests Gina had ever had. They had volunteered to cook the evening meals, producing gourmet food with ease. Lou in particular was also adept at thinking of small treats that would tempt Mel.

'I make sure they're fairly healthy,' she assured Gina. 'I did this short course about tempting titbits for invalids when my friend's sister was pregnant. I could get her to eat when no one else could.'

In the evenings, Simon put Emma to bed, then sat with his wife till she grew drowsy. The others used the family room, which looked out on to the pool. After helping Mel up to bed, Simon would join them downstairs for an hour or so but was too worried to be good company.

'I'm going for an audition tomorrow,' Rick announced over breakfast one day.

'Audition?' Gina asked, keeping an eye on Emma, who was a fussy eater, to make sure she ate enough protein. She'd read an article saying children should go to school on protein.

'Yeah. To become an artistic equivalent of a busker – sketching portraits in a big shopping mall.' He grinned and pretended to pound his chest. 'Big artist, me.'

'Are you good enough for that?'

'Oh, yeah. I've been doing it at home for ages. Sketching isn't what I want to do but it's a necessary step in my life's work.' He looked at her, serious now. 'I want to paint portraits eventually, real ones where silk gleams and hair looks soft and fluffy. But I dropped out of art college because they had their main focus on modern stuff. I don't want to waste my time painting meaningful blobs. I should have chosen a college with more care, but my art teacher said this one would be best for me to broaden my experience. I didn't know what to look for, and my parents knew even less so I took his advice. And anyway, I wouldn't have met Lou if I'd gone somewhere else.'

He gave her a loving look across the table. 'She was working nearby and once we met, that was it. We're going to get married one day, you know. We haven't told her parents yet and they'll all say we're too young, but we know we're right for one another.'

Lou pretended to thump him. 'You might have let me tell Auntie Gina about us.'

He shrugged. 'Does it matter who tells her?'

Her mock anger softened into a warm smile. 'No, not really.'

He turned back to Gina. 'I can earn good money sketching – I've done it before – and we need to finance the rest of our trip.'

'Are you allowed to work while you're in Australia?'

'Of course. They let backpackers do all the jobs other people don't want, like picking fruit and stuff. We couldn't have afforded to come otherwise. We do have our tickets home, though.'

'I'm going to look for jobs in cafés while we're here,' Lou said. 'It'll all be useful experience because they're bound to do things differently here. I want to have a café of my own one day, but I've a lot to learn yet. And I'll need to save the start-up money.'

Gina looked from one to the other. They seemed too young to be thinking of marriage and yet there they were making plans for the future with all the confidence of untried youth. 'I wish you both well, in marriage and in work. Now, I want to ask a favour of you. Would you mind staying here with Mel today so that I can go home and check everything's all right? I need to take in the mail and that sort of thing?'

Rick smiled. 'Sure. Glad to.'

Lou glanced at the clock. 'Mel should be waking up soon. I'm going to take her up a glass of ginger beer and a glucose tablet. No harm in trying it, is there? It helped my cousin.'

Gina drove home with a sense of relief. They were such a sensible pair, Mel would be all right today.

Her house seemed cramped after the spaciousness of her daughter's home. Strange, that. She'd found it cosy before.

She looked wistfully at the pile of brochures on the dining table. She'd been collecting information about flights, going on line to look at accommodation in England, had even picked out a hotel in Blackpool that had a special offer valid for the whole summer if you booked for a full week. With a sigh she shoved the brightly coloured papers into the top drawer and tried to put her dreams away with them. Just for the time being, of course.

When she'd finished, she packed some more clothes and drove back to Perth.

She found Lou sitting cross-legged on the floor by the sofa, where Mel was sitting up. The two of them were laughing about something. It was little short of a miracle to see Mel more cheerful.

'You look a bit better,' she said lightly, kissing her daughter. She kissed Lou's cheek too while she was at it.

Mel nodded. 'I do feel better if I rest and those tablets the doctors gave me are stopping me being sick as often. Even the ginger beer seemed to help today. Ginger beer! Stupid, isn't it?'

'And you'll be pleased to hear that I've been feeding her up today, Auntie Gina,' Lou said with a grin. 'Titbits for invalids.' She grinned at her cousin.

'She keeps nagging me to eat.'

'But only tiny helpings, you must admit. And most of them stayed down.'

'Yes.' Mel sounded surprised.

'Well, I'll go and put my things away, then,' Gina said.

As she walked up the stairs she heard Mel say to Lou, 'I feel so guilty. Mum was planning on a trip to England and now she's got to stay and look after me. I'm messing up everyone's lives – Simon's too.'

Well, at least Mel understood how she was feeling, Gina thought as the prison bars closed around her. She'd give Lexie a ring tonight, hadn't seen her and Ben for days. Might as well make the most of living nearer to her younger daughter.

But no matter how positive she tried to be, she still felt bitterly disappointed.

Chapter 20

England

At breakfast the following morning, the dining room was quite full, and the waitress asked Brad if he'd mind sharing a table since they had a lot of singles in the hotel this week.

'Not at all.'

'Choose any table with just one person on it, then.' She flourished one arm at the room and hurried off.

He glanced quickly round and his gaze fell on an elderly lady sitting in the bay window. She was very upright but there was a loneliness about her that touched him. He enjoyed the company of old people. When you got them talking, they were usually very interesting and some had done the most amazing things during the Second World War. He went over. 'Would you mind if I joined you? All the tables are occupied and I've been asked to share with someone.'

Her face brightened visibly. 'Not at all. I enjoy meeting new people.'

He went to get himself some juice and fruit from the breakfast bar, then sat down. 'Are you on holiday?'

'Permanently. I live here at the hotel. It's much more interesting than an old folks' home and people don't die on you all the time.' She smiled at her own feeble joke and added, 'I'm Bridie Shapley. Call me Bridie. You Australians prefer first names, don't you?'

'Yes. And I'm Brad. Is it so obvious that I'm an Australian?'

'It is to me. I used to have an Aussie family living next door, but they went back to the sun. I wished I could go with them. Unfortunately, I was too old to travel on my own by then.'

Bridie was a mine of information about things to see and do near Blackpool and in the end Brad invited her to go out in his car for a drive.

She beamed at him. 'I'd love to, if you don't mind the fact that I need a pit stop every hour and a half, and can't walk very fast.'

'I don't mind at all. I'd welcome some company, actually.'

'Give me half an hour to check my emails and powder my nose and I'm all yours. I'm expecting an important business email about some shares, or I'd not keep you waiting so long.'

He stared at her in surprise. 'Email?'

She shook her head, making a tutting noise. 'Don't judge a book by its cover! Us oldies are perfectly capable of navigating the internet. Wrinkles on the face aren't so wonderful, but wrinkles on the brain store a lot of extra information.'

'Do they really?'

She gave another of her rasping chuckles. 'I don't know, but that's my theory and I'm sticking to it.'

First she directed him to drive along the sea front to St Anne's and they stopped there for a while so that Brad could walk along the beach and Bridie could enjoy the bracing air from the comfort of a seafront shelter. Next she took him inland to a pub she knew which did excellent lunches, insisting on paying for that as a thank you for her day out.

After they got back to Blackpool, they sat for a while overlooking the sea and she helped him plan what he'd do with his daughter in the Lake District the following Saturday.

He went out in the evening to stretch his legs and buy some fish and chips, which was a lot cheaper than eating at the hotel. He walked further than he'd intended so it took him a while to get back, by which time he was feeling slightly nervous and had come to the conclusion that some parts of Blackpool didn't feel all that safe after dark.

He was looking forward to eating breakfast with Bridie again. He hadn't realized how lonely he'd been feeling. He was, he supposed, a gregarious type, not a loner. If it had been at all possible, he'd have travelled with someone. But there wasn't anyone and he didn't want to put off the travelling any longer. As Bridie had said today, you could get too old to travel. He was fit now. Who knew what he'd be like in another few years? He'd met people who were fit and active at ninety, others who were semi-invalids at sixty. You never knew what life would do to you.

His son had warned him he'd be lonely and he'd pooh-poohed that, but Michael had been right. Oh, well. Maybe after Brad had sorted out how and when he'd be able to see Rosie, he'd book himself on a guided tour of Europe. There were all sorts of places he wanted to see – Paris, Rome, Greece.

–

On Friday evening Stu came home in a foul mood after another clash with his headmaster who had got the removalists in to start packing up the contents of the resource centre without consulting Stu, and had tried to include some of Stu's personal possessions in the first batch.

'I got back just in time to make them unpack my things. That bugger hadn't even had the courtesy to discuss it with me or ask whether I was using them. And then Binnings had the nerve to ask me whether I'd made the teaching aids in my own time or the school's, because if it was the latter, they belonged to the centre not me. He even questioned where I'd got the materials for them from and whether I'd worked out the programs on the school's computer.'

'I remember you deliberately buying your own materials so that they'd belong to you,' she agreed. 'And making them at home in the evenings.' And he'd put untold hours into devising programs the kids would enjoy, ones which made spelling and arithmetic into a game and a challenge.

'Anyway, I soon set him straight about that.' He gave a snort of indignation. 'Binnings then had the cheek to say that if I cared for the kids that much, I ought to give the new centre copies of all my programs. I told him altruism went only so far, especially when what you'd done wasn't appreciated.'

She watched in surprise as Stu went back out to unload a carrier of six bottles of wine from his car, together with more of his equipment. It wasn't like Stu to buy booze. He didn't usually care whether he had a drink in the evening or not. She was the one who enjoyed an occasional glass of wine, so watched out for special offers when she did her grocery shopping.

'Stu, was it worth picking a fight with him? You'll still have to work with him next year, after all.'

'Yes, it damned well was! What he was doing was deliberately designed to rub it in that I was no longer in charge as far as he was concerned. Well, that'll backfire on him. If I'm not good enough to run the new centre, then my teaching aids aren't good enough to use there, either.'

'I've told you before: you should try to sell them for publication. It's brilliant the way you've written the reading enrichment program and those games are cute.'

'Maybe I will. In the meantime, let's open a bottle and drink to the downfall of Binnings and all like him.'

'It's a bit early to start drinking.'

'Not today, it isn't.' He opened the bottle and poured two glasses.

Rosie came downstairs, picking her way among the boxes in the hall. 'What's going on?'

'Your father's bringing home his own teaching aids before those belonging to the centre are moved to the new school.'

'Where are you going to store them, Dad? You must have dozens of boxes of things.'

'They can go into the garage. The car will have to stay outside for the time being.'

Rosie reached across the table for an apple. 'Well, it's only for a couple of months, isn't it? They'll be going back with you next term.'

'Not necessarily.'

She caught her mother's eye, read a warning in it and changed the subject. 'What do you think I ought to wear on Saturday, Mum?'

Jane frowned. She hadn't wanted to raise this yet, but it was too late now. Stu would have to know. 'Depends where you're going. Did he say? No? Well, something casual, I suppose.'

Stu leaned back, glass in hand. 'If you're fit enough to go out with a boyfriend, you should have gone back to school today.'

Rosie saw her mother's body go tense, though her voice remained casual.

'She's going out with Brad.'

The silence that followed was deafening.

'When was this arranged?'

'Yesterday.'

Stu's voice took on a sharp edge. 'And it didn't occur to anyone to consult me about that? Or am I no longer considered to be her father?'

Jane made a slight cutting movement with her hand to warn Rosie to leave this to her. 'You were upset when you came home last night and if you remember, you shut yourself up in the den all evening, so there wasn't much chance to talk.'

His voice was heavy with sarcasm. 'There is a door into the den. You've not hesitated to use it before.'

'You were drunk, so it'd have been silly to try to discuss something so important then. Anyway, I'm telling you now, aren't I?'

He folded his arms. 'I don't like the idea of her spending the day with that man. We don't know anything about him.'

'Brad's all right. You can trust him,' Jane replied.

Stu's voice grew even sharper. 'Correction. I don't know anything about him. I haven't even met him. So I'm not actually much inclined to trust him with my daughter's safety, however highly you think of him. If he wants to see her, if she won't let this matter drop—' He broke off to scowl at Rosie. 'Then he can come here for an hour or two and see her under our supervision.'

'But he's taking me out!' Rosie protested. 'It's all arranged.'

'Then we'll just have to un-arrange it, won't we?'

She burst into tears. 'You can't do that.'

'Can't I? Strange, but I thought I was your father and you were underage.'

'Stu, you're not being fair.'

He swung round to glare at his wife.

'Ganging up on me now? That man has only to turn up and it seems he winds everyone round his little finger. Get this straight, both of you! I don't want Rosie associating with him. He can see her a couple of times and that's it! Afterwards he can sod off back to Australia and leave our family alone.'

'Dad, please!'

'I'm not going to change my mind about this!' he roared, his face a dark red, veins standing out at his temples.

Sobbing, Rosie rushed upstairs to her room.

Jane turned to Stu. 'This means a lot to her. We shouldn't stop her seeing him.'

'We? It's you who decided this. I thought we had a pact about backing one another up and you knew exactly how I felt about him.'

'I only said—'

'Or perhaps you're still carrying a torch for him. Perhaps you want to see him again, too.'

'That's ridiculous and unfair.'

'Is it? I bring her up, give her everything my own son has and this is the thanks I get. Well, I'm not handing her over to him.'

'Stu, you know adopted children sometimes need to meet their biological parents. What she wants is perfectly reasonable and—'

'And I'm being unreasonable. Well, live with it. I'm not – repeat, not! – changing my mind.'

She threw up her hands. 'OK, you've made that clear and you won't discuss it, or even let me say what I want. So you can tell him you've put your foot down.' She plonked a piece of paper down in front of him. 'There's the number of his hotel. Ring him up. Beat your chest. Put on your caveman act!' She spun round, snatched up her handbag and marched out of the house.

Stu ran after her to the door. 'Where are you going? Jane! Where are you going?'

But she didn't answer just got into her car and drove off.

He stared after her for a few seconds then looked down at the piece of paper. Mouth a thin, tight line, he went inside, picked up the phone and dialled the number.

'Can I speak to Brad Rosenberry, please?'

'It'll take us a minute or two to find him – if he's in the hotel. Can I get him to ring you back?'

'No, it's urgent. I'll wait.'

He took a slurp of wine and sat tapping his fingers on the kitchen table, wishing they wouldn't pour schmaltzy music into your ears while you were waiting. Then he heard a man's voice saying, 'Thank you,' and someone picked up the phone.

'Hello. Brad here.'

'This is Stuart Quentin, Rosie's father. I'm afraid I don't approve of my daughter going out all day with a stranger. If you wish to see her tomorrow, you can come to the house for an hour in the afternoon. Two o'clock.'

Stu didn't wait for an answer but slammed the phone down and finished off his glass of wine then sat scowling into the distance. To quote the kids at school. This whole situation sucked big time.

Muttering 'Waste not, want not,' he picked up his wife's glass of wine with one hand, the bottle with the other and went back into his den.

Where the hell had Jane gone?

–

Brad put the phone down, frowning.

'Not bad news, I hope?' The receptionist gave him a bright professional smile that said she didn't really care then turned to the next customer.

He wandered into the bar and ordered a glass of beer. As he turned around, he saw Bridie sitting in a corner reading a magazine and sipping something pink from a tall glass. She wasn't looking in his direction so he went around to the other side of the bar, needing to be alone yet not wanting to go up to his room, because even the most beautifully decorated hotel room felt soulless and quiet, far too quiet for his present mood.

What had led to the Quentins' sudden change of heart about Rosie?

Was the decision Jane's or her husband's?

Brad took another sip of beer without really tasting it and frowned into space. What was he going to do tomorrow afternoon? Sit in the living room at Jane's and make stilted conversation in front of a man who clearly resented him? That was no way to get to know his daughter.

Stu's voice had sounded angry.

Brad tried to think how he'd feel if someone turned up and claimed to be Joanna's biological father? Angry, yes, and jealous too. He could see the other man's point of view, of course he could, but Stu had always known Rosie had been fathered by someone else. It was hardly a surprise to him.

He remembered his daughter's face, the shy hope on it. She had a lovely smile, with Jane's generous mouth.

Oh, hell, what a tangle! Whatever he did, someone was going to get hurt.

Maybe he should go and see Rosie tomorrow then cut his losses and move on?

He took a sip of beer. No! He'd come ten thousand miles to meet her. She clearly needed to get to know him, too. If he let Stu drive him away, he'd be letting Rosie down, so he'd just have to persuade the Quentins that he wasn't trying to usurp Stu's place as father, that all he wanted was to make a place of his own in her life. If they'd let him.

A group nearby burst into raucous laughter and suddenly he couldn't stand it any longer. He went outside for a walk, moving from one garishly lit space to another, hearing canned laughter, seeing hucksters and small-time gamblers, lingering to buy some sticky pink and white

Blackpool rock and then biting a chunk off and sucking it as he walked along.

He was lonely. Had been since his wife died, really. Wanted a woman in his life again. Why hadn't he taken up Judy's offer, gone out with her?

Because he wasn't attracted to her in that way. Even Jane didn't attract him this time round.

He had always been better at making friends with women than romancing them. The thought of chatting someone up made him cringe. How did one do it these days? Not to mention making love to a woman for the first time...

Oh, hell, he didn't know what he wanted, just – something, someone, not to be alone any longer. This trip had proved that to him already.

–

Upstairs, Rosie and Casey looked at one another as their mother's car door slammed and she drove off.

'What's going on?' she asked.

'More to the point, what about tea?'

'Trust you to think of your stomach.'

He patted his almost concave belly. 'I'm a growing boy.' He put one hand to his ear as the door to the den banged shut. 'Hark! I hear sounds of a man in retreat. Stay here and I'll go and see whether it's safe to get some food.'

'I'm not hungry.'

'Well, I am.' He hesitated near the door of her bedroom. 'I'll bring you something up, eh?'

She shook her head and stayed where she was, sitting on the edge of the bed, hands clasped, waiting for something. She didn't know what.

A few minutes later Casey came up with a plate of doorstep sandwiches, but she couldn't face eating so he demolished them, leaving one for her for later.

'I don't know where you put it,' she commented as he opened a can of lemonade to wash everything down.

He smiled and moved to sprawl on the floor beside her bed, leaning against it while he fiddled with her school bag straps. When she didn't speak, he shot a quick glance sideways. 'Don't give up, Rosie. Dad's wrong about this. He's chucking a wobbly because of his job.'

'It's not my fault he didn't get the new job. Though if he spoke to the headmaster the way he speaks to us sometimes, I'm not surprised. He's no diplomat, that's for sure.'

Casey let out a snort of laughter. 'No, it's Mum who smoothes the path in our family.'

'She's not getting very far with smoothing things this time. Dad must have said something nasty for her to storm off in a huff. Wonder where she's gone.'

'Who knows?'

Rosie sighed. 'If I'm not allowed out with Brad, how am I going to get to know him? From the way Dad was talking, he intends to be there with us all the time.'

'That is so un-cool.' Casey traced a pattern in the carpet several times, then said slowly, 'We need to get cunning.'

'We?'

Casey rolled over and looked up at her. 'Well, you can't do it on your own, can you? How about you and I pretend to go to the cinema tomorrow evening, but only I go and you take off with this Brad guy for an hour or two?'

She considered that, head on one side, then shook her head. 'I don't like to lie to Mum and I don't want to get you into trouble. And if they found out, they might stop me seeing him ever again. But I think what Dad's done is wrong. In fact, it stinks.'

'Mum and Dad have quarrelled a few times lately.'

Rosie sighed. 'I've caused some of that.'

'I think it's mainly because Dad's so upset about losing his job.'

She looked at him with tears in her eyes. 'I don't know what to do, Casey.'

'Me neither. We'll have to think of something.'

'Like what?'

He shrugged, gave her one of his wordless hugs, muttered something about 'science project' then walked out without looking at her again. He always did that after he'd hugged her, as if he was embarrassed by what he'd done. She smiled. He was OK, Casey was. Not like some younger brothers.

But her smile soon faded. This wasn't working out as she'd hoped. Only – she couldn't abandon Brad, she just couldn't.

Why was Dad acting as if he was the only person who mattered in the world? She was disappointed in him. Very.

–

Jane went to the Women's Wellness Centre. There was a meditation class starting that evening. She'd decided to give it a miss so she could be at home for Stu. Only if he was going to act like this, picking on poor Rosie, questioning Jane's loyalty to him, not to mention drowning his sorrows in drink, she needed to escape and do something for herself now and then.

She was a bit early, so registered for the class and went to wait in the big room at the rear. There was another woman sitting there and Jane introduced herself. The woman looked at her as if she didn't understand English then gave a little gasp.

'Oh, sorry. I was miles away. I'm Peggy. Have you – um – done this before?'

'No, but I've always wanted to. I'm hoping it'll have a calming effect because my husband is being an unreasonable sod at the moment.'

The other woman stared at her, then said in a near whisper, 'So is mine. I've just left him.'

'That must be hard. Mine's not that bad, but I have to get out of the house for a bit. I'll be glad when he's over this bad patch at work.'

Two other women came in then and there was no more time for confidences. But Jane found Peggy staying near her, looking so nervous that the instructor assured them all she'd never killed a student yet.

In the event, it was a very pleasant hour, soothing and relaxing, just as she'd hoped.

When it was over Jane smiled at Peggy. 'They're holding the classes twice a week. I think I'm going to come to both. Are you?'

'Yes. Well, I think so. I'm not sure what'll be happening.'

Jane had heard other women dither like that. 'It's up to you to make things happen, Peggy. Now that I've calmed down I'm going home to have a nice big row with my husband. I'm not putting up with his bad temper without making a protest or two of my own.'

But when she got home, she found Stu asleep in the den, an empty wine bottle beside him. If he wanted to booze, he could just stay there and live with the consequences tomorrow. She hoped he would have a very bad hangover.

She went to see the kids and found Rosie asleep with tear stains on her cheeks and a half-eaten sandwich on a plate beside her.

When she peered into Casey's room he was playing some game or other on his computer.

'Where'd you go, Mum?'

'To a meditation class. Did you get something to eat?'

'I did, but Rosie wasn't hungry.'

'Did your father come out of his den?'

'Nope.' Casey looked at her. 'He's being a total shit about this Brad guy.'

'Tell me about it.' Jane sighed. She and Stu had an unbreakable rule that they backed one another up when it came to the kids, whether they agreed or not with a decision. But it was going to be very hard to keep that rule this time, because he was being unfair and hurting Rosie badly. 'I'd better get to bed. It's going to be a difficult day tomorrow.'

'What's he like?'

'Who?'

'Rosie's father.'

'Tall, older than me and your father, wearing well. Has a friendly sort of face. You'd like him.'

'She's really upset.'

'We're all upset.'

'I can't see why Dad's getting so het up. She doesn't even call the other one "Dad", she calls him Brad. Can I meet him next time he comes?'

'Yes. Why not?' Unless Stu objected to that as well. Jane tried to hold back a yawn and failed. 'Well, I'm going to bed. Don't stay up too long.'

But tired as she was, she couldn't get to sleep for a long time. She kept expecting Stu to join her. Only he didn't.

Was that because he was too drunk or was he deliberately staying away from her?

Chapter 21

England

Jake heard something drop through the letter box on to the hall floor and went to see what the post had brought. He shuffled through two bills, three advertising brochures (did these people think he was made of money?) and found an aerogram letter from Lou, which he opened eagerly. He was glad to hear that she'd arrived safely, but her final paragraphs upset him.

> I've found some relatives. I'm sorry, but your father died recently. I'm really sad that I missed him. But he had another daughter (Gina) so you've got a half-sister. She's about Mum's age and I really like her. I know you would too if you gave her a chance. Her husband was killed a couple of years ago by a drunken driver and she gets a lost, lonely look on her face sometimes.
>
> She's got two daughters, Mel and Lexie, who are older than me. Rick and I are staying at Mel's house now, so you can ring us at this number if you want. Mel's pregnant and very sick, so we're helping Gina look after

her. Rick's got a job doing sketch portraits in a shopping mall.

I'm not sure whether to tell Mum about Gina and her family or not. You know what she's like. Perhaps you could mention it to her? She must still be busy settling into her new house. You know how fussy she is. I've sent her a couple of postcards, but she's probably still mad at me.

Oh, and could you tell Aunt Peggy about it too, please? I'm not on the sort of terms with her where you send postcards. And this is a bit of a touchy subject.

He re-read the letter slowly. It was cheerful and positive, so typical of Lou. Where that girl got her sunny nature from he'd never understood, because her mother was always very sharp and critical about the world, had been even as a child. Poor Mary had never been the same after her mother left them. He'd definitely give Lou a ring once he'd worked out the time difference. There'd be something to do that on line, no doubt.

As for telling his daughter about her relatives, he wasn't sure about that, though he felt obliged to tell Peggy. In his opinion life was too short to let hatred fester, especially over something which was long over and done with.

Only it wasn't over and done with now, was it? There were relatives down under, and he'd always believed blood was thicker than water. Family connections mattered.

Peggy came in from hanging out some washing. She looked so lost and unhappy, he kept wondering what would become of her. He already knew that he didn't want to live with her permanently. He had organized a pleasant life for himself now that he was retired, even if he did have to live on a rather small income, and it didn't include living with anyone else.

She looked at the letter in his hand.

'I've just heard from Lou in Australia!' He held it out to her. 'Do you want to read it?'

She looked at him in surprise. 'Don't you mind?'

'Mind what?'

'Me seeing it? Hartley used to—' She broke off and her lips wobbled for a moment.

'I wouldn't have offered if I minded.' He passed it across to her.

She read it through, stopping on the second page to exclaim, 'Well! I can't believe she's done this.' After she'd finished, she shoved the letter across the table to him with such force that it floated to the ground. 'It's disloyal!'

He decided to play dumb. 'What is?'

'Going to see those people, staying with them. How could you have let her go looking for them, Jake?'

'How could I have stopped her? Lou's grown up now and makes her own decisions. I wasn't keen but I've changed my mind. Actually, I'm glad she's got some family down there in Australia to turn to if anything goes wrong.'

Peggy got out her handkerchief and mopped her eyes. 'I've never forgiven him for leaving Mum, never!'

Jake sighed. Not that old stuff again. 'I've noticed.'

'Don't you care?'

'I did at the time, but I've got on with my life since.'

'Did you ever open that letter from our father?'

'No. I've still got it, though.'

'Hartley destroyed mine. He said the man didn't deserve a daughter.'

'I thought you chose to destroy it.'

She sighed. 'No. I've always been curious about what was in it. But I don't want anything to do with this female, half-sister or not.'

'You're never likely to meet her, so I don't see why you're getting so upset.'

Peggy flourished her handkerchief, obviously settling in for a good weep so he stood up quickly. 'I'll just go and do a bit of weeding. You've got to keep on top of it.'

'But I—'

He whisked outside, pretending not to hear her. Out in the garden he breathed in the fresh summer air with relief and bent to thin the new row of radishes.

A little later Peggy called out, 'Jake! There's someone at the door.'

With a sigh he went to answer it, knowing how afraid she was that Hartley would return. A courier's van stood outside.

'Box for Mrs M Wilkes. Sign here.'

'What sort of box?'

The lad indicated the back of the van, where a large cardboard box stood ready to be unloaded.

'Peggy! Could you just come out here, love?'

When he explained what it was about, she went over to stand near the box but not touch it. 'It's Hartley's handwriting.'

'Well then, I suppose he's sent some more of your things across.' Jake signed the piece of paper and helped the man carry it inside.

'Aren't you going to open it, Peggy?'

'You do it.'

He went for a knife and cut through the plastic tape, looking in puzzlement at the contents. 'It's all rags.'

Peggy came to join him, clapped one hand over her mouth, letting out a little mew of pain. 'Those are my embroideries. Look! He's cut them into pieces. He must have done it to all of them to fill this box.' She backed away from it, sobbing unrestrainedly.

Jake looked at the rags grimly. 'The rotten sod.' Then he frowned. 'I'm just going to fetch Bob from next door.'

'I don't want to see anyone.'

'Well, you'll have to because we need a witness.' He'd seen Bob peering out of the window at the van.

'Could you come and be a witness to something else for us, please?' he asked when the door opened.

Bob brightened up. 'What's the matter?'

'My sister's husband sent the box that arrived a few minutes ago. I want a witness to see the contents before we go any further.'

'Always happy to help a neighbour.'

And happy to find out the latest gossip, too, Jake knew. He led the way back into his house and waved one hand at the box. There was no sign of Peggy.

Bob peered into it, frowning. 'What's this?'

'Pick them up, have a good look.'

Bob fingered through the shreds. 'It's embroidery – or it was. Looks like someone's cut it up.'

Jake smiled grimly. 'Spot on. Peggy loves embroidering. She's been doing it for years. Her husband's cut all her pieces up and sent them over.'

'Nay, never!' Bob was silent, then let the pieces drop back into the box. 'I said he was a nasty piece of work when he came around here threatening you, didn't I?'

'You did indeed.'

'But this is worse. He must be sick in the head to do this.'

Jake nodded.

'You'd better watch your back, lad.'

'I shall. That's why you're here. I need a witness who'll tell the truth about what he's seen. I haven't had time to cut them up since the box arrived, have I?'

Bob straightened up. 'No, you haven't. And I'm not afraid to speak up if needed.'

'I know. Thanks.'

When his neighbour had left, Jake went to find his sister, who was sitting in her bedroom, weeping silently, rocking backwards and forwards. He kept patting her shoulders and making soothing noises, but it was a long time before she stopped crying.

At intervals during the day, she whispered, 'What'll he do next? Oh, Jake, what'll he do next?'

At teatime she looked at him. 'Could you burn them, please? I don't want them around.'

'Better not. They're evidence.'

'What of?'

'Cruelty.'

She frowned at him, then slowly nodded. 'It is cruel, isn't it?'

'Very.'

When they'd cleared up the tea she said suddenly, 'I really fancy a glass of wine.'

'I don't have any in, sorry. I've some beer if that's any use.'

'Could we go out and buy some wine? Would you mind? I'll keep track of everything I owe you.'

Before they went to the supermarket, he looked over the back fences at his neighbours, both of whom were outside enjoying the fine weather. 'Could you keep an eye on my place, please? As Bob will tell you, we're having a bit of trouble with my sister's husband. I don't want him waiting for me, even in the garden. Call the police if he tries to get into the house.'

When he escorted Peggy out to the car, she asked, 'Do you think he'll come and damage your things as well?'

'No harm in being prepared. After those shredded embroideries of yours, I'd not be surprised at anything that bugger did.'

He locked the side gate carefully from the inside, shooting the bolt with a thump. At first he'd thought only of giving Peggy somewhere to live temporarily. Now he was thinking of how to protect her – and himself.

What the hell had got into Hartley?

–

Brad rode a tram along the promenade at Blackpool the following morning to pass the time, getting off towards the south end at the Pleasure Beach. He wandered around the rides and sideshows, though not all of them were open yet. Places like this were more fun when you were with someone. He could have brought Rosie here. They'd have had fun together, he was sure.

For lunch he bought a sandwich and ate it sitting on the promenade, keeping an eye on his watch, feeling relieved when it was time to get ready.

Stopping the car outside Jane's house, he took a few deep, steadying breaths, feeling as nervous as a teenager calling on a girlfriend's family for the first time.

The door was opened by a balding man with close-shaven hair and glasses. He was a bit shorter than Brad. He scowled and said nothing.

'Stu?' Brad stuck one hand out.

After a moment's hesitation the man took it, letting go almost immediately after one cursory shake. 'I suppose you'd better come in.'

Brad followed him into the living room, where Rosie was sitting very upright and tense on a chair. 'Hi, there. It's lovely to see you again.'

She got up and came to give him a hug, but there was something defiant about the way she did it.

'I'm sorry we can't go out as planned.' She threw a resentful glance at her father. 'This isn't the best way to get to know one another.'

To Brad's dismay, Stu sat down in an armchair and folded his arms, watching them though not making any attempt to join in the conversation.

Brad tried to ignore the glowering presence. 'Tell me more about your life, Rosie. School, what you do at weekends, hobbies, that sort of thing.'

She shrugged. 'School is school. You have to go through it, but it isn't much fun.'

'What are your favourite subjects?'

'Biology,' she said with another defiant glance at her father. 'It has useful applications in the real world.'

Jane came to the doorway. 'Hi, Brad. Stu, can you just come and help me for a moment, please?'

Their glances locked then he stood up, 'Excuse me for a minute, Mr Rosenberry. I won't be long.'

When he'd gone, they saw Jane's hand reach out to close the door after him.

Rosie looked at Brad in despair. 'Dad's not usually like this. He's just lost his job and he's angry at the whole world. But I don't see why he should take it out on me. He and Mum had a row last night and he was so horrible, she walked out for the evening.'

Footsteps thudded down the stairs and the door opened again and a lad peered into the room. He smiled across at Brad. 'I just wanted to come and meet you.'

'You must be Casey.' Brad stood up and held out his hand again.

This time it was pumped vigorously then the lad stared at him openly. 'Mum was right. You do have a friendly face.'

Brad blinked at this frankness. 'Do I?'

'Yup.' Casey looked at his sister, who was sending him a silent message and threw up his hands defensively. 'I'm going, Row-zee abe. See you around, Mr Rosenberry.' He sauntered out, grinning broadly.

'I apologize for my brother. He can be a right little oik sometimes.'

'I like him. And he wasn't scowling at me, at least. Cheer up, Rosie love. We'll get through this.'

She relaxed a little. 'It's not easy, is it?'

'No, but I can't tell you how happy I am to have met you.'

She relaxed still further. 'Me too.'

In the kitchen Jane said in a low voice, 'Stop this now, Stu and let them go out together.'

'She's my daughter and I'm keeping an eye on her. He could be a paedophile for all I know.'

'Thanks for the compliment.'

'What's that supposed to mean?'

'That I'd choose my friends so badly.'

'That's not what I was implying and you know it.'

'How's the hangover today? Does being unkind to Rosie make it feel better?'

He looked at her, such a ravaged look that she suddenly rushed across to fling her arms round him and whisper, 'Don't.'

'Don't what?' he asked, cuddling her closely.

'Don't look so anguished. Things will get better, we have to believe that.'

'Do we?'

'Yes.'

They stood there for several minutes, not saying anything, needing to be close.

When he pulled away, she looked at him anxiously.

'I'll go and tell them they can go out for a couple of hours – but only because you asked me so nicely.'

'Welcome back, Stu. I didn't like the other man who's been wearing your shoes lately.' She cradled his cheek in her hand for a minute then stepped back.

Reassured by his wife's demonstration of love, Stu went back into the living room.

Rosie was engaged in animated discussion with Brad, but broke off to look at him warily and he felt even guiltier. She'd been spot on when she accused him of taking it out on her. But he still didn't really want that man intruding on their lives. He wasn't giving up on that, but would have to deal with things more subtly from now on. He cleared his throat. 'Now that I've met you, Mr Rosenberry, I don't mind if you go out for a couple of hours.'

Rosie's face lit up and she bounced across the room to fling herself into his arms. 'Thanks, Dad.'

He hugged her convulsively then held her at arm's length and smiled, too choked with emotion to say anything more. But her hug made him even more determined that no one was going to take her away from him.

'I will look after her,' Brad said as he followed Rosie out.

'Mm-huh.'

When they'd gone, Stu muttered something under his breath, wiped his forearm across his eyes and went back into the kitchen. 'Let's go out for a meal tonight, all four of us.'

Jane paused, cup in hand, then nodded. 'OK by me. Better ask Casey if he's got anything on. I know Rosie hasn't.'

Stu went upstairs and found his son hunched over his computer. 'You sister's gone out with *him* for a couple of hours. If you're not doing anything tonight, how about an Indian meal, all four of us?'

'Good one, Dad.'

Stu hesitated, then asked, 'What did you think of him?'

'Seems a nice guy.'

'Yeah. I suppose.' He'd thought so too. It made things worse, somehow. He didn't say damn Brad Rosenberry, but he thought it.

Casey gave him a knowing look. 'She isn't calling him Dad, you know. She calls him Brad.'

Stu shrugged and went back downstairs. Sometimes his son could be all too perceptive.

But it still felt dangerous to let that man into their lives and if he could do anything to put a spoke in Brad bloody Rosenberry's wheel, he would.

Chapter 22

Australia to England

Lou sat outside by the swimming pool in the sunshine, wishing it was warm enough to swim, but June was the beginning of winter down under and the water was surprisingly cold. Simon said it all depended on the night time temperatures and these had been quite low lately.

'This is bliss, isn't it? Fancy it being so warm and sunny in winter. Rick…'

He moved closer, put his arm round her and pretended to push her in, laughing as she squealed and clutched him.

'Stop messing about. This is serious. Would you mind spending a bit longer in Western Australia?'

'Not at all. The manager at the shopping centre has asked me about working for longer. I'm a popular attraction, it seems. Why?'

She looked at him fondly. He had the widest, most infectious smile she'd ever seen. He wasn't just a gentle giant, he had a friendly soul. 'I want to suggest something to Mel and Auntie Gina.' She leaned closer to explain, speaking very quietly, not wanting to be overheard till she was sure he'd agree.

'Hey, that's fine by me. If Simon doesn't mind us staying on, that is.'

'He's going to need us both if Mel agrees.'

–

Inside the house Gina was watching them, envying them their closeness, the love they showed towards one another in big ways and small. Seeing them made her miss Tom even more, though it was years now since he'd been killed. But you never stopped missing someone. She missed being a couple as well.

Footsteps made her turn round. 'Mel! Are you all right? Should you be up?'

'I was bursting for a pee. Even invalids have to do that.' She ran one hand through her hair. 'If I lie on that couch for much longer, I'll turn into a vegetable and put down roots.'

'The doctor said you were to have as near to bed rest as you could manage.'

'I know.' She came across to put her arm round her mother. She was so thin at the moment that it upset Gina. 'I'm so grateful to you for stepping in.'

'That's what family are for, helping one another.'

'Yes, but you should have a life of your own, too. We took you for granted before, didn't we? With the babysitting, I mean.'

'A bit.'

'Well, I'm not taking you for granted now. If there was any way I could manage without you, I would. But I can't, Mum.'

She sniffed and Gina gave her a quick hug. 'I can go to England next year, Mel. Once the baby's born and you're able to sort your life out, I'll be free to travel. Now, can I get you something to drink?'

Even as she spoke, Lou came into the kitchen. 'I was just going to ask if you wanted a snack.' She studied her cousin. 'Is it my imagination or do you look just a teeny bit better this morning?'

'If I do, it's partly thanks to you. Are there any more of those little apricot pastries left? I—' She broke off an looked at them in surprise before finishing her sentence, 'I'm hungry. That's the first time I've felt hungry since I got pregnant.' She smiled. 'It feels strange.'

'We'll bring our snacks into your parlour and eat with you, shall we?' Gina suggested.

Mel grimaced. 'Not if you're having coffee. I can't stand the smell of it at the moment.'

'I prefer tea, as you well know. Tea all right with you, Lou?'

'Sure.'

Later, when Gina had gone out to do some shopping, Lou went to sit with Mel again. 'Before you go to sleep, can I ask you something?'

'Yes, of course.'

'If Rick and I stayed on here for a couple of months, would you feel all right about your mum going to England?'

Mel looked at her in surprise. 'But don't you need to move on soon?'

'We can do that if we're in the way. But they want Rick to continue at the shopping centre and he's earning good money. And if we continue to stay here, we can save quite a bit.' She laughed. 'The picture shop is making a fortune framing his sketches and they've offered to pay him a retainer as well as what he gets from clients for his portraits. It's really nice getting to know you and Lexie, much more important than travelling round Australia, as far as I'm concerned. I don't really get on with Cheryl. She's about your age, but she's so up tight about the world.'

Mel stared down at her lower body, not looking forward to the small bump growing into a large one. 'I'd be fine about you staying. In fact, it'd be brilliant. Mum's been hiding her disappointment, but she was really excited about going to find her family in England. It was the first time I'd seen her so excited and alive-looking since Dad died. Lexie told her she should move on just before I got so sick, and now I've stopped her doing that. I've been feeling so guilty.'

'Then I'll suggest it to Auntie Gina tonight. She could go for two or three months, longer even if things work out well, and still be back in plenty of time for the birth.'

'She might not accept your offer. She's got a thing about family not letting one another down.'

'We'll have to persuade her that you'll be all right.' Lou smiled at her cousin. 'I'm family too, after all. Besides, you prefer my cooking.'

Mel stretched out her hand and as Lou took it they both smiled.

'That's one of the downsides of people emigrating,' Mel said. 'Cutting themselves off from their families. At least Emma and this baby have relatives here, on my side and Simon's.'

–

'Say that again!' Gina stared at Lou and Mel, unable to believe what she was hearing.

'Why don't you go to England as planned and let Lou and Rick look after me?' Mel repeated patiently.

'I couldn't do that.'

'Why not?'

'Because… I'm your mother.'

'I'm grown up now and you don't have sole responsibility for me. The trouble is, if I lie around like a queen with people waiting on me, I do feel better.' Mel grimaced. 'Well, I'm only throwing up a few times a day, which is a big improvement. I'm even managing to keep things down more, especially the food Lou prepares. You know, you could start a business delivering food specially to tempt invalids. You'd make a fortune. You'd have to get a dietician to endorse it, though. Or you could write a book about it.'

Lou gaped at her in surprise.

Mel smiled. 'When I'm working, I'm employed as an ideas person.' She turned to her mother. 'Will you go?'

'I'll think about it.'

Lou opened her mouth to argue, but Mel nudged her in the ribs and shook her head.

Later she explained, 'Mum's always like that. Has to think things through. She didn't say no, though, so I reckon she'll agree.' She smiled at her young cousin. 'I'll feel a lot less guilty if she does. Now, how about a tiny bowl of soup?'

The soup came with a piece of toast in the shape of a flower and somehow both slipped down easily.

-

Gina went up to her bedroom and stood by the window, staring down at the turquoise pool, which was sparkling in the sunshine. Could she go to England? Would it be right?

A feeling of responsibility for her daughter warred with her desire to meet her English family and in the end, she allowed herself to consider it seriously. What would she need to do? What should she take with her?

Without realizing it, she sat down at the dressing table and started making a list.

It was only when she went downstairs to tell them she was going to accept their offer that she realized how excited she felt – and how nervous.

She peeped in on Mel and saw that her daughter was asleep, so went to the kitchen to find Lou. Rick was out at the shopping centre, so for once she was alone with her niece. 'I wondered if you could tell me more about my brother and sister.'

'You're going?'

'Yes.'

'That's great! Well, I haven't seen my great-aunt Peggy for ages. Even Gramps doesn't see much of her. She married a horrible man, a real control freak. He bullies her all the time.'

Gina stared at her in shock. 'He beats her?'

'I don't think so, but he puts her down and won't let her do anything except run around after him. Gramps can't stand him, and my granddad is a good judge of character, who always gives people the benefit of the doubt. He must have been very hurt by his father leaving to hang on to his anger so long.'

'Any child would be. What do you know about your Aunt Peggy, then?'

'Not much. She likes embroidering and does beautiful pictures, but apart from that, she's rather colourless.'

Gina was disappointed by that description. She'd love to have a sister, but having lived with Lou for a few days, she already trusted her niece's judgement. Lou had a very sane view of the universe and was wise beyond her years. Rick was equally balanced about life. Some people just were.

'You'd better go and see Peggy during the daytime when the big bad husband isn't home,' Lou suggested.

'What about your grandfather?'

'He's great. I never think of his wife as my grandmother because I never met her. She left him years ago when Mum was thirteen, more fool her. So Gramps brought Mum up on his own. He's retired now, lives quietly, cares about the environment and sometimes goes to help clean up parks and things. And he grows the most amazing organic vegetables. He has a share of a community allotment scheme as well as his own back garden, and he has a greenhouse for tomatoes and for propagating stuff. He sells plants sometimes at weekend markets.'

'You sound fond of him.'

'I am. He wasn't happy about me coming to find you and stirring up old quarrels, but maybe he'll have got over that now.'

Gina felt disappointment sear through her and tried to hide it from her niece.

There was silence then Lou added quietly, 'But if Gramps gets to know you, I'm sure he'll like you – and you'll like him. I've already written to tell him about you. I can let him know you're coming, if you want.'

Gina thought about this, then shook her head. 'Thanks, but no. I think I'd prefer to stick with my original plan and not warn them. I'll simply turn up and insist on talking to them.'

'Good for you.' Lou eyed her sideways. 'So, you're going?'

Gina nodded. 'I want to, but we'll have to ask Simon if it's all right with him.'

'Mel told me to leave her to handle him.'

'She must be feeling better to say that.'

'She is as long as she rests, but she still gets sick if she tries to do anything.' Lou frowned suddenly. 'I hope this doesn't run in the family. I want lots of kids, but I don't want to go through something like that each time.'

'My other daughter wasn't sick at all, except for a bit of morning sickness, mostly just nausea, no throwing up. That passed after three months. Goodness, you do plan ahead, don't you?'

'You have to. Me and Rick know what we want in life so we're going for it. You should do that, too.'

Out of the mouths of babes, Gina thought as she waited for Simon to come home from work. She could learn a lot from her niece, was learning a lot.

-

A week later Gina got on the plane and it wasn't until she was sitting in her seat that she began to feel nervous. Not of the flight, but of what lay at the end of it.

Suddenly the longing for family which had been driving her for several months seemed to evaporate and she wished she hadn't started this.

The woman next to her said something and Gina forced herself to reply politely. But she was glad when the first meal was served and the woman stopped talking to devour every last morsel on the tray. Gina had lost her appetite. She wished she could sleep, but she'd never felt so wide awake, even though it was the middle of the night her time.

She was relieved when they landed at Manchester what seemed an eternity later. She'd dozed briefly on the second leg of the journey, but hadn't really slept and yet she didn't feel tired. Picking up her hire car, she studied the map book then set off for Blackpool, nervous of driving in a new country. The roads seemed much more crowded, even outside the city centre.

'I'm coping,' she said aloud and gave a little nod of satisfaction about that.

Mel and Lexie, who'd been overseas several times, had given her several lectures about what to do and what not to do when travelling alone. And even Simon, who'd driven her to the airport in Perth, had warned her to be careful.

She'd booked a hotel room in Blackpool, the place she'd found before on the Internet with a special offer for weekly accommodation. Rick knew the hotel and said it was a good one.

She'd studied a map of the city on line and done her best to memorize her route through it after she left the freeway – no, she had to learn to call them motorways now. Of course she got lost, but when she stopped to ask for help, people were very kind and their accents reminded her so much of her father that she felt comforted.

She would just take her time, find her feet and see how she felt about going to see Jake and Peggy.

She smiled as she parked outside the hotel. She'd done it!

Chapter 23

England

Brad dropped Rosie back at home just before the end of the two hours he'd been allotted for taking her out. They'd walked along the sea front at Knott End, talking about her, talking about him, not in any structured way, just following their impulses. Later they'd gone into a café and talked some more over a cappuccino, an orange juice and some pastries.

Stu answered the door but Brad could see Jane standing at the rear of the hallway, watching and listening. Who was she keeping an eye on? Him or her husband?

'You'd better go up to your room now and finish that schoolwork, Rosie.' Stu turned as if to shut the door in Brad's face.

'I'd like to arrange another outing,' Brad said quickly, putting a hand out to hold the door open. He could see Rosie standing halfway up the stairs, listening, her head bent as if she didn't dare look at anyone.

'I thought you were travelling?' Stu said in a clipped, tight voice. 'Surely you can get on with your holiday now you've met her, then, if you really have to, come back and say goodbye?'

'I'm not going anywhere for a while. I'm here for Rosie… and it's what she wants, too.' Brad could see Jane frowning now. She took a step towards them then stayed where she was.

Stu shrugged. 'Well, we're not sure about our family plans for next weekend, so perhaps you could ring towards the end of the week?'

Brad felt anger begin to bubble up and raised his voice so that it carried down the hallway. 'You're still trying to stop me getting to know Rosie, aren't you?'

'I'm trying to make sure this thing doesn't go too far. You've got your own life and family in Australia, so you won't be around for long.'

Jane moved forward to join them. 'We've nothing planned for next Saturday, Stu. She could easily go out with Brad again then.' She smiled apologetically at the visitor. 'We don't want to disturb her schoolwork during the week, though. Next year is her final year at school, so she needs to build a good foundation this year.'

'An evening out wouldn't be particularly disruptive, surely? I could take her to tea, have her back by eight thirty.'

'Let's just leave it till Saturday this time, shall we?'

Stu gave him a triumphant smile. 'Enjoy your holiday Mr Rosenberry.'

Behind him, Jane caught Brad's gaze and shook her head in warning.

He closed his eyes for a minute, breathed deeply then turned and left. Only when he lifted his hands to grip the steering wheel did he realize how deeply his nails had dug into the palms.

—

Stu closed the door with a thump and turned to look at Jane, but after one disgusted look, she walked away from him. He looked up as a door slammed, hesitated then went into his den and shut himself in. His whole world was breaking up, it seemed. Whatever he did, he upset someone. And all he wanted was hold his family together and stay in the home and town he loved.

Why was that too much to ask?

He switched on the computer and flicked through some of his resource program files, not getting the usual urge to create more. He kept seeing Jane's disapproving face. Why could she not understand how he felt? Was she still attracted to Rosenberry? Sighing he began to play solitaire.

Only when he was in here did he feel at all in control of life.

—

When the door closed behind her husband, Jane made her way quietly up the stairs. She found her daughter standing by the window watching Brad's car pull away. 'So... how did it go?'

'It went very well. He's really easy to talk to and I was finding out about his children. Just think, I have an older brother and sister.'

'Half-brother and -sister.'

'You don't correct me when I call Casey my brother. It's the same relationship.'

'Well, you and Casey have been brought up together. The others are much older than you and you're not likely to meet them, are you?'

'I could if I went out to visit Brad in Australia. I've got nieces and nephews there, too, you know.'

Jane stared at her in shock. 'Has he asked you to do that?'

'No. He hasn't said a word about it. But it's what I was planning to do before I knew he was coming to England, take a gap year, spend part of it earning some money, then use it to go to Australia.'

'I don't think your father would approve of that.'

'I heard my father just now speaking to Brad and if you want the truth, I'm ashamed of his attitude.'

'You're not to speak about him like that!' Jane snapped.

'Why not? He's drinking himself silly every night, acting the grouch all the time and being rude to people.'

There was silence, then Jane said quietly, 'You need to make allowances, Rosie. He's going through a traumatic time.'

'So am I! And you don't seem to notice that, either. You just notice what Dad needs. I come a long way second.'

They stared at one another, then Jane moved towards the bedroom door, using the tactic that had stood her in good stead at other times. 'Let's wait till we cool down to discuss this. I don't want to quarrel with you.'

'You never want to quarrel with anyone because you want things to go smoothly and if they don't, you back away. Sometimes people have to stand up for things that matter to them. And if you don't let me see Brad while he's here and see him more than once a week, too, I'll think a lot less of you as well as Dad. And what about my mobile? Are you still going to keep that?'

But she was talking to herself. Her mother had gone. Typical!

Casey came across to her room. 'I couldn't help over-hearing.'

'You always do.'

'Hey, I'm on your side here.'

Rosie looked up at him, tears still welling in her eyes. 'Sorry. I'm a bit upset.'

'You can use my mobile to ring him, if you want.'

'I don't want to get you in trouble. I'll use a phone box. I'll be back at school next week anyway, so they can't watch me every second. Dad's acting like a spoilt brat who can't have what he wants. Even I know jobs come and go these days. Has he had his head in the sand for the past few years or what?'

Casey propped himself against the doorpost and considered this. 'I reckon he has. He's so devoted to those students of his that it doesn't leave much time for anything but family and work. And even when he's at home, he spends half his life in that den of his. He hasn't come to watch me play soccer or cricket this year, you know. Not once. And it's pretty good to make both teams, like I have. He's always apologizing, saying he'll come next time. As if. Even you've come a couple of times and you're not into sport.'

With one of his shrugs, he slouched back to his room.

Rosie shut the door and went to sit on the bed, thinking through her talk with Brad, the things he'd told her.

He hadn't said a word of criticism against her father and mother, which she respected. Best of all, she was starting to feel very comfortable with him.

She hoped her dad would come out of this black mood soon, though. The whole house seemed full of unhappy echoes lately.

She could see why people grew up suddenly. Life wasn't easy and you became aware of that. Relationships were complicated and got more complicated as you grew older. But Mum had always said that family mattered most. Why couldn't she and Dad see that Brad was now part of Rosie's family?

-

Stu came home from school on the Monday looking even grimmer than before. Jane's heart sank as she saw him slam his car door and kick an empty plant pot out of the way. What now?

'Hi.' He came into the kitchen and went straight for the fridge, pulling out a bottle of wine. Catching sight of her disapproving expression he said, 'Don't start on me. If any man has a right to drown his sorrows, it's me.'

'What's happened now?'

'They've given the assistant teacher's job to someone from the other school. So I won't even be in the Resource Centre in the new school. It's Binnings' doing, of course. He wants to drive me out of the area.'

'Oh, Stu, I'm so sorry.'

He held up the bottle with a questioning look and she shook her head. 'I'm driving. It's the meditation class tonight.'

'Can't miss your bloody meditation, can you?'

'It's very calming. You should try doing something like that.'

'To borrow one of Casey's favourite expressions: As if!'

She sat down opposite him at the table. 'What are you going to do?'

'They've offered me a position as an English teacher.'

'You'll hate that.'

His words seemed to drip acid. 'I have a mortgage and family to support. I don't have any choice but to accept.' He raised the glass in a mocking toast and took a defiant swallow.

Casey came in, looked at his father and rolled his eyes at his mother as if to say not again. 'What's for tea?'

'Burgers, chips and salad.'

'Two out of three are good.'

'But you don't get those two till after you've eaten your salad.'

'You're a bully, Ma, do you know that?'

'Don't cheek your mother!' Stu said sharply.

'I'm not! It's a joke between—'

'And don't answer back!'

Casey looked at him in disgust. 'Whatever happened at your school today isn't my fault and I resent you taking it out on me.'

Stu glared at him. 'Go to your room!'

Casey picked up his school bag and stamped up the stairs.

Jane went to get him a snack to last him till teatime. When she picked up the plate and glass of milk, Stu snapped, 'Do you have to spoil him?'

'He's a growing boy, needs plenty of food.'

'Well, don't worry, he'll get it. I'll still keep working to provide it.'

When she went up, Casey was at his beloved computer, playing a lightning fast game that involved moving coloured squares around the screen. He turned around with a hostile expression on his face but relaxed when she held out the tray.

'It's doing my head in, Dad being like this,' he muttered.

She kept her voice low, too. 'It's been a bit heavy going lately, I agree. But he's just had more bad news today so please try to make allowances.'

There was the sound of raised voices in the kitchen and Rosie came running up the stairs. She didn't try to speak quietly as she called across the landing, 'What's with Dad? I hardly opened my mouth and he was telling me off, saying I don't appreciate what he's doing for me.'

'He's found out he won't even be working in the resource centre at the new school.'

'Oh. That's hard. But it's not my fault, is it?'

'Shall I get you a snack, Rosie? It'll be better if you stay up here.'

'No, thanks. I'm not hungry.'

'Tea will be a quickie tonight. I'm going to the meditation class again. There are two a week and I find them very calming.'

Rosie let out a little huff of anger. 'We could all do with some of that at the moment.'

'You could come with me. They're women only classes, but another woman brings her daughter.'

'No, thanks. I've got too much homework to do. I'm still making up for stuff I missed last week. You'd think so close to the end of term they'd relax a bit but no, they're piling it on.'

Jane went into the bedroom to give herself a minute or two to cool down before she confronted Stu. When the phone rang, she automatically picked it up, but he must have done so as well. She was about to put the receiver down when she heard Brad's voice. Oh, no! There couldn't have been a worse time to ring.

She winced as Stu was incredibly rude then slammed the phone down. She set her hand piece into the cradle rather more gently, then buried her face in her hands.

Things couldn't go on like this. And she wasn't backing Stu up on this latest attempt to keep Rosie away from Brad.

Only – she didn't want to fight Stu in front of the kids.

–

Brad went to sit in the bar just off the hotel lobby, still feeling angry about his phone call. Damn the man! he thought as he ordered a glass of beer.

When a newcomer walked in and approached the reception, looking uncertain and nervous, Brad watched her in idle curiosity. She waited and when no one appeared, she looked round for a bell to ring.

It was the label PER on her luggage that made him walk across. 'They're just changing shifts. The new receptionist will be here in a minute. Just got in from Perth?' He could see how exhausted she was.

'Yes. It's a long flight.'

'Tell me about it. I made it myself recently. Group torture, I call it.' He held out one hand. 'I'm Brad Rosenberry, another Aussie.'

She studied him guardedly as she shook hands. 'Gina Porter. How did you know I was from Perth?'

He pointed to her luggage. 'I had the same labels on my suitcase when I arrived. Ah, here's the receptionist. I'll leave you to settle in.' He moved back to his seat in the bar and took a sip of beer, wondering what to do with the evening. Stu had made it more than clear that he wasn't welcome to take Rosie out to tea during the week, then had hung up before he could answer, which was probably a good thing, because Brad was trying not to give Rosie's dad any reason to complain.

It was like dealing with a hostile porcupine, though.

On an impulse, when Gina turned from reception to go up to her room, he went across the lobby to her. 'Come and have a drink when you've settled in.' He gestured to the bar. 'I'll be here.'

'Oh. Well, all right. Thank you.'

He didn't know what had made him do that. He didn't usually invite strangers to have drinks with him, especially females. But Gina looked a bit lost and he was feeling lonely today. And tired as she was, she was attractive: natural-looking and maturely feminine. He didn't want her to think he was trying to pick her up with a sexual encounter in mind, though.

When Bridie stepped out of the lift, he realized how he could make Gina feel more comfortable with him and beckoned to the older woman. 'Fancy a drink? I met a woman from Perth in the lobby just now and she's coming down for a drink in a little while, so if you'd like to join our merry company…?'

'Why, thank you, Brad. I'll have a pink gin, please. On ice. They know how I like it.'

There, he thought in satisfaction as he ordered it. The woman from Perth wouldn't feel threatened with Bridie here. And he'd have some company to take his mind off his disappointment.

As Gina rode up to her room in the lift, she decided not to take the stranger up on his offer of a drink. She didn't know why she'd accepted, really, except that he had a kind expression and seemed friendly. But you never knew. Both her daughters had warned her to be careful who she got talking to. A woman on her own was such an easy target.

She dumped the suitcase on the bed and studied the room. It was perfectly clean and neat, but decorated in dull colours that wouldn't show the dirt. And the subtle lighting did little to brighten it up. Dimly lit rooms always made her feel depressed.

Which was why she changed her mind and decided to accept the offer of a drink. She whipped out a change of clothes without unpacking the rest and took a hasty shower.

Not bothering about make-up, she brushed her hair, picked up her shoulder bag and left her room. If the man wasn't in the bar, there was nothing lost. She could have a drink on her own and then see about some food.

Brad was in the bar, however, sitting talking to an elderly lady as if he knew her. That made Gina feel safer. When he saw her, he smiled and stood up, so she smiled back and walked across to join them.

'This is Bridie Shapley. She's a permanent resident at the hotel who's taken pity on a lonely traveller. Bridie, this is Gina, who's just arrived from Western Australia.'

They shook hands and she sat down.

'What can I get you to drink?'

'A glass of white wine, please.'

She fumbled for her purse.

'My treat this time.'

When he'd gone to the bar, Bridie smiled at her. 'He's quite safe, you know.'

'Pardon?'

'Brad. He's quite safe. He's just lonely, not trying to pick you up for the wrong reasons. He's taken me out for a couple of drives, which is a rare treat. I do miss being able to drive myself.'

'Oh. Well, I—' Gina broke off and admitted, 'I was a bit worried. You never know.'

'I'm not usually wrong in my judgement of people. That's one of the few good things about old age, you understand better what makes people tick. Mostly, it's an obstacle course, growing old is, I mean. You leap over one health hurdle after another as the years build up. But it has its benefits, too.'

'That's what my dad used to say. I do miss him. He only died a couple of months ago.'

'I'm sorry. It's sad to lose a parent. I was married once, but my husband was killed in 1943 and I've no children. I regret that now, but I turned into a career girl after I lost Peter and it was either career or marriage in those days. I do have a few relatives still, but I rarely see them nowadays. I live in the hotel and that's much better than being in an old folks' home where everyone talks about nothing but their ailments.

Every now and then I meet someone interesting to talk to, like Brad. I've friends I visit, though I'm losing them one by one.' She picked up the glass and smiled at it. 'And I can enjoy the odd drink whenever I want to here, without anyone checking up on me. Some people tend to treat us oldies as if we're witless children. So annoying.'

'There you are. Sorry it took so long.' Brad set a glass of white wine in front of Gina and slid into the edge of the circular booth. He raised his glass. 'To us all!'

Gina insisted on buying the next round and found out there were bar snacks of a substantial nature, so checked with her companions and they all ordered steak sandwiches, which Bridie assured them were excellent.

An hour or so after eating Gina felt her eyes growing heavy and was unable to hold back a huge yawn.

Brad grinned at her. 'The jet lag's catching up with you now.'

'Yes. I'll have to go and get some sleep.'

'Join us for breakfast – if you're up in time. It's better to keep to UK hours as soon as possible.'

'I'll do that.' She found her way up to her room and crawled into bed, feeling happier than she'd expected. What nice people Brad and Bridie were. But there was something making him look sad when he wasn't involved in the conversation. She wondered what it was.

Chapter 24

England

During the afternoon Jake said casually, 'I'll run you to your meditation class after tea, Peggy love.'

She looked at him pleadingly. 'Don't make me go tonight, Jake.'

'Is that how you think of it, making you go?'

She nodded.

'But it's your only chance to get out of the house and do something on your own.'

'I think I've lost the habit of doing things on my own.'

He fell silent, not wanting to sound like a bully but feeling quite sure she ought to go.

Peggy watched him shake his head and knew he was disappointed with her, but he didn't say anything so she got on with preparing the tea. The class hadn't been bad last time, actually, and the woman she'd met – Jane – had been very friendly. She ought to go, really.

She waited for Jake to urge her to do so, but he didn't, and perversely she was disappointed. In the end she said, 'I've changed my mind. I will go to the class. If that's still all right with you about the lift?'

He beamed at her. 'That's my lass.'

As she went into the centre, Peggy felt as if someone was watching her, so stopped behind a huge potted tree to peer outside. There was a car parked in the street with no lights on and someone sitting inside. It was a white Toyota like Hartley's, but she couldn't read the number plate at this distance. It couldn't be theirs, though, because it had a badly dented wing.

She was just being silly, seeing dragons where there were none.

She signed in for the class and went along to the big room at the rear of the building. To her huge relief, she saw Jane there already. She hesitated, but the other woman smiled so she went across to join her. 'You came again.'

Jane nodded. 'I certainly did. If I don't get away from the crises at home I'll go mad.'

'Things still bad?'

'Yeah. And you?'

Peggy found herself telling Jane about the chopped up embroideries.

'Anyone who does that sort of thing is sick in the head. My goodness, what have you been putting up with over the years?'

Peggy stared at her and it was as if the pieces of a jigsaw puzzled fell into place. 'A lot. Hartley's never hit me, but he's often hurt me with his cutting remarks. I can see that now, because my brother is so very different.'

Jane patted her hand. 'Well, you've come to the right place here to sort yourself out.'

'Are you getting counselling help too?'

'No, just doing these classes as a respite. My husband is usually pleasant enough, but he's lost his job and he's been in a foul mood, not to mention drinking too much. I'm giving him until the end of the school year and if he doesn't improve by then, I'll have to do something about him – though I haven't worked out what yet.'

Do something about him. Peggy wondered why she hadn't tried to do something about Hartley. Because she was a coward, that's why.

The instructor came in just then. There were only six women present for the class, so they got plenty of individual attention and by the end of it, Peggy was feeling more relaxed than she had for ages. As she turned towards the door, chatting to Jane, it banged open and a man burst in, glaring round the room until his eyes settled on her.

Hartley.

'Ah!' he said and moved forward.

Peggy screamed in terror, clutching Jane's arm. 'Don't let him get me!'

–

Rosie was angry with her dad on her own behalf but was also beginning to worry about the way he was drinking. He didn't seem like himself any more.

He didn't join them for tea and her mother looked tight-lipped as she served the food, not joking with Casey about eating his salad as she usually did, but ordering him curtly to get on with it, for heaven's sake.

When the meal was over Rosie and Casey cleared up, then went back upstairs, passing the door of the den, which was shut tight. They exchanged glances and then went into their bedrooms. Casey would muck around with his computer before he settled into his homework, she knew, but she preferred to get her assignments out of the way, then do what she wanted for the rest of the evening.

Only tonight she couldn't settle and though there was a TV programme she usually watched, she didn't go down because she heard her dad crashing about in the kitchen and swearing.

Casey came in to see her later on. 'You didn't go down to watch your programme.'

'No. You didn't, either.'

He shrugged. 'Not worth the hassles.'

'Tell me about it.' She started fiddling with her pen. 'Dad cares too much about that job of his. He always has.'

'Yeah. Fancy something to eat?'

'You can't be hungry already!'

He grinned and patted his belly. 'What can I say? I'm a growing boy. I'm taller than you now.'

That still made her feel strange. She'd always been the big sister, but he'd shot up like a weed this year. There were a lot of things making her feel strange lately. She suddenly realized why Casey had come to see her and was hovering near the door. 'I'll go down with you, shall I? I fancy a cup of hot chocolate.'

The kitchen was in a mess again where their father had made himself a sandwich. He'd left out the cheese without bothering to wrap it up and the butter container was open nearby, with a half-eaten sandwich left at one end of the breadboard.

And there was another wine cork on the draining board.

'That's the second bottle tonight. He'll be paralytic,' Casey whispered.

'Let's get some food for you and go back to our rooms quickly. Never mind about the hot chocolate.'

They crept up the stairs like two thieves, stopping when they heard a sound… Their father was sobbing.

They looked at one another in horror and separated at the top of the stairs without a word.

Everything was upside down lately, Rosie thought, as she put on some music and took out a novel her friend had lent her. But she couldn't settle to it. Her father's crying had been such an unhappy sound.

She looked at her watch. Her mother was normally back by this time. What was keeping her so long?

The instructor went to stand in front of Peggy and when Jane moved to position herself beside her friend, the other women followed, forming a protective half-circle instinctively.

Hartley took a quick stride forward but stopped and swung round as the door opened behind him. The receptionist came in, giving a quick nod in response to the instructor's questioning look. The newcomer stayed by the door, arms folded.

'If you touch anyone or interfere with these women's freedom in any way, you can be charged with assault,' the instructor told Hartley. 'Please leave the premises at once.'

'It's not assault to want to see my wife. I only want to have a talk with you, Peggy. A talk, that's all. If we go home, we can sort this nonsense out without interfering busybodies poking their oars in.'

Jane put an arm round her companion, who was shaking like a leaf. 'You don't even have to speak to him if you don't want to,' she said in a low voice.

At her words Hartley's face went a dark red, his anger almost a visible cloud around him. But his voice remained chill and controlled. 'You're coming home with me, Peggy. Home. It's where you belong, you know it is.'

She shook her head. 'No! No, I'm not coming. I'm never coming back.'

As he took another step forward, the group of women moved closer, protecting her.

Hartley lost it then, trying to push the nearest woman out of the way. When she wouldn't move, he shoved her hard with both hands.

She let out a yelp of shock as she staggered backwards and fell over from the force of his push.

He stopped to scowl down at her. 'I didn't push you that hard. Stop pretending.' He looked back at the group, took a deep breath and said slowly and emphatically, 'You should be ashamed of yourselves, coming between a man and wife.'

The woman on the floor scooted away from him before she stood up.

'I don't want to speak to him.' It came out as a whisper and Peggy was ashamed of that, so gathered her courage together and shouted, 'Go away, Hartley! I don't want to talk to you.' This time her words echoed round the room.

'Go away!' he mocked. 'I'm going nowhere without you, *Mrs* Wilkes.'

'I'll ask you again to leave, sir,' the instructor said. 'These are private premises and you're trespassing.'

He gave her a sneering smile. 'There's not one of you here able to make me.'

'No,' Jane cried, incensed, 'but together we can. Don't underestimate that, you bully.'

He turned to glare at her. 'I'll remember your face, you interfering bitch. You'd be wise to stay out of this. What's between me and Peggy is private.'

The outer door banged and he turned around in time to see two police officers come in.

'We got a call to say that there was trouble,' one of them said, her eyes scanning the room quickly and settling on Hartley.

'These women are keeping me from my wife,' he said at once.

'I've left him. I don't want to talk to him,' Peggy said.

'He's been asked several times to leave the premises,' the instructor said in her calm, quiet voice. 'And he's assaulted one woman already.'

Hartley spun round. 'I've assaulted no one.'

'You knocked that woman to the floor.'

'Your name, please, sir,' the male officer said coming to stand close to him.

'None of your damned business.'

'He's called Hartley Wilkes,' Peggy said.

'And he did assault me,' the woman he'd shoved out of the way said. 'He knocked me over and I bumped my elbow. Look. There's a bruise.'

'In that case, I'm arresting you…'

Hartley's expression of shock at this would have been amusing if this had been happening to someone else, Peggy thought. He always had considered himself above the law, speeding when he thought he'd not get caught, drinking and driving. And until now, he'd got away with it. Serve him right if they arrested him.

'Mrs Wilkes?'

She waited until Hartley had gone out of the room, then turned to the female police officer, who was standing patiently beside her.

'If your husband is frightening or hurting you, you may wish to consider taking out an injunction against him, Mrs Wilkes,' she said in a very gentle voice. 'Now, could you give me your name and present address, please, and tell me your version of tonight's events...'

There was a shout in the reception area, 'Peggy!'

'I'm here, Jake.'

He came running along to join her. 'I saw the police car – and Hartley getting into it.'

The police officer moved to stand slightly in front of Peggy.

'It's all right, officer. This is my brother. I'm staying with him.' She turned to Jane and the other women. 'Thank you for protecting me. I'm really grateful.'

'Some of us have been in your position,' the woman who'd been knocked over told her gruffly. 'Don't let him talk you out of pressing charges.'

'I won't.'

'What's happened?' Jake repeated.

Jane explained while the officer was taking down details from Peggy.

He looked at her in shock. 'I'd never have believed Hartley capable of this.'

'Your brother-in-law was so angry, I think he was beyond reason.'

Peggy finished talking to the officer and came to join them, feeling washed out. 'We can go home now, Jake.'

'I'm sorry I persuaded you to come here tonight,' he said. 'I won't make that mistake again.'

'You didn't persuade me, I chose to come. And I'm going to keep coming, because I really enjoy doing meditation.' She could see the surprise on his face. 'You were right, Jake, love. I do need to make friends and talk to other women. I've been like – like a prisoner for the past few years. And what's more, the minute we get home I'm ringing Cheryl up and telling her I've left her father for good.'

As soon as they got to Jake's house, she picked up the phone. 'Cheryl? I have something to tell you. Well, I'm afraid your friends will have to wait. No, listen to me. This is important. I've left your father and I'm not going back to him.'

Jake could hear Cheryl's screech of shock from across the room. He watched Peggy trying to speak her niece and not succeeding.

In the end, she said quietly, 'If you won't listen to me, I'm not wasting any more time on you.'

She put the phone down and leaned back in her chair, tears leaking from her eyes and smearing her glasses. 'She doesn't believe me, Jake. She's taking her father's side, won't even listen to mine, says it's no wonder he gets impatient with me.'

'Unkind, I call that.'

'She's always been Daddy's girl and he treats her very differently from me.' Peggy pulled off her spectacles and started to clean them on a tissue, staring blindly at the television, seeing nothing but a blur of colours. She was relieved that Jake didn't try to talk to her. It really hurt when a daughter wouldn't even try to listen.

But she wasn't going back to Hartley. His behaviour tonight had made her absolutely certain of that. It was such a relief to have made the decision! The peaceful little flat of her dreams seemed possible now.

She didn't want him to try to hurt Jake, though, because of her staying here. Or Jane. No, he wouldn't know where Jane lived, so her friend was safe. But maybe she should ask about that women's refuge when she went to see Gillah tomorrow. She still hated the idea of going to one, but she didn't want to put her brother in danger.

—

When Jane arrived home there were lights on upstairs and in the den, but the other rooms of the house were dark. She was still feeling shaken by the encounter with Peggy's husband. Fancy being married to a man like that!

She went into the den and found her husband sprawled with his head on his arms, an empty bottle on its side next to him and a half-full bottle standing so close that if he moved he'd knock it over.

Fancy being married to a man like this!

No, no! she told herself hastily, feeling guilty for even thinking that. Stu wasn't normally like this. It was just a phase he was going through.

She went and picked up the bottle with wine in it, then closed the door behind her. She could have used some comfort herself tonight, but not the sort that came in a bottle.

There were footsteps on the landing and she looked up to see Rosie staring down at her.

'Are you all right, Mum? You usually call out when you come in.'

'No, I'm not all right.' Feeling suddenly shaky Jane went and sat down on a chair in the kitchen, glad to hear

Rosie running down the stairs because she needed to be with someone. 'There was trouble at the meditation class and I—' She broke off, unable to continue, shuddering violently and holding herself.

Rosie was across the room in a flash, putting her arms round her mother, murmuring reassuringly as if their roles had been reversed. 'It's all right. I'm here. It's all right.'

The shuddering passed and Jane blinked at her daughter, her eyes full of tears. 'Sorry. But it was such an ugly scene and he – the other woman's husband – threatened me as well because I stood by her and comforted her. She was terrified, Rosie, shaking and white. How could I not put my arm round her?'

'Mum, that's terrible! We have to tell Dad. Or should we call the police?'

'The police were there. They said to be careful for the next few days, but he was probably just mouthing off because he was angry. And anyway, he doesn't know where I live. Only... you should have seen his face when we stood between him and Peggy. It was like one of those horror masks, grotesque, full of hatred.' She was still clinging to Rosie.

'Shall I fetch Dad?'

'He's out of it.'

'Not again!'

More footsteps on the stairs and Casey appeared, stopping in the doorway to stare at them. 'What's the matter? You OK, Mum?'

So Jane had to explain all over again.

'You need a brandy or something,' Casey said.

She looked at the half-empty wine bottle she'd brought in from the den. 'I think we have enough drinking going on in this house. How about a cup of hot chocolate all round instead?'

'I'll make it,' Rosie said.

Jane grabbed her hand. 'Thank you.'

'What for?'

'Being there, comforting me.'

'It's what you and Dad have always said. Families look after one another.'

Only Stu wasn't looking after them, was he? He was sunk deep in his own misery, thinking only of himself. Jane was disgusted with him.

Casey sprawled on a chair while Rosie got the hot chocolate ready. Awkwardly he patted his mother on her shoulder, giving her a little nod and a half-smile but saying nothing.

'What if that man comes after you?' Rosie asked when they were all sitting down with mugs of steaming chocolate.

Jane shook her head. 'I don't know. I've never been in this sort of situation before. What does one do?'

'We'll all have to keep watch,' Casey said enthusiastically. 'You wouldn't know what sort of car he had, would you, Mum?'

She shook her head.

'You could ask your friend Peggy. She'll know.'

'I suppose so. But I doubt it'll come to that. Being arrested will give him a shock, I'm sure. He wasn't a layabout and he wasn't drunk, he was wearing a smart business suit. And Peggy's going to take out an injunction against him. He won't even remember me in a few days' time.'

'But what if he does?' Casey worried.

'Well, you can keep your eyes open,' she said lightly, sure now that she'd overreacted. They were a great pair of kids. She was so lucky.

And Stu would come around.

Surely, he would?

Chapter 25

England

The following morning the wake-up call roused Gina at seven thirty, but she snuggled down for a few more minutes and didn't surface again until ten o'clock.

As soon as she'd showered, she rang her elder daughter on her mobile. Mel answered at the second ring.

'How are you, darling?'

'Mum! We've been wondering if the flight went OK.'

'I'm fine. It's you I'm worried about. Are you still being sick as often?'

Once assured that Mel was slightly better and that her cousin Lou was looking after her like a guardian angel, Gina cut the conversation short. 'These calls are very expensive, so I'll email you when I can find an Internet café.'

After she'd finished her breakfast, she got ready for a walk. Daylight on your face was supposed to help counteract jet lag. It seemed a waste to leave the hire car sitting in the hotel car park, but she really didn't feel up to a drive today, let alone an encounter with a possibly hostile half-brother or -sister.

The weather was brisk, with clouds scudding across the sky, and the sea air was invigorating. Gulls mewed and wheeled overhead, pouncing on anything edible, not seeming at all afraid of the humans. She walked briskly along the promenade and found herself at what must surely be the Golden Mile, so crossed the road to have a closer look. Her father had told her about it, and the stalls and show booths were just as garish and tatty as he'd said.

She watched in fascination as a man made some Blackpool rock, with the name of the town running all the way through, the letters neatly positioned in a circle round the edge of the round pink and white candy stick, which started out large and then was pulled into a much longer and thinner stick. When he'd finished making it, she bought a piece for herself, biting off the end and enjoying its sweet, minty taste.

Loud music beat around her as she strolled on, different tunes blaring out next door to one another; bright colours and lights assailed her eyes; and people standing outside the booths and shops shouted at her, assuring her of never-to-be-repeated bargains or marvels just inside their premises that would astound her.

Every now and then she'd see people playing what looked like bingo in seedy little rooms, sitting at machines with their backs to the sea. What a way to spend a holiday! There were even stalls selling sheets and bedding. Now why on earth would you go on holiday to buy things like that?

After a while Gina crossed the road and tramlines to get to the promenade itself and continued her walk, enjoying looking down on the smooth sandy beach below. The sea was different from at home, though, a brownish green in colour instead of aqua.

At two o'clock she stopped for a cup of tea and a scone, not feeling hungry enough for a proper meal. As she sat eating, she felt an overwhelming desire to sleep and worked out it would be getting towards bedtime at home. But she didn't give in and return to the hotel for a lie down. Only when she grew too tired to walk any further did she catch a tram back along the promenade.

What was she going to do with herself all day tomorrow? she wondered as she walked into the lobby. Maybe there was a coach tour she could go on? You saw so much more if someone else was driving. She went to look through a rack of brightly coloured folders, taking a selection into the café-bar and sitting down with them.

Bridie appeared, looked at her questioningly and when she gestured to the seat next to hers, came across to join her.

Without asking, one of the waitresses brought across a tray with a teapot and a few small cakes.

'You'll join me?' Bridie asked. 'I always have a snack at this time of day, then I don't need to come down too early for my meal. The evenings can be rather long otherwise.'

What must it be like, Gina wondered, living totally on your own with no family to turn to? She'd felt hard done to by fate when she lost her husband so young, but she'd had her daughters to comfort her and lately two lovely grandchildren. Bridie seemed to have no one. Her family should be ashamed of themselves for leaving her alone like this.

Brad came into the foyer, looking rosy-cheeked and windswept. Gina felt a sudden throb of pleasure at the sight of him. That astounded her so much she looked quickly away and it was left to Bridie to wave him across to join them.

'Looks like we're going to have a few showers this evening and tomorrow.' He ordered a coffee and sat down, eating the remaining cakes once he was sure the two women had had enough. 'I get hungry,' he said apologetically. 'Fast metabolism.'

'You're lucky,' Gina said feelingly. 'I have to struggle to keep my weight down. I really ought to lose a few pounds.'

He studied her frankly. 'I don't think so. You're just right. I don't find coat-hanger women at all attractive.'

Gina felt a warmth in her cheeks.

'I've never heard that phrase before,' Bridie said.

It was a minute before Brad seemed to notice that she'd spoken, because he was still looking at Gina, smiling slightly as if pleased with what he was seeing. Then he turned to Bridie. 'It's a word I use for fashionable women who keep themselves too thin on purpose. They look like those wire coat hangers we used to have.'

Bridie chuckled. 'You're a man after my own heart, Brad Rosenberry. In my generation, it was luscious curves that turned men on, not prominent bones. Some of those models look as if they've just come out of Belsen.'

'Curves still do it for most guys!' he assured her with a boyish grin.

Well, Gina thought, she certainly had those, and flushed all over again at her own reactions to him. Luckily the lighting wasn't too bright and the other two didn't seem to have noticed. Well, she hoped they hadn't.

As she went up to her room later, she marvelled at how comfortable she'd felt with both Brad and Bridie. It was a cliché but it was as if she'd known them both for years.

She sat on the bed and studied the brochures, finding a full-day tour to the Lake District. She'd always wanted to go there. It was late, but on the off chance, she rang reception to ask if they could still help her book a place on it and they assured her they could. She got ready for bed feeling she was coping well with being a tourist on her own.

She would contact her brother and sister later, but couldn't even bring herself to plan it yet. It wasn't just the jet lag. Now that she was here, she was terrified of being rejected by them. It meant so much to her to meet them, get to know them.

Surely, they wouldn't turn her away?

–

When Brad got back to his room, he wasn't sleepy, so decided to phone Joanna and Michael. He did a quick calculation of the time differences and was disappointed to realise they'd be in bed now. He needed to ring them in the morning or early afternoon because they were seven – or was it eight? – hours ahead of England.

He picked up the novel he'd been reading – trying to read, he amended, frowning at it. The story didn't seem to be sinking in. Perhaps he should buy another, one that was more cheerful.

What he really felt like was a long walk, but he didn't feel safe in this district late at night – well, he wouldn't in central Perth either. He'd go for a brisk walk in the morning then go out for a drive somewhere. Maybe Gina and Bridie would like to come with him? Gina had had a pile of brochures. Maybe he should look at coach trips too? They could go on one together.

Or would she think he was being too pushy? He sprawled on the bed, thinking of her. Why she should appeal to him more than Judy had, he couldn't work out, but she did.

He was going to have trouble getting to sleep, he could tell. He was not only worried about Rosie but also about how lonely he was feeling. He hadn't realized how much he'd miss the daily contact with people. His whole life had been spent working with others, meeting new people as he trained them, going home to his family or going out with friends.

He still wanted to travel round Europe, of course he did, but he didn't want to do it on his own. And he had too many days to fill in between his visits to Rosie. He'd definitely look at the coach tours tomorrow.

With a sigh he switched on the television and propped himself against the bed head to watch a film.

To his surprise Gina slipped into his mind again. He could imagine her beside him, gesticulating as she chatted. She had such a warm smile and a very expressive face. There was a gentleness about her that he liked, too, her voice was low and soft... her body was soft as well, very feminine. Stay away from thoughts of soft female bodies, Brad! he told himself as his body twitched.

Taking a deep breath, he tried to concentrate on the television, but there was no programme worth watching.

In the end he went and had a cool shower.

What a time for his libido suddenly to switch on fully again!

Was it Gina? Or was it just himself, ready for any attractive female? He didn't know. He was so out of practice with women he was terrified of making a fool of himself.

The following morning it was raining heavily and Gina was glad she'd booked a coach tour because you couldn't walk about in weather like this. She took breakfast in her bedroom, not wanting to seem too clingy with her new friends, then went to wait for the coach in the hotel lobby.

She would have enjoyed the trip much more on a sunny day because the scenery, what she could see of it, was gorgeous, lushly green after Australia. But as it was, the few passengers on the tour scurried for shelter at every stop and some of the views were obscured by mist or grey curtains of rain. And since everyone else seemed to be in pairs or quartets, and several of the groups didn't speak much English, she was on her own all day.

What she should really have done was go and visit her family. Got it over with. Why else had she hired that car? It was sitting there behind the hotel, costing her money she could ill afford. She'd go the very next day. She was being a coward about it. If they were going to reject her out of hand, it was better to find out at once, then she could plan some sightseeing – York, London, Hadrian's Wall were all on her list, perhaps even Paris. She'd always wanted to see Paris.

The weather cleared as they drove back into Blackpool and when the coach let down a couple at a hotel further along the promenade from hers, Gina decided to get out and walk back. It was still light, though there weren't a lot of people about. It stayed light much longer here in summer than it did at home. She looked at her watch. People were probably having their evening meal or getting ready for it.

She'd work up a nice appetite for hers with a brisk walk. She'd been sitting around for too long today.

Huddled in her lightweight jacket, because it was quite chilly, she didn't notice the young man with a hood pulled forward to hide his face until he grabbed her arm and yanked her into an alley, dragging her away from the street. She screamed, but he cut off her scream with one hand across her mouth, trying to pull her shoulder bag off her arm at the same time.

She fought against him desperately, but he was much stronger than she was.

–

Worried by her mother's phone call, Cheryl rang home. She waited, her foot tapping impatiently, for her father to answer but he didn't pick up the phone. Where was he? She didn't believe what her mother had said about him being arrested. Why would anyone want to arrest a respectable man like her father?

If her mother thought she could gain sympathy with wild stories like that, she had another thing coming.

At midnight, seriously worried now, Cheryl made one final attempt and at last he picked up the phone.

'Dad! Where were you? I've been so worried. I had the stupidest phone call from Mum. She seemed to think you'd been arrested.'

'I had been.'

'*What?*'

'Only because she and those friends of hers made up a pack of lies about me and the police believed them. Did you know your mother's left me?'

'She said she had, but I didn't believe her. I mean, how will she manage without you?'

'Try telling that to her bloody brother. Tonight I just wanted to talk to Peggy, that's all. I mean, what's the world coming to when a man can't talk to his own wife without her claiming he's harassing her? I blame those damned feminists at the Women's Wellness Centre. They're man-haters, that lot are. That's where it happened.'

He paused, breathing deeply. 'She's staying at your uncle Jake's. Did you know that?'

'She did say something about it. She'll be upset. You know how uptight she gets about small things and you can be a bit sharp with her at times.'

'Only to keep her on her toes. She's such a bad organizer, I have to point out what needs doing.'

Cheryl kept quiet, but he didn't seem to need encouraging to rant on about her mother. And some of the things he was saying weren't true and were very unkind. He'd never talked quite like this before. Her mother meant well, didn't mess things up on purpose. And her father was extremely fussy about things being done just so. She'd not like to live with him again, fond as she was of him. In fact, she'd never found a man she would like to live with until recently and was waiting to see how that panned out before mentioning Pete to her parents.

She realized her father was still speaking and tried to concentrate.

'…and why Jake persuaded her to leave me, I don't know. I suppose he wants a free housekeeper. In the meantime I'm having to cook my own meals and iron my own shirts. Peggy will no doubt change her mind in a few days and come crawling back. Well, she's got no money of her own, I make sure of that, so she'll have to. And I'll lay down some pretty stiff ground rules this time, I can tell you. I...'

Cheryl frowned at the phone. She didn't like to hear him talking so wildly. 'Look, Dad, just calm down and—'

'Calm down!' he thundered. 'Do you know what I've been through today? What if it gets out that I was arrested?'

'What did they charge you with?'

Silence, then, 'Assault'.

'You hit someone? Was it Mum?'

'No, some other stupid female. I pushed her away from Peggy a bit too hard and knocked her over by mistake. I said I was sorry, but no, she's one of those femi-nazis, has to put men down.'

'Perhaps she'll come around after a day or two, and withdraw the charges.'

'I doubt it. How do you think it'll make me look being taken to court? I've never been so embarrassed in my whole life.'

'Mum does get a bit upset when you shout at her.'

'Don't tell me you're taking her side against me! Of all the ungrateful—'

'No, Dad, of course not. When have I ever?'

'That's my girl.'

But he still didn't stop talking, repeating the same thing over and over again. Cheryl stopped trying to reason with him and made occasional noises to show she was listening. It was a relief when he said he had to get to bed.

She put the handset down and stared at it then began walking round the flat, trying to make sense of what had happened tonight. Did her father often blow his stack like that? He'd never done it with her before.

Her mother had wept on the phone. Her father had ranted and raved like a madman. She couldn't get the contrast between the pair of them out of her mind.

Well, one thing was certain. She wasn't going home again till things had settled down. She wished Pete was here, could have done with someone to hold her, but he was away on a business trip. It was frightening to hear your father ranting like that.

Her last thought as she slid towards sleep was that her mother had sounded really scared and she'd been brusque and dismissive. She felt ashamed of that now.

She'd ring Mum back in a day or two and see if she was feeling better. She might have gone back to Dad by then, probably would have. He'd settle down again once she did. He needed Mum more than he would admit, was helpless in the house. She'd not like to marry a man who had to be waited on hand and foot.

Chapter 26

England

A voice called out from the entrance to the alley. With a curse Gina's attacker kicked her so hard the pain drove every other thought from her mind. When the pain subsided a little, she realized someone was kneeling beside her. At first she thought it was her attacker and flinched away, then she recognized the voice.

'Brad! Oh, Brad! Thank goodness it's you.'

He helped her sit up but muddy as it was, she couldn't face standing up yet. She clung to him, shuddering. After a moment or two she began to get control of herself and noticed they were both sitting on the damp ground and she was pressed close to his chest. He was stroking her hair, murmuring soothingly.

When she drew away a little, he asked, 'Are you all right? He hasn't injured you?'

'I'm getting there.' Still leaning against him, she looked round for her handbag but there was no sign of it. That made her jerk upright. 'He's taken my bag! It's got my money and credit card in it.'

'Damn. I was so concerned about you, I didn't chase after him, though I'm not sure that I could have caught him. He was a lot younger than me and he chose his place well, used those dustbins to climb over the wall at the far end of this alley.'

'You might have got hurt if you'd chased him. I wouldn't want that.'

'Let me help you up.'

It hurt to stand up and she groaned, still clinging to him.

'We should get you to hospital. You are hurt.'

'He kicked me, but I think it's just bruising.' She looked down at her leg, which was throbbing now.

Brad pulled out a mobile phone with his free hand. 'I'm calling the police.'

She didn't try to stop him. She felt absolutely disoriented, kept needing something from her handbag, a tissue to wipe her face, a mirror to see what she looked like. But she had nothing, no familiar weight on her shoulder... only Brad.

'The police are coming as soon as they can. I hope you weren't carrying all your money today?'

'It was all the English money I had, but it's my credit card I'm worried about. There's a number to ring if you lose it – Oh, that's in my handbag too.'

'What bank are you with?

She told him.

'I'm with that one as well.' He glanced over his shoulder towards the far end of the alley. 'Let's just walk back to the street, where we'll be safer, then I'll ring the bank's emergency number. I've got it in my wallet.'

She shivered, still trying to sort it out in her head. 'That man pulled me right off the street. No one seemed to notice except you, or hear me screaming.'

'I was out for a stroll and I'd seen you in the distance, so was watching you. And people did stop, so they obviously heard you screaming, but no one tried to help you. Fine world it is when people stand by and let others be attacked!' He fished in his pocket and pulled out a wallet, fumbling through the contents. 'Ah, here it is! Look, we'll ring this number now while we're waiting for the police. Do you have any idea of your credit card number?'

'Yes, of course. I know it by heart.'

'My daughter's like that. I can never remember long numbers. I even have trouble with phone numbers.' He dialled swiftly and when someone answered, explained what had happened and passed the phone to Gina.

During the conversation that followed, she arranged to have a stop put on her credit card and was told to go to a certain bank in Blackpool the following day with proof of her identity to fill in the necessary forms. A new card would be sent to that bank in about a week's time.

As she handed the phone back to Brad, she realized something else. 'My mobile phone! They'll have that too.'

'We'll ring your phone company once we get back to the hotel.'

She was beginning to wonder how she was going to live until she got her new card. Tears welled in her eyes but she tried not to let them fall, because what good would it do. But a few escaped her and suddenly she found herself sobbing against Brad's chest.

She ought to move away, but she couldn't. Only with him holding her tightly did she feel safe.

'The police can't do anything now,' she said as time passed.

'No, probably not. But we should still report the incident. Facts gradually build up into a whole picture. One day, the details you give and the information from other victims may help catch your attacker.'

She sighed with relief when a police car drew up half an hour after the attack and two officers got out. Brad signalled to them and they strode across the pavement.

'You all right?' one asked her.

'A bit bruised, but that's all.'

'Come and sit in the car and tell us how it happened.'

She couldn't hold back the tears as she relived the attack. Brad's arm was still there, though, a band of warmth that made her feel safe.

When Gina had told them all she could remember, which wasn't much, one officer went to inspect the alley. 'This has happened a few times now, same MO,' the other said. 'One day he'll bite off more than he can chew and we'll catch him. Would you recognize him if you saw him again, Mrs Porter?'

'No, he had a hooded windcheater.' She frowned, trying to think of something that was nudging her. 'I might recognize his voice, though. He had a regional accent, only I can't say which. I'm Australian, can only recognize a Lancashire accent. It wasn't that, though.'

'Well, it's a help even to know that.' The officer smiled encouragingly. 'If you hear anything like his accent, will you let us know? Or if you remember anything else?'

'Yes, of course.'

The other officer came back. 'Nothing. It's paved so there are no footprints.' He turned to Gina. 'We'll drive you back to your hotel now, shall we, Mrs Porter?'

'If you don't mind. I'm feeling a bit shaky.'

What was she going to do now? she wondered as they drove slowly back. She still had her passport, but she had no cash in hand, apart from a few Australian coins and notes in her suitcase, and no means of getting at her money until she received her new card. She couldn't pay her hotel bill or buy food or anything.

'You'll need money,' Brad said, as if he'd read her thoughts. 'I can lend you some.'

She looked sideways at him. 'Are you sure? You don't really know me.'

He chuckled softly. 'When I look at your face, so transparently honest, I feel quite certain I'm going to be repaid.'

'Thank you for the compliment. Well, I think it's a compliment. But weren't you going to move on after a few days?'

'I was, but my situation's changed, so now I need to stay in the area. I might try to find somewhere cheaper to live, though, a self-catering place perhaps. It's a nice hotel but I'm not made of money.'

The thought of him leaving the hotel upset her and she blurted out, 'I shall miss you.'

'I'll miss you too. I enjoy your company. But we can still see one another – if you'd like to, that is.'

'I would.' His compliment made her feel warm, dispelling for a moment the chill and fear she'd been feeling ever since the attack.

As their eyes met, the street outside the car seemed to blur and all she was conscious of was Brad, his strength and kindness. His wasn't an overt, macho masculinity but it nonetheless touched something inside her, making her feel softly feminine.

Then the car stopped and they both jerked back to reality as the officer opened the car door.

–

The day following her husband's attack, Peggy got up late, coming downstairs yawning, looking strained. Jake nodded a greeting but didn't ask how she'd slept, just put the kettle on.

She went to stand by the window, looking out at the back garden. 'Even with vegetables, it looks pretty. No wonder you win prizes. You've got green fingers.'

'I do my best.' He went to stand beside her and raised one arm, intending to put round her, but let it drop again. Something about her body said don't touch me. And anyway, they weren't a family for touching and cuddling, never had been. He couldn't remember his mother ever giving him a hug. He'd tried to cuddle his daughter sometimes and she'd been like his mother, stiffening when held.

Thank goodness for his granddaughter. From when she was tiny Lou had flung herself into his arms more times than he could remember and that hadn't stopped as she grew older. When she became a teenager, she'd had the obligatory rows with her parents, but rarely with him. He was missing her, felt guilty that he'd been unkind to her before she left for Australia – though he still wished she hadn't gone raking up old embers like that.

He realized Peggy was speaking and tried to give her his full attention.

'I think I need to start planning a new life, Jake, and for that I need money.'

'I've been through divorce, so I can tell you that you've a right to a share in the family possessions, like the house.'

'Hartley has savings, I know he does. And the mortgage is paid off. But I doubt he'll give me anything! He keeps a firm hold on his money.'

'You'll need a good lawyer.'

'That's what the counsellor said. In the meantime I need to get my pension paid directly to me, not into Hartley's account.'

Jake looked at her in surprise. 'Did you even hand that over to him?'

She nodded, flushing slightly.

'Eh, it's a wonder he let you breathe on your own.'

'He's not been very kind lately, but I've never liked arguments and upsets, as you know. I'm going to try to – well, stand up for myself from now on, though.'

She didn't sound optimistic and the smile she gave him was so fragile and uncertain, he ached for her.

'Cheryl said—' Peggy took a deep breath. 'She said I needed Hartley to look after me, that I'd never be been able to cope on my own. I'm sixty-six, Jake. It's about time I did learn to stand on my own feet, don't you think?'

He nodded, letting her lead the conversation.

'I've got another appointment with the counsellor tomorrow. I – I'm going to ask her about a divorce lawyer.'

'Divorce?'

She looked at him solemnly. 'I was awake a lot during the night thinking. I'm never going back to live with Hartley. When I see how kind you are to me, it makes me think, it really does. How could I just accept what he was like in private? The way he mocked me, insulted me, said I was useless. No wonder my daughter despises me.'

She bowed her head for a minute and her voice came out muffled. 'What I don't understand is why I let him do this to me.'

'You were depressed after you'd had Cheryl. Hartley was always a bossy bugger, but after she was born, you were lost for a while and he took over. I think he got a taste for ordering you around then and never stopped.'

She nodded slowly. 'And I took so long to get pregnant and then couldn't have another baby. I felt ashamed of that and he was angry because he'd wanted a son. He idolizes Cheryl, you know, and she's always been Daddy's girl. If I divorce him… I don't think she'll want anything to do with me. But Hartley doesn't know how to cook or look after himself or anything like that, for all he mocks me.'

'Whatever you decide, I'll help you.'

She laid one hand briefly on his. 'Thanks. You're the best of brothers. You always looked after me when I was a child, even though I was the eldest. I needed it then, too, didn't I?'

She began eating some toast but stopped for a moment, head on one side. 'It's a good thing we went and got my clothes. Otherwise they'd probably have turned up here in rags as well.'

'You must be upset about those embroideries.'

She shrugged. 'Sort of. But I can do others. It's me I'm upset about, Jake. Me and the mess I've made of my life. Embroideries aren't important compared to that.'

When she'd finished eating, she looked round. 'I'll give the house a good clean, shall I? Pay you back a bit.'

'You don't need to pay me back. I'm glad to help you.'

She gave him a wry smile. 'To keep me occupied, then.'

'All right. And thanks.'

So he went outside to get a bit of sun on his face and do some weeding. He ought to go down to the allotment, but he didn't want to leave her on her own. Those shredded embroideries were still worrying him. It was such a cruel, vicious thing to do. In the end he decided to get extra bolts for the front and back doors and perhaps a fancy iron grill for the frosted glass pane in the top half of the front door. There was something to be said for old-fashioned wooden windows with frames and small panes like his. Not as easy to smash open as big sheets of glass.

You couldn't be too careful when someone was – unbalanced. Jake was quite sure there would be more trouble to come.

He hoped Peggy would stick it out and get a divorce, but he wasn't optimistic.

–

When Gina walked into the lobby, people stared at her and Brad. She caught sight of herself in the big mirror to one side and gasped in shock. Her hair was a mess, her face tear-streaked, her clothes torn and there was a bruise on one cheekbone.

'What happened? Have you been in an accident?'

She turned to see Bridie hurrying out of the bar and tried to speak, but couldn't, could only gesture with one hand, swallow hard and press the hand to her lips to hold back the tears.

'Oh, my dear!'

As the older woman put her arms round her, Gina began sobbing all over again, beyond words now. She heard Brad explaining briefly that she'd been mugged, could sense people nearby listening, muttering, and felt nearly sick with relief when her friends guided her across to the lift, away from the staring faces.

Brad kept calling out, 'Let us pass, please. She's been hurt.'

People fell back, still talking and exclaiming.

'Mugged? What do we pay the police for?'

'Look at her, poor thing.'

'Don't know what the world's coming to.'

Their voices seemed to echo in Gina's head as if they'd come from far away.

Brad stopped by the lift as something occurred to him. 'I'll have to get her a new key card so that we can get into her room.'

'In the meantime she can come to my room.' Bridie kept hold of Gina. 'Don't faint on me, dear. I'm not strong enough to hold you up. Ah, here we go.' She moved forward as the lift doors opened, saying in an imperious tone, 'Please stay back and wait for the next lift. My friend's been hurt and needs to lie down.'

The door closed on another group of staring faces and still that bony arm supported Gina. As long as it was there, she felt she could stay upright, but she couldn't speak a word of sense.

When they got out of the lift Bridie fumbled in her handbag and slipped a key card into the lock of a room at the end of the corridor. 'Come and sit down.'

Inside Gina collapsed on to a sofa, leaning her head back, closing her eyes, letting the silence and comfort wrap round her like a soft shawl.

'Here. Drink this, my dear.'

She became aware that Bridie was thrusting a glass into her hand.

'Brandy. Good for shock.'

She did as ordered and the fiery warmth felt good as she let a mouthful trickle down her throat.

There was a knock on the door.

Bridie hurried across to let Brad in.

'How is she?' he asked in a low voice.

'I'm able to speak for myself.' Gina looked up as they walked across to join her. 'I'm sorry. It seemed to hit me all over again when we came into the hotel. I'll be fine in a few minutes if I can just sit here quietly and – and feel safe.'

'That's a girl,' Bridie said. 'You can sit there for as long as you want. Take another sip.'

She moved closer to Brad and Gina heard her ask in a low voice, 'Ever dealt with someone who's been mugged before?'

'Well… no.'

'I've not gone deaf, you know,' Gina protested.

Bridie turned to study her. 'No, but you're still in shock and won't be thinking clearly. Your colour's better now, but if you're anything like my friend who was attacked, you'll not want to be left on your own. Would you like to stay here with me tonight? This couch pulls down into a bed.'

'I can't put you to so much trouble.'

'Of course you can!'

'Then yes, I would like to stay here.' The thought of being alone in her hotel room was suddenly terrifying and she knew she'd not sleep a wink.

'Go and fetch her things, dear boy.'

'No, I can…' Gina tried to stand up, but her legs felt so rubbery, she let herself fall back down on to the soft cushions. 'I can get them myself if you'll just give me a few more minutes.'

'I could easily get them for you,' Brad said.

'But you won't know what I want!'

'I was married for thirty years. I've a fair idea what a woman needs. If you don't mind me poking around, that is. Or I could escort you down?'

She couldn't suppress a shiver at the thought of leaving this cosy room. 'No, you go. I'd be grateful.'

He stopped at the door. 'I think I'd also better try to contact your mobile phone company. Give me the details and I'll ring them and explain what's happened. You don't want to be stuck with a big phone bill on top of everything else.'

'I'd forgotten that.' Bridie was right, Gina decided. She'd not been thinking at all clearly since the attack, still wasn't, however hard she tried. 'You're so kind.' She gave him the necessary details and when he'd gone, looked at Bridie. 'You must think I'm so weak to go to pieces like this.'

'I think you're coping very well, actually. I told you, it happened to a friend of mine. They had to sedate her for a day or two and she needed sleeping tablets for months afterwards. These young hoodlums don't realize what they're doing to their victims, how the effects linger down the years.'

Gina nodded, then confided the thing that was worrying her most. 'How am I going to live until I get my new credit card?'

'We'll sort all that out in the morning. I can lend you the money if necessary. For the moment, I think you should have a warm shower, then we'll get room service to bring you up something to eat.'

Gina reached out to clasp her companion's hand. 'You're so kind, yet you hardly know me.'

'I was brought up to think of others as well as myself. And anyway,' Bridie hesitated, her expression sad. 'You remind me of my sister. She died young, but she had hair just the same shade as yours. I don't see much of my relatives now, what few I have left.' She stared into the distance for a moment longer, then added more briskly, 'And anyway, if we can't help our fellow human beings, we're not worth much, are we?'

She then spoiled the solemnity of the moment by chuckling. 'Besides, I don't usually get much excitement in my life, so you'll be doing me a favour by letting me share yours.'

Gina smiled in spite of her worries and leaned across to hug her. 'I wish you were a relative of mine. I've had a shortage of them all my life because of my parents emigrating.'

'We lose a lot of people to Australia.' Bridie blinked furiously and turned to pour herself a brandy.

Gina wondered who her friend had lost. As she looked around, she felt relieved at how safe this place felt. She needed that right now. 'Even with you here, I keep getting flashbacks, remembering how helpless I felt when that man dragged me down the alley.'

Brad came back just then with her suitcase and she let them continue to fuss over her, marvelling at how lucky she'd been. If she hadn't met these two kind strangers, she'd be on her own in a hotel room now and she didn't know how she would have coped with that.

She didn't like living on her own, even in her own home. She didn't just miss Tom, she missed the family years, when she'd had him and her daughters for company, always something needing doing. In those days, time alone had been a welcome oasis in the bustle, not something to be managed carefully.

Since Tom's death she'd tried to make the best of her new life, so that she wasn't a burden to her daughters, but Lexie was right. She hadn't really moved on.

Until now. This trip was her rite of passage.

Chapter 27

England

In the morning Stu made no attempt to get ready for work. Jane studied him surreptitiously. He looked ghastly; serve him right for drinking so heavily.

When the kids had gone to school, she braced herself and went to sit in the breakfast area with him. 'We need to talk.'

'I'm a bit fragile this morning. Can't it wait until another day?'

'You're hungover, you mean. And you'll be hung over tomorrow as well, if you go on this way. You and I need to talk and I think we'd better do it now.'

He glowered at her and folded his arms. 'All right, talk away.'

'Very well. I have a few things to say, so I'll start. Firstly, I overheard your phone conversation with Brad because I'd just picked up the phone myself. I can't believe how rude you were to him, but even worse as far as I'm concerned, I can't believe you took such a decision on your own and didn't consult me about whether Rosie could see him.'

As she'd been talking Stu uncrossed his arms and began fiddling with the crumbs on his plate, arranging them one by one in a neat circle.

'You know how I feel about him,' he muttered.

'Yes, but do you know how I feel?'

He looked up in surprise, fingers suspended over the plate. 'Of course I do.'

'I don't think so. If you knew how I felt, you'd never have behaved like that.'

In the silence that followed she could hear birds trilling and cheeping outside and see the dust motes dancing in the sunbeams that were spearing through the windows. She had great trouble keeping her tongue still.

He didn't speak, not a word, not even a sigh.

When she could bear it no longer, she went on quietly, 'And you're taking absolutely no account of Rosie's feelings when you make these unilateral decisions, which isn't fair to her, either. You're not usually unfair, Stu.'

He went back to fiddling with the crumbs, rearranging them into a line this time.

She resisted the temptation to snatch the plate away from him and insist he look at her.

'Rosie needs to see Brad so that she can understand where part of her comes from. She needs that. It's not a whim and it's definitely not something she'll get over. I bought a book about it last week. You should read it too. If you stop her getting to know him now, she'll only do it after she leaves home.' Again, she waited and when Stu at last replied, it was so quietly she had to strain to hear what he was saying.

'He has no right to come here trying to take my place.'

'He isn't doing that. And she isn't trying to put him in your place.'

Stu shrugged, a gesture so like their son's when he couldn't articulate his feelings, that Jane was touched and her anger softened a little. 'Don't do this, darling. You'll alienate her if you stop her seeing him. Remember, it was Rosie who contacted him, not vice versa. Yet you're blaming him. What would you do if you found you'd fathered a child, if that child wanted to meet you? Tell her to go away? Of course you wouldn't. And neither would Brad. He came all the way from Australia to see her.'

'I wish she'd never found out.'

'I shouldn't have let you persuade me to keep it secret that you weren't her father in the first place. We were so wrong. But now she does know, we have to trust her. She's nearly grown up. She'll be flying the nest soon.'

Another silence heavy with emotion. This time she waited it out.

He shoved the plate aside so violently that crumbs spilled everywhere and it nearly fell off the edge of the table. 'It hurts.' His voice was harsh, his hands were clenched into fists.

'I know.' She waited for him to calm down a little. 'There's something else, Stu, something I didn't tell you before.'

He flinched as if she'd hit him. 'What?'

'Rosie told me she always felt she came second to Casey with you, which made her feel there was something wrong with her. Now she knows why, she's happier about herself.'

He looked at her in horror. 'She didn't come second. Jane, you know she didn't. I love her dearly. She is my daughter as far as I'm concerned.'

'I think – just marginally – you love Casey more. Oh, not intentionally, but he is flesh of your flesh, after all. And she comes from another man's flesh – only now that man

271

has a face.' She reached out to take hold of his hand. 'And you've all the other stuff hurting you at the moment, so you're not making good decisions about the Brad thing.'

He twisted his hand so that he could hold hers properly. She closed her eyes in relief, because it seemed like a sign. She made her final point bluntly. 'Darling, how long are you going to continue drinking? It's not solving anything.'

Stu shook his head, a blind, helpless sort of gesture. He was grasping her hand so tightly now that it hurt.

Time to break the tense mood. She stood up and pulled him with her. 'Let's go and sit outside. It's a beautiful day and if you're going to play hooky, you may as well take advantage of this weather. I don't have to start work till this afternoon.'

So they went to sit in the garden, holding hands like teenagers. Like lovers. Like old friends. They didn't say anything, just enjoyed being together, as they had done from the time they first met. There weren't many quiet moments like this with two youngsters in the house.

Stu didn't say anything more about himself and his problems, and Jane didn't know whether she'd helped him or not. She hoped she had, but as he had to trust Rosie, she felt she had to trust her husband now.

He'd never let her down before... but then he'd never had to face two painful crises at once before, either.

Nor had she. She hoped none of them guessed how painful it was for her to see Brad again.

–

The following morning Gina felt disoriented when she woke up. Still half-asleep, she pulled the covers up to her chin to protect herself against some nameless terror, then remembered what had happened and let out a little noise that was half groan, half sigh.

'You sound to be awake, dear.'

She turned her head to see Bridie standing in the doorway that led to the bedroom, fully dressed, not a hair out of place.

'For a minute I couldn't think where I was.'

'I'll make you a cup of tea – or do you prefer coffee in the morning?'

'Tea, but you don't have to wait on me, Bridie.'

'I'm having a cup myself now that it won't disturb you if I put the kettle on. Would you like to use the bathroom? There's a clean towel if you want a quick shower.'

When she looked at herself in the mirror, Gina was horrified. She looked haggard, with dark circles under her eyes and that tell-tale bruise on one cheekbone. She had a shower and washed her hair, found her own hairdryer sitting on the surface, complete with its adaptor for English sockets. When she'd finished blow drying her hair, she looked a lot better – well, a bit better. There was nothing she could do about the bruise or the dark circles. She didn't use much make-up and what little she'd brought had been in her stolen handbag, so she couldn't hide anything. Well, the bruise would be gone in a few days.

How long would her memories of the attack linger, though?

When she went out into the sitting room again, Bridie was standing by the window, gazing down at the promenade. 'There's always something to see. I spend a lot of time these days spying on my fellow human beings. There's tea in the pot. We'll go down to breakfast presently. Brad rang while you were having a shower. He'll meet us in the dining room if we let him know when we're ready.'

'You're both being so kind to me,' Gina said wonderingly. 'A complete stranger.'

Bridie smiled. 'Not a stranger now, surely? A friend now, I hope. How did you sleep?'

'Not very well. I kept jerking awake. I can't tell you how relieved I was each time to know you were next door.'

'I was glad to be of use. Sadly, I'm afraid I have to leave for a few days, though you can stay in this room if you prefer it to yours. I can get you a key card.'

'Are you going somewhere nice?'

'I have to see a specialist in Preston every twelve months. I had breast cancer a few years ago and they like to check up on me, then I go to stay with an old friend who lives there afterwards. She's housebound now and I know how much she looks forward to my visits, so I don't like to let her down.'

'How do you get there? Can I drive you?' Gina flushed as she realized she had no money. 'Oh! I'm sorry. I've no money for petrol. But if you'll pay for some, I can take you.'

'I've ordered a car, dear. I always use the same driver and I booked him last week. No need to trouble you. But I'll give you my mobile number in case you need someone to talk to. I don't go to bed until late and I'm usually up quite early. I'll ring Brad now, shall I?' She picked up the phone.

When they left the room, Gina could feel herself tensing up, which was silly, because what could happen to her here inside the hotel when she wasn't even on her own?

She was glad to see Brad waiting for them in the lobby. And surprised at how much better she felt with him beside her.

She wanted to clutch his hand like a frightened child. Oh, dear, she really must pull herself together.

–

Brad watched Gina walk across towards him, her hair shining but her face pale and strained. The bruise standing out lividly on her cheekbone made him feel angry all over again. 'Are you all right? How did you sleep?'

He saw Bridie watching him with a slight smile as if she could tell he was attracted to Gina and approved. Well, he was attracted. But now wasn't the time to do anything about that.

Once they'd finished breakfast, Bridie said she had to start packing and Gina went to get her things from her friend's room. He could tell at once that she was nervous of staying on her own, but didn't say anything, except to offer to carry the suitcase down for her.

'I can manage. I shouldn't be taking your time up like this,' she protested.

'I've nothing else to do with my time but hang around. I'm waiting to make a phone call. And actually, I'd welcome some company today... if that's all right with you?'

'You're not just saying that?'

'No.' He saw Bridie giving him a nod, as if to encourage him to continue, but he'd have continued anyway. 'I'd really enjoy spending the day with you.'

'Oh… well… that'd be great.'

By the time they'd said goodbye to Bridie, the banks were open.

'I'd better take my passport,' Gina said, looking round for something to carry it in and only finding a plastic bag.

'That's not safe. Let me put it in my inside pocket.'

He went with Gina to fill in the forms. To her relief, when she produced the passport, the bank was willing to advance her some money from her account, but they could do nothing to hurry up the new credit card. Brad had to put the money in his pocket as well as the passport.

'Thank goodness I kept my passport in my suitcase,' she said as they walked away. 'If I hadn't, how would I have proved who I was?'

'Why worry about that? You did have it.'

She gave him a warm smile. 'Yes, and I had two good friends as well. Even more important.'

'It's my pleasure to help you. Bridie's, too, I'm sure.'

'She's a lovely woman. Her family should be shot for leaving her on her own.'

'It happens.' He saw an expression of pain cross Gina's face and stopped walking to ask, 'What did I say to upset you?'

'Oh, talked about family. It's a sore point. All my life I've wanted family and had none until my daughters were born. And here are these people ignoring Bridie.'

He nodded. 'I regard my family as a precious gift – even when they're infuriating me.' They began walking again. 'What do you want to do now?'

'Go shopping. I need a new handbag and purse. I'll manage without makeup until I get my credit card back. I want to make this money spin out.'

He noticed how she kept glancing round nervously, how she shrank back when someone came too close, so offered her his arm. She gave him a shy smile as she took it and didn't draw away when he pulled her closer. It felt good to be walking so close to a woman again. No, be honest, he told himself, it felt good to be walking close to Gina.

She bought a handbag then they found a shop dealing in mobile phones. After explaining the situation, to a chorus of oohs and ahs from the two sales assistants, Gina was asked to prove who she was and then was sold a basic phone on special offer with the same phone company she'd used before.

'My handbag doesn't feel as empty now,' she said with a smile as they came out of the shop.

'My arm does.'

She gave him a long, considering look and he held his breath, hoping he'd not overstepped the mark. Then she moved closer.

Be careful, Rosenberry, he told himself. Only he didn't want to be careful. Why should he?

It was as they were walking along a side street that he saw the sign in a real estate agency and pulled to a halt again, pointing to it: Self-catering holiday accommodation. 'Do you still want to live more economically?'

She nodded, staring at the sign. 'I have to. Even with the special offer, the hotel costs more than I want to spend.'

'I'm the same. How about we find what it costs to rent a flat? We could share one.' When she stared at him, he added hastily, 'A two-bedroom one, I'm not propositioning you. We both need to stay in the district for a while and it's a bit lonely being a solo traveller, don't you think? Outings are so much more pleasant when you've someone to share them with.'

She remembered her lonely day in the Lake District. 'Definitely.'

'Let's go in and at least find out what they have on offer.'

-

As Peggy got ready to go out, she stared at herself anxiously in the mirror. Her disturbed nights had given her a drawn, tired expression and her cheeks were a faded greyish white rather than pink. Her spectacles seemed to emphasize the wrinkles around her eyes. How long had she been looking so old and careworn? She'd always been more concerned to see to Hartley's needs and get the house as perfect as possible than to think about titivating herself.

Talk about attempting the impossible! She just wasn't the sort to achieve perfection… not in anything. So today she'd be content to look neat and tidy for her counselling session.

When she went downstairs, Jake was waiting for her, smiling. He smiled a lot, her brother. He was so easy to live with, she kept thinking she was dreaming.

This time, when they got to the centre, she had no hesitation about waving goodbye to him and walking inside on her own. The receptionist greeted her cheerfully by name and in spite of the incident with Hartley, Peggy felt quite safe here because people stood by you if anything went wrong.

Gillah came out to greet her and clasped her hand for a moment, holding it in both of hers and studying Peggy's face, nodding as she let go of the hand as if she approved of what she saw.

When they were settled in her cosy little room, Gillah leaned back and waited.

Peggy knew it was up to her to initiate a conversation. It was hard to say it aloud and the words came out in a breathless rush. 'I've decided I want a divorce, only... I don't know how to do it. And... I want to get my money back, my pension and I think I ought to have a share of the house. That'd be fair, wouldn't it?'

'Are you sure about the divorce? Isn't it a little early for such a decision?'

'That's the thing I'm most certain about. I didn't really know how other people lived because Hartley and I didn't go out much, and we didn't have any real friends only his business associates. Oh, I was so nervous whenever we went to company functions! He got furious if I said the wrong thing.'

She looked at Gillah and at a nod, continued, 'But even in the short time since I've left Hartley, I've learned so much and – and I know I've been a fool, a doormat. I just can't understand why I put up with it for so long? Maybe he's right. Maybe I am stupid.'

She cried then, she couldn't help it, she was so ashamed of her own cowardice.

When the counselling session was over, Peggy left the centre with her head spinning with information and her hands full of leaflets about divorce.

Jake was waiting for her outside and she hurried towards him, eager to share her treasure trove of information, sure that he wouldn't mock her. It was a long time since she'd felt eager about anything. So they sat in the car and she told him what she'd discussed today.

'And Gillah says it'd be much cheaper to get a divorce myself,' she ended. 'I'm not sure I can, but I'm going to try. There are sites on the internet which offer do-it-yourself kits and support if you need it, she says. I'm not very good with computers, but you've got one, haven't you? Could you help me find out what I need to know?'

'Of course I can. Nothing easier.' He hesitated and added, trying to be fair, 'If you're really sure.'

'I am. And… if you don't mind bringing me here again and picking me up, I'd really like to continue with the meditation classes.' She dared put a secret longing into words, knowing her brother wouldn't mock her. 'I want to try to make a few friends.'

She wasn't sure she had much to offer anyone as a friend, because she wasn't clever or interesting, but she was going to make the effort. She really liked Jane. Perhaps something would come of that, in spite of the difference in their ages? Oh, she did hope so!

–

Gina went to her room to ring Mel privately on the new mobile phone. She felt nervous as soon as she left the lift, worse when she shut the door, and she shivered as the room seemed to close around her. She couldn't help it, she had to check the bathroom and wardrobe before she could do anything. Only then did she dial.

Her daughter picked up the phone. 'Mum! How are you?' She listened as Gina explained about the mugging and gave her the new mobile number. 'I can't bear to think of someone hurting you like that. Please be careful where you go in future. You were crazy to walk back to the hotel on your own in the evening.'

Gina tried to make light of it but shivered involuntarily. She was dreading sleeping here alone tonight. 'It was just bad luck. Now, the other thing is, I won't be at this hotel after tonight. Brad and I are going to share a self-catering holiday flat for a couple of weeks to save money and—'

'You're what?'

'We're going to share a flat. Two bedrooms and the tiniest living room-cum-kitchen you ever saw. We went to look at it this afternoon and rented it for two weeks. Well, Brad rented it. I can't pay my share till I get a new credit card. I don't want to carry big sums of cash round with me.'

'Mum, are you crazy? You've only known this man for a short time. He may be a serial rapist or… or a murderer.'

Gina smiled at the thought of Brad being anything else but straight and decent, then her amusement vanished as she heard what her daughter said next.

'You can't do that, you just can't. It's asking for trouble. When I think of all the lectures you gave me when I was a teenager and now… Mum, have you gone crazy?'

'You don't have much faith in my judgement, do you? I know Brad well enough to trust him, thank you very much. He saved me from a bad attack and has been supportive since, a true friend. And he's not only been kind to me but to an elderly lady we've both made friends with at the hotel.'

'That could just be a ploy to lull you into a false sense of security. And actually, if you must know, I don't trust your judgement where men are concerned. You've not dated anyone since Dad died and you don't sound as if you knew many before you met him. Mum, please don't do this.'

'I have to live my own life, Mel.'

Silence, then, 'Are you – involved with this Brad?'

'Not yet.'

'What does that mean?'

'Exactly what I said. Not yet. I may or I may not get involved in the way you mean. I certainly find him attractive and I think – I hope – he's attracted to me.'

As she put her phone away, Gina felt a thrill run through her at the thought of Brad. She was hoping... well, you could hope, couldn't you?

And her daughters could just mind their own business, for once. She wasn't old yet, so why act it? She twirled round and flopped down on the bed, lying beaming at the ceiling, arms outstretched.

It was such a good feeling to have a man wanting you. It'd been too long, far too long, since she'd made love to anyone.

As she sat up, her euphoria dimmed and reality intruded again. She was absolutely dreading sleeping here alone tonight, though she was trying not to betray that to Brad. It was stupid, really, because she'd not been mugged here, but that was how she felt.

Chapter 28

Australia

When she'd put phone back into its cradle, Mel turned to Lou and explained what was happening. 'My own mother!' she finished indignantly. 'Doing something as stupid as walking round on her own at night.'

'This Brad sounds like a nice guy. Maybe she'll enjoy a little holiday romance.'

Mel shook her head. 'Mum's not like that. She doesn't approve of casual sex. Anyway, it's dangerous, living with a stranger. What if he's only doing it to get her into bed? When he tires of her, he could drop her like a hot potato. Just think how that'd hurt her.'

'Then let's hope he's a kind and considerate lover, and they have some good bonks before they part company.'

Mel covered her ears. 'Do I want to hear this sort of thing about my mother?'

Lou laughed. 'Auntie Gina's not a fossil. She's young enough to remarry and she's very attractive for a woman her age. She has beautiful eyes.'

'You don't understand.' But Lou refused to be drawn into an argument and Mel gave up trying. She hadn't the energy.

She rang Lexie as soon as her sister got home from work and explained what was happening.

283

'Good for Mum!' was Lexie's immediate reaction. 'It's about time she got a man.'

'I don't happen to agree with you. I can't bear to think of her sleeping around.'

'Do you expect her to be celibate for the rest of her life?'

There was silence as Mel tried desperately to work out what to say.

'Hallo? I can hear you breathing so I know you're still there. You do expect her to stay celibate, don't you?'

'She was happy with Dad. How can she turn to anyone else after him? And she's got us, so she's not alone.'

'Oh, Mel. You always want everything to stay the same. Look at how angry you got with me when I started to go out with other guys after I split up with the Rat. I think Mum should go for it and enjoy some good sex while she still can.'

Did no one understand? Mel wondered angrily as she put the phone down and lay back on the sofa. Was she the only one worried about her mother's safety? Look at what had happened already on this stupid trip. Mum had been mugged. That was bad enough, but what if it'd been worse? What if her mother had been killed?

Chapter 29

England

Gina waited in her hotel room until it was time to meet Brad for dinner. He'd assumed she needed time to get ready, but that hadn't taken long and then she sat and waited, feeling nervous, keeping an eye on the door.

How long was she going to feel like this? She'd heard of people going to pieces after violent incidents and had always felt mildly scornful of them, sure that she'd never be like that. You had to pull yourself together when something went wrong and get on with your life, she'd thought.

Only it wasn't that easy. She understood that now.

She looked at the clock again. Only five minutes to wait. Maybe she'd go down early.

On that thought she picked up her new handbag and went to the door of her room. Her heart started beating faster as she opened it and peered down the corridor. No one in sight. She rushed for the lift.

Standing there waiting, she felt naked, vulnerable, kept glancing over her shoulder, breathed a sigh of relief when there was a ping and an empty lift stopped at her floor.

The lobby was brightly lit, full of people, with a concierge standing near the main entrance. She closed her eyes and let out a long, shuddering sigh of relief.

'You're early.'

She jumped in shock at Brad's voice behind her.

'Sorry. I didn't mean to startle you.' He studied her in concern, as if he could see the fear behind her attempt at a smile.

'I'm a bit jumpy. Silly, really.'

'Not silly. A perfectly normal reaction.' Without even asking, he put his arm round her waist and she was glad of it, leaning against his warm, strong body. They walked like that into the foyer café and she relaxed still further as they sat down in the corner they'd occupied before and ordered something to eat.

It was when they were going back to their rooms a couple of hours later that fear clutched at her belly again and she stopped, catching her breath, then forcing herself to move on again.

'You're still afraid to sleep on your own, aren't you?' he said quietly as they waited for the lift.

She couldn't pretend and nodded her head.

'Would you like me to sleep on your sofa?'

'No sofa.'

'Are there two beds or one?'

'One.'

'Same in my room, unfortunately. I could stay with you for a while, just till you get to sleep.'

The lift doors opened and they went inside. 'I couldn't trouble you like that. I'll be all right with the door locked.' She had to be.

It wasn't until they were standing in the open doorway of her room that she said in a rush, 'I don't think… Brad, it's a big bed. Please…'

'I'll stay with you, then. I'll better go and fetch my things.'

'I'll come with you.'

'That bad, eh?' He pulled her into another of his lovely hugs.

You could get addicted to hugs like this, she thought. 'After dark, it feels – more dangerous. And that's silly, because I was mugged in daylight.'

They went for his things and with him there, her room seemed ordinary again.

She should have been embarrassed, getting ready to share a bed with a man who'd been a complete stranger a week ago, but she wasn't. She didn't know what there was about Brad, but being with him was so comfortable. She liked him as well as being attracted. They hadn't stopped chatting all evening, no awkward pauses, no racking your brain about what to say next, no treading carefully around a topic.

He went into the bathroom to get ready and she took the opportunity to take off her dressing gown and slip under the covers.

'Do you want the light on or off?'

'Off.'

But as the room plunged into darkness, fear surged through her and she let out a whimper. He hurried to sit on the edge of the bed at her side. 'Oh, Gina, I'm so sorry it's left you like this.'

'Could you – hold me?'

He gathered her in his arms and she nestled against him, feeling the terror subside.

'Better?'

'Yes. But it's not just because of the mugging. I love it when you hold me. Will you kiss me?'

'I don't want to take advantage of you.'

She answered that by pulling him towards her and kissing him, aware that he was aroused. Well, so was she.

'Are you sure?' he asked as he pulled away, breathing deeply.

'Stop being honourable and make love to me.'

Her worries about making love to a man other than her husband slid away, because this was Brad and he had only to touch her to start currents humming through her body. She caressed him and sighed with happiness as he began to caress her.

The shadows receded, to be replaced by happiness... and by an ecstasy that surprised her.

–

The following morning Gina woke early, feeling shy, lying with her eyes closed for a minute or two wondering how to face him.

As if he'd sensed that she was awake, Brad rolled over and ran one fingertip down the side of her cheek.

'Good morning, lovely Gina.' He pulled her into his arms and kissed her.

'What a nice way to say good morning,' she said, smiling at his sleep-flushed face then returning the kiss enthusiastically.

When they came up for breath a second time, she asked idly, 'What time is it? The clock's on your side.'

He rolled over and squinted at it, then sat up. 'Hell, it's half past eight! I hate to stop cuddling you, but if we don't get up quickly, breakfast will be over and we'll not be out of our rooms in time. Do you want to use the bathroom first?'

She reached for her nightdress.

He grinned and snatched it out of her hand. 'Do you have to put this on?'

She flushed. 'I've not got the sort of firm young body I want to parade in front of people.'

'I don't want a firm, bony body. It's your softness that turns me on.'

She compromised by grabbing her dressing gown and heard him chuckle as she closed the bathroom door.

After that it was such a rush getting ready to leave that she didn't have time to worry about what came next between them. Something, surely? It had felt so right last night. She'd enjoyed making love and it'd had the added bonus of banishing the demons. And what's more, her body felt great this morning, relaxed and yet full of energy.

Sorry, Mel, she thought, but I'm not going to be careful. If this is only a holiday romance, then I'm going to enjoy every second of it.

But already she was hoping it would be more than that.

–

They drove to the flat separately in their hire cars, parking in the marked bays behind the building.

'You know,' Brad said as they carried their luggage up to the first floor, 'we could give up one of the cars and save some more money that way.'

'I think we should wait a day or two before doing that. You might hate living with me and need to get away on your own.'

289

He stopped halfway up the stairs to smile warmly at her. 'I doubt it.'

It was another of those moments that took all the oxygen out of her lungs and she could only stare back at him. Neither moved for a minute or two, then he hefted his case and strode up the last few stairs, opening the door of the flat with a flourish and waiting for her to trundle her wheelie case inside first.

The place wasn't very big at all, but tiny as the kitchen was, it had the necessary equipment to cook simple meals. She went to open a cupboard and smiled at the few pieces of mismatched crockery inside, which included three red bowls, two yellow checked plates and some pink mugs with Blackpool written on them. She pulled two of the latter out straight away. 'I'm so looking forward to choosing my own food and being able to make a cup of tea whenever I want one. I thought I'd enjoy having all my meals cooked for me, but you can tire of it very quickly.'

'Me, too. We need to buy some teabags, though.'

'What I'm longing for is hearty Australian-style salads and lots of big crunchy vegetables, not fancy towers of food with no substance to them, or steak sandwiches with two curls of lettuce and half a tomato.' Her mouth watered at the thought.

'We didn't say which bedroom we'd each have.' Brad walked from one doorway to the other – all of three paces – then looked at her. 'Or may I have the pleasure of sharing your bed from now on?'

'I'd like that.' She'd have been upset if he hadn't wanted to.

She wheeled her case into the room with the double bed, grimacing at the dark, old-fashioned wardrobe, wishing the owners had painted the walls white, not sickly lilac.

He followed her in. 'Shall we go food shopping now or unpack first?'

'Shopping. I'm hanging out for a cup of good tea and we need to buy some food.'

'Lots of food. I don't mind what I eat but I need plenty of it.' He looked at her very determinedly. 'And there won't be any nonsense about halving the food bills. I eat more than anyone else in my family, and definitely more than you, from what I've seen.'

'All right. You can pay for two-thirds. I'll do the cooking, if you like.'

'We'll share it. You're not here to wait on me and anyway, I enjoy cooking.'

They found a supermarket and selected their food amicably, then returned to the flat to sort everything out.

It felt strange sharing a kitchen with someone who wasn't her husband. Gina had to stop for a moment as memories flooded back.

'You all right?'

She turned to see Brad staring at her in concern. 'Just – remembering my husband. Tom didn't cook at all, except for barbecues, but he loved to hover near the kitchen when I was working in it.'

'Helen was a brilliant cook, made the most wonderful cakes, but she didn't let me do any cooking. It was most definitely her kitchen.' His expression was sad, then he shrugged. 'When she died, I went through her cookery books and taught myself to do some of my favourite meals, but I've never tried to make cakes. Maybe I will one day.'

It was as Gina was turning to find a bowl for the fruit that they collided. His hands steadied her and he didn't let go, pulling her into his arms. The kiss started off gently, but soon she found herself melting against him, wanting him again. When he pulled away, she dragged his head back and continued the kiss because she didn't want it to stop yet.

Strange how comfortable she felt taking the lead with him, making her own needs felt.

They broke off the embrace and stood quietly, clasped in each other's arms.

'I'd forgotten.' Her voice came out husky. It was a wonder she could breathe at all, she felt so roused by his nearness.

'Forgotten what?' His voice was slow and sounded deeper than usual.

'How it feels to be thoroughly kissed.'

'I'm a bit out of practice. You're the first woman I've been attracted to since Helen died. I missed the sex, but I'm not into quick sex with strangers, never have been.'

'You and I are nearly strangers.'

'No, we're not. We're good friends already, have been from the very start. There was something sparking between us from the start.'

She couldn't deny that, with her whole body tingling merely from his touch.

–

That night, Jake heard a noise he couldn't explain. He usually slept very soundly, but since Peggy's husband had tried to snatch her from the women's centre – and he was sure that had been Hartley's intention in going there, not merely a desire to speak to Peggy as the bugger had claimed – Jake had found himself waking up at the slightest sound. Like tonight.

There it went again, a very soft sound from the rear of the house. Had he locked the side gate last night? He couldn't remember so he got up, slipping into his dressing gown and opening his bedroom door.

'Jake?' The door next to his opened.

'Shh. Don't put the light on. I thought I heard something outside. I'll just go and check.'

'I'm coming too.'

'Don't make a noise, then.'

They crept downstairs in the darkness and went into the kitchen. As he squinted through the window, Jake thought he saw something to the right, so switched on the outside lights.

Caught in their glare, Hartley froze, then turned and ran around the side of the house.

Angry, Jake went down the hallway and flung open the front door, seeing a dark figure running away down the street, feet pounding on the pavement. As he watched, Hartley tripped and fell, but was up again immediately, disappearing into the distance.

Jake didn't attempt to pursue him. Why bother? The sod had probably got his car nearby.

As if to confirm that, they heard the sound of an engine starting, Peggy came to stand beside him.

'It was Hartley, wasn't it?'

'Yes.'

'What was he doing in your back garden?'

'I don't know. Let's go and find out.'

The first row of vegetables had been deliberately stamped flat. Jake scowled down at the poor battered plants. Such a waste. And such a petty thing to do.

Peggy threaded her arm through his. 'Oh, Jake, how awful!'

'It's only a few vegetables lost. Not much harm done. I can easily plant more.'

'He knows how proud you are of your garden, how you win prizes at shows, so he was trying to hit you where it hurts most – as he did when he cut up my embroideries.'

Jake could see that the lights had come on in the next house. 'I'll just have to check the side. I must have left the gate unbolted. I'm not used to living in a fortress.'

But before Jake even reached the corner, Bob stared over the fence, holding a rounders bat in one hand and a torch in the other. 'I thought you were intruders.'

'We had one, but I chased him off,' Jake said.

'It was my ex-husband. He's damaged my brother's garden.'

Bob flashed the torch across the nearest rows. 'Spiteful bugger. You're better off without a fellow like that, lass.'

Jake watched her lift her head and straighten her spine.

'Yes, I am. That's why I'm getting a divorce.'

This time her voice didn't wobble.

It'd be worth losing a few veggies to see Peggy gain a little confidence. Sometimes nasty tricks could misfire. If this one stiffened her resolve not to return to Hartley, it was well worth a few runner beans.

He went around the side and found the gate swinging open. He'd have to remember to close and lock it from now on. It was so alien to his nature to live like this.

He resented it, resented it deeply.

Chapter 30

England

'I need to make a phone call before we get tea ready,' Brad said when they came back from a gentle stroll along the promenade. He shut himself in the unused bedroom and pulled out his mobile.

A man's voice said, 'Hello?'

Oh, damn, he'd got Stu again.

'It's Brad. Could I speak to Rosie, please? I'd like to arrange to see her.'

The silence at the other end went on for so long he began to wonder if Stu had put the phone down.

'I'll fetch her. You'll have to ask Jane about seeing her, though. I'm having nothing more to do with this.'

Brad heard a thump, as if the other man had dumped the phone somewhere, and the sound of receding footsteps. Well, at least Stu hadn't told him to go away this time.

Someone picked up the phone. 'Hello?'

'Hi, Rosie.'

'Hi, yourself.'

They chatted for a few minutes, mostly her telling him about her school day and her friend Mandy. He smiled at the way words poured out of her and encouraged her to continue by making appropriate noises and asking questions now and then.

When the torrent of words slowed down, he made his bid. 'Would you like to come out for tea with me tomorrow evening? Your father said we'd have to ask your mother.'

'He did? That's great. I'll fetch her.'

More waiting, then Jane's voice, cool, as if he was a complete stranger. Hope fading a little, Brad repeated his invitation.

'All right. You can pick her up about six. There's an Indian restaurant nearby that she likes. You won't need to book mid-week. Only I don't want her staying out late. It's a school day.'

'I'll bring her back at whatever time you say. And Jane… Can I take her out on Saturday as well? For the whole day?'

'Probably. I'd better check with Stu first, though. I'll confirm it when I see you tonight.'

She broke the connection and he sat for a minute, staring at the phone. He'd never taken to mobile phones until now, hated the way some people didn't seem able to function without them, blaring out their private affairs in the street or in shops. But his mobile was a lifeline here in England, keeping him in touch with his two Australian children and their families. They didn't seem as far away when you could phone them. He must ring them again tomorrow morning.

He wondered if he should tell Gina about Rosie but didn't want to confess that he'd been unfaithful, not at such early stage in a new relationship. He wasn't proud of his affair with Jane.

He went back into the kitchen. 'Just arranging to see one of my relatives tomorrow evening. Will you be all right if I go out?'

'Of course.'

He knew Gina would be nervous, but he couldn't see any way round that. He had to see Rosie. 'I'll make sure the lock on the door is OK. In fact, I could put a bolt on if it'd make you feel safer.'

She put up her chin, in a way he was starting to recognize. 'I'll manage, Brad. I can't be clinging to other people all the time.'

But he felt guilty about leaving her – and about not saying who he was going to meet.

–

In Poulton Jane went into the den. 'Thanks, Stu.'

He looked at her with no hint of a smile. He'd come home from school in a strange mood again, shrugging off her queries about his day.

'I'm still not happy about this,' he said at last.

'Well, you'll have to get used to it while Brad's in England.' She took a deep breath and got it over with, 'He wants to see her on Saturday as well.'

'What if we want to see her at the weekend. Don't we have any access rights now?'

'Stu, don't start.'

'I haven't started anything.'

'You've rarely wanted to do things with the family at term-time weekends before. You've always been too busy with school work.'

'What do you think pays for this house?'

She wasn't having that. 'The money both of us earn. You've not been the sole provider since the kids were small.'

He scowled at her so blackly she spun round and walked away before she said something cutting, something which might lead them into a destructive argument. She was not only tired of him taking out his disappointment on the family but also of him giving everything to his job and putting his family second – and not even a close second.

When she went into the kitchen, she couldn't settle to cooking and was relieved that no one else was there, because her thoughts were so bleak something must be reflected in her face.

She heard Stu go into the living room and peeped in to see him sitting morosely in front of the television news, pretending to read the newspaper but more often frowning into space. He hadn't come to see if she needed any help. How long since he'd pulled his weight in the house?

'Don't you have school work to do tonight?' she asked as she went in and out to set the table.

'Nope. I'm doing nothing extra for them now.'

'Right. I'm going to the meditation class.' She couldn't help adding, 'Will you be OK?'

'You won't find me drunk when you come back, if that's what you want to know.'

She rolled her eyes at her daughter as she went into the kitchen to finish cooking tea.

'Is he still angry about Brad?' Rosie whispered.

'He's angry about a lot of things. I'm going out tonight. You all right with that?'

'Yes. I'll be up in my room doing homework. I'm not staying down here with Mr Grumpy.'

Casey came trampling down the stairs. 'Is tea ready yet?'

'Soon. And it's your turn to wash up tonight, don't forget.'

'Aw, Mum! None of the other guys wash up. It's girls' stuff.'

'Don't start that again! We all dirty the dishes, so we all share the washing up. This is the twenty-first century, not the nineteenth.'

'Dad doesn't do any of it and he dirties things too.'

'He's usually working in the evenings.' She listened, knowing Stu could hear them and hoping he'd volunteer to do his share for once. But he didn't.

'He's not working in the evenings now. It's not fair if he doesn't take his turn.'

She gave Casey *the look* and he said nothing more.

It was a relief to get out of the house.

There were no interruptions to the class that night by angry husbands, and Peggy's whole face brightened up when Jane went across to sit by her, which was pleasing. Jane hated seeing any woman look as downtrodden as Peggy. If a little friendliness helped the other woman build a new life, she was happy to offer it.

Heaven knows, she could do with a friend herself at the moment.

As she drove home, Jane noticed a white car with a battered front wing in her rear view mirror. It clung to her tail like a leech, even turning into her street after her, though it was a dead end.

When she parked on the drive the other car came to a halt across the road, its engine idling. She couldn't see the number plate and was reluctant to go out on to the street to look at it.

Anyway, why would someone want to follow her? It was probably just someone who'd lost his way.

Only if so, why was the driver still sitting there? And why was he staring at her? She could see quite clearly in the light of the street lamp the paler blur of a face turned towards her house.

Even as she watched, the car started moving and drove slowly out of the street, but she couldn't shake off her conviction that its driver had been following her.

There was only one person she could think of who might want to annoy her. Peggy's husband had threatened her.

Oh, no! Please, not that! She didn't need any more problems at the moment.

–

When Brad had left to meet his relatives, Gina hesitated, then placed a chair under the door handle. She hated being so cowardly, but at least she hadn't tried to stop Brad going out. She looked at her watch and did a quick calculation. Too late to call home now. Her Aussie family would be in bed now. She switched on the television but there didn't seem to be any programmes worth watching.

Every few minutes she glanced at the door to check that the chair was still in place.

'You're going to have to snap out of this, Gina Porter!' she said aloud. But the sound of her own voice then the silence that followed only seemed to add to her nervousness.

In the end she left the bedroom light on and turned off the one in the living room, going to stand by the window and stare down at the people walking past. Bridie had said she spent a lot of time doing this, which had seemed sad. But it did make you feel more connected with the world when you were on your own.

After a while she drew the curtains, put the light on again and got out the papers about her father's family, studying them one by one. Tomorrow, she vowed, she'd go and see her relatives. Lou had suggested it might be better to contact her aunt Peggy during the daytime when her husband would be at work. The grimace that had accompanied the words 'Uncle Hartley' spoke volumes about the girl's feelings about him.

Just before nine thirty she heard footsteps coming up the stairs and tensed. But Brad called out before he even tried to open the door, so she had time to snatch the chair away.

She flung herself into his arms without thinking.

'Was it bad being on your own?' he asked, stroking her hair.

'Not good, but I coped.'

'Hopefully your fears will gradually subside. They should vanish completely when you return to your own home in Australia.'

She was glad her face was buried in his chest and he couldn't see her expression. The way he'd said that seemed to make very clear the fact that she'd be going home alone. She asked how his evening had been, astonished to see a guarded expression on his face, which was so unlike him.

'You don't need to tell me if you don't want,' she added sharply.

'I'm still trying to come to terms with it all. I'll tell you the details later. Tonight my relative and I went out to an Indian restaurant and we just – talked. Getting to know one another. You know how it is.'

'No, I don't know. But I've decided that tomorrow I'm going to try to contact my own relatives, so maybe I'll find out what it's like. I'm well over the jet lag now so I hope I'll be able to talk sense. Though what they'll think of this, I don't know.' For a moment her hand went up to the bruise on her cheek.

'Don't you know them at all?'

'I didn't even know I had relatives in England until my father died. I may not get on with them, or them with me, but it's worth a go, don't you think?'

'Definitely. Family is what matters most in the world.' He went and picked up the little plastic box he'd put on the table, handing it to her with a little bow. 'I brought you back some gulab jamun.' He saw her puzzled look and opened the box to display the contents. 'It's an Indian dessert, very sweet and sticky – also very delicious.'

She looked at two balls of what looked like dark brown sticky cake, sitting in syrup, and probably containing a million calories. 'You'll have one with me?'

As they sat down to eat and chat, she felt pleased that he'd not forgotten her. And the dessert was delicious.

She and Tom had never tried Indian food because he'd disliked spicy food. It was only after his death that Lexie had started taking her to restaurants with more exotic cuisines.

Brad smiled at her as they cleared up their supper things. 'It was lovely coming back to you, not to an empty room.' After they'd finished, he drew her into his arms and said in a low voice, 'I'm still hungry, though.'

'Me, too.' She was amazed at herself for falling into bed with him so quickly... falling in love, too. Oh, no! She mustn't expect anything permanent. Things had changed since her youth.

But the worries about leaving herself vulnerable all vanished when he touched her. She felt so right with him, had done from the start.

-

The following morning Gina woke first and slid carefully out of the bed, going to make a mug of tea and staring down at the promenade as she drank it.

When Brad joined her a short time later, she took a deep breath and said, 'I need to go out on my own today. It's time I contacted my English family.'

'Did you ring them last night?'

'No. I want to surprise them. They don't know I'm coming.' She hesitated, then explained in more detail about her father's papers and the second marriage.

Brad was frowning now. 'Surely it'd be better to get their phone numbers and ring them first?'

'I don't want to give them a chance to refuse. At least this way I'll see them, even if they refuse to have anything to do with me afterwards. But Lou doesn't think her granddad will refuse to see me.'

'So you'll go and visit him first?'

'No. I'm going to my sister's. Surely I'll stand more chance of being accepted by another woman? I can't tell you how much I've always wished I had a sister.'

'I could come with you. I don't mind sitting in the car and leaving you to it.'

She shook her head. 'Thank you, but I'd rather do this on my own.'

So after they'd cleared up the breakfast things, she got ready, staring at herself in the mirror and wondering what they'd think of her. She looked nice, at least she thought she did. This was a favourite skirt and top that reminded her of happy times. Even the weather was smiling on her, she thought, as she went down to her hire car.

She turned the key in the ignition and there was a click then absolute silence. Getting out, she went to look under the bonnet. She wasn't very good mechanically but had learned to check battery leads, at least, and to look for leaks in the water hoses.

But she could see nothing wrong with any of those.

'Damn!' She got her handbag and went back up to the flat, catching Brad on the point of going out.

'Something wrong?'

'The car won't start. I'll have to ring the hire company. I've got the info somewhere.'

'Why don't you let me take you? Ring the company before you go, but tell them you won't be home till later this afternoon.'

She hesitated, but it seemed that fate wanted him to go with her. 'Thank you.'

'I'll keep out of it, stay in the car.'

'I'd appreciate that.'

Her sister's house wasn't hard to find. It was on the outskirts of Poulton, a detached, red-brick residence located in a cul-de-sac of similar executive dwellings. The garden looked rigidly neat and there were two bottles of milk standing on the front doorstep in the full sunlight. Why hadn't someone taken them in?

Gina braced herself and rang the doorbell. She didn't know what she was going to say, would just have to play things by ear.

To her disappointment, a man opened the door, a man who hadn't shaved for a couple of days and whose eyes were red-rimmed and angry.

'Didn't you see the 'No hawkers' sign?'

'I'm not selling anything. I came to see Peggy Wilkes.'

'Well, she's not at home, so you bloody well can't.'

'Could you tell me when she'll be back? I've come all the way from Australia to find her.'

He'd been turning to go back inside, but at her words he spun round. 'Why the hell would anyone come from Australia to see Peggy?'

Gina hesitated. She didn't want to tell her business to strangers and she didn't like the looks of this man, but if he was her brother-in-law he'd find out soon enough. 'I believe she's my half-sister.'

He stared at her so fixedly she nearly turned tail and fled.

'Her father did run away to Australia with some whoring husband-stealer.'

Gina gasped. 'Don't you speak about my mother like that! You know nothing of what happened!'

'Oh, don't I? You should have heard Peggy's mother on the subject.'

'Just tell me when your wife will be back, please.'

He reached out to grab her arm. 'Come inside. We'll phone her up together. I'm sure she'll come running when she hears who you are. What did you say your name was?'

Suddenly all Gina's instincts told her to get out. Early in the day as it was, he was unsteady on his feet. He must have been drinking. She tried to pull away, but he had hold of her arm and wouldn't let go.

'Oh, no, you don't!' he said harshly. 'You want to see Peggy and so do I. You're my ace in the hole and you're coming inside to wait for her.'

Gina screamed for Brad, struggling to get away. She couldn't believe this was happening twice in a week, but she was angry about it this time rather than terrified, kicking out at him and scraping her shoe hard down his shins.

Abruptly Hartley let go of her and she would have fallen if someone hadn't caught her. 'Brad! Oh, thank goodness!'

'What the hell do you think you're doing?' Brad demanded, pushing Gina behind him.

'Inviting my sister-in-law inside,' Hartley said, clutching the door post. 'Sorry. Maybe I was a bit over-enthusiastic. But I'm sure my wife will be delighted to see her.'

'Where is your wife?'

'She's out. I was going to phone her.'

'He was going to keep me here to fetch her back,' Gina said. 'And I think he's drunk. He's slurring his words.' She rubbed her arm where he'd gripped her tightly, sure it'd be bruised.

'Let's go back to the car, Gina.' Brad moved backwards along the path, keeping an eye on the man, who seemed to be having a little trouble staying upright.

'At least tell me where she can find you,' he called after them. 'I'm sorry if I frightened you. I'm a bit upset today. It won't happen again.'

'You won't get the chance to assault her again,' Brad said grimly. 'For two pins I'd go and lay a complaint against you with the police.'

The other man's face turned chalk white and he took a hasty step backwards, slamming the door shut.

Brad hurried back to the car and slid in beside Gina. 'Are you all right? He didn't hurt you?'

'He probably bruised my arm where he grabbed me but apart from that I'm fine.'

His eyes were searching her face. 'After what you've been through...'

'I think this incident has had the opposite effect on me. It's not made me feel worse, it's made me too angry for that. Who the hell does he think he is? And where's my sister? He said she was out, that he'd have to phone her. You don't suppose she's left him? Because of the drinking. I couldn't smell any booze but he was definitely unsteady on his feet.' Gina shook her head in bafflement. 'I'm certainly meeting some delightful people in England, aren't I?'

'No. But I am.' Brad kissed her lightly on the cheek and started up the engine. 'Where to now, milady?'

'My brother's house. Maybe he'll know where Peggy is.'

Inside the house, Hartley leaned against the wall, feeling sick and dizzy. He didn't know what was wrong with him today, had been feeling strange ever since he got up. And left leg and arm were slightly numb. He rubbed them with his right hand, but it didn't seem to help. He must have slept in an awkward position.

He stumbled along to the kitchen, which looked dreadful.

'You're coming home, you bitch,' he muttered and went to the fridge for some milk, staring at it angrily when there was none.

In the end he left the tea brewing in the teapot and went into the living room, supporting himself on pieces of furniture.

He'd have a nap. That'd make him feel better.

Then he'd work out a way to get Peggy back.

–

Brad and Gina consulted the satnav again and drove to Jake's house.

'I'm coming to the door with you this time,' he insisted.

'All right. But let me do the talking, if you don't mind.'

This house was much smaller, semi-detached and old-fashioned in appearance. The street didn't look nearly as affluent as her sister's did.

Taking a deep breath, Gina knocked on the front door. The man who answered it looked so much like her father that she was shocked rigid and for a moment, she couldn't speak.

'Are you all right?' he asked.

'Sorry. I was just a bit startled. You look so like Dad.'

He went very still and the smile vanished from his face.

'I'm your half-sister, Gina. I've come from Australia to see you,' she went on, desperate to make him talk to her.

A voice spoke from behind him. 'Then you should have found out first whether we wanted to see you or not – and we don't!'

The woman who had come up the hall behind him looked much older than he did. Gina stared at her. 'Are you – Peggy?'

'I'm nothing to you,' she said harshly. 'Jake, come back inside.'

'Just a minute, love. You go and put the kettle on. I'll be with you in a minute.' He turned back to Gina. 'Sorry. Peggy's never got over our father running off with your mother and she's in a bit of a fragile state at the moment. I don't want to upset her.'

With an apologetic shake of the head, he shut the door in her face.

Gina stared at it in shock then burst into tears and ran back to the car, with Brad following.

—

From behind the door Jake heard her crying and felt terrible.

Peggy's voice sounded sharply from the kitchen. 'Jake!'

He looked from one to the other, torn, not wanting to hurt either of them, but the crying seemed to echo in his ears and in the end he ran back to the front door to call his Australian sister back.

But the car was driving away by the time he got to the gate and it disappeared around the corner.

Feeling like the greatest villain unhung, he walked slowly back to the house.

Peggy was sitting in the kitchen. 'You went after her,' she said accusingly.

'Aye, well, I was too late.'

'Good.'

And Jake, normally the most peaceful of men, lost his temper. 'How can you say that? She was crying. You've been hurt yourself. You know what it's like. I wish I hadn't listened to you, you've so little compassion in you. I'm ashamed of myself, Peggy, really ashamed. And I don't even know where she's staying, so I can't go after her.'

It was Peggy's turn to cry, but Jake didn't feel like comforting her and went out into the back garden, slamming the door behind him.

How could he find that poor woman and apologize?

Chapter 31

England

By the time they got back to the flat Gina had stopped crying, but her expression was so lost and sad, Brad could have thumped her bloody brother for doing this to her.

'We'll go out tonight, take our minds off this. I'll see if there's a show we can go to or a decent restaurant.'

She shook her head. 'Thanks for the thought, but I'm not a child to be comforted by such things. This is too important to me.'

'Then what can I do to help you?'

'Nothing. I have to face the fact that they don't want to meet me. It was always on the cards. I just persuaded myself they'd give me a chance if I turned up in person.'

'I hate to see you so unhappy.'

'I'll get over it.'

'Do you want me to leave you on your own?'

She gave him a grateful look. 'For a while, if you don't mind. It's such a beautiful day, I'm sure you'd enjoy a long walk.'

Dismissed, he could do nothing but get ready and go out.

Gina was beyond tears now. She went to sit by the window but saw little of what was happening outside as she tried to work out if she could have done anything better. Should she have written to Jake and Peggy first? No. They'd have refused to meet her then she'd not even have seen them. And she was glad that she'd at least done that. Goodness, Jake had looked so like her father.

She was so lost in thought that she didn't at first realize someone had knocked on the door. She went to open it, then hesitated and called out, 'Who is it?'

'Me. Bridie.'

Gina flung the door open. 'Come in! I'm so glad to see you. How was your check-up?'

'Fine.' Bridie moved forward then stopped to study her, eyes narrowed. 'You've been crying. What's wrong.'

'Oh, dear, you're always catching me at a bad moment, but Bridie, I really need some advice.'

'Then put that kettle on and we'll discuss it over a cup of tea. I'm parched.'

'Have you walked from the hotel?'

'Of course I have. I'm not yet in my dotage. Use it or lose it applies to all ages and activities.'

'How was your friend?' Even before she replied, Gina saw a spasm of sadness cross Bridie's face.

'She's not able to cope on her own now so I didn't stay for my usual week. She's going into an aged care facility and is absolutely dreading it. I would too. I'm so lucky that I have better health than her, not to mention the money to live in the style I choose. Though I am considering finding an upmarket residential home instead of the hotel here. I'd like a little more space and a garden to walk in. I can always go back into a hotel if it doesn't work out.'

Her friend's thin elderly voice was soothing and as Gina made the tea, she could feel herself relaxing.

When they'd both got a cup of tea and biscuit in front of them, Bridie took a few sips and said simply, 'Now tell me what's wrong, dear.'

Gina explained everything, her voice catching as she explained exactly what had brought her to England. When she faltered to a halt, she looked up and saw that Bridie's eyes were also brimming with tears. 'Oh, no! I shouldn't have told you. You've enough troubles of your own.'

Bridie reached out and took hold of Gina's hand. 'I'm glad you told me, more than you could ever have realized.' She gave a smile that had both warmth and sadness in it then said quietly, 'My surname may be Shapley now, but I was born Bridget Everett.' She waited, head cocked to one side.

Gina stared at her in shock. 'Then that means – are you my father's sister… my aunt?'

'I am indeed. Isn't it wonderful that fate has brought us together?' Bridie leaned forward to plant a kiss on her niece's cheek, then sat back and studied her face. 'No wonder you reminded me of my sister. I received a letter from my brother after he left England, explaining why he'd run away and wishing me well. It didn't have a return address. That was the last I heard from him.'

'I think Mum and Dad must have decided to cut all ties with their families. They never told me about my English relatives or even that Dad had been married before.'

'I met your mother before they left and I liked her. I was less keen on his first wife, who was sharp and suspicious in her ways, no softness in her. I always suspected that Daniel wouldn't have married her if he hadn't got her in trouble. But then she had another child the year after, so he was well and truly trapped.'

Bridie was tapping her fingers on the table now, her brow creased in thought. 'I'm surprised that Jake treated you so badly yesterday, though. He's usually much kinder and fairer to people. Peggy's a washed-out copy of her mother, very inept and lets that ghastly husband bully her. I've not seen her for years because I can't stand him.'

Gina was smiling now, joy singing through her as it all began to sink in. 'Well, at least I've met one relative over here, as well as Lou in Australia. Isn't it wonderful? You are – glad about it?'

'Of course I am. So glad that I'd like to invite you and Brad to have dinner with me in the restaurant at the hotel tonight to celebrate. And come in a taxi, because it calls for good champagne.' She looked at the clock. 'And now, I'd better be getting back to the hotel. I do need an afternoon nap these days, I'm afraid.'

'I'd drive you, but my hire car won't start.'

'It's all right. I'll call a taxi.' She pulled a phone out of her handbag. 'So useful, this little gadget, but I have trouble with the tiny keypad. They're not designed for older eyes.' Holding it at arm's length and squinting slightly, she pressed a pre-set number and ordered a taxi.

When it arrived, Gina escorted her downstairs and then went back up again, feeling happy. Yes, this did call for a champagne celebration. She wished Brad would come back, so that she could share her good news.

When she got into the flat a phone was ringing and she saw Brad's mobile on the end of the kitchen counter. Without thinking she picked it up. 'Hello?'

A woman's voice asked, 'Is Brad there?'

'No, he's out.'

'Oh. Can I ask who you are? I thought he was in England on his own.'

'I'm a… friend.'

Silence, then, 'Well, will you tell him Jane called. I'm another friend of his, a very old friend, and I need to speak to him urgently and privately. Have you got something to take down my mobile number with?'

Gina picked up a pen and dragged the newspaper towards her for lack of a notepad. 'Yes.'

After she'd switched off the phone, she pushed it away from her, wishing she hadn't picked it up. Who was this Jane? And why had Brad pretended to be here to see relatives? The woman had said she was a friend. How close a friend? If Gina wasn't mistaken there'd been resentment in the other's voice. Surely he wasn't stringing two women along?

–

A few minutes later there were footsteps on the stairs and Brad called out before unlocking the door.

Gina busied herself getting him a mug of tea as she told him about Bridie. After that she fell silent.

'There's something else, isn't there? What's wrong?' He saw her move uneasily and bite her lip. Already he could tell how she was feeling from her body language, because she hadn't a sneaky bone in her body.

She hesitated, then told him about answering his mobile. 'I shouldn't have but I was so happy I wasn't thinking straight.' She explained about her conversation with Jane. 'You didn't tell her you were with someone and that seemed to upset her. How close a friend is she exactly?'

His heart sank. He'd rather have explained this later, when they knew one another better. He didn't feel proud of having been unfaithful and didn't want to do anything to risk losing Gina. As he looked at her, he realized how much he felt about her.

'It's fine if you don't want to tell me, Brad. I have no right to ask. We're just – holiday friends, you and I.'

She turned away and he couldn't bear it. He walked round the table and put his arms round her. 'I hope we're more than mere holiday friends, Gina.'

She looked up at him uncertainly. 'Do you?'

'Oh, yes. But it's time to explain exactly why I'm here, which will also explain who Jane is.'

'You don't have to.'

'I do. I want us – you and me – to stay together and, well, see how things go, so I need to be honest with you.'

He could see the uncertainty still clouding her lovely eyes and tossed caution to the winds. 'Oh, dammit, Gina, haven't you realized that I've fallen in love with you? I didn't mean to and it's happened so quickly it's taken me by surprise. I'm out of practice at romancing someone, but I'm hoping…'

Her smile lit up her whole face. 'Oh, Brad.' Then she added softly, 'I've fallen in love with you, too. Only I didn't dare hope for anything. I got such a scolding from my daughter about holiday romances and being careful.'

So of course he had to kiss her and as one thing led to another, they wound up in bed, touching, caressing, reinforcing what they'd said in the way lovers always have.

Lying there afterwards, with Gina nestled in his arms, Brad braced himself to make his confession. 'I still have to tell you why I'm here and I don't come out of it too well, I'm afraid.'

She listened intently as he stumbled through the tale of Rosie and Jane. When he'd finished, he waited for her to say something, but she didn't speak for so long he began to worry.

'Were you ever unfaithful again?'

'No. I'm not normally a cheat. And anyway, it was too costly emotionally. It took me ages to recover. I think I'm very old-fashioned about such things, can't take sex and love casually.'

'And how do you feel about Jane?'

'I don't want to hurt her, but there's nothing left of the old flame between us, I promise you. We're neither of us the same people we were then and anyway, she has a husband. But there's Rosie, you see. My – our daughter.'

'Jane sounded… as if she still cared for you.'

He pulled away and held her at arm's length, shocked rigid. 'You can't mean that! I haven't given her any encouragement, I promise you. I only wanted to see Rosie. In fact, I don't think I've even been alone with Jane this time, except when I was standing on the doorstep. No, you must be mistaken.'

'I could be, I suppose.' Gina glanced at her watch, lying beside the bed. 'Oh dear, we'd better get ready for our celebration meal with Bridie now.'

'I'd rather lie here and cuddle you.'

Smiling, she pressed a kiss on the part of him nearest to her, which happened to be his bare shoulder, and swung her legs out of bed. 'Come on. We have to celebrate.'

As the evening passed, he watched Gina smile and show affection to Bridie – which wasn't hard to do, he really liked the older woman himself. He wanted her to show the same unalloyed affection for him, as well. But there was still a slight constraint between them that had not been there before he told her about Jane. He could sense it and he rather thought Bridie had noticed it, too.

It took him a long time to get to sleep, he was so worried that Gina might not be able to trust him now.

–

When her niece and Brad had left the hotel, Bridie stayed up for a while, sipping a glass of her favourite cognac and worrying. Something was not quite right between those two, she could tell it. There had been a hint of anxiety in the way Brad watched Gina. What had caused that?

She'd arranged for Gina to come to tea on her own the following day on the excuse of showing her some family photos. She'd do that, of course she would, but she wanted to use the occasion for something else as well. Glancing at her watch, she wondered if her nephew would be in bed yet. Only one way to find out. She picked up the phone and dialled his number, delighted when he answered almost immediately.

'Jake? Bridie here. I need to see you about something.'

'I'm a bit busy at the moment. How about one day next week?'

'Tomorrow. It's extremely important or I wouldn't ask.'

He sighed. 'Very well.'

'Three o'clock sharp. Don't let me down or I'll come and hunt you out.'

'If it's that important I'll be there. Still in the same hotel?'

'Of course. And don't be late.' Smiling, she put down the phone.

There had been enough feuds in the family. Time to end them once and for all. It didn't matter which side of the globe you lived on, family connections mattered.

Chapter 32

England

Jake stared at the clock. He had to stay up till midnight if he was to be sure of catching Lou in Australia at a reasonable hour, and he wasn't a late night person.

Peggy came in from the kitchen. 'Who was that?'

'Aunt Bridie.'

She grimaced. 'What does she want?'

'She didn't say but she insisted on seeing me tomorrow, so I'm going over for tea at her hotel.'

'Did you tell her about me leaving Hartley?'

'No. I'll tell her when I get there. I don't know what time I'll be back. I may stay and have a meal with her.'

'Oh dear. I've got my meditation class tomorrow evening and I'm supposed to be seeing Gillah in the afternoon.'

'Well, I can drop you off to see Gillah, but you'll have to get back here under your own steam. I'll give you the money for taxis.'

'I feel safer when you take me.'

'I can't always be available, Peggy.' He wasn't going to set a pattern of being at her beck and call, was already chafing at the way she hovered near him whenever he was inside the house. And his allotment had been very neglected since Peggy came to live with him. He was missing the circle of friends he'd made there.

His sister would be perfectly safe at the centre. More than anything, he wanted to put things right with his half-sister – if he could. But how did you find a woman whom you only knew as Gina in a big city like Blackpool?

You're still upset, aren't you?' Peggy asked. 'About her?'

'You mean our sister? Yes, I am. It was wrong of me to turn her away, especially when she'd come so far to see us.' He stopped to picture the woman he'd seen so briefly. 'She had a nice face, but I didn't even give her a chance. I feel dreadful about that.'

Peggy was silent, staring down at her hands, but she looked up quickly at his next words.

'I'm going to try to find out what her surname is and where she's staying, then I'll go and see her. She met Lou in Australia, so Lou may know how to contact her, or at least how to contact her daughters. I'm going to ring my little lass later tonight. Eh, old age can make you selfish and crotchety sometimes.'

'You're the least selfish person I know.'

'Thanks for the compliment, love, but I'm still ashamed of what I did today. It was such a shock, though, hearing her say she was my sister. I don't know… perhaps I need to be shaken out of my comfortable rut, perhaps we all do when we get to a certain age. Peggy, if I find her… will you meet her too? Give her a chance, at least?'

He watched sadly as his sister's face closed up, then had an inspiration. 'Why don't you ask Gillah about it?'

'I've too many other things to sort out. This woman is the least of my worries. Half-sister or not, she's a stranger to me and quite frankly, I'd be happy for her to stay a stranger.'

'Promise me you'll talk to Gillah about her.'

Peggy's shoulders slumped and she looked at him pleadingly.

'I really want you to do that for me. Promise.'

'Oh, very well, I promise. But Gillah won't make me change my mind. It'd be disloyal to our mother.'

'Mum never did get over Dad leaving her, but I don't think it was because she loved him. I think she made such a fuss because she felt humiliated. I can remember them arguing many a time and we both know how inflexible she could be if you didn't do things exactly her way.'

'You never said that before!'

'I've thought it, though. I heard him asking her for a divorce several times and her refusing, so he did try to do the right thing.'

'Well, he never tried to contact us afterwards. He could at least have written.'

'I've never understood that, either. But it was years ago and who knows what his new life was like? And he did try to contact me once a few months ago, only I've not opened the letter. Maybe I ought to now. Anyway, about you – it's the here and now that matters and if you're going to change your life, my lass, maybe you should get rid of some of your old prejudices. But you've promised me you'll speak to Gillah and I know you won't go back on your word.'

Peggy scowled at him and turned to watch the television, not saying much from then on.

The clock hands seemed to be moving very slowly tonight. He'd rather have been in the small bedroom, playing with his computer, but he felt he had to keep Peggy company in the evenings.

At last the clock fingers moved into position and he went to get the phone. 'I reckon I could ring Lou now. It'll be early morning there, but she usually gets up with the birds.'

But though he got through to Australia easily enough, there was no answer. After a while, voice mail clicked in, so he left a message, explaining his problem. He waited up for a while longer, hoping Lou would call him back, but she didn't.

As he lay in bed, he racked his brain but couldn't think of any other way of finding out where his half-sister was staying. What could he have been thinking of to turn her away?

-

The next day Gina was glad that sorting out her hire car left her little time for thought about herself and Brad. She felt a little awkward with him, not a lot, but enough to make her stand back from a total sharing of confidences and intimacies. She couldn't help it, she absolutely hated infidelity. And look how Brad's one affair had bounced back at him years later. It just proved that it wasn't worth it.

If it was his one affair.

She pressed one hand to her breast as this thought slid into her mind yet again. She wanted very much to trust him, but felt she needed time to get to know him better. After all, they'd rushed headlong into this relationship. She smiled. Like a pair of randy teenagers. She'd never thought she'd feel like this again.

It wouldn't hurt for them to slow down a little.

She took him for a drive in her new hire car to test it out, pleased that it was as easy to drive as the first one. They parked for a while, walking along the sea front at St Anne's, which was much more restrained and elegant than Blackpool, and buying a pot of tea and some scones for Brad in a little café.

It occurred to her at one stage that she'd hardly thought about the mugging today, what with her happiness about finding her aunt and her worries about Brad. She smiled wryly. It took one major crisis to dispel the after-effects of another, it seemed. As she remembered the attack, however, a little shiver ran down her spine. She caught Brad watching her as if he understood how she was feeling.

'You all right, Gina?'

She caught his hand for a moment. 'Yes. Just remembering. But I'm getting better every day.'

'I can see that.'

Her spirits lifted a little as she realized she hadn't even had to explain to him. Surely with this easy communication between them she'd soon get over her worries about him?

When it came time to go for afternoon tea with Bridie, she felt excited at the thought of seeing the family photographs and learning more about her father's family. She intended to find her mother's family one day, but might have to employ that detective to do so. Her mother had always said she had no close family left and there had been no clues among her father's things.

'You're not walking to the hotel, surely?' Brad asked as she got ready.

She shuddered. 'No. I thought I'd drive.'

'Parking isn't easy this close to the centre of town. You might have to use that multi-storey car park and those places can be a bit scary.'

She shivered at the mere thought. It was irrational since she'd been mugged in the open air, but she didn't like the thought of going into the gloom of a car park alone. 'You're right.'

'Look, I can drive you to the hotel and pick you up afterwards. You can ring me when you're ready to come back.'

She hesitated then nodded. She would definitely feel better going with him.

When they got into the car, he didn't start it at once, but began tracing his forefinger to and fro across the top of the steering wheel. 'Gina… I know you're upset about what I once did, about Rosie, and I'm sorry for that. Please don't let it come between us permanently.'

She placed her hand over his and gave it a little squeeze. 'No, I won't. But it's made me realize that we do need time to get to know one another. We're too old to rush heedlessly into a relationship.'

That made sense, didn't it, she told herself? But she could see a downturn to his lips as he started the car and drove off. And if she was honest with herself, she had been enjoying rushing heedlessly into a relationship. It had made her feel young again. And anyway, she did love him, she was sure of that.

So why did she feel she had to hold back now? She didn't know, hadn't felt sure of anything since her own brother had refused even to speak to her and shut the door in her face. That had hurt so much, more than she could put into words… to anyone.

Just before she got out of the car, she turned to Brad. 'My emotions are in a turmoil at the moment, for all sorts of reasons, not just about us. Please bear with me.'

His face lit up and that made her feel better. He had the most gorgeous smile.

–

Bridie had deliberately told Jake to come earlier than Gina. She sat him down and gave him one of her severe stares. He always joked that when she looked at him like that he didn't dare do anything but listen meekly and say yes to whatever she wanted.

'I've something to tell you, Jake, something very important.'

'I've got news for you too, Aunt Bridie. But you go first.'

'Did you know you had a half-sister?'

He stared for a moment then leaned forward. 'Yes. Lou met her in Australia. How did you find out?'

'I gather you sent the poor woman away with a flea in her ear.'

'You've spoken to her?'

She nodded, keeping her expression disapproving.

'You – know where she is?'

'Yes.'

He closed his eyes for a moment, then let out a great sigh. 'What a relief! I changed my mind almost immediately but when I ran outside, she'd driven away. And I didn't even know her surname. I felt dreadful about hurting her like that, wanted to say I was sorry, give her a chance.'

Bridie leaned back, relaxing a little. 'Ah. I'm glad I wasn't mistaken in you, Jake. Actually, she's coming to tea with us in half an hour, so you can do all that.'

He gaped at her. 'How did she find you? Or did you find her?'

'We met and became friends without knowing we were related. I really like her.'

'What's her surname?'

'Porter. But I'd better warn you that she's rather fragile at the moment. She was mugged a few days ago and it's left her jumpy.'

He stared at her in horror. 'And I sent her away on top of all that!'

Bridie hid her satisfaction at his reaction and tried to keep her expression stern. She wasn't forgiving him completely till she saw how he got on with Gina.

After that she'd deal with Peggy. Her niece must be persuaded to give Gina a chance as well, whatever that ghastly husband of hers said.

–

Peggy followed Gillah into the cosy little room, her promise to Jake weighing heavily on her mind.

Of course her counsellor noticed. 'Something wrong?'

Peggy explained about her half-sister.

'And you turned her away after she'd come ten thousand miles to see you?'

Peggy stared down at her clasped hands and waited for a tirade, but there was only silence and when she looked up, Gillah's face showed only an attentive calmness as she waited for an answer.

'Yes.'

'Did she seem upset?'

'She cried.' Peggy could feel tears welling in her own eyes suddenly. 'I've been trying not to think about that, but she sobbed so loudly as she walked away that I could hear her even from the kitchen.'

'It must have taken a lot of courage to come and face you two.'

Peggy mopped her eyes with a tissue then reached for another one as the tears continued to flow. 'I suppose I ought to agree to meet her? If Jake finds her, that is.'

'That's up to you. But you've been hurt yourself and you know how it feels...'

After the hour ended, Peggy went to wait in reception for a taxi. She kept her eyes resolutely down, not wanting anyone to see how reddened they were.

And when she got home she wept again. She'd not known she had so many tears inside her. She hated the thought that she'd been cruel to someone, really hated it.

The phone rang and she picked it up quickly, in case it was Jake. But it was her daughter.

'Mum, I've just had Dad on the phone. He was crying. Dad! Don't you think this has gone on for long enough? Isn't it time you went back to him?'

'I'm not going back to him. I'm getting a divorce.'

'I can't believe I'm hearing this. Mum, he can't manage without you. He's useless in the house.' There was a minute's silence, then Cheryl added in a softer tone, 'Won't you at least see him and talk to him? He's really sorry he's upset you.'

'I can't believe he'll change, whatever I say or do.'

'Oh, sod. They've just called a special meeting here. I have to go. I'll ring you this evening.'

'I'll not be here.'

But the phone was buzzing in Peggy's ears. Was Hartley really upset about her leaving him? Or was he upset about losing his house slave? The latter, she was sure. She'd spent a lot of time going over what her life had been like the past few years, couldn't believe how she'd waited on her husband hand and foot. And how unloving he'd been.

When was the last time Hartley had made her a cup of tea? Or even offered to? Or said a kind word? Or noticed how she was feeling?

She couldn't remember.

But if he was truly remorseful, promised to be kinder – wouldn't life be easier if she went back to him? It was going to be so hard to build a new life on her own.

How could you know what was best?

–

When Bridie opened the door to her at the hotel, the two women embraced and then Gina saw a movement at the other side of the room. She gasped as she recognized the man standing by the window.

'Come and meet your brother,' Bridie said, 'properly this time.'

Gina hung back. 'He doesn't want to—'

Bridie put an arm round her. 'Give him another chance, dear.'

Jake moved forward quickly. 'I was a fool yesterday. I realized that soon after as I'd closed the door and ran out to stop you, but you'd driven away.' He held out his hand. 'I'm glad to meet you, Gina, truly I am.'

She was overwhelmed and her voice wobbled as she took the hand and tried to speak. But the words choked her and she could only shake her head blindly.

'Come and sit by me on the sofa, then, and tell me about yourself – and how you got on with our Lou.'

Gina smiled involuntarily at the thought of her niece. 'She's such a delightful girl. We all liked her.' After that it grew easier.

'Jake, what are we going to do about Peggy?' Bridie asked a bit later. 'She really ought to be part of this reunion.'

He sighed. 'She's not thinking clearly at the moment. She's just left her husband.'

'Oh, good! I never did like him.'

He gave her a wry smile. 'Me neither. Gina, why don't you come and have lunch with us tomorrow? Peggy will be a bit stiff and distant, but if you can ignore that, we'll make a start on mending things between us.'

'I'd love to come.'

'You too, Aunt Bridie?'

She shook her head. 'I've got a luncheon engagement I don't want to break tomorrow.' She fetched some old photo albums from the bedroom. 'Now, come and sit at the table. We've got time to go through a few of these with Gina.'

It was wonderful seeing her father as a boy and Gina lingered over those photos in particular, her fingers tracing his beloved features. 'We grew very close after Mum died, and my husband was killed.'

'I could scan these into my computer for you,' Jake offered. 'Then you'd have your own copies.'

'Would you do that?'

'Of course. You're family. You have a right to them.'

Those words made Gina feel as if her cup was over-flowing with joy. Family. Other generations. Passing down the family lore through the photos. So much that she'd never had before.

Even for those who knew about their families, the distance from Australia made it hard to keep in touch properly. For her it had been a tunnel without any light at the far end.

–

As Jane drove to the Wellness Centre that evening, she realized she was being followed again by the white car. It was unmistakable with that battered front wing. This time she could see the number plate quite clearly, so repeated it to herself several times. When she turned into the centre, the other car drove past.

After she'd parked she went back to the car park entrance and looked up and down the street. The white car wasn't anywhere in sight. Perhaps it hadn't been following her. Perhaps it was just a coincidence and it was someone who lived in the area who had been going in the same direction as her twice. Still, you couldn't be too careful, so she wrote the car number down on a scrap of paper and shoved it into her handbag.

A taxi drew up as she was about to go into the centre and when she saw Peggy get out, she stopped to wait.

'My brother usually brings me.' Peggy looked round as if she was worried her husband might be lurking nearby. 'But he's had to go and see our aunt in Blackpool.'

'I can give you a lift home afterwards, if you like.'

'I don't want to be a nuisance. I can get a taxi.'

'It's no trouble. Honestly. Come on, we don't want to be late.'

–

When they were driving away from the centre after the class, the white car fell in behind them.

'Have a quick look behind, will you?' Jane asked. 'Do you recognize that car.'

Peggy did as she asked and let out a muffled shriek. 'It's my husband! What am I going to do if Jake's not home yet?'

'If he's not there, I'll take you home with me and you can ring your brother later to fetch you.'

'Thank you. You must think I'm very silly, but—'

'I don't think you're silly at all. Don't forget that I've met your husband. He seems – unbalanced.' Full of suppressed violence, actually, but she wasn't going to say that. The thought that he was the one following them made her shiver.

But when they got to Jake's house, there were lights on inside and his car was parked in the drive so she stopped. The other car overtook them, slowing down so that the driver was right next to them. The look the driver gave them made her shiver again.

Peggy whimpered at the sight of her husband's glaring face, separated from her only by the car windows, and didn't move until he'd driven away.

Jane looked sideways. 'Has he always been so full of anger?'

'No. But he's never been easy to live with.'

Jane waited until the other woman had gone into the house then drove home.

She half-expected the car to appear behind her again. It didn't, but the damage was done and she kept looking in her mirror, her heart pounding if she saw a white car coming up behind her, even if it was the wrong make.

When she got home, Stu was sitting in front of the TV and the kids were upstairs in their rooms. She hesitated, then called them all together to tell them what she suspected.

'You must be mistaken,' Stu said at once.

'I saw that car when it followed you home before, Mum,' Casey said. 'I've got its number.' He pounded up the stairs and was down again brandishing a scrap of paper.

They compared numbers.

'It's the same,' Jane said with a shudder. 'I'm going to call in at the police station tomorrow and ask their advice.'

Rosie came to sit on her chair arm. 'Be careful, Mum.'

Casey came to sit on the other arm. 'If that man hurts you, I'm going after him.'

Jane looked across the room. Stu had a worried expression on his face, but he hadn't come to touch her and offer comfort. In fact, it was as if the three of them were the family and he was the stranger.

How long had this been going on? She needed to have another talk with him. About their marriage this time.

Or would that be the straw that broke the camel's back for him?

Chapter 33

Australia

In Australia, Lou picked up the message from Gramps when she got back from a couple of nights away with Rick. She'd left meals and snacks prepared for Mel and a neighbour had picked up Emma from school, then Lexie had come over after work each day to look after her sister.

Lou and Rick had had a glorious couple of days 'down south' in the wine country. As Mel was getting better, he'd insisted they leave their mobile phones behind so that they could have a relaxed time. Lou had missed having one, though, and pounced on hers as soon as she got in, waving one hand to stop little Emma interrupting as she listened to her voicemail messages. When she'd finished, she looked at the clock. 'Just got time to ring Gramps.'

When she got through to him, he was not only still up but was bubbling with excitement about meeting his sister.

'There. I knew you'd like her. How did Auntie Peggy take to her?'

'She's not met her yet, but I'm sure they'll get on all right.'

'This is me you're talking to, Gramps, and we both know Auntie Peggy doesn't take a breath unless Uncle Hartley approves.'

'Well, Peggy's left Hartley and she's talking about getting a divorce. Yes, you may well gasp but I'm glad. He's been bullying her for years.'

'He'll nag her into going back to him.'

'She's living with me for the time being and she's taken out an injunction against him to keep him away, so he'll not be able to get at her.'

There was dead silence then Lou said, 'Maybe there's hope for her then. Anyway, give Auntie Gina my love and tell her Mel is feeling a lot better as long as she keeps resting. Oh, and Gramps, I nearly forgot to tell you…'

'Yes, love.'

'Me and Rick just got engaged.'

Another silence, then, 'You're a bit young for that, aren't you?'

'That's what everyone says, but I don't agree. When you meet the right person, it doesn't matter if you're eighteen or eighty. You'll see. Me and Rick are good for the long haul. But we won't be getting married for ages yet, only when we're ready to settle down properly and start a family.'

'Well, I hope you'll both be very happy. He's a nice lad.'

'Mum and Dad don't think so.'

'It's you not them who'll be marrying him, is it?'

When Lou put the phone down, she went to pass on the news to the others.

'Mum's actually met some relatives?' Mel asked. 'Why didn't she ring us herself?'

'She's probably busy with this new guy she's met.'

Lou chuckled at the scowl on Mel's face. She hoped Auntie Gina had met someone nice and was madly in love.

In a day or two she'd ring Gramps again and ask what the new friend was like.

Chapter 34

England

The following day Brad found Gina inattentive and fidgety, unable to settle to anything, so since it was sunny, he took her for a tram ride along the seafront in the morning.

'Nervous about meeting your sister?'

'I've met her already, sort of, but if looks could kill...' She grimaced. 'Yes, I am a bit nervous. But Jake will be there and I do like him.'

'Shall I drive you over to Poulton to see him?'

'I can't keep using you as a taxi. No, I'll drive myself.'

'I'd rather you weren't on your own.'

'I'd feel guilty if you were sitting outside in the car and it'd hamper me. I don't know how long I'll be.'

'I've got a good book.'

'Why do you want to come, Brad?'

'In case this Peggy upsets you again.'

Gina smiled then, the best smile she'd given him all day. 'You're very kind but I've got Jake on my side this time.'

'Well, how about because I love you? Is that a better excuse?'

'I love you, too, but I'm still going on my own.'

If they weren't in such a public spot he'd kiss her till she melted against him like butter. He stirred uncomfortably as his body responded to the thought of making love to her.

Back at the flat he watched her get ready and waved her off with a smile glued to his face. But it faded the minute she'd left because he was worried about her. He didn't know why, he just was. It was one of his hunches and he'd learned not to ignore them. They only happened with people he cared about. But she'd probably have thought him crazy if he'd told her.

He paced up and down the flat, three steps in one direction, two and a half and bump into the table in the other direction. After a while he made a cup of coffee but even as he took his first sip, the feeling returned more strongly.

Maybe nothing was wrong, maybe he'd look like an idiot… But he just couldn't sit at home with this feeling of apprehension churning around in his belly. He had to make sure Gina was all right.

–

Jake let Peggy take over the food preparation for the lunch with their sister. If it'd been up to him, it'd have been a much simpler affair: cheese and ham, crusty bread and a few bits of salad from his own garden, followed by a bought cake. For all her annoyance that he'd invited Gina to lunch, Peggy insisted on making a quiche and a chocolate cake, as well as a salad, and they looked good too. His mouth was watering long before their visitor was due.

She also fussed about the table, setting the one in the dining room that he hardly ever used, ironing the table-cloth and getting out the best crockery.

'Gina's coming to meet you, not judge a catering contest,' he grumbled, then relented and added, 'You've got it looking nice, though, really nice.'

'Hartley's always been fussy about how his meals are presented. He'd not have approved of paper serviettes.' She flicked a scornful finger towards them. 'Are you sure you haven't got any real ones?'

'Certain. And that's the umpteenth time you've mentioned Hartley this morning. It's as if you keep thinking about him. Is there something you're not telling me?'

She hesitated then confessed, 'Cheryl rang yesterday. She said her father had been on the phone to her and he'd been crying.'

'Now that I find hard to believe.'

'Me too. But if he was crying… it must mean he cares about me… mustn't it?'

Jake looked at her in alarm. 'You're surely not thinking of going back to him?'

'N-no. At least, I don't think so.'

Bugger being tactful, he thought. 'If you do, I'll wash my hands of you!'

She stared at him, looking so distressed he didn't know what to say or do next. He was relieved when the phone rang and he could go into the kitchen and answer it.

'Hello?'

'Hartley here. I wonder if you could spare me an hour. I need to talk to you about Peggy.'

'Sorry. I'm busy today.'

'If you won't come to me, I'll come to you and to hell with that injunction. I mean it. This has gone on for long enough. I want my wife back.'

'I've nothing to say to you. You've treated my sister shamefully over the years and I'm glad she's left you.'

'I'm coming round, then. She has to listen to me. I know I can make her see sense.'

'You're not allowed to come near her.'

Deep breathing at the other end, then Hartley spoke in jerky words, as if dealing with an idiot. 'How – can we – sort this out – if I can't speak to her?'

Jake saw Peggy standing in the kitchen doorway, listening. 'Just a minute.' He covered the phone with one hand and explained what Hartley wanted.

She stared at him for a minute as if he'd been speaking a foreign language.

'Peggy? Don't get upset, love. I won't let him near you.'

'It's not that. It's what Cheryl said, he's upset. If he really is sorry... Oh, I don't know what to do, whether to believe him or not. Couldn't you go and see him for me, find out if he's genuinely sorry, if he'll see a counsellor and get help?'

'A leopard doesn't change its spots. And anyway, let me remind you that we have a guest coming in a few minutes. I'm not abandoning her to jump to Hartley's tune.'

'You only need to be out for half an hour. I can look after her till you get back.'

'You didn't even want to speak to her yesterday.' The phone squawked and he uncovered it to snap, 'Will you wait your bloody turn! I'm speaking to Peggy.' He looked questioningly back at his sister.

'I need to know about Hartley. After what Cheryl said – I need to know if he's really sincere, regrets what he's done... Please, Jake, go and see him for me.'

'You're sure?'

She nodded. 'I can't just throw away all those years of marriage without making absolutely sure it's the right thing to do.'

He shook his head but didn't refuse. He was quite certain Hartley hadn't changed and never would, but it was her life. 'All right.'

'If you think there's a chance, maybe he'll agree to seeing me with Gillah present?'

Jake nodded and uncovered the phone again. 'I'll meet you at the Fountain Shopping Centre, Hartley. In the centre, near the fountain. How soon can you be there? All right. In fifteen minutes' time?'

He put the phone down and picked up his car keys. 'You'll be kind to Gina? Promise me. She was upset last time.'

'I know. I heard her sobbing as she ran down the path. I won't hurt her again.'

She watched him go, adjusted the one of the knives on the table because it wasn't quite straight then went to sit in the front room to wait for their visitor. It had been much easier to get things ready without Hartley peering over her shoulder, criticizing.

Did she really want to go back to him?

Could he change his ways?

She wished… oh, she didn't know what she wished. She felt all adrift.

–

Gina drove to Poulton, amazed as always by the number of cars on the road in England, not only those driving around but those parked along the edges of every street. Her thoughts kept turning to the coming meeting. Surely, now that Jake and Aunt Bridie had accepted her, Peggy would give her a chance too?

She got stuck in a one-way system and had to stop and consult her satnav, which kept telling her to go down a street that didn't exist. She took a guess and was relieved when the satnav took over again, directing her to Jake's street. As she parked the car outside the house, she stopped to take a deep breath. She was feeling more than a little nervous about meeting her sister. It was so important to her.

A sister. Just imagine having a sister!

–

Peggy only had to wait a few minutes before she heard a car draw up outside. She went to peep out of the window and saw Gina getting out of it, looking apprehensive. Oh dear, she didn't want this meeting, it felt like such a betrayal of her mother, but she'd promised Jake to treat their visitor kindly and she never broke her promises.

She watched Gina pause by the gate, square her shoulders and take a deep breath. Trying to smile, she went to open the front door. 'Hello.'

'Hi, Peggy.'

'Jake's been called out but he'll be back soon. Won't you come in? Would you like a cup of tea while we're waiting for him?'

Gina followed her into the hall. 'I'd love one.'

'We'll go into the kitchen while I make it. Do sit down.' Peggy hesitated, then explained, 'It was very important or Jake wouldn't have gone out. He's seeing my husband. I've left Hartley and taken an injunction out to stop him coming near me, but he says he wants us to get back together. Only I'm not sure. So Jake's gone to talk to him, see if he's really changed.'

'It must be very difficult for you.'

Peggy nodded then jumped up to pour the boiling water into the teapot and rinse it out. 'I love my cups of tea. They're my big weakness and I'm a bit fussy about making them properly.'

'Me, too. I've got several sorts of tea at home, for different times of day.'

Peggy looked at her in mild surprise. 'What's your favourite?'

'Ceylon Breakfast Tea. Though I usually drink it at lunch time.'

'It's mine too. But my husband says he can't taste the difference. He likes his tea really strong. And Jake doesn't care which sort he has, either, as long as it's got sugar in it.' Grimacing at the thought, she got two china mugs out. 'This is a difficult situation, isn't it? You and me, I mean.'

'Yes. I only found out after my – I mean, our father died that I had family in England.'

'You don't have any brothers or sisters in Australia?'

'No, but I always wished I did. I longed to have relatives like other girls. When they talked about their grandmas or cousins, I felt so left out because I had no one, not one single relative.'

Peggy tried to imagine being totally without relatives, but couldn't. In spite of her determination to keep the other woman at arm's length a certain sympathy crept into her thoughts.

Gina beamed at her. 'And now I not only have you and Jake, but Aunt Bridie too. I'm so lucky to have found her before it was too late. Isn't she wonderful for her age? So lively and interested in the world.'

'I haven't seen her for a while. She and my husband don't get on.'

They picked up their cups of tea and sipped, both nodding in pleasure. 'You make a perfect cup of tea.' Gina took another mouthful, wondering what to say next. She hoped Jake wouldn't be too long. He was much easier to talk to.

But at least Peggy hadn't turned her away this time. At least they were sitting together trying to build bridges. She smiled. Bridges made of tea leaves.

—

Hartley sat in his car, smiling as he watched Jake arrive at the shopping centre. Once the other man was out of sight, he edged between the rows of cars, cursing when he stumbled. His damned leg wasn't getting any better. He checked that no one was watching and got out the screwdriver he'd sharpened last night. Making sure that no one was watching, he stuck it into one of the rear tyres of the car, stabbing several times and watching in satisfaction as the tyre went flat, then doing the same to the other rear tyre.

'See if the spare does you any good now!' he muttered gleefully. He didn't want his damned brother-in-law coming back and interrupting him while he was talking to Peggy. If necessary, he would have to insist she went home with him.

He rubbed his forehead as he went back to his car. It was aching again. It was Peggy's fault for upsetting him. As he drove away from the shopping centre, he smiled. It was all falling into place, though. He'd soon have everything sorted out and his home back to rights again.

He parked the car away from Jake's house, in case Peggy looked out and realized he'd come, then tried to nip in via the side, as he had done before. But the gate was locked by very solid bolts this time, and they were padlocked as well. The anger that had been simmering in him throbbed more strongly. How dare anyone keep him away from his wife?

As he was standing there, wondering whether she'd open the front door to him, the people on the far side of Jake's house got into their car and drove off. Keeping his face turned away, Hartley walked briskly along the street, rang their doorbell and when there was no answer, opened their side gate. No bolts here and the fences in the street were old-fashioned wooden ones, with places to put your foot and climb over. He'd noticed that the other night.

'I'll teach you to leave me, you bitch,' he muttered as he peered over into Jake's garden. Pity he needed to be quick or he could have had some more fun trampling the plants. But he didn't want to attract Peggy's attention until he was inside the house.

Not without difficulty, he boosted himself up on the dustbin and dropped into the garden, stumbling as his bad leg gave way under him. He hid behind a bush while he waited to see if anyone had noticed him.

But everything lay peaceful in the sunlight. Ah, there was Peggy at the kitchen window. He kept very still.

When she moved away, he ran across the garden and wrenched open the back door.

'Do you think—?' Before Gina could finish her question, the door burst open and a man erupted into the room, grabbing Peggy by the arm and shaking her like a dog shakes a rat, shouting, 'You stupid, stupid bitch! What do you think you're doing?'

Kicking the back door shut, he began to drag her across the room towards the hall, one hand across her mouth. Peggy went limp, not attempting to fight him off, her eyes blank with terror.

For a moment shock kept Gina still. This had to be Peggy's husband. Just so had her attacker kept her quiet as he dragged her. Fury sizzled through her at men who attacked women like this and she looked round for a weapon.

'You're coming home with me now and if you ever do this again, I'll make you really sorry. You can't—' He broke off as he noticed Gina. 'Who's the hell's she? Don't tell me Jake has a fancy woman now.'

Peggy was trembling visibly and seemed incapable of speaking.

'I can see why you left your husband,' Gina said.

The anger was still zipping through her in a burning tide, but she was pleased she'd kept her voice steady. She couldn't do anything about the man who had mugged her, but she could do something about this one. She picked up the fruit bowl and hurled it at him, fruit and all, with an accuracy born of years of playing ball games with Tom and the girls. The wooden bowl hit him on the side of the head and fruit rained down around him. He yelped and put up one hand instinctively to the wound. A trickle of blood began to flow down his temple.

Gina moved out from behind the table, holding a chair in front of her for protection, hoping to get Peggy away from him. She jabbed it at him as if she was a lion tamer and he stepped hastily back, cursing.

His face was such a dark red and his expression so ugly, she hesitated to follow up with another jab. He shoved Peggy aside and as his wife stumbled and fell, he went for Gina. Laughing scornfully, he grabbed the chair by its legs and after a short tussle, yanked it out of her hands.

'You must be another of those bitches from the women's centre. Well, all you man-haters need teaching a lesson and I'm in the mood to do exactly that!' He grabbed Gina by the arm and threw her against the wall.

She was stunned for a few seconds by the impact, but managed to jerk aside and avoid the punch he aimed at her. 'Help me, Peggy!' she begged, backing away from him.

Her sister whimpered and cowered back, hands pressed against her cheeks.

'We're two against one, Peggy. Help me!'

Hartley stopped to laugh at that, a harsh, jeering sound. 'She wouldn't dare. Look at her. She's always been a coward. All she's good for is looking after me and my house, and by hell, that's what she's going to do from now on.' Then he turned his back on his wife and advanced on Gina again.

Peggy stared at him for a moment or two, stung by his scorn, then scrambled to her feet and picked up the heavy wooden fruit bowl that had fallen nearby. She smashed it down over his head, standing like a frozen creature as he crumpled to the ground. She opened her hands and it fell on top of him.

Gina could see that he was only partly stunned. 'Come on! Quick!' She grabbed her sister's hand and hauled her along the hall out of the front door. 'We need to get help.'

–

Brad saw Gina's car parked further along the street and waited. He didn't know what he was waiting for but something was still making him feel anxious.

When he saw the two women rush out of the house, looking dishevelled and upset, he flung open the car door and ran towards them. 'Gina! Over here! What's happened?'

'Oh, thank goodness.' She pulled her sister towards him. 'Peggy's husband's inside the house. He tried to force her to go home with him and then he attacked me.' She glanced over her shoulder as she spoke. 'He was like a madman.'

'You were wonderful,' Peggy said. 'The way you stood up to him.'

Gina smiled. 'You weren't bad yourself, smashing that bowl over his head.' She turned to Brad. 'He was only partly conscious when we left him, but he may be recovering now. I think we should call the police.'

'We'd better check that he's not seriously hurt first. Stay behind me.' Brad led the way towards the front door.

As they entered the hall, footsteps echoed from the side of the house and there was a clunk that sounded like a bolt being shot before the footsteps resumed. Brad swung round, pushing the two women behind him. The person wasn't coming towards them, however, but moving away from the house. 'Wait in the doorway!'

He ran outside again and saw a man running away down the street with a strange lurching gait. For a moment Brad was tempted to run after him, but he didn't, because it was far more important to make sure Gina was all right.

–

The phone rang just before lunch time, as Jane was getting ready to go to work.

'Mrs Quentin? I'm afraid your son's been hurt. Not badly, but he has a sprained ankle and it'd be better if he came home and rested it. He may also have mild concussion. Can you pick him up?'

Jane sighed. Casey was going through a very clumsy stage at the moment and had had several small accidents like this. He'd grown so fast he didn't seem able to manage his own body properly and walked into things all the time. 'I'll come straight over to pick him up.'

'Your daughter was nearby when he fell down the stairs and she got rather upset. She wants to come home too.'

'They're very close, those two.' Jane smiled as she said that because it was something that had always pleased her greatly.

When she got them home, she pretended to scold Casey for his carelessness, but he hopped across to the sofa and dropped on to it. 'You know I don't do it on purpose, Mum.'

'Sit there with that foot up and I'll put a cold pack on it. I've learned to keep one in the freezer for you over the past year or two.'

'I'll do anything as long as you feed me.' He put his hands into a praying position. 'They wouldn't let me eat any lunch.'

349

Rosie tossed her school bag on the floor and opened the fridge. 'You don't deserve it, but I'll get you a glass of juice and a sandwich, Mr Clumsy.'

Casey grinned at his mother. 'See. I've got my big sister to look after me. You can go to work now. You don't have to stay at home with me. I'm a bi-i-ig boy.'

'Too late. I've rung them to say I can't come in. So we'll all have a lazy afternoon together.'

'Cool. When I've had something to eat, I'll go and work on my computer.'

As she was helping her mother put some food together for Casey, Rosie asked, 'Is it still all right for me to go out with Brad tomorrow?'

'Yes. I thought we'd agreed about that.'

'I know. Only Dad's like – well, he won't speak to me about it.'

'That's his problem, not yours, love. He won't talk to me about anything at the moment, either.'

Rosie looked at her with a troubled face. 'I didn't mean to cause trouble between the two of you. I just wanted to know where I came from.'

Jane nearly brushed this off, then decided her daughter was old enough for the truth. 'Maybe your father and I needed shaking up a bit. We seem to have drifted apart lately.'

'That's because he cares more about his school stuff than he does about us.'

Jane didn't know what to say to that, didn't even know if it was true. In the end she sighed. 'I don't think it's only his fault. I've been a bit busy lately, doing extra hours at work.'

'You're not going to leave Dad or anything, are you?'

'Heavens, no! It'd take too long to train another husband.'

Rosie let out a sigh of relief.

'I'll just clear the kitchen up, then I might as well go and do the main shopping.'

'I'll come with you if you like, Mum.'

'I'd rather you stayed here and kept an eye on the boy wonder. Don't let him overdo things or try to fly down the stairs again.'

'Yeah. All right.' Rosie shuddered. 'He bounced down the stairs, Mum. I thought he'd killed himself. I felt sick till I saw him move.'

Jane gave her a hug, then drove away wondering what Stu would he be like next year, working as an ordinary teacher. It was stupid to waste skills and enthusiasm like his, and he'd got such good results from kids other teachers had given up on. Had the Education people gone crazy?

–

Jake waited inside the shopping centre, getting more suspicious by the minute. Hartley knew this area well, so there was no chance of him being lost and he hadn't far to drive. Maybe he wasn't coming. Only, why would he make the arrangement if he didn't intend to keep to it? Worried sick, Jake fumbled in his pocket for his phone so that he could ring Peggy and warn her to lock the doors. Then he realized he'd left it behind on the sideboard where he'd put it so that he wouldn't forget it. Fat lot of good that had done him!

He scanned as much of the shopping centre as he could see, but there was no sign of Hartley's large figure ploughing through the crowds in that arrogant way he had of expecting others to get out of the way.

Right then. Better go home.

At his car he stopped with a muttered curse. The rear tyres were both flat and when he went to examine them he found holes, several of them, so he guessed then that Hartley had done this to delay him getting back.

Terrified for his sister, Jake ran across to the taxi rank, pushing to the head of the queue and calling out, 'I've got an emergency at home and someone's slashed my tyres. Can I please take the next taxi? It's a matter of life and death.' Which might not be all that much of an exaggeration.

The people in the queue nodded and the lady at the front said, 'I've been waiting so long, another few minutes won't hurt.'

It was a minute or two before a taxi drew up and Jake kept looking anxiously at his watch. When one arrived he jumped into it and begged the driver to get him home as fast as he could.

As they began to turn into his street, another car squealed round the corner coming towards them and the taxi had to run up on to the pavement to avoid it.

That was Hartley's car. Jake would recognize it anywhere. 'Did you get his number?' he asked the taxi driver.

'No. It happened too quickly. We're lucky there wasn't a lamp post here.'

'I know who he is. We should contact the police. He's been behaving erratically lately.' He scribbled Hartley's name and address down and handed it to the driver as the taxi drew up in front of his house.

'I'll report it straight away. There are too many lunatics on the road. Here we are.'

Jake fumbled in his pocket for the money. 'Could you wait, please? I may have to go out again. It'll only take me a minute or two to find out if I need you.'

'OK. And I'll want your name and address as well for the police.'

'Jacob Everett,' he called over his shoulder as he rushed into his house.

Three people swung round to face him as he ran through into the kitchen. He'd expected to find Peggy in tears if Hartley had been here, but instead she was flushed and bright-eyed, seeming energized not crushed.

'Are you all right, love?' he asked. 'I thought I saw your Hartley driving away.'

Peggy explained quickly what had happened, ending, 'We fought him off, Jake. Gina and I did it together.'

The two women clasped hands, smiling mistily at one another, then Peggy bit her lip and the worried look came back into her eyes. 'What am I going to do about him if he won't obey the injunction?'

'I can't drive you anywhere till I get my tyres changed, but I've got a taxi waiting outside,' Jake said. 'I think we should report this to the police and ask their advice.'

'Gina and I both have cars if we need to go anywhere,' Brad said. 'I don't think you'll need the taxi.'

When Jake came back into the house after thanking the driver and sending him away, Peggy was pacing up and down, arms wrapped tightly round herself as if for protection. 'I can't get what Hartley said out of my mind. He said Gina must be another bitch from the women's centre and that man haters like her all needed teaching a lesson. Jake, he's been following Jane when she went to and from the centre, I saw him myself. What if he's gone after her now?'

The others stared at her in dismay.

'Nay, surely he'd not—' Jake began then broke off. 'But then I'd not have expected him to slash my tyres or attack anyone.'

'Jane?' Brad asked. 'Jane who?'

'Jane Quentin. She goes to my meditation class. Only I don't have her phone number or address.'

Brad felt sick at the thought of either Jane or Rosie being attacked by a man who seemed to have gone crazy. 'I know her and I've got her mobile number. I can phone her and tell her to lock the doors.'

'Oh, thank goodness!' Peggy stopped her pacing to listen as he dialled.

But when he got through, Jane said she was out shopping so he explained quickly what had happened and suggested she get home immediately. 'I'll meet you at your house. Can you ring Rosie's mobile and warn her?'

'Have you got her number with you, Brad? Right, you phone Rosie and I'll ring Stu. The school where he works is only a couple of streets away. He can get there more quickly than anyone.'

As the phone rang, Brad muttered, 'Answer, dammit! Come on, Rosie.'

There wasn't a sound in the room as everyone waited.

Chapter 35

England

Casey yelled suddenly from upstairs, 'That guy in the white car who's been following Mum just pulled up and hey, he's coming towards the house. Rosie, he looks like Hell Man on the rampage. Lock the front door, quick.'

She ran down the hall but the door was thrown open before she could get there. A burly man whose eyes were wild and angry limped inside and grabbed her arm before she could run away.

'Where is she?' he demanded. 'Where – is – she?'

Rosie tried to pull away from him but his hand was clasped tightly around her upper arm. 'Where's who?'

He looked at her then, as if he'd not really seen her before. 'The woman who lives here. Jane, she's called.'

'Mum? She's out, won't be back for ages. She's doing the shopping. And you're hurting me.'

He ignored that. 'Then you and I will just have to wait for her, won't we?'

'You've no right to come in here and tell me what to do.' She struggled to get away.

He shook her hard and thrust his face closer to hers. 'If you know what's good for you, you'll shut up and be still.' He dragged her from one room to the other, checking them out, muttering to himself, then looked up the stairs. 'What's up there?'

'Three bedrooms and a bathroom.'

He shouted up the stairs, 'Anyone there?'

Rosie prayed Casey wouldn't reply. He'd be no match for this brute.

Before the intruder could go upstairs, Rosie's mobile rang from the kitchen, so he dragged her back towards the sound, staring at it. 'Whose phone is that?'

'Mine.'

'Answer it. But not a word about me or I'll knock you out.'

Hands trembling, she picked up the phone and clicked on answer. 'Hello?'

Brad's voice. She cut off what he was saying quickly.

'Oh hi, Paul. Are you ringing about our date tonight? I'm sorry but something's cropped up, so I won't be able to make it. See you soon.'

The silence that followed seemed to echo round Rosie. She prayed that Brad would understand her hidden message, that Casey wouldn't make a single noise upstairs, that this madman wouldn't hurt her.

-

Casey had started to go to Rosie's aid, but it all happened so quickly that the man was inside before he could do more than move out on to the landing. So he stayed back, listening, terrified for his sister's safety.

When her mobile rang, the man dragged her off to the kitchen to answer it. Casey realized this was his own opportunity. Picking up his own mobile, he dialled the police emergency number, whispering a plea for help, praying they'd take him seriously. 'Mum came to see you about this man,' he finished. 'He's been following her car round.'

'Stay where you are. Don't attempt to confront him,' the voice ordered. 'And stay on the line.'

'Can't. He might hear. Please hurry up.'

Casey disconnected and stayed where he was, afraid to move a step because the bedroom floorboards creaked.

Then an email arrived and his computer chimed a merry announcement. He stared across at it in horror. Why had he set it so loud?

Downstairs he heard a chair scrape and footsteps come along the hall.

'It's only one of the computers,' Rosie said loudly. 'They do that when an email arrives.'

'We'll just go upstairs and check, I think. Hurry up!'

'I can't move properly with you holding me like that.'

Guessing that she was trying to warn him, Casey looked round frantically for somewhere to hide.

—

Jane phoned Stu. She insisted the school secretary have him called out of class and waited impatiently, hearing his name echoing in the background on the PA. It took longer than she'd expected.

Running footsteps were followed by his voice. 'Jane? What's wrong?'

'That lunatic who was following me the other night has gone round to our house after attacking Peggy. Can you get home quickly? Rosie and Casey are there and I think they're in danger.'

'I'll be there as fast as I can.'

357

After that she rang the police and begged them to go round to her house.

'We've already had a call from a young man called Casey about an intruder,' she was told.

'He's my son.'

'Officers are on their way.'

She got into her car and set off for home, praying she'd get there on time, breaking the speed limit most of the way.

–

The man shoved Rosie up the stairs ahead of him. 'Where's the computer?'

Since she hadn't switched hers on yet, she led the way into Casey's bedroom and pointed. 'It's my brother's.' To her relief the screensaver was on, so it didn't give away the fact that someone had been using it recently.

While they were upstairs, the man peered into the other bedrooms, but there was no sign of anyone. She didn't know where Casey was hiding, could only hope he'd not give himself away.

When they went back into the kitchen, the intruder took one of her mother's kitchen knives out of the rack, pointing it at her. 'Don't – try – to escape.'

She stared at it in horror, then at his face. He looked as if he was on drugs or something, because his face looked wrong, with one side drooping slightly. 'I won't.'

'Make me a cup of tea. Strong. Two sugars.'

This wasn't the time to argue so she went to put the kettle on.

As she was turning round, someone rang the doorbell.

The man was on his feet in an instant, grabbing her arm. 'Are you expecting anyone?'

'No.' She could see he didn't believe her, though, and her heart lurched in fear. 'Honest, I'm not. If it was Mum, she'd not ring the doorbell.'

'Then we won't answer it.'

But the doorbell rang again and she looked in that direction, hoping it was someone who'd help them, wondering if she should scream for help, but not daring to, not with the knife blade shining in a beam of sunlight.

The man let go of her arm and gave her a shove towards the sink. 'Make the tea, you silly bitch. They'll go away when you don't answer.'

-

Upstairs, Casey also heard the doorbell. He eased himself out of the cistern cupboard, which had been a very tight fit, and limped as quietly as he could into his parents' bedroom, which looked out on to the street. Once, a floorboard creaked beneath his foot and he froze for a moment or two, hardly daring even to breathe. But there was no sound from below, so one careful step at a time he made his way to the window.

He looked out to see a man walk away, then saw him crouch down with two women behind the front hedge. It was Rosie's Brad. They must know something was wrong from the strange way they were behaving.

Casey waved and waved, trying to attract their attention, but they had their heads close together, talking. Then, just as he was about to stop waving, the older of the woman looked up and saw him, nudging Brad.

Trying to signal that a lunatic was in the house and had Rosie downstairs was difficult, but Casey had to give it a go. Then he had a brainwave and mouthed 'Wait'. He tiptoed across to the dressing table, picked up his mother's lipstick and scrawled. 'Madman got Rosie in kitchen' on a tissue, dropping it out through the small window at the top, which was open.

He watched, heart thumping as it fluttered this way and that, finally landing right in the middle of the path. He listened, but the voices below were still coming from the kitchen so he pointed to it and nodded. Brad darted out, picked up the tissue and darted back again to read it and pass it to his companions. He looked up at Casey and raised one thumb to show he'd understood.

Letting out a long shuddering breath, the lad stayed where he was. Then he suddenly jerked to attention as his dad's car came roaring into the street and drew to a screeching halt in front of the house. He heard sounds in the kitchen, a chair falling over, Rosie saying 'Ouch!' and went to the door of the bedroom to try to see what was happening downstairs.

There was the sound of a key in the front-door lock.

The man had hold of Rosie by the hair and was dragging her forward. As the door opened, he yelled, 'You'd better not come any further or the girl will get hurt.'

Casey bit his finger hard to keep from calling out as the man placed a kitchen knife against Rosie's throat. He had to do something or she'd get hurt. He looked round and picked up a heavy cut glass vase from the landing table. Give him half a chance and he'd brain that lunatic with it.

In the doorway his dad stood very still. 'If you hurt Rosie, I'll kill you.'

The man laughed, a harsh jangling sound. 'That'd be too late to help her. Anyway, I don't want to hurt her, I want to see my wife. I'll give you Peggy's brother's phone number and you can ring and tell her to come home. Tell her I'll let your daughter go as soon as she does. Now, get away from the door. We're going to my house. If you make one wrong move, your daughter will suffer.'

Casey saw the old woman who'd been crouching behind the wall stand up suddenly. 'Let her go and I'll come with you now, Hartley.'

At the same time there was a sound from the kitchen and the man jerked round, staring from Stu to the woman, then over his shoulder at the kitchen.

Casey seized his opportunity and lobbed the vase carefully down over the landing banisters. Although he missed the man's head, he hit him on the shoulder and the knife dropped out of his hand.

Stu grabbed Rosie and thrust her behind him, facing the intruder as he backed away.

Hartley picked up the knife quickly and raised it threateningly, but by that time Brad had come in from the kitchen and grabbed him from behind.

'Run!' Shoving Rosie outside Stu went to help Brad and the two men struggled to overcome the intruder.

Casey saw through the landing window that another car had driven quietly into the street. Two police officers got out of it, running towards the house. He looked down, hearing yells, curses and crashes as his dad and the other men rolled to and fro. The hall table fell over sending all its ornaments flying.

Then the two policemen came in, though even with them helping, it took a while to subdue the intruder and handcuff him. He didn't stop cursing and yelling and threatening the whole time they were taking him out to the car and when he saw the two women, he renewed his attempts to escape.

'I think he really has run mad,' Peggy whispered to Gina. She stood very upright as Hartley was dragged past, not speaking, not even clutching her companion's arm just staring at him.

Rosie flung herself into Stu's arms, sobbing. 'Oh, Dad! I thought he was going to kill you.'

Tears were pouring down his cheeks as he hugged her close. 'I thought he was going to kill you too, Rosie darling, and I couldn't have borne that.'

When her sobs had died down, Stu looked over her head to Brad. 'Thanks. I couldn't have managed without you.'

Brad nodded but didn't move towards them. They were very much a father and daughter just then, and he was only a bystander.

Another car drove up and Jane came rushing towards them. Stu and Rosie turned to include her in their hug and explain what had happened. Casey limped down the stairs and went to join them.

Gina edged past them and walked into Brad's arms, clinging tightly to him. 'I was terrified he'd hurt you.'

'I felt the same about you.' He glanced in the direction of Rosie and Stu, sadness in his eyes.

'He'll always be her father,' Gina said gently. 'You can't change that now.'

'I know. I missed so much. She's a great kid.'

'You can still be her friend, sort of like an extra uncle.'

The sad look faded a little and he pulled her closer. 'And you? Are you still my friend?'

'Not exactly.' She could feel a smile creeping over her face, something she'd not have believed possible an hour ago.

'Oh?' His eyes roamed over her like a caress. 'What are you then?'

'Your lover.'

'My beloved,' he corrected. 'When I thought he'd hurt you, I was ready to pound him to a pulp.' He looked at her wryly. 'I've never thought of myself as a violent man, but I came near to it today. First because of you, then Rosie.'

'It's all ended well.' She turned to beckon Peggy inside. 'And I hope I've made another friend today.'

Peggy smiled. 'Not a friend, a sister. Thank you so much for helping me.'

'We were a team.'

Peggy looked at them. 'Did you two come from Australia together?'

'No, we met here – what, two weeks ago?' Gina looked at Brad for confirmation. 'Such a short time, really. And yet so much has happened.' She put one arm round her sister's shoulders. 'I'd come to England to trace my family, Brad had come to meet Rosie. We met at the hotel and fell in love – if not at first glance, pretty soon afterwards.'

Brad smiled at her and for a moment or two, she forgot about everything else.

'How brave of you to come so far on your own!' Peggy said.

'Me? Brave? I don't think so.' Gina shook her head. 'I'm a very ordinary person.'

'I think you're extremely brave,' Peggy said firmly. 'You've gone out and lived. I've stayed home and cowered like a mouse in a hole. I've wasted most of my life running round after Hartley and—' She broke off and sucked in a long, painful breath. 'But I'm not wasting the rest of it, not one single second from now onwards.'

Jake had come into the house to join them. 'Peggy love, did you think Hartley's face looked strange?'

She frowned, trying to picture it, then nodded. 'One side of his mouth was sort of droopy and he was limping.'

'I reckon he's had a slight stroke, a TIA they call it. A friend of mine had one a couple of years ago and he behaved very strangely for a while afterwards.'

'Perhaps we ought to ring the police and let them know.'

'They asked me to take you down to the station, to make a statement.' He looked from one woman to the other and smiled. 'The only good thing about today is the way it's brought you two together.'

'I think we were coming together even before that,' Gina said. 'Goodness, it does seem a long time ago now since I found those documents. Mel will scold me again for getting into trouble. It was just like one of those police dramas.'

'My daughter probably won't speak to me,' Peggy said bitterly. 'She'll be more upset about her father.'

Jake patted her shoulder. 'I'm going to have a word with that young lady. I think they'll have to put your husband into a mental hospital till they've worked out exactly what's wrong with him. Well, they did with my friend. I've always thought Hartley was a bit strange, but today, he went way beyond that.'

Jane came over to them. 'Won't you come and sit down? I think we could all do with a strong drink. Stu, could you get the whisky?'

'I'd prefer a nice cup of tea,' Gina and Peggy said together, then smiled at one another.

'I'm not driving,' Jake said. 'I enjoy a good whisky.'

As they were saying goodbye in the street afterwards, Gina suddenly remembered the letters she'd brought with her and pulled them out of her handbag. 'I think you should have these. And maybe this time you'll open them.' She gave one bundle to Peggy, the other to Jake.

They both stared at the envelopes in puzzlement.

'I've never seen them before,' Jake said.

'That's Mum's handwriting saying not wanted,' Peggy said.

They exchanged glances then Jake bit his lip and said in a voice thickened by tears, 'So Dad did try to contact us. And he tried again recently, but I didn't open the letter. I'm going to read all of them when I get back.'

Peggy held her bundle close to her chest, clasping them with both hands.

'You'll read them, too?' Gina asked her.

She nodded. 'I need to know my father cared.'

'I'm sure he did.'

Epilogue

When all the fuss had died down, Bridie insisted on giving a very special dinner to celebrate not only the family being reunited, but also Brad finding his daughter and falling in love with her niece. The Quentins were invited as well as Jake, Peggy and Cheryl.

'I'm hiring one of the small banqueting rooms,' Bridie told everyone, 'then we can be private. You're all to wear your very best clothes and I'll book you rooms in the hotel for the night, so you won't need to drive. My treat.'

Protests were useless. She insisted and got her own way.

'It'll cost you a fortune, auntie,' Jake said. 'I could easily drive home afterwards.'

'I've plenty of money, but only one family. Humour me this time, Jake.'

—

On the following Saturday morning, while the Quentin women were shopping, not only for groceries, but for new outfits for the celebration, the front doorbell rang.

Stu went to open it and found a woman he felt he ought to recognize standing there.

'Mr Quentin, isn't it?'

'Yes.'

'Clare Lester. We met at an area conference. I was one of the organizers. Look, I wonder if I can come in and have a word with you? It's about your job next year.'

He looked at her in surprise, but offered her a seat in the living room.

'You haven't been in touch,' she said, frowning.

'Should I have been?'

She stared at him. 'Mr Binnings said he'd passed on my message.'

Stu shook his head. 'He didn't pass on any message.'

She frowned. 'That's strange. But it explains why you've not contacted me about the job.'

'What job?'

'With the area program development unit.'

He couldn't speak. It was a small, elite group and he'd give his eye teeth to be part of it.

She smiled. 'I heard you give a talk back in February about the work you'd been doing with reluctant learners. What you said impressed me, but I had to make sure we had the funding before I could speak to you. If you're agreeable, I'd like to second you to the unit next year. After that, we'll have to see, but I can at least promise you a job in your own area afterwards.'

'Binnings must have forgotten to pass on your message.'

'That's what he'll claim, no doubt.' She smiled conspiratorially. 'He's a sod to work with, isn't he? I've tangled with him a few times and I was really sorry when he got the job at the new school.'

'To hell with Binnings, tell me more about the job.'

By the time Jane and Rosie came home, the visitor had left.

As Stu rushed out to the car, they looked at one another.

'It can't be more bad news,' Rosie whispered. 'He's smiling like he used to.'

Stu flung open the car door and pulled Jane out, taking her in his arms and dancing her down the garden path.

Laughing and protesting, she let him lead her inside and Rosie followed, eager to find out what had happened.

Casey came down the stairs. 'What's up?' he whispered to his sister.

'Don't know, but whatever it is, it's put Dad in a good mood. Good thing, too, after all the money me and Mum spent this morning. You should see my new outfit.'

'Come in here, you two,' Stu shouted. 'I've got some good news, for a change.'

–

Brad tried several times to propose to Gina, but somehow he couldn't get the words out. In the end he decided that actions speak louder than words and took her out on the afternoon of Bridie's special dinner.

'I really ought to be doing my hair and getting ready,' she protested.

'You're missing one accessory.'

'What?'

'You'll find out.'

They walked into town and he stopped in front of a jeweller's shop. Taking a deep breath, he clasped both her hands and pulled her closer to him. 'I'm hoping you'll let me buy you an engagement ring.'

People pushed past them, muttering that they were blocking the pavement. Gina stared at him, then someone said loudly, 'Excuse me, please!' and poked her in the ribs. Moving into the shop's entrance she asked with a smile, 'Couldn't you think of anywhere more romantic for a proposal, Brad?'

He went pink. 'I've been trying to do it all week, couldn't get up the courage. What if you'd turned me down?'

'You fool. You must have known I wouldn't do that.'

'I couldn't be sure.' He waited. 'Well, will you? Marry me, I mean, and let me buy you a ring?'

'Oh, yes. Yes to both.'

She surfaced from a passionate kiss to see people standing staring at them, some in amusement, some with disapproving expressions.

'She's just agreed to marry me!' Brad announced.

There was a smattering of applause, followed by a few good wishes, then the crowd dispersed and he led her into the shop, his neck bright red with embarrassment.

It took her several minutes to stop chuckling, then she chose a beautiful ruby engagement ring, saying quietly, 'Not a diamond this time.'

He raised her hand to his lips and kissed it.

The assistant had to clear his throat twice before they realized where they were and stopped kissing.

–

Peggy twisted to and fro in front of the mirror. 'Are you sure this dress is all right?'

Cheryl nodded.

'They told me they can help your father, you know.' Peggy had said this several times, but it hadn't cheered her daughter up.

'But it won't be the same. You won't be married to him. How will he ever cope on his own?'

'The way the rest of us do. By using his own hands, not expecting someone else to give up their life to act as his slave,' Peggy said quietly.

'Can't you try living with him – after he's been treated, I mean?'

'No, dear. I told you that yesterday and I don't want to keep having this argument. I have a lot of wasted years to make up for. Now, are you ready? Your uncle Jake will be here for us in a minute.'

'I don't know why you want me there tonight. It's not as if I get on with the rest of the family. And I don't know these other people.'

'It's about time you tried to get on with the family. And you certainly ought to meet your new aunt. She's come all the way from Australia to see us.'

Cheryl gave an aggrieved sigh and Peggy mentally threw her daughter's remarks into an imaginary waste paper bin, a tactic Gillah had taught her and one she'd found very useful during several recent encounters with her daughter.

'That dress must have cost you a fortune,' Cheryl said.

'Jake bought it for me. I still have to get access to my own money. You look very – smart.' Sharp would be another word for it, Peggy decided, more suited to a business meeting than a family gathering. But at least Cheryl had agreed to come with her.

To her relief she heard a car draw up and led the way to the door. She was going to buy herself a flat with her share of the money from this house. Gillah said the rest would be kept in trust for Hartley. So the sooner Peggy could sell the house the better, as far as she was concerned. She'd would never be able to feel easy here again. But she couldn't impose on Jake any longer, so she'd moved back to her home.

They said Hartley would need to go into sheltered housing after he left hospital, because he'd had another stroke, a bigger one this time, that had left one hand completely useless. She didn't envy anyone who had to look after him and whatever Cheryl said, she didn't intend to see him again, if she could help it. She still had night-mares about the way he'd treated that poor girl.

–

Bridie was waiting for her guests at the hotel, looking elegant in a powder blue beaded dress. It was one of those classically elegant, slender, mid-calf evening dresses that never date and it went well with her silver hair and softly pink complexion.

The dinner was superb, consisting of several courses to which everyone did justice, especially Casey. With much laughter and joy, they shared their week's news, the engagement ring was admired and toasts were drunk.

When it got near midnight, people were yawning, but everyone was reluctant to end the evening. Bridie tapped a spoon on her wine glass to get their attention. 'I have a little surprise for you before you're allowed to go to bed, but we'll have to go up to my room to see it.'

In her sitting room Jake went across to the computer, which stood on a desk at one side and switched it on.

'Sit down everyone,' Bridie ordered. 'This'll take a minute or two.'

Casey went to hover near Jake and a whispered consultation was held between the two of them when something didn't work as it should have done.

Eventually, however, they smiled at one another and stood back. On the screen another group of people was smiling out at them.

Gina gasped and clutched Brad's hand tightly as she saw her daughters and their families, as well as Lou and Rick.

'Surprise!' the Australian contingent chorused.

Everyone tried to speak at once, so Jake shushed the English group and Lou shushed the Australian group.

Gina brought Brad forward and introduced him, took a deep breath then held out her hand. 'We're engaged.'

'Mum! You didn't!'

Lexie jabbed an elbow in her sister's side before Mel could say anything that would spoil the moment. 'Congratulations, Mum. When are you bringing him back to meet us properly?'

'We've not decided yet. We want to do some sightseeing in Europe first.'

Lou came closer to the webcam to wiggle her hand at them. 'You're not the only one to get engaged, Auntie Gina.'

'Oh, how wonderful! I'm so glad for you.'

Half an hour later Bridie said, 'Mel, you need to rest now and so do I.'

–

When Brad and Gina got back to their hotel room, she blinked furiously and whispered, 'Hold me please.'

'What's wrong?'

'It made me homesick, seeing my daughters and grand-children. I do miss them.'

'We can go back any time you like.'

'What, and not have any adventures?'

'Your happiness is the most important thing to me. Our being together is the most exciting thing as far as I'm concerned.'

'Then how about we have a small adventure this year, then when I've seen Mel safely delivered of that baby, we can go off and have another adventure or two?'

'Sounds good to me. And tomorrow we'll phone my children and give them the news that I'm engaged.'

She nestled against him and gave a happy sigh. 'Who'd have thought that tracing my family connections would bring me so much love?'

He felt something wet against his hand. 'You're not crying?'

'Just happy tears.' Very happy tears.